Answer Key

page 19
Who Won?

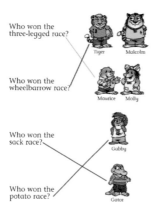

Who won the three-legged race?

Who won the wheelbarrow race?

Who won the sack race?

Who won the potato race?

page 21
Name-Writing Practice

Tiger

Malcolm

Gabby

Maurice

Molly

page 22
Pronouns

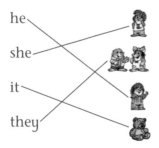

he

she

it

they

page 23
Give a Cheer!

Avis Blackthorn and the Magical Multicolour Jumper

Book 2 of the Wizard Magic School

S

JACK SIMMONDS

Jack Simmonds'

Avis Blackthorn and the Magical Multicolour Jumper

Copyright © 2015 Jack Simmonds

Cover copyright © 2015 Jack Simmonds

Thank you for supporting my work.

Avis Blackthorn
and the Magical Multicolour Jumper

CHAPTER ONE
The Return of the Brothers

Hello. My name is Avis Blackthorn and I am thirteen years old. I belong to what is, the most evil family in all of the Seven Magical Kingdoms and even, perhaps, in all of your kingdoms too. We call your world the *Outside*. My best friend Robin is from there, a place called *Yorkshire?* He goes to the same school as me — Hailing Hall School for Wizards — I started last year and it was my sanctuary. A sanctuary from my evil family with whom I play a constant battle, because I am not like them. Not at all. My parents and nine siblings are all very evil and work for Malakai — the most powerful, evil Sorcerer ever known — well, they did, until I defeated him at the end of last year.

My family hates me because I am not evil. I am treated like the runt, kept away at parties in case I embarrass them in front of all the other Malakai supporters. Some would disagree when I say *I am not evil* — only because of what happened in first year — I was set up. Framed for the attack of one of my friends by no lesser than the most evil and high lord of darkness (or whatever it was he called himself), Malakai. Fortunately, and with a great deal of luck and bluffing, I, yes me, managed to defeat him! In the process I saved Tina Partington and her brother Ernie Partington, who was a ghost for ten years and is thankfully, now a human again. It was my best friend Robin who saved the day, he raised Ernie and me back to our bodies! No mean feat, let me tell you.

Right now, I am scrubbing the floor high up in one of the twelve turrets. It's absolutely filthy! I mean black with dirt. I doubt it's ever been cleaned. This is not a voluntary decision either, I am being held at spell-point, practically, by my parents who need the castle to be in ship-shape ready for a thousand or so guests to turn up for the wedding of the bloody year. My sister Marianne and her poor deluded Prince finance are getting married in the grounds of our castle *Darkhampton*. She has him under a love spell I just know it. My parents encourage them who to marry — usually rich and influential families to increase their own reach and power. I heard that the family of the prince are really angry, they want nothing to do with us, knowing its a scam.

So far over the past week I've scrubbed floors, dusted every wooden surface within a four mile radius, whacked every drape to within an inch of its life, then dusted again as centuries of dust and muck came spewing out everywhere... I mean it really is the dirtiest castle ever! I finished each day without a thanks and looking like a Slackerdown Yeti (black, dirty, and very, very moody.) And I did all this cleaning without magic! My parents don't trust me, and... I don't have a bloody channeller do I! If you don't know, a channeller is a thing that allows you to do magic, as per the name, you channel magic through it. If you don't you could blow yourself up. I had one at the start of last year from the schools lost property. Which turned out to be the young Malakai's! That's how I worked out how to defeat him, he had his True Name written on it in hidden ink. I used his True Name to defeat him — the most evil Sorcerer ever, in all of history! And now I'm scrubbing floors. Mind you, if my parents ever find out what I did I would be in for a fate worse than death. They absolutely love him, and would do anything he asks. I wondered if they knew he had even been defeated? To be fair, they were rushing round the castle every minute of the day making beds up for guests, decorating, organising the chefs and all stuff like that.

Let me zap back a week and tell you what happened after I got out the carriage on the way back from school. I had fallen asleep in the plush ceremonial carriage pulled magically through the sky without any horses and started dreaming about killer rainbows that began attacking me… (I know, but it had been a stressful year). I woke just as we pulled up over my home and castle, Darkhampton, as my parents insist on calling it. I forgot how dark and gloomy it looked, it's held in a perpetual cycle of darkness while sunlight passes right around it. No trees, no plants, in fact, life was barely visible as I gazed down, the old feelings of being mistreated by my big evil family crept over me again. I suppose I'd got used to living in comfort, Hailing Hall had life, sunlight, walking trees, talking statues, the place buzzed with life… this was… deader than a lump of spent charcoal.

I was curious when the ceremonial carriage pulled up for me outside the school (and a little anxious), for I was rarely treated to such comfort by my parents. It was certainly suspicious. Just in case though, when I was in the carriage I put on my new, centuries old Seven League Shoes— a gift from the Lily, the Headmaster of Hailing Hall. I had no flipping clue how they worked, but according to the myth, they allow you to… it's either walk great distances fast, or run away quicker than you are normally able to… something like that.

When we touched onto the baron carriageway outside the drawbridge front door, my Dad rushed out to greet me… which was odd.

"Oh Ross, there you are…" he barked, not looking. "Quickly, quickly we need the carriage to go and pick up Wilso— you're not Ross! Avis?" He said looking down his nose at me with a scrunched up bearded face. "This wasn't for you… Oh well… get inside quickly!"

So a lovely warm welcome home for me after nearly a year away. I traipsed into the big Hall — a huge space that they use for receptions and parties, with a couple of big fireplaces, the biggest staircase you've ever seen and all adorned with stuffed magical animals in undignified poses on plinths. The room was miserable, the carpet was the only colour, blood red of course… but it was miserable because the walls were full of paintings of old, mostly dead family members — none of whom were smiling. We have a long history of evil family members and it's rather uncouth to smile, or be in any way charismatic, humorous or nice.

"There you are," said a spiky high voice. It was my Mother, scaring the hell out of me as she popped into existence out of nowhere. "Come on Avis! Bags down, let's get to work…" she clicked her bony fingers and a rusty mop and bucket appeared in front of me.

"Erm…" I squeaked under her dark stare.

"I trust you know how to use it?" she smiled viciously. "Start in the turrets, immediately." With a puff of dark vile smelly smoke she vanished. Well, she hadn't changed, not at all. My Mother was still tall, thin and haughty with a face like thunder, all sharp and pointed as if she's got a lemon wedged up the back of her throat. And she was bossy. I sighed and made my way up to the turrets — I certainly didn't have the guts to defy her.

My parents grudgingly allowed me meal breaks in between all the scrubbing. Believe me I tried to get out of it, but they seemed to know when I was slacking… I had just started a particularly stubborn black corridor, and thought I would have a sit-down. My body ached, every muscle pleaded with me to stop and as I sat against the wall my consciousness slipped into a deep sleep, before out of nowhere a burst of bright blue electricity struck my bottom!

"*AHH*!" I called.

"Get to work!" called my Fathers voice along the hallway. Seriously? I mean come on! I needed a break. Why did they have to have the wedding here anyway? I felt like Cinderella, being treated like a slave! Mind you, I could do what she did... sue her family and live in comfort for the rest of her life on the settlement. Apparently it bankrupted that family and they all had to move into a council flat with relatives on the *Outside*. I imagined my parents all living in a tiny flat after I sued them for mistreatment. I held onto this fuzzy dream as I scrubbed and scrubbed.

During one meal break sitting at the huge long table in the Hall eating my hard, mouldy cheese and bread that Butler Kilkenny brought me — there was a great big noise from the carriageway outside. Like a thunderclap my parents appeared out of nowhere by the front door. The drawbridge lowered and in walked my eldest three brothers Wilson, Simon and Harold.

"Mamma!" they cooed, doing air kisses for about ten minutes. My brother's entourages then proceeded to go back and forth to the carriages bringing in box after box of stuff and piling it up in the hall.

"You can't leave them all there," said Mother, snapping at one of the men who was sweating profusely as he lugged the heavy boxes.

"Where would you like us to put them ma'am?"

Simon, the second oldest and dimmest, said: "In our rooms of course... oh, we don' have rooms yet. What rooms Avis in?" I sighed and sank a little lower down the table, but not before Wilson spotted me.

"Avis!" he called, their beady evil eyes coming to rest on me. "Which room are you in?"

"I don't know what room it is," I lied. "You can't have it anyway… I'm in there, why do you want it?"

"Because, we've travelled an awfully long way," said Simon. "And must rest."

"We are guests," said Harold grinning. "Only fair we get pick of the rooms and if you're in it, that is rather unfortunate." I smiled at them as best I could, there was no point arguing with these three. Wilson looked like a dog with a smashed in face, due to a fight with a Wolfraptor. He wore blood red ceremonial gowns with gold trimmings… I rather thought he looked like a baboon in a cape. Simon was simple, very simple, when he looks at you there's clearly nothing much there. He's dead behind the eyes and brainless — slime always drips from the corner of his mouth and his choice of clothes is beyond strange. Today's selection is: chrome trousers with a neon yellow shirt and pastel green trimmings. All the brains went to Harold, he is exceptionally clever and cunning, I would never, ever decide on him as an enemy — he's the one sibling I am most scared of.

"Let me vanish all the stuff from my room first," I said.

"No, no," said Wilson. "Leave it, I want to have a play with it."

I grimaced. "Well you can't, it's mine," I called. Mother turned and caught me with a piercing stare.

"Don't argue Avis. Family dinner starts at seven," she announced before disappearing.

***

I didn't see any of my other siblings cleaning. They just stood around conversing with a few early arrived guests.

"Well, of course Mr. Vasbender," said Wilson in a sickening voice. "The media know their role in the new situation. I am seeing a girl currently who is the executive manager of the Herrald. It helps."

"Very good," called Mr. Vasbender. "I suppose the illusion of it all will carry on making the intended effect."

"Of course," said Harold.

I pretended to be dusting the banisters again, so I could get a good listen to what they were talking about — hoping I would hear something about Malakai. Where was he? What was he doing? If anyone would know it would be these lot. A little twinge in my stomach rumbled, but it wasn't food related, I was scared. Scared that Malakai would come for me and get revenge for what I did to him. Suddenly a great racket from one of the corridors caused everyone to turn and look. Gertrude and Wendice, were shouting at the top of their voices at each other.

"I WANT THE BLUE DRESS, IT LOOKS BETTER ON ME!"

"YOU LOOK FAT IN IT! I SHOULD HAVE IT!"

"GIVE IT TO ME!"

"NO! YOU GIVE IT TO ME!"

There was an awful tearing sound, and as they came into view in the Hall I saw them both holding one half of a flouncy blue dress. There was a rumble from somewhere deep, before the highest pitched squealing you've ever heard erupted around the Hall.

"*AHHHHHHHHH!*" they both screamed.

Guests and all manner of life that valued it's hearing, covered their ears as the shrill, terrible noise made every bone in your body shudder for its life. In a scorch of black smoke Mother arrived. The screaming stopped.

"What on earth is happening here."

"Wendice tore my dress in HALF!" Sobbed Gertrude. "You fat cow Wendic—"

"Enough of that," Snapped Mother. "Give me it…" They both handed her the two parts, in a wave and a flash it sewed itself back together.

7

"Now," she looked at the dress and then at the girls. "It will suit Wendice more, here…" she said, handing it to Wendice.

"But, but…" said Gertrude, her fat lip wobbling. "That's… NOT *FAIRRRRRR!*"

"Oh for gods sake," said Mother. "Get a grip of yourself girl, you're too big for that dress… go and find something more suitable, a shower curtain or something." In a puff of black smoke, she was off again. Now, as an Outsider you probably think that was harsh, your all very… what's that phrase that Robin told me… *politically correct?* Which means you're not allowed to say anything nasty to each other. But we are an *evil* family. Get used to it.

The Hall stood in silence for a bit, before my brothers began laughing. Gertrude ran off, well, more of a quick waddle, sobbing her eyes out as guests chuckled.

Wendice stood about smugly, waving her dress, before announcing: "You know actually I think she was right, I don't think I like it," with a click of her fingers, the blue dress caught fire and she dropped it on the floor, where it burned to a blue dust. "I'm going to find something nicer for the wedding." She flounced off back the way she came smiling to herself. Wendice had changed — last year she was as fat as Gertrude, but now she was skinnier than me, with long hair and a golden complexion. It was quite a transformation. She was already saying she'd had twelve proposals for marriage. I hope she didn't get married in the castle again, that's all I'm saying. I don't fancy cleaning it all again!

When they allowed me a toilet break, I raced back to my room and placed Sedrick, my teddy rabbit, inside my jacket. I had missed him — before, when it was just me on my own in the castle, I used to talk to him, sad I know, but I had no other friends. In my old school, down the road, everyone was too frightened to come here to play, knowing that my family was the most evil family ever.

I wondered what Robin and Tina and Ernie were doing. I would have loved to see Ernie's face when he went back to his old house after all those years — you see, last year I made friends with a young ghost, who, it turned out was the dead brother of Tina — he helped me defeat Malakai and Robin brought him back to life, all in the nick of time. He had been a ghost for ten years!

WHOOSH!

"OUCH!" I cried as a stinging electric bolt struck my bottom as Mother's voice rang true around this new room:

"Get to work, there's toilets need cleaning on the third floor!"

For gods sake, when will this end!?

I carried the mop and bucket to the third floor and looked around for the toilets, they should be behind one of these doors. That's the problem though, all the doors are the flipping same, so how am I supposed to tell where the toilets are? If *I* can't find them, then I'm sure as hec a guest won't.

But then a strange noise floated towards me — a scratching noise, water too... *slop, slap, scratch, scratch, scratch... slop, slap, scratch, scratch, scratch...* it was coming from around the corner. Cautiously I poked my head round a stone effigy of a near relative and saw...

"Ross?" Whoops. I couldn't help it, he was on all fours scrubbing the floor!

He looked up with bloodshot eyes, which winced as they saw me. He stood, clicked his fingers and the brush carried on scrubbing the floor. "There making *you* clean as well?"

"I was wondering when I might bump into you..."

"Why?" I said.

"Why? *Why?*" he said a little too loud, his face twitchy and dangerous. "Because you had something to do with the downfall of *him*."

I swallowed hard. "I don't know what you mean."

"The Lily said as much... you and the Partington's... that sodding ghost boy... it all adds up. You did *something*."

His voice dripped with indignation and resentment, he was livid that he'd been made to clean and somehow it was all my fault. His dark sunken eyes twitched. His thin lips chapped and curled inwards, skin pale and pasty, a green hue surrounding it — he looked like he hadn't seen sunlight in years.

I backed away slowly as he came closer. "How could I do something? I'm a first year?"

Ross rolled up his sodden sleeves. "I'm not stupid Avis. I know you did something, by sheer bloody luck or whatever… and I'm gonna get to the bottom of it. Your just lucky our parents are too busy with this wedding to realise what's going on." His eyes looked dead and black. "*I* was supposed to go and work for him, soon as I left that awful school… but now look, I am at home… scrubbing bloody FLOORS! All because of *you*," he began talking in a strangely high voice, which scared me even more — "*Didn't believe me did they… when I told them…*. and now look at *ME*! All *your* fault… all *your* fault…" he repeated.

I backed around the corner slowly. I did not like the look in his eyes. "You've got it all *wrong* Ross."

"I'm gonna make you *confess* to what you did. They will be able to read your mind and see that I am right."

"No ones reading my mind," I said, slowly putting the mop and bucket down. Ross raised his hands slowly. "Stop that," I said. "Put your hands down."

"I'll tell all our brothers first. Get some of Harold's *truth infusion*, make you confess. Then what do you think our parents will do about you? Or rather, do *to* you…" He cackled.

"They won't do anything because I am innocent. Now put your hands down."

Ross smiled. "No!" In less than a second, a bright red chain flew out of his hands at me.

"*Dancidious!*" I called, ducking as the chains shaved the top of my head. "Stop it Ross! *Stop it!*" But he wouldn't.

More red chains came flying towards me. "Dancidious! *Dancidious!*" I called in vain, for it made no difference! I ducked and dived out of the way. But it was time to run. I stood up and charged round the corner for the end of the corridor. There was a short golden flash beneath my eyes, I thought Ross has got me. But it wasn't that at all... it was something much better... my Seven League Shoes, the ones I put on in the carriage had lit up gold! As I ran, my legs felt different and I noticed time change around me. It slowed down. I got to the end of the corridor in the blink of an eye. I turned around and saw Ross, in slow motion, his face contorted into mad fury, spells fizzing and popping as they exploded against pictures, expelling plumes of dust from the floor. Speeding down the next hallway, which was at least a hundred feet, I put one foot before the next and without thinking or doing anything, the shoes carried me all the way to the end. It felt like walking through treacle, little effort was expelled, yet they carried me that hundred feet in a second. It was magical. The golden fizzing light died down as the shoes stopped moving, corridors and hallways had passed me by in a blur... but now I was... god knows where. It was dark and high up, for the pictures on the wall were all of magical creatures that we hang in the turrets. How did I get all the way up here in a matter of seconds? Still, they'd probably just saved my life.

All I could see was darkness and... an open door with a faint orange glow. There was no where else to turn so I walked forwards.

It was one of the turrets, small and dusty, dim and dark. Facing the fire was a high backed chair. A head of silvery hair just visible over the top.

"Come in boy," said a barky voice. I froze, ice shards splintering my spine. The voice echoed softly around the turret. "Sit, sit..." beckoned a long bony hand.

CHAPTER TWO
Granddad's Gift

"Granddad?" I said sitting down where he asked me and staring in disbelief at the old man with silvery hair. "No way... this isn't real... I thought you were... *dead?*"

My Granddad sat as still as a rusty nail, and looked as gnarled and grizzled as one. His face scarred and lined, due to all the fights he'd had. But all in all, for a dead person he looked pretty good — dressed in long black day clothes and a navy blue cape. His magical cane stood next to his chair, small colourful lights fizzing just under the surface. I was always fascinated by it as a kid and could watch for hours. We sat in silence for a long time, my mouth open, just staring at him.

He sighed. "So, you found me then."

"... I didn't mean to... I was just... running away and..." I stammered.

"Ross was after you. Thinks you ruined his life. You did something," he said in his characteristic barky, clipped tone.

"Yeah," I said. "He does, mind you, none of the Blackthorns like me."

"Nonsense. They just have a funny way of showing it," he said still looking into the fire. "So you came here by accident did you. That's a *coincidence*," he smiled. "Why were you up here in these turrets?"

"I wasn't, I was on the third floor. I was cleaning and ran away from Ross and..."

"Cleaning?" he sniffed, his brow furrowed. "They make you *clean?*"

"Yeah. Mum wants the castle clean for the guests coming to Marianne's wedding."

"Marianne?" he barked. "That jumped up little twerp? Sorted herself out and found a fella' ahy? I don't doubt with a personality like hers, she had to use quite the arsenal of love spells?"

I nodded, a small smirk gracing my face. "I think so yeah," I was itching to ask him what the hell he was doing up here, he was dead, I mean I'd been to his funeral and everything.

"Don't worry yourself about *that*," he said suddenly, dark glaring eyes coming to rest on me, commanding attention. "We are Wizards, we can do strange things. And as Blackthorn's we are well versed in black magic. Don't worry yourself about how. Just listen…" he held his hand out and a long poker appeared in it. He poked the coals as some fresh ones moved slowly into the air from the coal basket and landed in the renewed flames. "Don't worry yourself about Malakai."

I nearly fell off my chair. "Wha— wha— whaaaat? I mean, you know? But how?"

Granddad leered at me through the darkness, grinning a black-toothed smile. "Never liked him. You did us a favour I say… not sure *they* will see it that way," he said flicking his eyes downwards. "You didn't come here by accident, I made sure you came here. We never spoke much when I was alive."

"Er… alive?" I said, unsure if this was a joke or not.

"I probably don't need to remind you of the fact that you are different from other Blackthorns," he grinned his black grin at me again. "You're a *seventh son*. You did well against *him*. And I am sure you will find out what you need to in the upcoming year." He licked his lips, as if he was about to carry on, but then slumped back in his chair.

"Find out what?" I said.

He shrugged. "What you need to," his eyes moved to a place just above the cluttered fireplace, along which three items stood: a porcelain dalmatian dog, some magic nails and a red urn with a funny mark on it. But now, something was hanging down in front of the mirror — where there had been nothing before. "I had better give you something that will help." He reached forwards, stretching out his cane and unhooked the thing from the mirror. As he drew it towards him I saw it was a pendant. On the end of the sleek silver string was a small metallic shard of indistinguishable shape, which slowly came towards me on the end of the cane. "Take it," he said gruffly, I reached forwards and took it. There was a short rumble like thunder, before a flash of blue light lit up the room, temporarily blinding me.

"Ahh!" I cried, shielding my eyes. "What on earth was that?" The pendant was spinning in my hand now and Granddad, who didn't look like he was shocked at all, nodded happily to himself. The metallic shape on the end was a thin metal, but sturdy and a worn golden colour. In the very middle was a clear, black mark — I didn't know what it was, but had an inkling that it was a rune.

"It's a channeller," said Granddad, putting his cane back to his side. "A very old one."

"Forgive me Granddad, but this is strange... I mean, you're a Blackthorn... you're not supposed to be on my side. They all hate me..." I said, pointing down at the floor. "No one in this family has *helped* me before."

Granddad sighed. "You realise this as you get older — not everything is black and white, or good and bad. There is a lot of grey too," he gruffed. "You must tailor your vision to read the grey. Oh, and take this before you go," He handed out a small, red velvet drawstring bag.

"What is it?" I said, then realising as it touched down in my palm, it was a bag of gold! I couldn't help but gasp. "But, but, I..."

"It's embarrassing having a Blackthorn that walks around looking like a corpse... get yourself some smart clothes."

I couldn't help the grin that grew across my jaw. "Thank you, thank you so much!" Granddad didn't say anything, he just sat and stared at the fire.

"Take care," he barked, then with a wave I was dismissed. I stood, carrying my bag of gold and new channeller, unsure if I was dreaming or not, or whether these shoes were in fact casting a strange illusion of my dead Granddad being nice to me. But as I walked back out of the hazy darkness, I found myself high up in the castle, nowhere near the turrets... how strange.

I put the pendant channeller round my neck and tucked it beneath my robes. Then, put the bag of gold down the back of my trousers, into a secret compartment that I had installed in the shop when my Mother wasn't looking. No one would be stealing this bag of gold from me. I raced back to the cleaning cupboard to get another mop and bucket before I received another thunder clap to the butt.

Over the proceeding week, many unsavoury characters arrived. Slowly but steadily each room filled. Now that I had a channeller again I could do magic, but I had to make sure Mother and Father didn't see me otherwise I would be in for it. They would start questioning me about where I got it, and I'm a rubbish liar. But, I did have a few mop and buckets scrubbing the floors by themselves on the second and forth floors. And I casted the Riptide chameleon spell *Goaternut*, over myself at the top of the stairs while hiding behind a statue, so I could watch Father greeting the Hennessy Warlock Clan, who trod mud all the way up the stairs.

Then I saw Nasty Luke make his way in with his similarly nasty, pasty faced family. Followed by some wicked witches, twelve piggy bankers, who *oinked* all the way around the Hall, valuing the goods. Then came the Chelsee family. The wicked head of the family was old Marge Chelsee, a particularly foul woman — with her six, very ugly, daughters in huge ridiculous dresses, waddling behind her. As they chatted away to each other, I had trouble making out the difference between the piggy's oinks and the inane gigglish chatter.

I sat watching for a good few hours, it was better than cleaning, and noticed many important people. King's and Queens, Princes and Princesses, Head's of Kingdoms and Prime Ginisters (or whatever they're called on the Outside). Anyone who was anyone was here, it was crazy. If someone dropped a bomb and took this place out, you would have no leaders of any Kingdoms.

Father stood and with half a look at Mum, took out his magical megaphone and spoke, his voice cast magically throughout the whole castle. "Greetings to all who have arrived today here at Darkhampton. As you all know, we are here to witness the wedding of Marianne Blackthorn and Edward James Burrows..." There was some cooing from the people that remained in the hall. "Dinner this evening will be served in the hall at *seven* sharp." There was a small clap and everyone began to make their way upstairs to their rooms. I displaced myself from behind the statue and scuttled away back along the corridor to my mop and bucket on the forth floor.

Before I knew it, the sickening circus was ready to begin. Mother had found out what room I was in, and had made my wedding attire appear over the door. It was hideous. Green layers of jacket accompanied a yellow shirt — I didn't know it was fancy dress? Obviously I was going as a lump of mouldy cheese. I know Marianne wanted a colourful wedding, but this was ridiculous.

The week leading up to the wedding was hell. I'd been worked like a donkey: cleaning, scrubbing, washing clothes in the laundry room, washing drapes, washing dishes, bowls, cups and cutlery — Butler Kilkenny looked like he was going to have a nervous breakdown. "They haven't hired any extra staff like they said they would!" he called, as the piles of dishes tottered ominously on the creaking draining board.

"You should have learnt by now, that their *word* means nothing."

He huffed, creaked then whimpered. "Ridiculous... *ridiculous!*"

Fortunately, I didn't see Ross at all. I had no idea where he was. All my other brothers were milling around talking to guests, taking them on tours of the grounds — the black, dusty, bracken filled grounds — and leading dinners and parties.

Surely enough Marianne, (the bride) finally arrived. With everyone seated at the huge table, elongated until it was as long as the Hall, the doors suddenly burst open and a fanfare of rambunctious trumpets resounded ear-splittingly loud — announcing her arrival. She burst through the doors with enough gusto to blow a herd of Hubris over. The Hall stood, clapped and cheered. I couldn't clap because I had serving gloves on. Yes, you guessed it, I was a bloody waiter as well.

"I AM *HEEEEERE!*" she screamed. "Please, please..." she said in her sickeningly faux sweet voice. "Please sit, sit, it's only little old *meeee!*" She then proceeded to hug and kiss almost every one on the table, take her presents and hand them to her poor entourage. It nearly took all flipping night.

The morning of the wedding I was awoken by an alarm set up by my mother, which zapped my bed with an electric current — so naturally I shot out of bed. I got into the mouldy cheese costume, washed and sat on the end of the bed. I put the Seven League Shoes on, a golden tinge reflected off the dull black leather. It was early, too early. But something was different. Usually, in this house, we wake up to darkness, eternal darkness all day long. But today, sun light, glorious, wonderful sunlight peered through the window. I walked in front of the rays in a daze. It hit my face and made me tingle all over. For a moment, I thought I might be back in Hailing Hall.

"Well Sedrick," I said. "One more day of hell." I knew that if I just did whatever my parents asked, I would kind of get left alone for the rest of the holidays. And with three weeks left, I didn't want to do anything that would hinder my chances of going back to Hailing Hall.

***

It was the gaudiest wedding I'd ever been to. As I went downstairs everlasting rainbow confetti rained down from the roof, as guests descended slowly, taking in the whole god dam ugliness of it all. Cherubs, or fat, ghostly babies serenaded the crowd with trill tunes. Flowers sprouted from the banisters with bright colours, setting my hay fever off. Banners read *Celebration*, and *The Union of Blackthorn and Burrows*, and *Wedding of the Year* and other cringe-worthy things swung from the rafters at every angle. The Hall table was decked out with so much fancy glass, porcelain and cutlery that I am sure they'd had to enlarge it again. As well, the biggest black cake you've ever seen sat in the corner of the Hall with a huge glass dome standing over it. I mean it must have been twenty feet tall.

My parents were struggling with the sun, I could tell, they were shielding their faces and wincing like vampires. But they had no choice, you see Marianne had decided that for her wedding day that's what she wanted, so they had to make it happen. Removing whatever charm it was that made darkness eternal around the castle and letting the sun in once more. It showed off all the worst bits about the castle though. I mean, in the rays of sunlight that streamed in through long ceiling to floor windows, you could see streams of dust floating around. No wonder I'd always had bad lungs.

Our family is strange you see, their evilness has led to several strange traits: Marianne lives in the sunniest part of the Seven Kingdoms and has a palace with a glass roof that she calls Crystal Palace. It gets near twenty hours a day sunlight — she loves it. My parents however, love darkness. My brother's Wilson and Simon love the cold, and live in a big ice castle in Slackerdown. Wendice loves silence and darkness, and lives in a sound proofed palace in Farkingham. Whereas Gertrude loves noise, shouting, parties and dances and her palace in Golandria, has a permanent dancing troupe, band and party guests. It's a flipping strange family, this one.

"Avis!" cried Mother, spotting me. "*You're* over here, with Butler Kilkenny and the *staff*," she pointed and I traipsed over to a line of Butler Kilkenny and some stunned looking staff, standing to attention. Ross stood at the end of the line glaring at me in a red, orange and pink tuxedo, he looked like a dead flamingo.

Outside, in the charmed grounds which, today only, looked like a lush green paradise with actual grass, palm trees, white seats and a white tent thing.

The cherubs and the band piped up. I was at the back and saw for the first time, the tall, dark and handsome, if not a little dazed looking Edward Burrows. He made his way to the front where he stood next to a slim, fair-haired and rosy-cheeked man, who must have been his best man or whatever. Then, I mean you couldn't have missed her, in the hugest dress you've ever seen, Marianne began to walk to the front. The best man of Burrows looked really nervous, more so than Burrows, he kept looking around and checking his watch. As Marianne reached the front, Burrows gazed dreamily towards her — probably wondering what on earth was going on.

A man, dressed all in long black robes and golden buttons began speaking. "We are here today to celebrate the union between Marianne Louise Blackthorn and Edward James Burrows." The crowd clapped. I sighed, please let this be over already.

***

It was done. The *I do's* and the kiss and all that gushy nonsense was done. The poor bloke was officially part of the Blackthorn family, god help him. Like I usually did at my parents parties with mostly evil people, I stayed well clear for as long as possible. I walked over to this big collection of trees and found a quiet spot in the shade, settling down underneath. I took off the purple tie, and green jacket. *Ahhh*, that was better. It was so hot I was sweating! I said the spell that would hide me and wondered if it would work with all these clever, highly trained Wizards?

I snoozed under that tree for a long, lovely, dreamy hour. Until voices from the party got louder and louder.

"I thought he might have made an appearance," said a man's voice, followed by a cackle.

"Haven't you heard?" the voice screeched. "He's gone… Malakai was defeated by a boy!" the voice laughed, sending a chill down my spine — they were talking about *him*. I trained my ear towards the nearby conversation.

"I should wind your opinions in Sir Humphrey," came my Father's voice, deep and commanding.

"I should, but it's true isn't it?" screeched Sir Humphrey. "What hope is left for the darkness without its *leader*?"

My Father gruffed. "You just concentrate on *your* job, and remember who *placed* you where you are."

"He's right though Nigel," (that's my Father's name — Nigel, funny isn't it?) "He's gone, the opposing force is probably mounting an attack as we speak. I am surprised they're not at the wedding already." Father said nothing else that I could hear. So, they were worried that their evil empire would fall without its leader? So did that mean that Malakai had disappeared? I mean, I didn't kill him or anything, I saw him get away — maybe someone else had got him?!

"Hello, little brother," came a long, slow drawn out voice. "We know what you did," I opened my eyes slowly. All my brothers stood over me. Harold at the front, Simon, Wilson, Rory, Gary and Ross just behind. He'd told them. I just knew it. Fear rippled through me at the sight of these six pairs of dead, evil eyes staring down at me.

"What's wrong?" I said, as innocently as I could.

Harold judged me and rocked his head. "You don't look indignant at being accused, as you should be if you're innocent," he smiled.

I frowned. "I don't know what you mean," I said, playing dumb was the best option. "What am I supposed to have done now?"

Rory blurted it out. "Ross told us!" Harold held up a hand for silence.

I scoffed. "Oh, so you believe him do you? He's just annoyed because Mother and Father made him clean, he'll do anything to have me do it all instead."

Harold raised an eyebrow. "But it's also true that our Lord of Darkness hasn't been seen or heard of since the end of school, when the sanctimonious little creep Partington claimed to have defeated him."

"You helped him!" cried Simon.

"You did you did! Insider knowledge!" followed Gary.

Harold raised his hands again. "Quiet!" he waited, my brother's mouths opened and closed, ready to shout obscenities whether I was innocent or not. "Ross's story sticks. He thinks you had some *inspired insider knowledge* that helped this dead Partington boy end Malakai. Just tell me if

21

this is true or not, it will be a lot easier in the long run if you just admit the truth to me."

I swallowed. "Whatever I say will be wrong."

"The truth…" said Harold.

I couldn't tell them the truth could I? Even though I was tempted to under Harold's intense stare. For if I admitted that I'd helped Ernie, it would still be a lie. I didn't help Ernie, I did it all. "I had nothing to do with any of it," I said.

"Any of *what*?" said Wilson.

"Well, whatever Ernie said."

"*Ernie*?" said Harold. "So you're on first name terms?"

I swallowed. "No, I…"

Wilson huffed, then charged towards me. "I've had enough of this, there's only one way we can find out the truth… pin him down!" A few people began looking around at the commotion.

"Get away from me," I said, holding my arms out at them, making them laugh.

"What on earth are you gonna do to me?" said Wilson. "*Tidicidious*…" he called lazily. A whistle lit the air, as a turquoise triangle shot towards me like a thrown dagger.

I reacted as quickly as I could, wishing beyond all else that it would work. "*Dancidious*!" I cried. The whistling spell Wilson said, hit an invisible reflective shield in front of me and bounced off.

"Oh no…" I said — coming out of the doorway were ten entourages carrying the humungous twenty foot black cake. The dagger spell flew across the heads of guests and in one sickening, smashing sound the dagger shattered the glass. The force of the spell caused the men to fly into the air, the cake falling, falling… SPLAT! Across the cobblestones now lay black mush. There was utter silence. No one dared move. Slowly, one by one, eyes began moving from all around, following the turquoise contrail left by the dagger — to me. My brothers didn't react either, they stood dumb, shell-shocked. They didn't think I had a channeller, let alone could do magic. Then, the loudest, most ear-splitting, earth wrenching scream lit the air.

"*AHHHHHHHHHHHHHHHH!*" Marianne howled, her face contorted with a frenzied, berserk rage. Black sparks rained into the sky from her fingertips as guests ducked under chairs. Then calm. She stood breathing heavily. There was murder in her eyes, I had to do something to save myself.

Then, in the silence, a small voice called something. Out of the corner of my eye I saw the best man of Edward Burrows, blow a small horn. Small white flashes lit the forest behind and all around, as new people arrived. I was utterly confused. But then, realising what was happening, my parents stood and roared. Arms extended outwards pointing at the forest, as spells suddenly exploded from their palms.

I jumped to the floor as Burrow's best man called out: "*Assemble!*" Then, white lights fizzed through the air at the guests, leaving them to scatter in all directions. People in white robes were attacking the wedding! Spells and lights popped, whistled and crunched above my head and from all around. The guests, in one quick moment, drew up their sleeves, pulled out their staff's, canes, wands and sticks and threw return fire. Suddenly, from all around were leaves exploding into the air, bits of tree's cast in every direction as they were sliced by sharp spells.

It was time to run. I had no idea who these people were that had just appeared through the forest, what they were doing here or why. But I had to get out of here! I ducked and ran as fast as I could through the smoke and dust that clouded the air. I clattered into chairs and scrambled for the way out, slipping across skiddy cake and back into the Hall. I turned quickly and saw my six brothers firing off black spells in every direction.

Inside the Hall, the echoes from the battle outside rang deafeningly loud. "Oi you!" called Wilson and Rory bursting into the Hall behind me. "You can stay where you are!"

"Sod off!" I called, turning to run. I'd better be quick, because I felt a big spell brewing behind me. *Come on shoes! Please, please, please do your thing, like you did before!* I repeated, urging them on. But they didn't work. Orange fire burst past me, missing me by an inch. It hit the statue at the top of the stairs, which fell over the banishers casting a choking dust over everything. I jumped the last step and glanced behind me. My brothers turned, and were throwing spells at someone who had come into the Hall.

"Who *ARE YOU?!*" they screamed. Glancing down through the banisters at the man who was dancing away from their spells, I saw the best man of Edward Burrows. The man who had inadvertently saved me.

Without any more waiting, I turned and ran. My breath caught in my throat as my sides began to burn. Who were those people? Why were they attacking the wedding? Who was I kidding, it had probably just saved my butt. I reached my room on the forth floor and shut the door. The loud noises sounded far off, small bangs, pops and rumbles shuddered the floor. I pulled out a bag from under my bed and began pilling in clothes and stuff. I had to get out of here as soon as possible. But where did I go? School didn't start for another three weeks! I hid Sedrick inside an alcove in the wall. "*Avertere,*" I said, the shadow inside the alcove surrounded Sedrick until he became invisible. I glanced around my room, I think I had everything I needed. It was time to go.

But where? And how? How did I get out of the castle without getting attacked? I glanced out the window. Just below was our fleet of carriages. I had to get to them. I slung the bag on my back and moved out of my room. I needed to get downstairs and out the window in the kitchen.

Jogging along the corridor and past the Hall, I saw it was clear — my brothers and Burrows best man were gone. I slipped down the stairs, through the clouds of dust, as quietly as I could. Then, scuttled down into the servant hallways to the kitchen. My heart was beating so fast, all I knew was, if I was gonna make it out of this alive, I had to get away, far, far away. I pushed open the door to the kitchen which was crammed with food. The window was open in the corner, I thanked my lucky stars.

A bumbling, muttering noise made me stop in my tracks. "Errr, mehhh, whhhaa…"

"Hello?" I said. "Who's there?"

"Waaaahhh!" wailed the terrified voice. I followed the wails under the table, where a gibbering Butler Kilkenny sat trembling and hugging himself.

"What are you doing under there?" I said.

"Safe, safe…" he gibbered. "Safe from them," he turned and grabbed my jacket.

"Get off me!" I tried to push him away, but his bony claw hand gripped like a vice.

"You have to do magic to get us out of here! Do magic, magic boy!"

"I said get off me!" I cried, yanking his hands away.

He wailed again. "Snivelling little runt!" he cried, matted grey hair flying everywhere. "You little runt!" he pointed at me again.

"You nasty old man, I've never liked you… *Pasanthedine*," the Spell flashed before zapping Butler Kilkenny into the air. He screamed as he was flung upside down, hanging useless, flailing around madly.

"Get me down you little runt! Get me down!"

"Get yourself down you miserable old git…" With that I saluted him goodbye and jumped out the window.

About twenty carriages of varying grey, brown and black colours were lined up on the gravel in perfect order. Sprinting across to the only one I knew would fly itself, I opened the doors to my parents ceremonial carriage, threw my bag inside and jumped in. A loud bang rumbled the grounds, just behind the castle I could see what looked like hundreds of fireworks being let off.

I swallowed, it was time to go. I heard the carriage start to whizz as it lifted gently into the air, hovering slowly. "Take me too…" I thought frantically, where could I go? Butler Kilkenny had found a way down, I saw him poke his head out the window and shake a fist. I had to go somewhere they wouldn't find me. But where? "Take me… to *the Outside.*" I swallowed as the whizzing sound grew louder, the carriage rising higher into the air. Butler Kilkenny was joined at the window now by my brothers Wilson, Harold and Ross. A long arm reached out into the sky. I sat back away from the window.

"Go now! *Quickly!*" I called as the carriage whizzed a little louder. A blue blast of fire shot past the carriage window. They were trying to shoot me down! "Quicker!" I cried as they threw spell after spell at me.

BANG! The carriage was suddenly engulfed in a blast of black fire! "GO NOW!" In a flash of purple light, the carriage exploded forwards. I was thrown back into the leather seat. All sound was reduced to a high pitched whistle. I shut my eyes and prayed for it to be over as the carriage blasted upwards into the sky. I didn't know what the carriage did to get to the Outside — but knew it wouldn't be usual. And I was right, a second later the carriage began to spin. We shot at the speed of light through a spinning purple vortex — a terrifying, bright purple tunnel. At the end a white dot, which grew bigger and bigger until…

CHAPTER THREE
The Percevius Denn Inn

The carriage sailed into the white dot. I shielded my eyes before seeing green grass and brown earth, before falling, faster and faster. I clung on for dear life as the carriage seemed to lose all power and careered for the ground.

"*AHHHH!*" I cried in vain as I braced myself for the inevitable.

CRAAAAASSSSHHHHH! We smashed into ground, casting mud and earth into the air from all around as a sickening *eeeeeekkkkkkkk* sound erupted. I flew to the front and face planted the glass. I heard a sickening crunching noise, then pain, glorious, horrible, stinging pain! The carriage skidded through earth, before flipping over and over and over... me and my bag turning summersaults as it repeatedly smacked into my already sore face. I grabbed it as we span, round and round like some tortuous fairground ride. I prayed for it to be over already. Then, the carriage turned upside down, my body rose into the middle of the carriage in one glorious floating moment... before the leather seat, all at once, came crashing into my midriff, winding me completely — and then all was still, as darkness set in. I couldn't help close my eyes, and let my aching body rest.

The pain echoed through me even in sleep. When my eyes finally opened, all I could see was a pounding white light in front of my eyes where my nose throbbed. All down the front of my jacket was blood. All over the carriage roof, or floor, was blood. I blinked and sat up. The carriage was upside down in, from what I could make out from the gap in the window that wasn't buried in mud, the middle of a field. My stomach groaned as I sat forwards, the winding I received coming back in painful spurts like invisible stabbing needles. The carriage was making a weird whizzing sound and emitting a large amount of purple smoke, I had to get out of here quickly. With my head throbbing, and nose crying, I leant round and kicked the carriage door. Every pore of my body begged me to stop, as the pain rippled around me. *Stop being such a wuss,* I said to myself, hoping that it could make the pains just sod off. I gave another kick and caught the window which smashed. Purple smoke began billowing out of the carriage as if it was a race. Kicking the glass out of the panel I crawled out through the small gap, catching my robes on the shards and hearing small tearing sounds. But I didn't care, I was out of the carriage at last and… in the middle of a big field.

Sssssssssssssss… came the hissing sound from the carriage. Before purple flames suddenly engulfed it from all around. I stepped back into slippy mud. This was bad, really bad — it was my parents best ceremonial carriage, and now I'd crashed it and it was on fire. I couldn't even think of a spell that would put it out? I suddenly realised how little about magic I really knew, for I couldn't even think of a spell that would shoot water, or foam or anything that would put it out! And so, I turned my back on it, as if, childishly, it would just vanish and go back home good as new and there would be no problem and I wouldn't be in trouble at all — as if I wasn't in enough already.

I didn't know where I was. Like not just not knowing where you are in a town you sort of know — but not knowing where I was in a town, in a kingdom, in a world I didn't know — the *Outside*. Somewhere I'd never been, somewhere big and terrifying. I walked on though, despite being terrified that I might be killed at any point. I followed a track next to the field and walked, with my bag bobbing up and down on my back, until I saw the first signs of civilisation.

Huge shiny castles shot into the sky — or was it one big castle? But all different shapes and sizes, the tallest one looked like a dagger, all pointy, the next looked all rounded and bulbous, like a gnome's head, all the rest were big and square — so this was the Outside? I looked around, nearby was a road. A sound like a roaring Troll pierced the air, and I ducked, suddenly realising how exposed I was. But then, on the road the thing that made the roaring noise came shooting along it. Sounding like a big Troll was one thing, but it whizzed past with all the speed of a carriage. What was that? It had wheels like a carriage, the speed of one, but was all shiny and metal. Why did I tell the carriage to take me to the *Outside*? I suppose in some vain attempt I thought I would come and find Robin. How was I gonna get back to Hailing Hall now?

"Oi! Oi you little oik!" someone behind me called in a strange tongue. The man was standing near the burnt out carriage, and dressed like a servant. Is that how all Outsiders dressed? In slacks and dirty undershirts? Good god I hope not, otherwise I'd stick out like a sore thumb. He continued to yell, marching over the fields towards me. Perhaps he wanted to help me? The idiotic side of my brain reckoned, as I waited patiently for him to march angrily to my side.

"What on this bloody earth do you think you're playing at?" he said, all huffing and puffing hot stinky breath towards me. What do you Outsiders eat? He had a big bushy beard and long hair, I don't suppose he knew what a brush was? You don't need magic to operate one of those for goodness sake. "So, you gonna start telling me what you think you're doing young lad? Joy riding I expect were ya? Lost control of that vehicle… or whatever it is, and thought you'd crash it into' me farm did ya?" said the man getting angrier still. "And now you'd thought what a great idea it would be, ta' walk across me newly planted crops."

"Erm…" was all I could manage. "I'm terribly sorry could you repeat that, it's just, I didn't have a clue what you just said." It was true, I didn't and thought myself polite, bowing down to this, what looked like, beggar. But this remark clearly made him livid.

"Posh little tyke's like you think you can come and trample all over me farm without any consequences don' ya?!" he cried.

I frowned and backed away, trying to work out what he said, something about being posh… "No, I'm not posh, I mean I talk posh and live in a castle, but so do most people who…" I stopped.

"GET OFF MY LAND!" he exploded, then out of nowhere produced a pitchfork and began chasing me across his field! I tried to reason with him as I jumped the divots in earth and mud. "DOGS! CHASE HIM!"

Suddenly I heard vicious barking as huge dogs began leaping across the dirt towards me. Oh my god! I was about to be ripped to shreds! The breath became thick in my throat as my bag bobbled against my back and I tried to run uselessly. My heels clipped together in a divot and I tripped. Splat! With a face full of mud I scrabbled to my feet as the barking noise ascended, they were gaining! The shoes lit up again. Golden light around my feet shone radiant. In one second I was up and running at the speed of light. The farmer and the dogs disappeared in a flash, the field gone. Then the next one gone. Flash, gone. It was miraculous, I didn't even need to send the message to my legs to move and yet they worked. Then… there was a sudden burst of golden light all across my vision, followed by darkness. I felt myself falling through an ice cold and silent, black void. The fields vanishing, the Outside world gone, the only thing visible the light of the shoes.

Then light and sound filled my vision again. I was somewhere else. Somehow, either the shoes, or some magic I did not know — had taken me back to the Seven Magical

Kingdoms. I was in Gnippoh's the shopping capital of Happendance. A magical place filled with brilliant shops and stalls selling just about anything you could imagine. I'd been here a few times with my parents when I was younger. They always hated it and would never buy my anything, always there on *business*. I remembered people cowering in the street as they passed. Me just bobbing along and gorping at all the brilliant stuff in the windows.

I gazed around now, shaking off the strange feeling from that teleportation (or whatever it was), blinking as my consciousness returned. Up ahead was the entrance to Gnippoh's — a big, long, magical bridge with the hot River Tooze beneath, steam and mist rising over it clouding the town ahead in a mysterious white haze. The bridge was covered all the way over in statues of famous Wizards, Witches, Warlocks, and Warlords, which all stood high and opposing in their stoney forms.

"Come on! Get a move on!" said a little voice, I wheeled around to see where it was coming from. "Oi you, dozy!" it called again. It was coming from a small fat gnome dressed in a tartan kilt who was urging me forwards.

"What do you want?" I said affronted as he waved me forwards.

"How dare you speak to me like that!" he called, jumping up to his full height of two feet and pointing a minuscule finger at me. "There's other people wants to use this fairy ring than you, ya know!" I stepped back and looked around. He was right — I was standing inside a fairy ring. It was basically a small grassy knoll covered in flowers and a hazy green light. As soon as I stepped off and onto the cobble stones, there was a small thudding sound as another person landed inside it.

"Ouch…" called the man. "What was the hold up back there?" he said at the gnome, who gesticulated towards me, then urged the man off the ring. I looked around. I had just walked off a fairy ring? But just a minute before I was on the *Outside* and now I was back in the Magical Kingdoms. I didn't know where I was more in danger — get murdered by my brothers or spiked to death by a *Outsider*. Choices, choices.

I looked down at the fading gold of my shoes. I didn't know how they worked or why they had brought me here, all I knew was — I was blooming grateful.

There were more fairy rings dotted all the way around the entrance to the bridge, as well as high-pitched whistles from trains pulling into stations that built themselves as they pulled in. I crossed the wide Tooze bridge, taking in the wonderful spindly gothic buildings that were arching into the sky like it was a competition for who could stretch the tallest. All of them looked dangerously uneven as they teetered and tottered, the only thing keeping them where they were being Magic. With thatched roofs, mullioned windows and every building being a different colour — it really was unlike anywhere I'd ever seen. Father had always remarked that the lack of town planning in Gnippoh's let it down, he refused to go unless necessary. I liked it, I thought it was charming.

How I would have loved to shop, but the day was setting in and my eyes were stinging with tiredness. I marched into Old Poh Town, the main square of Gnippoh's with it's tall, white obelisk cathedral, tall five story roofless shops with bridges across to each other and the circle market complete with ravaging purple pigeons that would peck your face off for a bit of bread. I took a dark back street northwards and saw a sign for a place I remembered staying at before. *The Percevius Den Inn.* I sighed my thanks, my weary legs carrying me beyond the threshold and booking into a small, grim room with a view across the town square.

Zzzzzzz…

I slept like a cursed princess. Not even the drunken celebrations in the square woke me. I must have been tired when I paid for the room, because it wasn't the best. This place was not exactly how I remember it as a kid. It was small. Very small. I could just about fit in the bed and I'm small. It had brown, or once white, sheets. The walls were green and black. The floor was a blackened stone covered in a grey rug which I reckon used to be colourful, but not anymore. Next to the window was a desk and chair. The desk was covered in stains and old food. Grim. I put some of my clothes away and cleaned the room a bit. I mean, after living in a big dirty castle I'm used to dirt but not this much.

Sitting in the chair I blinked away the heavy sleep, which clung to me like a goblin. I didn't even know what time it was. The square was grey and raining and devoid of people. The white steam rose up from the river behind the buildings. Just then there was a knock at the door, before it opened.

"Breakfast orders?" said the scullery maid looking bored. She looked about my age but I hadn't seen her at Hailing Hall.

"Right," I said, my stomach rumbling. "What is there?"

I sat in a chair that seemed to be sinking down further and further the longer I sat on it. The bar area downstairs was equally shabby, but I didn't care, I was too hungry. I woofed the bacon, sausages and eggs down with toast and kiwi juice. Yum! Then, I got up to pay the ruddy-faced man at the bar.

"'Ere, ain't you the Blackthorn kid?" he said leering over a pump at me.

"Who me? No…" I said as all my insides turned to jelly.

"Yeah you are I'm sure… your little erm… Aver… no, Avis!" he clicked his fingers as he remembered.

"I'm not a Blackthorn," I scowled, the jelly wobbled inside me as I tried to think of a story. "I'm a Wilson, Robin Wilson…"

"*Wilson?*" said the man, his red face turning perplexed. "Aint never heard of no Wilson. You sure your a Wil—"

"Positive!" I cried as I rushed back upstairs. I was stupid, so stupid. Why hadn't I disguised myself?! Of course people would recognise me, I had the most evil parents in all the Seven Magical Kingdoms. All I could do now was hope the bar man didn't snitch. Otherwise I was for it.

Later that day I pulled out some clothes. I needed to wear something that wasn't going to shout '*Blackthorn*!' — I needed to stay hidden. Looking at the clothes I realised there was no way, I'd hardly packed anything in the mad rush. Unless I could change my own face there was no way I could even go out. I mean, I had sat and watched out the window earlier as Wizard after Wizard walked past whom I recognised from the meetings with my parents. I would be captured immediately. I wondered what happened to them at the wedding. I didn't doubt that they were ok, I've never seen better Wizards than my parents. But who were those people all in white? And why were they attacking the wedding?

I had three weeks until the start of school. Three weeks of hiding, hoping no one would find me, of being bored in an amazing city I couldn't go out in, and three weeks of missing my best friends — Tina, Robin and Ernie. As I sat alone up here in this cramped room with little to do, all I wanted was to be able to speak to them. I didn't even know their addresses, so I couldn't even send a telegram. I had consciously not taken their addresses. Think about it, what if my brothers got hold of them? Exactly.

Gnippoh's is a funny place, it has an entire year of seasons in a week. So on the Monday I sat and watched rain, then sleet. Tuesday, more rain and wind followed by all the leaves falling out of the trees. Wednesday, it snowed so hard they had to close the market. By Thursday it thawed out and turned into a river, before melting away completely and new buds and shoots began appearing on the trees all around. By Friday everything was in full bloom. Saturday and Sunday were really sunny, all day and by Sunday night it had gone back to cold and rain again.

Each morning I had to sit and watch the market sellers shouting and demonstrating their amazing fruit, or fish, or contraption. Out on the square was every market stall you could imagine, even a guy selling channellers. How I yearned to go out and explore, but the image of being back at Hailing Hall, safe, kept me up here. I didn't want to risk it.

So I just sat, the scullery maid would give me a knock when it was time for breakfast, or lunch or dinner and I would sit and draw it out for as long as possible. The food was ok, sloppy sausage and mash that looked more like soup, and lasagne that looked more like, well, porridge. Never mind, it was better than the food at home. And the scullery maid was nice to me, sometimes if she wasn't busy she'd come and sit with me while I ate, she was pleasant enough, a bit thick, but I don't judge.

I had memorised the route to school so much that I was sure it had bored straight into my memory for life. The letter from last year had instructions on it for how to get to Hailing Hall from Gnippoh's. And so I resumed my place in the chair by the window; watching, snoozing and dreaming, wondering about how my life could have been different if I just had a normal family. That is, until, one day when I spotted some people I knew through the window. I wouldn't have believed it, would've have put it down as wishful thinking. Robin and Tina were walking slowly through the square, down the steps towards the main shopping town. I rubbed my eyes and looked closer. It was the last day of the summer holidays and the last day I had to stay here at this dirty Den Inn. I jumped up and threw clothes on, grabbed my bag and ran out of the room without a backwards glance.

"Thanks Jenny, thanks Hamish!" I called to the bar man and scullery maid as I legged it out the doors and into the dark alley. Running, I pushed through the crowd, trying to see above their heads for where Robin and Tina went. I skipped the steps three at a time and jumped through a gap in the market stalls. I was outside the tall white obelisk cathedral now and looked around but they were nowhere to be seen. I'd missed them!

"Avis?" said a voice. I turned, Tina and Robin stood mouths open in pleasant surprise.

"There you are!" I called and ran at them.

"Ahh!" Robin called laughing as I practically tackled him to the floor. "Missed you too."

"Oh Avis..." said Tina giggling and hugging me. "How have you been?" she scanned me up and down, for injuries probably.

"Fine, yeah, just fine... ah I've missed you guys. Had no way of finding you. Been staying there..."

Tina's eyebrows raised. "What the dirty Den?" her nose shrivelled up at the thought of it. "Why?"

"Bit of trouble at home, you know."

Robin nodded. "We did know actually," he said, taking off his thick glasses and polishing them as they had got all steamed up. "Tina sent me a copy of the Herrald, apparently some people attacked the Blackthorn wedding?"

"Yeah they did..." I said. "Do they know who?"

"Let's go somewhere," said Tina. "A nice cafe — Slippy Spoons is nice and quiet, come on it's just down here..."

"Thank you," I said taking the quite frankly humungous mug of hot chocolate.

"Told you it was good," Tina smiled taking the cherry from the top of her teetering mountain of cream and marshmallows before eating it. The cafe was quiet, cheap and tucked away down a dark alley. The table and seats were strange, they were made of orange plastic. "It's an imitation of a cafe on the *Outside*. They call it a *greasy spoon*, don't they Robin?" Robin nodded straight into his mountain of cream, and now looked like Father Christmas. I couldn't help but laugh.

"I am so glad I bumped into you guys. I was gonna go mad in that Inn."

"So," said Robin slurping his chocolate. "How did you get away?"

"Stole a carriage." I grimaced. "Crashed it too, on the *Outside*."

Tina nearly choked. "You did *whaaaaat?*" she put a hand to her temple as if she was an exasperated parent.

"So did they say who the attackers in white at the wedding were?" I said.

Robin shook his head. "They don't know, just said that it was a group that used to exist a long time ago or something. Didn't really understand it." I looked to Tina for a better explanation, but she shrugged.

"I was glad to get away to tell you the truth, treated me like a slave when I got back. Cleaning, scrubbing, sorting out stuff for the wedding. God knows what they would have done to me if there was no wedding," I shuddered.

"Well, think yourself lucky…" said Robin. "I can't talk about magic or anything to my parents, friends, no one."

"Why not?"

Tina sighed. "He's an Outsider. It does strange things to Outsiders when you show them, or expose them to magic. Sends them *maaaaad*," she said rolling her eyes round her head and sticking her tongue out.

I blinked. "Who was it who said if you show an Outsider magic then they *spontaneously explode?*" Tina and Robin spluttered into their drinks.

"Perhaps it was someone having a laugh?" said Tina giggling. "To be fair, it's not a bad allegory. It messes an Outsider up if they are shown it. Most can't handle it. They call it *Exspelling*, when you send an Outsider mad by exposing them to magic."

"I dunno," said Robin. "I mean I reckon my parents would understand if I told them. Outsiders are more open minded these days."

"Where do they think you go all year?" I said.

Robin smirked. "A boarding school for talented young men to become spies for the British Government." We all laughed heartily, which felt weird, my mouth wasn't used to it.

"How's Ernie?" I said. "Where is he?"

"At home with Dad still packing, they both hate shopping!"

"So do I…" said Robin.

"Ah, but not *Gnippoh's?!*" Tina said, throwing her arms wide. "No one hates shopping in Gnippoh's. I seem to remember telling Avis at the end of last year that I needed to take him clothes shopping…" she winked.

There were more robes in this shops than I had ever seen in my life. "This is the place to get them. You could do with some more as well Robin, I seem to remember you grew out of last years," Robin grimaced.

"Welcome to Ruben's Robes!" called an excitable man coming around his desk. He had a pencil behind his ear and a big bushy moustache. "Right… Hailing Hall?" he said looking at me.

"Yes Sir," I said and he nodded, his eyes scanning me all over before narrowing as he twisted his moustache, deep in thought. A notebook and pencil jumped into his hand as he began to write what I presumed to be measurements. After a few flicks through all the rails in the shop he stopped.

"Aha! Here we are. Just the right sized ever-changing robe… you'll be a first year will you?"

"No! Second," I said a little sourly.

"Second, right, well this should do you," he handed me a long, brilliant robe. It felt heavy and as I touched it, turning bright blood red.

"Wow," said Robin just behind me.

I was so glad I now actually had robes that would fit me properly, I wouldn't look like a leprechaun anymore! Robin was measured and bought some robes that extended if, or as, he grew. Once we had our new robes wrapped, bagged and paid for, we moved on together and shopped. It was the best day I could have imagined. We went to Sordina's Sweet Emporium which had sweets in jars all the way up a huge glass wall that reached high into the sky. It was so full of children and adults fighting for space that we had to take a few breathers outside before jumping back in. The sweets were alive! Robin got bitten by a jelly snake, before biting its head off. Tina got half attacked by a gnome as we left who thought she stole something — she promptly told it to sod off. And I bought the biggest packet of wriggly worm sweets in the world.

Later on we went to a clothes shop and I let Tina choose me some clothes, like I had a choice! She chose me a pair of smart jeans, a new white school shirt and a very fancy red and green tartan shirt — I was actually quite pleased with her choice, she was too, she kept gloating about it. "Oh you do look lovely Avis, you really do!" Robin rolled his eyes at me every time he heard her say that.

As the sun began to set we decided it was time to set off for Hailing Hall. At last.

CHAPTER FOUR
A Crash in the Night

I huffed and puffed up the hill to Hailing Hall. This time my bag floating behind me. I don't know how I did it last year.

This time though, it was stuffed full of brilliant new stuff I'd bought from Gnippoh's.

Our school was perched high on a huge canyon, with views all the way around Happendance, the nicest of all the Seven Magical Kingdoms. To the right of the track was a huge drop — Robin kept pointing it out to me. I wish he wouldn't, I hated heights. The canyon spread right off into the distance for as far as you could see. Perched on the opposite cliff edges were some brave looking cottages, smoke rising slowly into the air, wavering in the haze of the summer sun.

We followed the flow of people up the hill from the train station, bags all floating behind our heads. Some, third years I think, were all playing a game of trying to hit each other's bags down. One, a rather large boy, was complaining, "Oi stop it, there's some things that could smash if my bag drops!"

"Why, what you got in there? Your Mum's best china?" they all laughed.

The big iron gates opened wide revealing paradise. Huge, lush gardens greeted us and statues stood to attention smiling gleefully. Loud peacocks strutted around weaving in and out of the individual hedges shaped like magical creatures, who all bowed low. Carriages zoomed overhead and landed in the carriage courtyard. I smiled, at least this year I wouldn't have a git brother to try and avoid at all costs.

"What are you smiling about?" said Tina.

"I was just thinking how good it is to be back!" We walked right on up that gravel path slowly together, taking it all in. Whoops and cheers filled the air as people bumped into their best friends again. The new first years quietly weaved through the crowd and collected silently in front of Magisteer Dodaline on the grass. She was a funny looking Wizard, with long grey hair tied up in a plat, with big baggy brown robes and a funny triangular brown hat. She didn't like me, I just knew it, she thought I was responsible for the attack on my friend Hunter last year, which I wasn't. The first years all sat around nervously, glancing around at us, they looked so small. Smaller even than me. I heard Tina go *awwww*.

David Starlight and some friends pushed past us laughing and joking, he didn't even realise it was us. Robin and I didn't like David Starlight, he was a show-off and an idiot. His Riptide team, the Eagles, beat ours last year, well *beat* is an understatement, they humiliated us. I shivered at the thought at having to play Riptide again, out of fright, not excitement. The school grounds was busier than I had ever seen them. Carriages zoomed over head, people hugged and laughed, statues bowed, ghosts — barely visible — busied about with carrying things around.

Straker was waiting for us in the Hall, smiling pleasantly, which was weird. Straker was a strange Magisteer, he wore an impeccable grey suit and appeared to have no neck. His skin was tight like a snake and his eyes blacker than the night. He was moody too. So now that he was smiling, it just looked weird — I am not sure I saw him smile for the whole first year.

"Bags on the floor," he quipped. "As they will be taken to your dorms."

I dropped my bad next to Robin and Tina's as the little parchment labels suddenly popped into the air with our names on, before the whole thing disappeared in a flash.

Tina nudged me in the ribs. "Ah! What is it?" I said. She was staring up at the roof. Robin and I followed her gaze. All around the hall was the usual armour and flags of all the different forms, the Riptide schedule and all sorts…

"I don't see anything?" said Robin.

"Nor me."

Tina huffed and pointed to each corner of the room. Now I saw them. On small plinths around the perimeter, and each corner of the high Hall were big eyes. It sent a shiver down my spine as I saw them watching us. It was literally a big eye ball. White and staring. They were new.

"They're Occulus…" said Tina gravely.

"Never heard of it," I said. Tina seemed perturbed by the big eye balls. But now all around the hall, others had noticed them too.

"Sir, Sir?" said Jack Zapper tugging Straker's sleeve. "What are those eye's up there?" the Occulus seemed to hear him, and leaned in for a closer look, causing a few people to whimper. Straker pretended to look up and tried to pretend he didn't hear him.

"Come on, off to the Chamber," he managed.

I turned to Tina. "Why do we have them?"

Her face was scrunched up with concentration as she thought. "Dunno. Dad never mentioned it. Bet you anything the Lily says they are for *our own protection*…"

Straker pushed open the doors to the Chamber. Noise erupted from all around, the other five years above us were already in here causing an awful racket. There was much shouts of excitement, and fast garbled talking about their summer off. Robin and I gave a quick wave goodbye to Tina whose table squealed as they saw her, pulling her into a group hug. We walked slowly through the melee, over to the Condor's form table and *ahhhh*, it all returned to me…

the smell of preparing food drifting up from the kitchens below, the burning coals, the feint flowery incense, and the centuries of old dust. The Chamber was a funny old room, it was huge, round and domed. The roof was brick and curved over like a big upside down fish bowl. All over the walls and ceiling were suits of armour, pictures of famous Witches and Wizards, flags, drapes, quotes, old Riptide kits, swords and magical regalia that had been donated by famous Wizards that had been schooled here over the years. It was stuffed full. Dangerously close to all this stuff hung fire brackets which blazed different colour light depending on the mood of the Chamber, as well as huge chandeliers that hung in mid-air and dripped hot wax on you. I took a seat next to Robin, we were the first back on our table. "I'm starving!" said Robin rubbing his stomach.

"We just ate like three hours ago?" I said.

Robin smirked. "Well, Mum says I'm a growing lad," he winked.

"Robin, I doubt you'll ever stop growing, it's gonna turn out that you're of Giant lineage," I said pointing to a picture on the wall of a Giant, sweeping twenty Wizards into the air.

He laughed. "It could certainly come in handy! I meant to ask you…" he said, his tone changing as he leaned in closer and whispering. "Have you found out anything about, you know, the whereabouts of… *thingy*."

Glancing around our table, there was a fourth year form and a seventh year form table nearest us. So I kept my voice low. "Not much, we'll find a better place to… *talk*," I glanced around again to make sure no one could hear. "But, I did overhead some people at the wedding… they reckon he's gone for good, they're all terrified…"

Robin raised his eyebrows and smiled. "Nice, but er… what do your parents think about it all?"

"I don't think they have yet. Knowing them, they'll have a plan lined up." They always do, trust me.

43

Suddenly a big booming laugh echoed around the Chamber. Robin and I looked at each other, we knew that laugh. Through the crowd bounced the larger than life Hunter.

"Here they are!" he boomed pulling us both into rib-cracking hugs. "How ya been!?"

"Go—ood." I managed with the little air I had remaining. He laughed again and ruffled my hair.

"Nice to see ya' Avis..." his scars were still horrific, starting at his neck and working upwards to his temple like a shadowy rock face, they were deep and pronounced. Last year Hunter had been attacked by a demon, set on him by Malakai after we tried to trick the Eagles form and David Starlight. It was a horrible time, for everyone.

"Where's everyone else?" said Robin.

"On the way now Robbie!" Hunter pointed, sure enough the rest of the Condors came pushing through the crowd and came to sit down on our table. I felt a trickle of nerves at seeing them again, we hadn't been the best of friends last year and I really wanted to prove myself this time. I wouldn't be shy, or nervous this year. For some reason, being a Blackthorn I feel like I need to prove myself more than anyone else, prove that I am not evil like the rest of my family.

"Hi Ellen," I said coming to hug the clever, shy, be-speckled girl with long poker straight hair.

She looked up at me with big, bug eyes and seemed to recognise me, eventually. "Avis..." she said dreamily. "How've you been?"

This carried on for a while, I shook hands (very formally) with Graham who was tall, dark-haired and well mannered, he was from Scotland on the Outside and sometimes it was hard to tell what he was saying. Simon, his best friend shook my hand limply, he didn't like me much and I shared his disapproval. He was short with blonde hair and a puffy face, big nose and snooty demeanour. I said a quick hello to

Dawn too, as Graham and Robin hugged for they were quite good friends last year, especially when I was barred from the rest of the school and spent months in an old clock tower. Dawn was a very big girl and seemed to have got bigger over the summer. She was dressed in a big floral blouse that my Mother would have called a bath curtain, her hair was fair and shaped to a small bob. She always looked a bit gormless too, her mouth slightly open like she was waiting for someone to tell her to shut it. Jess and Florence waved at me across the table, they were best friends. Jess has the reddest lips and whitest skin you'd ever see, and would give Snow White a run for her money. Florence was very tanned with big dark freckles and long wavy ginger hair. I swear it wasn't ginger last year. Joanna half waved at me shyly as she joined Ellen, her big bushy hair falling over her reddening face.

Someone tapped me on the shoulder. "Hello," said the boy who was taller than me and looked faintly recognisable.

"Hello?" I said confused. "Who are you?"

The boy smirked. "It's me, Dennis."

"No way?" It was too. Last year Dennis was a small, squeaky boy who hung around with the girls. Now he was taller than me, and had a voice deeper than Hunter's. "What happened to you?"

"Dunno, voice broke I think. Anyway… good to see you again." He took my hand and shook it, I nearly flinched as his hands were huge, they looked troll-like.

"Sure," I said turning and tapping Robin as Dennis walked away. "Robin? Did you see Dennis?"

Robin laughed and nodded. "Someone must have put a growth Spell on him… no other explanation — he's taller than me!"

Jake and Grettle, the two blonde Golandrian twins, took a seat at the table and shook hands, but refused hugs. Golandrian's didn't do hugs.

"Avis… 'ow are you?" said Jake, whose English had transformed, the first time we spoke it was non-existent. He shook my hand with a strong grip. "Not goin' to murder anyone 'dis year 'den?"

I laughed nervously. He had a dark stare that I couldn't look at for long, it was hard to tell if Jake was joking or not.

"Attention all," called a voice from the front of the Chamber, as noise and chatter barely died down. "I SAID ATTENTION ALL!" the voice boomed, magically enhanced across the Chamber.

Silence fell, as all turned to see the Lily standing proudly at the foot of the Magisteers table. He was a very charismatic man, dressed head to foot in white robes, his bald head shining, a short white beard glistening as if it had been dipped in glitter. He opened up his arms in welcome and everyone rushed to take their seats. "Welcome back one and all to another year at Hailing Hall. I trust you had a good summer off and recharged your batteries. Soon enough the new first years will enter the Chamber for the first time to learn and live here amongst us for the next seven years. I want you to be welcoming, pleasant and show them warmth and understanding. You will all remember what it's like to be on the other side of that door." The Lily glanced around once more, then nodded his big bald head at the Chamber door.

It opened at once and in piled the new first years. They followed Magisteer Dodaline who marched fervently to the front of the Chamber where they all turned and faced us, looking terrified. The Lily moved slowly around the staff table, smiling softly, his hands in prayer. "Welcome, welcome!" he called. "I am the Lily, your Headmaster here at Hailing Hall."

And then, just as he had done when we were first years, he moved slowly along the line and looked at each terrified person in the eyes.

"At this school, we pride ourselves on our ability to learn the most sacred art of magic. Something denied to ninety-nine per cent of the world. You are the privileged ones, and I needn't remind you of the great power that comes with these abilities. You are all very powerful people, in your own right, and together even more so. The fate of humanity is in your hands whether you like it or not. Many assume this means they have power over those less fortunate. But the true nature of man is not his ability to rule others but to treat those less fortunate exactly as they would like to be treated themselves."

BONG! It came out of nowhere, scaring the life out of me. Robin laughed as he saw me nearly jump out of my skin. "Not funny..." I mouthed at him. A small pedestal grew from the ground as the poor first years took to the stage and announced their name and interesting fact. Robin was still laughing at me jumping, so I poked him in the ribs.

"H-hello my name is Glenda Compton-Campbell..." there was muttering in the crowd, then a woop from a sixth year table. It was Marshall Compton-Cambell's sister. Marshall was well known as the top scorer in the Centaurs Riptide team. "And my interesting fact is that I can run a hundred and twenty boots in ten seconds." Everyone clapped and *ooooed*. Impressive, (if it was true).

"What the hec's a hundred and twenty boots?" said Graham. Simon tutted and told him it was what Wizards measured things by.

One by one, the poor things got up and announced their name and interesting fact. Half way through Ramid Kahn, the fourth year joker snuck through and lined up with them, and he just about managed to announce his name, the crowd who knew what he was doing in hysterics, before he was chased off the podium by a very angry Magisteer Mallard. Some of the names I just about recognised, brothers or sisters or even cousins of people who already went here. Like Duncan Herrald, brother of Ursula

47

Herrald in our year — their descendant was the one who started the Herrald newspaper. There was Ingrid Bloaters little sister Margret Bloater, who looked identical to her — big and round, much like the name. Apart from that there was no one else of note, that I recognised anyway. No one that was going to give me a run for my money by being more evil than the Blackthorns. The first years took their new tables and settled down tentatively with their new forms.

The Lily stood once more, Robin licked his lips as it was nearly time for the food to come out. "Before we start our wonderful feast I had one more thing to mention. Some of you may have noticed the Occulus around the school. I am afraid these will be a permanent addition to our time here. The school councillors have deemed it necessary to aid the *security of the school...*" we all knew he meant Malakai. Tina was frowning and watching avidly. "Please do not try to tamper with them, they will alert us if you do. If you have nothing to hide it won't report you. They are here for your protection, so please just pretend they are not there." I smiled and glanced back to where Tina was, she caught my eye and nodded as if to say *I told you so.*

After a huge dinner we walked back to our room together.

"Eighteen, nineteen, twenty..." said Robin who was counting as we tried to remember the way back to our dorm room.

Hunter rubbed his huge, round, full tummy and glanced at Robin. "What you counting Robbie?"

"Twenty-one... I am counting the amount of Occulus's there are on the way to our dorm room. There's loads... and don't call me Robb—"

"What the hec are Occulus's?" said Hunter as if he thought they sounded made up.

"Them," I said pointing up at the big white eyeball watching us over its plinth in the corner of the corridor. Hunter looked around vaguely.

Jake cleared his throat. "It's a watchers tool. They want to watch everything we do, like a fascist dictatorship. Means we cannot sneak out of bed, cannot go where we are not supposed to, not skip lessons, stay outside at lunch, because these things will see us and report back to the Magisteers," he sighed. I never thought about it like that, what if I needed to go to the Library in the middle of the night like I did last year? Or go off to find something important? I wouldn't be able to. An Occulus would spot me.

"What does it do if it spots you then?" I said.

"Wails…" said Jake. "We had them at my last school, just after the riots…" he and Gret smiled at each other. "They wail like a siren."

"Freaky stuff," said Robin who had stopped counting and was now frowning up at the Occulus's with disdain.

The carpet in the hallway to our dorm had changed colour, from a bright first year turquoise, to a dark blood red. And the pictures of semi-famous Wizards, Giants and Magical creatures still lined the walls leading to our door. Inside, everything was the same, except the now blood red carpet. Seven beds were spaced equidistantly around the room facing each other, laden with blood red top sheets. The tall brick fireplace now burned a welcoming orange fire, surrounding it were the three comfy couches that were unofficially known as our homework seats, as we always sat in them together to do our homework.

My bag was already on my bed, I undid the zip and pulled out the heaped mass of stuff which I'd piled in rather haphazardly. Next to my bed was a flimsy wooden wardrobe. Hanging up my clothes I realised how pointless it was, they were so crumpled. I should just leave them in the wash bag for the laundry ghosts now. I put my new clothes up on hangers, Tina was a good dresser, I was really pleased with my new clothes.

"Very flashy," said Graham, pointing over at my tartan top. "Tartan eh, that's my people's spiritual pattern." I laughed, but truthfully I didn't know what he was on about. I put my pens and parchment in my similarly flimsy desk and lay on my bed to relax. *Ahhhh...* the bed was bliss. Beds at home were so old and lumpy, whereas these beds at Hailing Hall were like sleeping on clouds, or unicorn feathers.

Robin was being fussy and folding his clothes just so and so while Graham laughed at him. Simon was very quietly trying to do a smoothing spell on his ever-changing robes and tie, but kept huffing.

"What's up with you?" Hunter boomed.

Simon grimaced sourly. "Got a new channeller, but I am not sure if it's working properly. It better be, cost enough..." I sniggered as I recalled Simon's last channeller, a big pearl necklace, he'd probably begged his parents all summer to get him a new one. "Something funny?" he called across the room to me.

"Oh come on boys," said Graham. "Let's not start this again, you two will get on this year."

Simon swallowed, but the sour look remained. "Yeah we will, as long as he promises not to try and kill any of us in our sleep."

My heart began pounding, how could he say that? After even the Lily came out and said I was innocent? "That's not fair Simon," said Robin putting his neat pile of jumpers down. "You know Avis had nothing to do with that, it was Malakai."

"Yeah, here's the proof," said Hunter, pointing dramatically at his face.

"Okay, okay!" called Simon, throwing his ever-changing robes into his wardrobe with a thud. "Just don't like it, that's all."

Jake hissed. "You've never liked 'im. You don' even need an excuse. Just man up." Simon was scowling and glanced across to me, I smiled, which wound him up even more. They had all stuck up for me, I wasn't used to it.

"Well, what if I can't do magic? With this faulty channeller?"

Jake threw his book down on the bed. "I don't know, just tell Partington when we see him!" Simon sniffed after his telling off and walked out the door in silence muttering something about getting washed.

Robin turned to me when he left and pulled a face. "I don't think you're on his Christmas card list!"

"I know," I said giggling a little. "I don't know what I am meant to have done?"

"He's just being a little girl because his channeller isn't what he hoped," said Graham. "He'll get over it."

Magisteer Partington bounced into the classroom with a flick of his brown robes beaming around. "Hello! Hello! How are we all? Good summer I trust?" he moved around the table and shook each of our hands. He looked much the same, rosy red cheeks, square-shaped head with a triangular brown hat perched on top, short receding brown hair and a kind face, pinched like an owl. "It looks like everyone made it through the summer," he said silently counting heads.

I really liked Partington, he was genuinely kind and a patient teacher, which I supposed you had to be if you were tutoring first years. "Second year!" he clapped. "The best of all the magic years."

"Really?" said Dawn greedily. "Why's that Sir?"

"Well, not really… just an expression I use sometimes," he backtracked. "It's a good year, you're using what you learnt in first year as a foundation to push on and learn much, much more, with many excellent Magisteers. Of which I shall announce soon, for you shall be going in partly *mixed classes*. They are not ability based, they are random classes so you'll get to mix with other forms, which is exciting isn't it?" he smiled round hoping we would too. A small gurgling in my stomach told me that no I wasn't excited, I was nervous. Why couldn't it just stay like this? I knew these people.

ACHHOOOOO! Hunter sneezed the most gigantic sneeze you're ever likely to hear. Poor Partington jumped for the door, Ellen's glasses fell on the floor and Simon dropped his channeller which he was closely inspecting. "Well it's definitely broken now isn't it," he muttered slamming it down and proceeding to stare upwards at the ceiling with a right face on.

"It's the dust in here Sir," Hunter sniffed, taking a big tissue that Partington made appear out of nowhere.

Partington wrinkled his own nose as he judged the dustiness of the room. "Yes, I suppose, it is a little… You know, I think the ghosts have forgotten to come and clean up here during the summer. Lazy so-and-so's…"

I ran my finger along the table and thick grey dust came up. "Ewww," I said, chorused by others around me who did the same.

"Perhaps they're on strike!" called Jake waving a fist.

Partington waved his hands impatiently. "Doubt it. Anyway, don't worry about all that now, I'll get some ghosts up here soon to give it a quick once over. We've got a lot to get through."

The room we were in was high up the middle and tallest school tower. Up about a hundred flipping stairs too, round and round in a spiral, it felt so high up you could literally feel the air getting thinner. Out the mullioned windows behind us encircled silent, white bobbing clouds. Messy piles of books teetered around the outside of the room, along with instruments under grey cloths that were indistinguishable. The urge had never taken me to see what they were.

"Hold on," said Partington pointing at someone in between Dawn and Jess. "Who are you? You weren't in this class last year." I craned my head round to see who it was.

"It's me Sir, Dennis?"

"What?" said Partington unconvinced. "You look nothing like…" he stopped. Robin and I nudged each other and laughed. So did the girls. Jess and Florence creased with laughter at Partington's perplexed frown.

"It is Dennis Sir!" said Jess through giggles. "He's just changed a lot over the summer."

Partington stared for ages, until it became slightly uncomfortable, then he seemed to come to himself. "Yes, of course, of course you are… my goodness, how you young things change." We laughed again, which eased the tension and poor Dennis' embarrassment. "So your timetables…" said Partington reading from a sheet he now had in front of him. "Form is with me every morning. Monday morning's you have Mental and Physical Training with Magisteer Simone—" he stopped as muttering broke out. Magisteer Simone was infamous for being the most evil Magisteer in Hailing Hall. She was very tall and wide with one eyebrow and was as mean as they come.

"Why her?" said Simon whining.

Jess and Florence dropped their heads too, they had a run in with Magisteer Simone last year. Whereas Graham, Joanna and Ellen shrugged at each other, they had no idea.

"Oh she's lovely when you get on her good side," said Partington.

Hunter slapped the desk. "Good side? It will take us all year to find that!"

Partington smirked slyly, before carrying on. "Magisteer Wasp will take you for your studies of the AstroMagical chart. Magisteer Commonside for Numerology, Magisteer Yearlove for Spell-craft, and myself for Riptide."

"Riptide?" called Dawn looking into the ceiling. "I'd forgotten all about Riptide!"

"Of course Riptide!" said Partington enthusiastically. "It wouldn't be Hailing Hall without Riptide. Oh and I am sure you'll all be told soon but, just to give you a heads up, the way we play the games will be changing."

"Changing?" chorused Jake, Gret and Joanna looking concerned.

Partington nodded fervently. "Yes. Back to the old ways, how we used to do it. Not sure if its all been finalised yet, so I can't tell you anything, but of course I will. Now, the first training session will be in a few weeks when we have the stadium booked."

"Sweet," said Jake. "'Opefully we will be better this year."

"Here's to hoping. Right, put your robes and ties on because we're back down to the Chamber for the communal breakfast with everyone. Make sure you talk to the first years, make them feel welcome. I'm sure you remember what it was like for yourselves." I certainly did — it was this time last year that my brother Ross had made embarrassing photo's of my flash up on my robes for all to see.

Simon sidled up to Partington who was waiting by the door. "Sir, just before we go down can I ask you about my channeller?"

"*Again* Simon?"

Mental and Physical Training, I wonder what that involved. Robin looked a bit sick, he said it sounded like we were going to be lifting weights and running. "I'm no good at all that sort of thing," he moaned, beady eyes flickering with nerves as we trundled through the lower ground corridors towards classroom 27e on the west wing.

"At least it's not a high up classroom, you got to think of the positives," I said. "Those high up ones make me giddy."

"True. But you just know this Magisteer is going to be a nightmare." I couldn't disagree with him, I knew she would be, just from the one experience of her. And her renowned reputation amongst all the other years, who'd told us that morning that she was a '*complete taskmaster*'. A little part of me felt that they were embellishing it, as half of the Jaloofia form regaled ours on the nightmare lessons with Simone.

The Jaloofia's included a snooty lad called Fry Ferry, who reminded me of my brother Ross, who said: "If you don't do what she asks, or she takes a dislike to you, she has a tendency to lock you in her spiky, sprat infested coffin for the night!" I shivered, I hated sprats (they are like rats, but bigger with red eyes and some say they have a modicum of magical power). Robin scoffed at Fry Ferry when they left and said he'd never heard such drivel in all his life. Hunter looked terrified as we walked to her lesson, his top lip wobbling.

Outside number 27e we waited. Robin, Hunter, Joanna, Ellen, Gret and I lurked nervously. The others were in another class, which Gret wasn't very happy about — she was always moody without her twin brother. Another form appeared looking apprehensive in the dimly lit corridor.

"Is this the class with Magisteer Simone?" said a timid girl coming to face me in the grey light.

I nodded. "Yes."

They all came forwards and lurked with us.

"Oi?" called a voice. "Where did you guys go?" this voice wasn't timid or scared. Around the corner came a girl — the first thing I saw was her hair. It nearly lit up the dim corridor all by itself, for it was bright white, curly and fell down to her waist. But now she was frowning. "Why didn't you wait for me?" she berated her classmates, who shrugged sheepishly. "Hello!" she said waving around at us all. "We are the Snares form with Magisteer Blackthorn."

I blinked as my heart did a little jump. A part of me must have misheard her. "Who did you say your form tutor was?" I said.

"Magisteer Blackthorn," she said confidently. "He's new I think. Who are you?" I didn't say anything, I couldn't. My breath caught in my throat.

"He's Avis Blackthorn," said Robin and the girls face brightened.

"I see, how nice for you."

I shook my head. "No, it's not nice," I managed. "Do you know his first name? What does he look like?"

The new girl looked around at her classmates for reassurance. "Don't know his first name... but he's erm... tall, dark, confident, very clever, erm... he has nice skin and his eyes are dark?" she managed, shrugging at her lack of description. But I didn't need any more, I knew exactly which brother this was after she said *clever*... it was the eldest of all my brothers, Harold. The one I was most scared of.

This must be a wind-up? I leaned on Robin for support. Yes, it was a wind up that's all, David Starlight had come to scare me to death by getting someone to tell me my brother was working in the school. The white haired girl looked at Robin for an explanation, but not before Hunter said: "They don't get on. The Blackthorn's are an evil family. But Avis isn't evil, so he's an outcast and they don't like him." The girl frowned, before the boy just behind her stepped forwards.

"Magisteer Blackthorn doesn't seem that evil to me."

"Yeah," said the white-haired girl. "He seems really nice."

I didn't say anything, I couldn't. The shock had pulverised me. If it was true, then I was done for. I thought I was free from my family after Ross left last year, but now I had to deal with another — the cleverest, most cunning, out of all my family, except my parents. He'd come to get me hadn't he? Come here to pull me out of school and take me home, let my parents deal with me.

Suddenly a great booming voice erupted through the corridor causing us all to jump. "LINE UP AND WAIT QUIETLY!" It boomed from a shadow in the alcove of door to the classroom. It was a big shadow, about three normal people wide and two up. Hunter was holding his chest, panting and whimpering in equal measure. Magisteer Simone came out of the shadows slowly and stared down at us. "Well, why aren't any of you MOVING!" she blasted.

I jumped up and scrambled after Robin who'd made a bee line for a half-orderly line in front of her. She glanced up the line and smarted. "Did I say make the line in front of me? Make it by the DOOR!" She snapped. The line shuffled next to the door, images of being locked in a coffin made me submit to her barky commands. "And in we go…" I risked a glance at Robin who caught my eye and rolled them as if to say *a whole year of this?* The girl with the white hair in front of me was scowling, she did not look pleased.

We put our bags in a pile on the dusty floor and stood together in the classroom, which was grey and cold. Not as cold as Straker's room, but cold enough to make me yearn for a jumper underneath my robes, in the middle of summer too. The walls, floor and ceiling were grey, it had no redeeming features, no blackboard, no books, no instruments, nothing. There were even cast iron bars over the one window in the room.

"Mental and Physical Training," started Magisteer Simone slamming the door. "Makes a Wizard what they are. The best Wizards are the strongest. Fact. To be a Wizard at all you have to have tremendous inner and outer strength — that's why most of you are hopelessly pathetic at magic, because you are weak, feeble, with no more mental strength in your molly-coddled lives than a Witchetty Grub. You're useless…" she was enjoying herself as she spat these words, I say spat, because I felt some of it land on my face from six feet away. She was really ugly, and

I don't mean that lightly. One bushy, bristly eyebrow went right across her brow which all but buried her narrow, beady eyes. Her skin was patchy and pockmarked, her lips thin and taut, her body huge and suspended on tight, skinny legs. Her dress was even weirder, and added to the strangeness. Knee high boots, fastened tightly, with tight green trousers blended in no way with a tight brown and green collection of garments buttoned up to her neck. A black cane, or it might have been a whip also donned her right hand and she swung it round at opportune moments to emphasise her point, causing us all to duck. "I will work you hard, build the mental strength you require to be great. Of course most of you will fail and enter the world as another *moderate Wizard*, like we need more of those!"

***

With a click of her fingers five mop and buckets popped up in the middle of the floor. "And you will clean your own mess up!" she barked leaving the room. I stood slowly, I think all of the vomit was out of me. My stomach twinged again, and I clutched it groaning along with the others. Robin was sprawled across the dirty floor heaving into one of the buckets. Hunter had passed out in a corner of the room and the white haired girl was scrambling to open the window. The rest of her friends were sprawled on the floor clutching each other.

"You alright Robin?" I said, as a little blob of stuff fell out the corner of his mouth. Gross.

Robin heaved again and looked up, his eyes bloodshot, his face red and blotchy. "What do you think?"

I grabbed the mop and bucket which swelled with soapy water as I neared. I slopped it on the floor and guided it around my patch of yellow sick. My arms felt incredibly weak, like they had been beaten by a troll for an hour. My legs didn't feel like my legs, they felt like someone else's —

numb and wobbly. Grettle was propping up Ellen and helping her mop the sick up with a disgusted expression.

Joanna looked up through thick bushy hair at me. "We can't do that twice a week surely?"

The white haired girl was tilting her hair back and fanning herself, trying to pull some of the air from the open window inside. I noticed as I stood, feeling very sick, how utterly stunning she was. Her face was mischievous like a pixie, and her hair was like a beautiful mermaid's — long, bushy and silky. Some strange feelings gurgled inside me and I wasn't sure if they were the guilt of looking at this new girl over Tina, or whether it was more sick ready to come up. I shook my head, hoping it would expel any thoughts of the white haired girl.

All the sick was just about mopped up. Robin was leaning on his mop for dear life in case he might topple over and Hunter didn't know what part of his body to clutch, so settled with lying in a foetal position. It had been the hardest, most gruelling hour of my life. Magisteer Simone was an absolute git, and made us do so much physical exertion that it drove most to be sick — and she didn't even let us stop when we were, she made us do press ups in other people's sick. That's what set me off being sick, having to come face to face with Robin's! It stank! She really enjoyed barking: *"Twenty press-ups!...Fifty sit-ups!...Another thirty press-ups!...A hundred squats!"* Then when we did, it was never good enough: *"Hunter missed a rep, that's five more for everyone!"* or *"You must touch your toes on a sit-up!"* And you couldn't just not do something, like Hunter did, halfway through refusing through absolutely exhaustion, to do another hundred star jumps, she screamed in his face: *"YOU PATHETIC EXCUSE FOR A WIZARD! A HUNDRED MORE SITS-UPS FOR EVERYONE!"* It was torture. And now everything hurt, my back, my sides, my legs, arms, neck, head, even parts of me I didn't know existed.

One good thing I supposed was that it gave me no time to think about my brother Harold being a Magisteer at the school. Every time I thought about it, I went even weaker. So I stopped, putting it out of my mind until it was confirmed properly — when I saw him with my own eyes. A part of me thought maybe they were mistaken, it was someone who sounded like Blackthorn, or coincidently had the same name but was of no relation. Yeah, that would be it… hopefully.

Everyone exited the room as quickly as we could (waddle was a better word), down to lunch where I for one, ate nothing. I couldn't. Robin didn't either, he just sat making moaning noises whenever he moved. "Pass me a drink of water please Simon," said Robin.

"Get it 'yerself!" said Simon grinning at Robin's apparent pain.

"You stupid idiot," Robin smarted, before reaching across the table for the water jug. "AWWOOO!" he cried clutching his side, and causing people from the surrounding tables to look in both parts sorry for him and knowingly. He poured himself a glass gingerly and looked up at Simon menacingly. "You will see mate, when you get up there later, how you enjoy it! Then we'll see if anyone passes you the water." Robin slammed the jug back on the table and moaned again.

I just sat in silence trying not to move, for when I did, it hurt. About five or six tables away was the unmistakable white haired girl. She was suffering too and was nibbling on the end of a baguette and rolling her eyes skywards. I glanced across at the Magisteer's table again to see if my brother was there. Only Magisteers Trunwood, Mallard and Dodaline were up there, no one else.

"Here he is," said a voice behind me. Then, the most agonising pain — I screamed as a heavy hand clapped me on the back.

"*Ahhhhwwwwa!*" I whimpered turning my stiff neck, my eyes watering as I came face to face with the blue eyes and charismatic charm of Ernie Partington.

"Woah, sorry Avis didn't mean to. What's wrong with you?" he said.

Hunter glanced up from his slumber and said, "Simone."

"*Ahhh*! I see, well I'm sorry and if it helps, it does get better, no not better, easier."

"Thanks, I think," I said as Ernie sat on the empty seat next to me. Last year Ernie was a ghost, and found me when I was locked up in one of the high turrets, he remained a great companion for me during that time, sneaking me food and doing work with me. I found a way of bringing him back to life at the end of the year using the Book of Names that Malakai was trying to keep. Robin was the one who actually raised us both back to our bodies in record time — for I had become a ghost too, it was all part of my plan to end Malakai. We agreed afterwards for Ernie to take all the credit for ending Malakai, instead of me, because think about — Malakai is my parents employer. They would kill me if they found out the truth. Now Ernie had come back to life, he could retake his last year. He chose Magisteer Nottingham's from the Phoenix's, who were very pleased to have a celebrity amongst their ranks.

"How was the summer with your parents?" he smirked.

"Hell," I grimaced.

He laughed. "That bad? Well I'd hate to rub mine in your face. It was great to go home again," he looked up into the ceiling and smiled, then blinked. "Tina says they gave you trouble? You had to escape and live in the Percevius' Den Inn, in Gnippoh's?"

"Yep…"

"Avis, that place is dangerous, lots of unsavoury characters,"

I sniffed. "Yeah that's why I didn't go out. Didn't want them spotting me, they'd recognise me wouldn't they? And tell my parents immediately. Anyway, I didn't know where else to go."

"You could have come to ours?"

"I could, except I don't know where you live."

Ernie frowned again. "Did Tina not give you our address?" I shook my head. "She must have forgotten," he said looking over towards her on the Hubris table. "Weird coming back to life after ten or whatever years… all the friends I had are gone, moved on with their lives, had children, working and all that," he smiled meekly.

It must be hard to lose all those people and have them grow up and forget about you. "Even went and saw my own grave. Next to Mother's. So, that was strange."

"I bet."

"Anyway, if you want or need anything just come find me, my dorm is on south wing, room 33y." He got up, then just as he went to go, turned back. "And er a little drop of mango perry will help ease the pain. Promise."

"Cheers," I smiled, before grimacing. "Oh but there's no mango perry at lunch."

Ernie leaned in closer and whispered: "Just tap the table three times and ask for it, you might just get some," he winked.

As Ernie went back to his table, I turned to Robin, my neck turning stiffly. "Did you hear that?"

Hunter leant a hand forward and wrapped the table three times. "Mango perry please," he said. "Literally, I will do anything to get rid of this pain."

After lunch half our form limped upstairs to another new class with Magisteer Wasp. Trust it to be up about a hundred flights of stairs! Robin, Hunter, Joanna, Grettle, Ellen and I limped up each one as if it were a mountain peak, a grunt and moan after each hurdle. The other half of our form, who hadn't had the most gruelling physical workout of their lives (yet), had got bored of waiting for us and zoomed off ahead.

We finally made it, up to the very topmost point of the tallest spire in the school. We held each other, panting and wheezing as we came through a huge midnight blue drape at the top of the widening stairs. Through that was a small hallway with a moss covered glass roof. It didn't help my stomach knowing that we were so high up in the school, it made my knees go giddy again just thinking about it. We stumbled forwards through big oak doors.

"Aha, here are the late ones!" called a flittish voice. "And what are your excuses? Too many steps I presume? Well, your compatriots managed just fine." The voice was coming from a small man dressed immaculately in the middle of the room. He had curly blonde hair with greying sides and a boyish complexion — the overall look could have easily likened him to a Cherub in a suit. He stood with an expectant look, fingering his lapels.

I saw Jake, Graham and Simon giggling to one another at our apparent uncomfortableness. "Sorry Sir..." said Grettle, stepping forwards. "We had a lesson... with... Magisteer Simone... this morning," she panted.

"Oh I *see*," said the tiny man, understanding suddenly. "You poor things, come in and take a seat wherever you like. I'll fetch up some Mango Perry for you," he said kindly. I was a little-taken aback at the kindness after having the evil Magisteer Simone, that now I wondered if Magisteer Wasp was playing some horrible trick. But sure enough, after sitting down gingerly, Magisteer Wasp returned with a big bottle of chilled mango perry and a large tray of glasses.

The room was huge and round, above was a giant blue glass dome with markings that were hard to make out in the daylight. There were no seats as such, but cushions that were spaced apart around the circular stone steps that went right around the room. In the middle was a tall wooden plinth that Magisteer Wasp took. Tall wooden rafters reached all around the top of the room. Goodness knows how high up we were and no way would I intentionally try and think about it.

"Lovely to have you all here and to meet a new class," said Magisteer Wasp who had a slight twang to his voice that was hard to place. "My name is Magisteer Wasp and we will be learning the AstroMagical chart together. A little about me — I am born of an Outsider Italian father and a Golandrian mother. My first job was an apprentice to the now famed Wizard author and explorer Arthur Hape-Heath. I became Heath's trusted AstroMagical Chart advisor over the twelve years I worked for him. But in the end, I found a love for teaching in an environment I found more tailored to my advancing years, giving me time to study other things. Now, enough about me, who do we have in here?"

I found Magisteer Wasp very pleasant and AstroMagic interesting. I imagined that it could have been really boring if someone other than Magisteer Wasp was teaching. Robin found him really funny and laughed as Wasp squeaked the full table of signs out in one breath. AstroMagic, he explained, was basically the effect of the gravitational pulls of planets, stars and moons on our Magic. He said that there are certain infusions you can only make in the sign of Kreller, which is in November and December, or Spells that work better under certain signs. And once one knows fully the AstroMagical chart, then you can tailor your magic to these unseen forces.

"It reaches such an extent," said Wasp. "That one could perform a Spell and it be utterly ineffectual, for the sign you are in, renders it useless. Of course it depends when you are born yourself of course."

It was already a very long first day and with two lessons left and a mountain of stairs to climb back down, I sighed. Don't get me wrong it was good to be back, great in fact, but with my muscles already hurting, the fact that my brother might be teaching at the school, as well as lots of new magic to process — made my poor brain feel like a heavy drooping weight at the top of my spine. The Mango Perry seemed to be working, it felt as if it were greasing my creaking bones, rendering them slightly useful again.

Half way down the stairs Robin turned to me. "I just thought," he said, frowning so hard that his round glasses nearly disappeared into his cheeks. "You didn't get your channeller back last year from... *thingy*. So... did you buy a new one?"

I looked around to make sure no one was listening, Graham and Simon had shot ahead, while Hunter and Ellen were still at the top of the stairs looking down at them feebly. "I forgot to tell you," I whispered, for in all the fuss and excitement of seeing Robin and Tina in Gnippoh's and then returning to school, I had completely forgotten about the meeting with my Granddad. "I'll tell you when we see Tina. Two more lesson's first." Robin groaned, he, like me, just wanted to go to bed.

"This must be a joke," said Robin. "The classrooms are so far apart! How do they expect us to get to each lesson on time?" he was really grumpy now and shuffled along scuffing his feet, I hated that.

"Pick your feet up!" I said. Mind you I had to agree with him, the next lesson was Numerology with Magisteer Commonside, back down all those stairs and all the way over to the other side of the school, on the first floor! Pushing our way through about fifty heavy drapes, down numerous corridors that looked identical, we finally found classroom number one-hundred-and-eleven.

"Oi, wait for us!" called Hunter, trailing behind with Ellen.

"We're here now anyway," I said, getting rather annoyed with Hunter calling after us all the whole way. I didn't want to be late again.

"COME IN!" boomed a voice from behind the door. I looked at Robin.

"Why do I have to push the door?" he said. I sighed and pushed, ducking inside the new room. Graham, Simon and the others were already waiting.

"You're not late," said Commonside with as little expression as a person can. He stared dreamily as we crossed the threshold into this rather cramped room with a raised seating area and tiny desks. "Yes, the room is a little cramped, used to be a broom cupboard I think, anyway it was number one-hundred-and-one, so I couldn't resist," he said, not looking at anyone in particular. Robin and I took the last remaining desk near the front as they were the only seats remaining. All around the tiny room were numbers, plastered to the ceiling, the walls, the seats and chairs. They covered everything. Numbers were not really my thing, words were, so I had to force myself to take an interest. Robin eased himself into his chair very slowly, causing Dawn and Jess to laugh.

Robin huffed. "It's not funny!" he called, levering himself in sideways.

"Now then," said Magisteer Commonside who was gazing into the ceiling. He was incredibly plain looking — with plain beige clothes, half a head of fair hair and about as much charisma as a chewed pencil. His face, while plastered with absentness, was beige too: a long beige nose, beady beige eyes and thin beige lips. He was just so plain, he had no redeeming features whatsoever. "Numerology is the study of numbers. Obviously," he said, and I felt a sigh echo inside me. "While it's hard to prove their effects magically, they have sure popped up throughout the centuries and shown their worth to those fortunate enough to be allowed to study them properly."

Robin leaned towards me, ever so slightly and mouthed: "What a load of waffle."

Magisteer Commonside was immensely boring. As we left the class, I was still none the wiser as to what Numerology actually was. "One more lesson!" said Hunter whizzing past us in the corridor. At least the next lesson wasn't too far away.

"We're with another two forms in this next lesson," I heard Joanna say to Ellen, just ahead of us.

"Do you know who?" I called. Joanna turned and shook her head.

"Good luck," called Gret, giggling as half our form including Jake, Simon and Graham turned away down a corridor towards Magisteer Simone's — it was their turn.

We carried on along the biggest corridor in the school, dubbed 'The Big Walk' as it was the longest and most used. It connected the Hall and the Chamber and numerous classrooms and corridors. It was lined with all the most important paintings, donated to the school over the years. Partington said we will study them in a few years with the Magical Art Teacher — Magisteer O'Connell. That didn't fill me with excitement, they were just boring paintings.

As we passed the Hall to the left below, over the wooden bannisters we saw some unfortunate people going out to practice Riptide already.

"They're keen!" I said to Robin. And then I spotted the white haired girl, dressed in a green and black Riptide kit. My heart leapt into my throat with utter shock. Not because of her, but because of someone else — she was right. My brother Harold was standing ahead of the line. His dark eyes still and focused on his form. This was a dream, I was sure of it.

"Watch it!" said someone behind me as I stopped stock still gorping down into the Hall at him. Surely my eyes were playing a trick on me? Was it an illusion? A trick? But then, his dark eyes drifted upwards, ever so slowly to me. And he smiled. A vicious, evil Blackthorn smile.

"Right, come on Snares, let's go practice!" he called. His form, the Snares, including the white-haired girl, cheering.

Then I felt Robin tapping me on the shoulder. "Avis? Earth calling Avis! Come on we're gonna be late... What's up?" he said.

"My brother, Harold. He's here," I said. Robin's face dropped.

"So that girl was right? What you gonna do?"

"What can I do?"

"Go tell the Lily?" said Robin clicking his fingers.

I scoffed. "He was the one who employed him?"

"Oh yeah..."

I sighed, nothing was ever simple was it? "Come on, let's get to lessons."

As me and Robin approached Magisteer Yearlove's, me in a dream with my stomach churning with anxiety about my brother being a Magisteer at the school, I heard Robin suddenly call out.

"Tina?" he said.

"Robin? Avis?" I looked up now as Tina was waiting outside the same classroom with half her form. "Are you with Yearlove now too?" she said, her excitement rising.

"Yes, we are!" said Robin and Tina jumped on him causing her form to look on perplexed. Then she launched herself at me.

"You ok?" she said. "You look like you've just seen a ghost!" she laughed.

Robin grimaced as he whispered. "He's just found out properly that his brother now works here as a Magisteer."

"No way!" she said. "Who?"

Robin raised his eyebrows. "Magisteer Blackthorn of course, of the Snare's form."

Tina looked guilty now. "Not that tall, dark, handsome new Magisteer?" she laughed. "Oh god, it is isn't it? Avis, I'm so sorry. What do you think he's gonna do?"

I shrugged as another half of a form came round the corner. "I just want this day to be over." I said.

"Come sit with us at dinner," Robin said. "Avis has something else to tell us that he forgot in Gnippoh's."

Tina's beautiful face lit up with excitement again. "What? Tell me now, go on, *pleeeease!*"

"Not here," I said, as a man's head poked out of the classroom door, piece of paper in hand.

"Form's… Hubris, Condor and Swillow?" he said and we all nodded. "Right, in you all come then…"

"Too many men Magisteers if you ask me," Tina whispered under her breath as we all filed in. As my eyes adjudged I saw with amazement, that this room was different to the others. Compared to Simone's grey room, Wasp's circular dome, or Commonside's tiny broom cupboard — Magisteers Yearlove's room was magnificent. It looked like a cathedral. Golden beams stretched from ceiling to floor propping up a colossally high pitched roof. Stone arches held up a second floor, which ran around the outside of the room. Under these stone archways, stuffed into the shadows were piles of old stuff: battered books, silvery instruments and old paintings, mostly covered in large cloths.

The ceiling was decorated with the most elaborate magical paintings of the scenes of the magical war and the Jermain and Shaun-John magical revolution. The images were so cool, popping out of the ceiling whenever you looked at them — like real cool magical art should be — not like those boring paintings in the corridors. Colour streamed in through the stain glass windows, casting a rainbow of light across the white stone floor. Stairs floated in mid air at the far end of the room, in a spiral with no hand rails — right to the very top of the ceiling. It was so magical and awe-inspiring that it made me completely forget about Harold.

At the very end of the room was a miniature version of Hailing Hall. A life-size model of the entire school complete with Riptide pitch, floating island and grounds — and it was moving! The trees swayed, the statues moved and the sun beat down upon it. The top of the centre spire of the model was complete with a blue glass dome — where we had our lesson with Magisteer Wasp.

"Hmm…" hummed Magisteer Yearlove looking about with the rest of us. "I suppose it is rather special isn't it? Have you seen the *Magiexempla*?" he pointed to the model of Hailing Hall. As we moved closer to it, we realised it was behind a thin, nearly invisible, glass dome. Magisteer Yearlove, who was tall, with short black hair and a black beard flecked with grey, approached the, whatever he called it, and waved his arms. It gave a small cracking sound as the miniature school split in half and opened outwards.

"*Woah…*" we chorused. Inside were tiny paper models of everyone in the school. It was incredible. I saw the Chamber, just below the school, with it's domed roof and circular tables with a sparse amount of people eating or working. Their little papery form busy with eating, writing or messing about. And the Library, all the way over on the third floor with its own cathedral-like room, with huge tottering walls of books and the river right in the middle complete with mini boats. I spotted Magisteer Simone with the rest of our form lining up in a very straight line. The paper models of our form mates moving ever so slowly. High up in the spire was Partington sitting at his desk eating an apple. A blue fizz of light erupted from the Riptide stadium, and I saw the green and black kit of the Snare's jumping around the Habitat, which looked like a sandy desert — my brother Harold in the stands, stood arms crossed. Yearlove pointed a long finger to the middle of the school, where, in a big cathedral room, twenty or so paper models were staring ahead at a tiny life-size model of Hailing Hall.

"Incredible isn't it?" he said. And we all sort of nodded, open mouthed. "If you get a magnifying glass, you can see you looking at models of yourself, and the models of models... makes your brain hurt after a while..."

After getting over the glory of the room and its many distractions, Yearlove summoned twenty comfortable leather chairs into a horse shoe around him. The girls were paying a lot of attention to Yearlove, their eyes swimming with dreamy adoration. "We try to keep things informal here. I am not going to push you to learn, that's up to you. If you want to do well and learn what can be one of the most complicated and dangerous magics then you'll do well to take in as much as you can. But, if it's not for you, please take yourself away — I have no problem with that. There's nothing worse than one person infecting the rest with apathy," he paused for dramatic effect. "With Spell-craft, your imagination is the only limit. There are an infinite amount of combinations, some mix well, others don't, they come with trial and error. That Magiexemplar," he pointed. "Was made with the forging of hundreds of Spells, which enchanted it, giving it life."

"Did you make it Sir?" said a boy from one of the other forms, who looked longingly towards the model.

Yearlove nodded. "It was a labor of love. In fact, I must confess, that I created much of this room too. It used to be just a classroom, but I thought... how awfully boring, let's make it an interesting place to learn."

Tina, next to me, cleared her throat. "I couldn't help notice Sir, that it's bigger on the inside than on the outside..." she said pointing towards the small door we entered through.

"Another forging of Spells that you will learn toward the end of your sixth year. It's only really Wizard architects and a handful of builders that know that enchantment. But I, as an advocate experimenter and amateur inventor, made my own."

It was hard not to like Magisteer Yearlove, he was modest and interesting, good looking and charismatic. He introduced us to the world of Spellcraft by getting us excited, even though my whole body ached and head hurt as the sun dipped beyond the horizon come the end of the lesson. Yearlove also committed every name in our class to memory in one go. We went round the circle saying our names.

"Tina Partington," she said, blushing.

"Aha, Partington eh? Well, let's hope you have inherited your father's skill!" Tina smiled and whispered something like *not likely*, before he came to me.

"Avis Blackthorn," I said, a lot more confidently than I would have last year. There was a little breakout of muttering from the boys of one of the other forms, and I could have sword I heard '*told you so.*'

Yearlove bowed his head and smiled. "Ah yes, the *non-evil* Blackthorn. Glad to hear that Avis," he smiled.

"Robin Wilson."

"The very clever Outsider?" Yearlove offered. "I remember the end of school assembly," he winked, causing Robin to go a deeper scarlet than our robes. "Whose next?"

"Jasper, Jasper Gandy…" said a good looking, very sure of himself boy. "From Swillow form Sir," he said as Yearlove raised an eyebrow as he tried to remember Jasper.

"Gandy? *Gandy*?" he said, twisting his beard in thought. "I remember, your father works for the King doesn't he?"

Jasper coughed a little awkwardly before muttering. "Yes Sir, he *did*…"

Yearlove blinked before asking, "Did? You mean he left?"

"No, he died Sir."

Yearlove, who was crouching slightly, swallowed and got up, touching Jasper on the shoulder before adding. "I'm very sorry to hear that," a tiny bubble of tension filled the air. Robin glanced sideways at me and grimaced. Tina was staring across at Jasper with a pained expression, her eyes swimming with empathy, or something.

We all made our way down to dinner, talking excitedly about the excellent lesson with Magisteer Yearlove. "I am absolutely starving!" said Robin. "I could eat ten plates of sausages right now!"

"Me too!"

Robin laughed. "How do you reckon the others got on in their first Mental lesson with Simone?"

"*Pfft!*" I spluttered, imagining Simon limping around and moaning. "If they're lucky we'll teach them how to summon some Mango Perry from the table."

Robin gave me a funny look. "Well, I am not revealing that little secret, unless they're nice to us…"

"Oh you boys!" said Tina who caught up with us, hearing the end of our conversation. "What's that noise?" she said. There seemed to be some commotion coming from up ahead, in the Hall. We rushed forwards, Robin and me slightly behind Tina, our bones creaking and cracking as we jogged. Reaching the bannisters at the top of the Hall, all I could see was the tall ginger and purple cloaked Magisteer Nottingham berating two men and a woman. They were not dressed in school robes, and looked to be scrabbling for the exit. Notebooks and pens jumping up and running after them.

"And take your camera with you!" called Magisteer Nottingham, throwing the boxy metal camera towards a be-speckled man who caught it, then turned and shouted back.

"If you just let us interview him, it will save all this nonsense!"

"YOU ARE NOT WELCOME HERE!" blasted Nottingham, charging forwards. "If Ernest Partington wanted *another* interview, he could find you! He knows where you are, now... SOD OFF, before I set the *ghosts* on you."

The three reporters yelped and ran for the door. Tina jumped down the stairs five at a time. "Good riddance you filthy SPRATS!" she bellowed at the top of her voice. Magisteer Nottingham turned to her, looking very red in the face.

"No need for language like that Miss Partington," and with that he turned with a flick of his purple robes and marched back to the Chamber.

Robin and I exchanged glances, before Tina said a little loudly: "Coming to dinner or what?!"

Tina pushed peas and mash around her plate, deep in thought. Robin was making awful noises as he walloped down sausages and mash with hefty portions of onion gravy. "Slow down mate, or you'll give yourself indigestion."

"So... hungry..." he said in between swallows.

Tina shook herself from her dreamy expression. "So what was this thing that you wanted to tell us?"

"Oh yeah," I said, as Robin looked up putting his knife and fork down, as a bit of mash on the end of his chin fell into his lap. "At home over the summer..." And I told them all about escaping from Ross with the Seven League Shoes (which I had hidden in my bag upstairs), and then coming face to face with my Granddad who I thought was dead. Tina was frowning as I continued to explain that he gave me a channeller which lit the room up and then, he and the room vanished.

"Show me it," she said. I reached under my shirt and pulled out the thin, black marked, golden metal channeller. "Hmmm," she hummed inspecting it closely. "Looks like it's a part of something else doesn't it, the way the jagged metal forms this shape? And this rune will mean something. Typical we don't study runes yet. At least if the room lit up, it's meant for you," she winked.

"But what about my Granddad?"

"What about him?" she said distractedly.

"He's supposed to be dead?"

Robin burped. "You sure it happened, could it have been an illusion?"

"He gave me this channeller didn't he? So it can't be."

Tina sighed. "Anyway, sorry I can't help. I'm just going go and speak to my friends," she said, standing and pushing her mash and peas away.

"Ok, well I'm going up to bed now, it's been a long day," I said. "Coming Robin?"

"Sure," he said clutching his stomach. "Think I did eat it a bit quick actually."

As we left I saw Tina go, not to her own form table, but that of the Swillows. I didn't know she had any friends in the Swillow form?

Robin and I traipsed out of the Chamber, pushing open the big oak doors, before coming face to face with Graham, Simon, Jake, Jess, Dawn and Florence who stood (just about), looking like zombies and dripping with sweat.

"Er, you do know dinners nearly over?" I said trying to hold back the smirk, they didn't look so cocky now.

"Yes, well, we've only just made it out of the class haven't we?" said Graham through pursed lips.

Jake waddled forwards toward the Chamber door. "Yes, if one person cannot do all ov' the press ups we all do more!" he said shooting a glance at Dawn, who looked shell-shocked.

Robin smirked. "Treat yourself to some Mango Perry — oh no you can't, we just finished it," he said, before spluttering with laughter.

Graham shot Robin a murderous stare. "I'm not aching enough to come and box your ears!" he said. Jake stood in front of the doors and looked at me pleadingly.

"Oh fine," I said opening the door for them. "Night all."

I nearly fell asleep as I brushed my teeth, nearly accidentally squeezing Moss Moisturiser on my toothbrush instead of Spider Leg Toothpaste, *ergh*, can you imagine? Robin looked disgustedly at my black toothpaste before pulling out his vile minty smelling stuff that you Outsiders use. The boys bathroom was big and long, with white and black tiled floors, long rows of sinks and mirrors, followed by five bathtubs next to each other with a magic curtain that pops up when you get in (so no one can see you in the nude). As well as a long wall of grubby toilet cubicles, with a soggy old looking mop going from one to the other wiping the floor fruitlessly. Opposite them was a big display cabinet full of magical washing bits like Bernard's Butterfly Lotion, Vampy's Blood Hair Wash and Shaun-John's Own Spider's Eye Face Wash, amongst others. There were also large iron metal grates along the bottom of the walls, where the excess water flowed out — and, as me and Robin found out last year — one of them led, via the underground river, all the way to the Library. As I recalled, the loose grate that gave easy access was the one nearest the display cabinet. After washing I was just about to leave, before I turned and saw Robin, with his shirt off, checking himself in the mirror.

"What on earth are you doing?" I said, trying not look at his pale posterior.

He was turning and trying to check his back. "Think all those exercises have done some damage to my back."

Robin was so white and pale that he resembled some kind of transparent fish, you could almost see all his organs. "Put it away before you blind me," I chuckled.

"Oi! Don't say that, I don't like taking my shirt off in public, you'll ruin my confidence…" he scorned.

I couldn't help but let out a long and extremely satisfying *ahhhhhh* noise as I got into bed and stretched. It felt better than anything. The soft crisp sheets, the lighter than air pillow and mattress, the laying down of all those tired muscles. Robin was asleep and snoring almost immediately, but I lay wallowing in the beautiful relaxed feeling that now swept over me. The orange embers sparking lightly in the fireplace, casting a dim orange glow around the room as the lights outside the window from nearby towns flickered in the distance. I wondered dreamily about Tina — something seemed different about her this year and I couldn't put my finger on it. Before I knew it, the white haired girl from the Snare's form jumped into my mind — a small wriggling feeling in my stomach writhed. Sweet sleep gently drifted over me. Even when the others slowly limped into the room and went to bed, I hardly stirred.

Zzzz…

A channeller pendant just like mine waved in front of my face in a hypnotic fashion. My Granddad's gaunt, lined face turned twice around on its axis and began laughing silently at me, his mouth opening black and huge, like a tunnel. Then Tina, standing at the end of the tunnel, in the light, looked up and saw me, but then, she looked straight through me as if I wasn't there. Before, a giant crashing sound echoed around us, as the tunnel rumbled and fell on top of her and she disappeared in a flash of smoke. And then screaming…

I woke with a start and looked around. Everyone was sitting up in bed peering through the darkness. "What is it?" I said through the gloom.

Jake leant forwards. "'Der was a noise outside, did you 'hear the *crashing* noise?"

"I heard it! Nearly scared me half to death!" Hunter cried.

"Came from over there," Robin pointed out the window. I shook the dreamy sleep away and pulled my legs out of bed. Or I tried to. They were thick with pain, I couldn't help but yelp.

"What is it?" said Dennis pulling his sheets closer.

Simon snorted. "Not another ghost was it?" He was a git, just because a ghost had scared me in my sleep last year, he never shut up about it.

"No. If your gonna get out of bed, do it slowly…" I said, slowly edging myself out from the covers.

"Where are you going?" said Graham.

"To see what the noise was." The dorm above us must have heard the noise as well as small thuds echoed about our room. "Come on." I said to them, marching over to the curtain and gently drawing it back. Jake and Robin joined me — just off in the distance the lights leading down the path to the Riptide stadium were lit… illuminating utter devastation ahead. We all gasped, plumes of dust were spilling into the air over huge piles of strutting wood.

"Oh *no*…" said Jake in a terrified voice.

Hunter jumped up, before yelping. "What is it?" he called.

"It's…" I couldn't say.

Robin, who was blinking rapidly at the sight without his glasses on cried: "The bloody Riptide stadium has collapsed!" Simon and Graham, still in bed, looked to me and Jake to confirm, maybe they thought Robin couldn't see properly without his glasses on.

"It's completely demolished," I said.

"Is anyone out there?" said Simon. I scanned around but couldn't see anyone.

"What's the time?" said Jake, looking at the clock on the fireplace. "Nearly *four*," he said, as if this added to the mystery.

Simon sniffed. "Who would be out there destroying the Riptide Stadium at four in the morning? Surely they'd have been spotted by the Occulus's?"

"Doesn't have to be someone from the school does it?" said Dennis before whimpering something about preferring the girls dorm.

Graham came over to the window now. "Who says someone demolished it?" he said. "It was mighty old, might have just fallen?"

"Hmm," I hummed. "Could be. There was a lot of magic holding it up I reckon."

Simon threw off his covers and charged over, thinking we were winding him up. Dennis was shaking his head. "That can't be true. They wouldn't let hundreds and hundreds of children into a stadium that was in danger of collapse!"

I felt myself nodding along with the others. But it wasn't long before the blue light of ghosts gently swam into our room.

"*Off to bed…*" droned the most expressionless ghost I've ever seen. "Come on now, away from the windows and back into your beds." We did as it said, before another two ghosts drifted into our room and began singing soft low lullabies. I don't know how it worked, but rather embarrassingly I was out like a shot.

The next morning it was all we could talk about. The curtains opened promptly at seven, revealing, in the new light of day, the utter devastation of the collapsed Riptide Stadium. We had to strain to be able to see it over the hill in the distance, but stone pillars and wooden struts stuck out from all directions. The dust had all but vanished now, but around the grass on the hillside were scattered bits of debris.

"Do you reckon this means we won't have to play Riptide this year?" said Dennis, rather excitedly.

Jake, who was scowling, huffed. "I 'ope not! I've been looking forward to it all summer."

When we got to Partington's classroom he immediately announced that there was an assembly that all second years must attend. "Why only second years?" said Dawn. But Partington just shrugged, nonplussed.

Florence dumped her bag on the table. "Did you hear the crash last night?"

"Of course," said Dennis. "It was so scary!"

"I am surprised Avis didn't scream like a girl," droned Simon. "Because the ghosts returned, three of them this time. I seem to remember it was only one that scared the daylights out of you last year, when you screamed like a girl." He laughed forcibly, as a few people in the class tittered lightly. Remembering what Tina told me the previous year — I smiled sweetly, even though my blood was boiling and all I wanted to do was spell Simon through the window.

"They were pretty the ghosts weren't they?" I said sweetly. "Sure I saw one of them wearing a lovely *pearl necklace*," I said raising my eyebrows at Simon's sheepish face. Robin, Graham and Hunter sniggered, even Partington was smirking and I revelled in the moment as Simon tried to hide his red face with an AstroMagic Chart.

As we walked to the Chamber, we passed several higher year forms, but the strange thing was, none of them were talking about the collapsed Riptide stadium, or looked worried about it. "Perhaps they are glad, I kind of am," Robin whispered. "Might mean we won't be humiliated again, if we don't have to play."

Once inside the Chamber, we saw Magisteer Simone prowling around the front, smiling to herself. Nearly all the second year forms were in here already and had taken the tables near the front. Tina's form, the Hubris piled in, followed by the Swillow's. Tina was walking next to...

Jasper Gandy? The boy who had told us all about his dead Dad in Yearlove's lesson? After them was the Snare's, led by my brother Harold looking proud, taking a seat as close to us as he could. Git. Although I did notice the white-haired girl glance over at me, I think, but then she rather dreamily looked away. A confused mass of feelings bubbled inside my stomach like a complicated potion. It was too much to think about on a cold September morning. I wrapped my robe closer around me, and sunk back down in the chair as Magisteer Simone began.

"I am sure you all heard the commotion in the night," she raised her eyebrows slightly and smiled viciously to herself. "No one? *Hmmm.* When we checked, you all had your faces plastered to the glass windows like labradors..." She barked over the top of our heads, I saw the first line of people directly in front of her, rub their faces as they were seemingly plastered with a thick layer of spittle. "In an *unfortunate accident* the Riptide stadium collapsed. We don't know why, however, foul play has been ruled out. It is after all, a very old building of near four hundred years. And..." she said, turning on the spot and grinning evilly. "Someone must be charged with the rebuilding of it. As the school's budget is tied up in other things we must come up with an alternative. And... as your Mental and Physical Training Magisteer I thought it suitable to volunteer *your* services." It took a second or two, before muttering broke out.

"What's she talking about?" — *"She means us? We have to rebuild a stadium?"* — *"She's gotta be kidding, I ain't doing it!"* People cried out, voices rising higher as they realised our new reality. The second years would be rebuilding the Riptide Stadium!

Simone raised a hand. "This would... QUIET!" she cried, waiting for silence. "This would serve two objectives: getting the stadium rebuilt, and... teaching you all the very serious and practical mental and physical training you all need to be truly helpful, practical Wizards." Caretaker

81

Ingralo, with his belly hanging out from his shirt and a cigarette perched in the corner of his mouth, entered quietly from the back of the Chamber. "Myself and Caretaker Ingralo will be overseeing the project and the rebuild will be taken in stages through your lessons and, if needs be, *after lessons.*" More talking broke out as Robin looked to the heavens with an exasperated expression.

"When are we gonna have time to do homework?" he muttered through clenched teeth.

Hunter huffed loudly. "Just when you thought you couldn't hate her anymore!" he said before falling off his chair with a loud crash.

Simone held up a thick hand once more. "I forgot to mention, even though it's obvious... *no magic* will be used whatsoever in the rebuild. If anyone — QUIET!...If anyone is caught using magic, it's an instant *detention*. And I assure you, my detentions will be a whole lot worse than rebuilding a stadium..."

As we upped and left I saw Tina talking fervently with Jasper about the situation. Then, Harold, my brother and his form stood and walked out. The girl with white hair talking to her small ferrety-looking friend — "I know," said the short girl, their faces close. "She's evil. But there's nothing we can do, we can't get out of it Zara."

Zara? That was the white haired girls name. Zara.

CHAPTER FIVE
A Ghostly Detention

"You are all here to repair this glorious stadium back to its full heritage," Magisteer Simone prowled around the front of the crowd of second years who had collected a short space away from the destruction. "I will repeat, no magic, no moaning and no whimpering. You will take orders from myself and Caretaker Ingralo." She pointed to the filthy slob of a man behind her, who grinned, cigarette ash falling down his front. "Detentions will be granted for anyone who doesn't do as they are told."

Hunter, who was standing just in front of me and Robin turned and whispered, "I think I'd rather do detention than this!"

"This is as much a learning experience as anything else..." Simone grinned again, revelling in the disgusted looks she was receiving from all around. Behind us, back in the school I could see faces at windows, checking out what was going on. I felt a little ball of jealousy squirm. Why were they in there, all warm, and we were out here in the cold and drizzle and grey of a late September evening? It wasn't fair.

"Miss? Miss?" called Kenny McCarthy with his hand up. "Why is it only the second years have been chosen to rebuild it? Why not the other years? It would get built quicker if they helped, especially the seventh years!" he fired off quickly, before Simone could stop him. Mutterings of agreement circled.

After a very loud and uncomfortable dressing down from Simone, in which she made at least five people cry, including Kenny McCarthy, we proceeded with the build.

As we interspersed into our groups of three and set upon our own tasks of clearing the wood into sized piles where Simone had specifically stated, I saw Tina with her own form, she had seemed to make much better friends with them this year. I should have been glad, pleased for her, but... I wasn't. I couldn't help my eyes drifting across to the curly, if not dampened, white hair of Zara, carrying a big log. Robin nudged me in the ribs. "Come on slacker, me and Hunter are not doing all the work!"

"Your bloody right we're not!" said Hunter giving me a deep stare before attempting to pick up a huge wooden rafter.

By sun down I was absolutely exhausted. I couldn't tell if this was real or a dream anymore. We had lugged countless wooden logs across to the mounting piles. Simone and Ingralo just marched around and barked nasty commands. Hunter was getting visibly angrier the more Simone passed us, and I thought we may have to hold him back from launching himself at her. The darkness set in quickly, small lamps popped on all around us but barely illuminated the sodden wood logs. They became heavier and harder to pick up. The biggest ones that had been left until the end were a six person job at least. After each one was put on corresponding pile, I had to stop and catch my breath. My arms were on absolute fire. My thighs felt like they were made of biscuits — like they could crumble at any moment, and my stomach was so empty I was looking at the grass and wondering if anyone would notice me take a chunk of it! Brian Gullet feinted as he and his form carried a large log to the pile. This should have been the impetus for Simone to call time on it. But no, she just smiled and called him a weakling. Ingralo picked him up and splashed icy water into his face until he awoke. We witnessed the sun going down behind the floating island and the thick forest. The lights in the school popping off as the clock struck five past ten. Only the light blue glow of the ghosts floated past the windows now. We slipped around the sodden, muddy grass, over the large wood splinters. Back and forth, back and forth, the piles of wood mounted higher than the hills.

I couldn't even remember anyone saying stop. The elation that should have flowed at those words was stuck, dampened by the impending despair of this horrible situation. I just remember following everyone. Tripping and sliding back up the hill to the school. The ghosts snapped angrily at us as we trailed mud all the way up the corridors. I traipsed after Robin and the other boys, none of us speaking. We quickly washed. Hunter stood under a shower with all his clothes on, eyes closed. I couldn't move my arms. The cold and wetness that had seeped all the way through, seemingly to my bones, would not budge. The hot water burned my hands, which were wrinkled, pink and sore, especially after Robin did an anti-splinter spell on them, removing the numerous barbs of wood. Like zombies we climbed into bed. I just about managed to pull off the wet material that clung to me. Thankfully, it was a Saturday tomorrow, so we could sleep in.

***

"GET UP! *UP! UP! UP!*" Cried a loud, shrill voice scaring the life out of me. My bedsheets were swept from beneath me, flying into the air. Freezing cold air hit me like a wall, as I shot up with a start.

"W-w-what's g-going on?!" I cried shivering uncontrollably. The blue pulsing light of a ghost was whizzing round our room doing the same to everyone.

"AHH!" Graham cried, clutching himself as his sheet rose high into the ceiling. The fire was unlit, and my breath was visible in front of me. The unfriendly ghost seemed to be emitting an icy coldness. Simon screamed and fell out of bed, followed by Jake who jumped up and tried to swing for the ghost. But it simply blew freezing cold air at him. Jake stood, stunned, as ice crystals formed on the end of his nose.

"What's going on?" Robin called at the ghost, as he jumped into his dressing gown. "Just tell us!"

"Magisteer Simone says your all LAZY! It's SIX o'clock, and you should be *out there!*" he pointed out the window. "She said the wind has blown the logs down, so you have to go out there early and sort it all out!" cackled the ghost, who had pointed ears and an evil face.

"No, no, NO!" Hunter cried despairingly. "This is not real, it's a nightmare!"

I reached out at the fire and clicked my fingers, an orange flame burst into the grate. "Leave us!" I called at the ghost. "We will be down shortly."

"NO!" It screamed shooting an icy breath at the fire which went out immediately. "You go *NOW!*"

With every part of my body aching and with very little sleep we went back out into the freezing cold Saturday morning and carried on.

But it didn't take long for the gruelling schedule to take its toll. By midday, Hunter was at his wits end. "I've never been this hungry in my life," he moaned, pulling at the big log that was stuck on a tuft of grass.

"YOU!" called Simone marching over to Hunter. "What are you doing with that? Keeping it as a pet?" she smirked.

"No," said Hunter affronted, his face contorting with rage.

Simone raised her eyebrows as people began looking over. "Then *WHY* are you simply standing there caressing it?"

"BECAUSE I'M KNACKERED AND STARVING YOU EVIL WITCH!" Hunter bellowed. What followed was a tirade of swear words and screams from Hunter, the like of which I have never seen or heard before. He was enraged. "... AND YOU ARE A SAD, UGLY, SOUR

FACED, MONOBROW COW…" Hunter finished and took stock of everything he'd just said as a stunned crowd of second years barely moved as silence befell.

Simone smiled, her face shaking with concealed rage. I was scared of what she might do. Her one eyebrow had turned a puce green round the edges. "Detention," she said simply. "After you've done working here, you'll go to an *all night detention*. I think that should teach you to speak out of turn to me."

"Oh sod this!" said Hunter, slamming down the log, which narrowly missed Simone's foot and marched off up the hill.

"Oh no you don't!" cried Simone, raising her hands at him. Hunter's feet left the floor and he dangled upside down, flailing around in the air like a useless fish. Slowly, he sailed through the air, limp and useless back next to the log with a resigned look. Thud. He hit the ground, and proceeded to lay there, in the wet grass. He really was the most stubborn person I'd ever met. He only got up and back on with the work once Simone charged up a big black cloud to follow him, striking him with thunder every time he slacked. Hunter muttered something about going to the Lily and complaining about Simone being racist, whilst glancing up at the cloud with contempt.

***

A few weeks passed. Things had calmed tremendously. Hunter still walked around with a face like a teenage troll. Most probably owing to the fact that he had to go straight to detention after every session of the stadium rebuild. I didn't envy him at all. At first he refused point blank to go, Simone even threatened to fetch the Lily, so now Hunter had to be escorted by a two ghosts. Robin and I barely spoke during the rebuilds, in fact hardly anyone spoke, we were all still in a state of shock. There was some talk though, at lunch which was allowed — a quick twenty minutes grudgingly granted to us by Simone, with a tray of sandwiches brought out by some ghosts. One boy Aaron, who was from London on the Outside, started talking about the ghost that had woken us up with freezing air. Apparently it wasn't a ghost at all, but an *apparition*, set on us by Magisteer Simone. Everyone's disgust of her increased a hundred fold.

"What I would do to get a chance to spell her," said Hunter through a half grimace, half face full of egg sandwich.

It became easier though. Something I never thought I'd say at the start. The aches and pains slowly became less painful. The logs became lighter and the days shorter. Our lessons suffered, no doubt. Yearlove and Partington were definitely worried and would ask us if we were sure we were okay every ten minutes — for Ellen and Joanna had repeatedly fallen asleep in Yearlove's lessons. He didn't disturb them mind, but summoned some blankets. Partington was frowning around at us each morning in form. I had about twelve plasters in various positions, eight on my hands, three up my arms, and two big ones on my leg and face. Don't ask. He would come round the desks inspecting our hands, a pair of magic tweezers clicking in his pocket — the anti-splinter spell had been so overused by Robin and me that it had stopped working.

"I'm fine Sir honest," said Graham, as Partington turned on him and asked him how he could carry on with that many splinters in his hands. "You get used to it!" said Graham proudly. Partington just sighed and shook his head gravely.

I'd settled into a rhythm. I like rhythms, routines and order. That's why I get excited about timetables. It's a structure, I like to know where I am and what I will be doing. Even when I was at home in the summer holidays, I would write myself a daily timetable. That's just how I work. So when things come up that upset my rhythm, it upsets me. And I had settled into this routine of:

Getting up early at six o'clock with the boys.

Lighting a fire.

Grabbing something to eat from the Chamber.

Going straight out to work on the Stadium.

At eight o'clock we would go to form with Partington (who would complain about how tired and malnourished we looked).

Then depending on our timetable we would go to lessons, or go back to the stadium.

Lunch time we would get a tray of sandwiches to quickly much on (while watching the other years frolic in the sun, which had all of a sudden decided to come out — jealously watching them play Riptide or just laze around doing homework. How I wished I could laze around doing homework now!).

The pattern continued with a lesson, back to building, lesson, back to building. All lessons finished, back to building until nightfall when Simone would let us leave at around ten o'clock to grab some cold dried up dinner, yet most of us just went straight to bed.

I would go with Robin and the other boy's in our form to our bathroom and wash in the showers before heading to bed.

Repeat.

Yes, she made us come and work on the Riptide stadium during *all* our free time. This meant that during off periods, where we had no lessons, we would have to go straight to the stadium. Kindly, our other Magisteers relented from giving us too much homework. Ingralo stayed at the stadium at all times, leaving Mr. Jenkinson a ghost of enormously boring proportions in charge of cleaning the castle with a team of randomly chosen pupils. Ingralo had a small canvas tent near the stadium with a big comfy sofa in it. Jack Zapper and Bernie Boppet sneaked inside it and stole one of Ingralo's very large iced cakes, sharing portions of it round to us starving workers. "He's got a mountain of the things!" said Jack.

Strangely, I looked forwards to Thursday and Friday afternoons when the Swillow's had lessons. It meant that Tina, who had become very friendly with them, would come and speak to us. "Decided to come and see us now have you?" I joked.

"You keep saying that!" she said, her golden face contorted into a dark frown. "If you're going to be like that I'm off..." she said, flouncing away again.

"Typical isn't it," said Robin, who shared my soft spot for Tina. "You save a girls life, and what do you get in return?" I sniffed, I was thinking the same thing.

The stadium was actually getting somewhere. The base of the seven quadrants had been erected, which was immensely hard work. Simone had repaired the broken splintered wood with magic and replaced the ones which were too broken with wood from freshly fallen trees, cut to size by Ingralo. It involved using massive ropes to pull them into place. But now we were climbing up very tall ladders and laying wood in sections across the quadrants. It was dark under there, for the huge waterproof drapes covered the top of the stadium, blocked most of the light.

I had a bad feeling in my stomach. Simone had forced me to go up the ladder to the middle of the immensely high quadrant. It was terrifying. Standing on a wooden slat, in the darkness, very high up, I took the wooden beams being passed up to me. Hunter at the bottom, passed them to Robin, he to Bernie Boppet, him to Jack, then to Jasper Gandy, to Simon, and eventually to me. Above me was Graham, Jess, and Jake, like me trying not to move for fear of falling off the massive drop. All around the other quadrants the same thing was happening.

But then the worst possible thing happened — as I took the huge wooden slat from Simon and pulled it up, heaving it to Graham, I saw a flash out of the corner of my eye. Something small and black had danced across my vision below — I looked closer, but whatever it was had gone.

Strange. Suddenly, a huge wooden rafter on the end of a rope swung out of nowhere. And it was coming straight for me at a dizzying pace. I hardly had time to notice what was happening.

"AVIS!" Robin cried. As screams echoed all around the stadium.

To avoid being hit I stepped back... onto thin air. My heart leapt into my mouth, as I fell backwards off the quadrant. I flapped, clawing at thin air. Panic flashing before my eyes. The drop below opened up as I began to plummet hard towards the ground.

My heart leapt into my throat. I fell, surely to my death, as screams of horror erupted all around me.

Everything passed by in slow motion. Dropping down past Simon, Jasper, Jack, Bernie and Robin... their horrified faces plastered across my retina as wind wailed past my ear.

Just past them, on the ground, hidden by shadow and darkness something was darting away. A small, hunched figure under a dark ragged cloak was watching, grinning.

The ground approached fast. I clutched myself, bracing for impact.

As I was about to hit the ground, I suddenly felt soft something cushion me. Then I bounced off, like a trampoline and sprawled through the muddy floor gasping for breath before falling face first into mud. Icy water brought me back to my surroundings. Magisteer Simone's livid face bared over me.

"Stand up!" she barked. I did, my legs felt wobbly. I looked up at the drop and shivered. "WHAT ON EARTH DO YOU THINK YOU ARE DOING?" She screamed in my face. The sound took a little longer to reach me as my ears were still ringing from the fall.

"What do you mean?" I said.

"He didn't do anything!" called Robin, who was descending the ladder as quick as he could.

"Didn't do anything? Can you please tell me who cast that spell then?!" she cried, looking around at everyone. My dizzy head managed a glance around at the perplexed faces.

"Honestly Miss…" I said wobbling again. "I didn't do anything."

"LIAR!" She cried. "I saw you. So did Ingralo. You used magic to try and make the build go quicker. You thought I wouldn't notice?"

I didn't know where to start. "But honestly, I didn't do anything…"

"And it's your own fault, nearly killing yourself!" she said judging me and what she could do next.

"I saw…" but I stopped. It sounded ridiculous didn't it? I saw a tiny, hunched figure running away.

She sighed pleased with herself. "I don't care what you saw. You will do detentions."

"*What?*" I cried, too weary and tired to properly argue.

"Miss!" someone cried. "Avis didn't do that."

"It wasn't him," said Robin rushing to my side. "There was a flash miss, a blue one, over there…"

Simone and Ingralo looked at each other, then laughed! "Ha-ha! How amicable! Lying for your friend like that. You foolish boy. Avis, extra detentions for having liars as friends."

I couldn't believe it. Two months of detentions for something I didn't even do. But I was too weary to argue. Too tired and dazed after the fall to properly state how unfair this was.

I must admit, after the initial shock had worn off, a sense of resentment began to course through me. Others were saying how unfair it was too, but that didn't help me. I felt like shouting at the Lily for employing this evil woman in the school. It wasn't enough that others thought I was innocent. I still had to do detentions. But had I seen the perpetrator? That little-ragged thing that scuttled away. What was it?

The next day at five o'clock in the morning! (Yes, five!) I was awoken by two haughty ghosts who beckoned me silently out of my bed. I sat up for a moment hoping it was a dream. But no, it was a nightmare. At least they were not freezing me like that other thing did. I put my burgundy jumper on and lit the fire with a click of my fingers.

"Are you here to take me to my detention?" I whispered. Slowly, they nodded. I followed sleepily down cold draughty corridors wondering what god awful detention I was in for. They drifted ahead of me slowly, going downwards. Down to the ground floor, into the Hall, then off through one of the huge drapes. It faded into a big doorway when the ghosts approached. This tall dark passageway sloped downwards, through the dark place under the school. At the end was a wall. A dead end? But my stupidity, or tiredness, was saved as the ghosts drifted closer the dark wall evaporated. Sound and light burst across my still, sleepy senses. Clatters and bangs, whizzing and whirring filled the air. Blue light erupted down the hallway, a hundred ghosts filled the huge room ahead of me. All the ghosts in here were busy, rushing around from here to there. The humungous room opened out as I stepped through the invisible wall. I jumped back as one ghost nearly knocked me over as she whizzed past with a tray of hot croissants. I gasped. This was a kitchen. A giant, stadium-sized kitchen. Tall stained glass windows reached down in long stretches showing the blue darkness of the early morning. It was very bright in here with so many ghosts, but no actual light. It was cold too. No fireplaces were lit. The only heat seemed to be coming from these huge fire ovens to the right of the room covering almost the entirety of one wall.

"Here to help are you?" I spun around. An expectant looking young girl ghost handed me an apron. "Hurry, you're over here…"

"Right," I said putting on the apron. "What will I be doing?"

"Here's your place," she drifted to a small work surface in the middle of the packed room. Ghosts tutted and hissed as I walked through — I was getting in their way as they busied themselves with baking and preparing. "You're going to start by chopping up this box of fruit and vegetables... apples need to be in slices of twelve, the carrots into circles, mango into around fifty small pieces, and..." she went on like this in a very fast voice — I would never remember all that. Now I looked at her I realised how young she was to be a ghost, was it rude to ask? I assumed so. She had a bow in her hair and a kind, fraught face. "And," she said finally. "You must work fast. Speed is the game! Okay?"

"Okay," I shrugged and in barely the blink of an eye, she was gone, whizzing off to a food prep area the other side of the stadium-sized room. I began to chop. It was weird in here. All the food preparation tables were in lines along the room, like a classroom. Facing the huge fire ovens were busy looking ghosts fussing themselves with putting in huge trays of meat, vegetables and sweet pastries. Call me stupid, but I never really thought about where the food came from — I just thought it was magic. Obviously that was a ridiculous idea. But, I never knew it was such a busy operation, that was for sure.

"AVIS!" boomed a voice behind me, I turned and saw Hunter was grinning wide, a large knife in his hand.

"Hunter?" I said completely surprised and pleased in equal measure. "But when did you get down here? You were asleep earlier."

"Know a shortcut," he winked, his tall white chefs hat falling off into his pie. "It's okay in here isn't it?" he said putting a spoon full of pie meat in his mouth.

"They let you eat," he said taking another spoonful, before putting it down again as a tall ghost stopped next to him and shook his head. "Sometimes," he added.

Every moment of my spare time was now taken up. Once we'd done an hour or so in the kitchens it was back to building the Riptide stadium. Hunter and I would leave the kitchen together to go and work on it, the ghosts questioning us non-stop as we left. Hunter would say to them: "I tell you every day, we have to leave now under orders from Magisteer Simone, to go and build the stupid stadium," before turning to me and saying: "Every day I have to tell them!"

The first day back building the stadium Magisteer Simone kept her beady eyes trained on me, grinning to herself.

"Don't worry about her," said Robin just above me on the quadrant. "She'll get what's coming to her."

From up in that quadrant I could see all the way across, through the patches of light, to where Tina was. I can't remember the last time we had properly spoke. Nor had I spoken to Ernie. To be fair, we were very busy.

Over the coming weeks I grew more confident in the kitchens and the ghosts slowly trusted me to do more. More than Hunter was allowed to do. Perhaps they had found out first hand how accident prone he was. They let me carry the bakeries to the fire ovens, at first they said I was too slow, but I told them that I couldn't fly like they could. The ghosts were strange, hard to get on with, dreamy, so wrapped up in their tasks that they hardly knew who they were. Their personalities worn away by the centuries, like waves beating a rock face. It was sad really.

***

During this time I was being failed left, right and centre by Simone, Commonside and Wasp for not handing in any homework. When the hec was I supposed to do that? Making my way back to the kitchens late at night, I walked slowly rubbing my sore hands which ached and were growing increasingly numb. David Starlight and three of the Eagles form came out of a corridor near the Hall. David Starlight was my nemesis and my stomach tightened as I saw him and his friends. Last year, he was the reason I was excluded from the rest of the school, Robin and Hunter dressed up as Malakai, and we tried to scare them, but it all went wrong. He smiled sweetly as they came closer, and I noticed he had his arm in a sling. His friends were taking the mick out of him and he was pushing them away with his good arm.

"Oh Avis," he said stopping in front of me. "Long time, no see."

"Yes, it's been lovely," I smiled as his friends guffawed.

David raised his eyebrows. "So one Blackthorn leaves and another arrives. Do they not think you can't cope on your own?" he said in a sour voice. "You need protection, because you're afraid that people will realise you're *the enemy*."

"What are you talking about?" I said.

"The Blackthorns are the evil enemy, I'm surprised no one has realised that already. The things your parents are up to!" he sniggered. "Hope you're having fun on that building site. I would have loved to have participated, but…" he indicated his strapped up arm. "Healer just said it's not possible. Simone understands."

"Good for you," I muttered, jealousy scorching my insides.

David grinned. "That fall you had was mighty close, you should be careful, using magic up that high."

"Shove off," I said, pushing past him, I was nearly late. He laughed and turned away — I wanted to say something clever, but I was to tired.

The ghosts had systems, which I learnt quickly. When a meal was ready, like the tray of bacon and sausages for

96

breakfast, they would put it all on this great big long translucent table. When it was breakfast time they would make sure everything was on the table, then they would wrap on the ghostly table three times. The food shot upwards through the ceiling. The ghosts then listened intently, in utter silence. Once they heard cutlery and shouts at the food, they would scream with joy, hug each other and whiz around the room excitedly. It was bizarre.

Over these coming weeks I hardly saw Robin, or Tina. Sometimes I would see her, in the off chance that I made it into the Chamber for some dinner. Her table, the Hubris form, and her friends Karma Zhu, Jessie Emms and Tow Taylor-Smith (Jess named them for me, she knows everyone), always surrounded Tina — but more than that, the Hubris form and the Swillow's were virtually interchangeable. They all sat on each others tables intermingling. Tina seemed happy though and I didn't blame her for not talking to me, I mean, I was never around. Partington even questioned whether me and Robin had fallen out with her.

"No Sir," said Robin. "Think she's made good friends with the Swillow's…"

"Ah yes, I did notice," he whispered leaning on our table gently. "You don't think it has anything to do with that Jasper fellow do you?"

A gurgling pit of green jealousy writhed inside my stomach. So even Partington had noticed it. I put it out of my mind quickly, there was no way… Tina was *my* friend. My mind skipped to the memory of us swimming in the lake at the end of last year, lying in the sun and spending all that time together. She couldn't just forget about me. And yet, she never sat next to me in Yearlove's lesson, preferring to take a seat up next to Karma Zhu and Jasper. I swallowed.

The person I spent the most time with was Hunter. We carried each other through the painstaking days of little sleep, physical torture and countless, busy food preparations. We worked together preparing the food, which was also the only time we got to eat. If we were late at all, a swarm of apparitions would rise up out of the ground and pelt us with icy water — our hatred of Magisteer Simone, the filthy tyrant, was at fever pitch.

It pains me to say this but gradually, the work in the kitchens became exciting and interesting. I never thought I'd say that about manual work. Even Hunter enjoyed it, I think that was because he was around food. Ok, the ghosts were bossy, but once you knew what you were doing they would leave you alone. Then one day in mid-October, Hunter said something that made the nearest ones who heard him stop and glower.

"It is a lot of effort thought all this isn't it?" he said. "I mean, I don't know why they don't just use magic to make the food…" Then he stopped as blue ghostly eyes stopped what they were doing and turned. "What? What's wrong?"

One of the nearest ghosts drifted down. "To talk of such a thing is sacrilege amongst us ghosts," he said. Then he turned to the others who were staring. "Carry on…" they did as he said.

"Sorry," said Hunter. "I didn't mean to—"

"You're not to know," said the ghost before taking out a small cloth and wiping his ghostly glasses. "A little lesson in food and magic… the two cannot mix. It's dangerous. Food is information, energy, vibration. It's this that sustains a Wizard. You cannot even use magic near or around food for it will then be contaminated. Ingesting magic is serious for a Wizard. It can cause serious health problems. You'll get the *Twitch* for one."

"What's that?" I said.

"The Twitch? A disease that you get when you ingest too much magic. It's very nasty. Mostly, it's prisoners, or the trapped, or the homeless who develop the Twitch. If you are without food, what do you do? You will get it any way you can, and that means using an illusion of food to feel full. There's nothing worse than hunger." I found myself nodding. "We are very careful to make sure we use no magic around our food here. Look…" he pointed to the translucent table with the trays of food set out on it. "The Tollo Table for example is a ghost invention, it uses no Wizard magic at all. It's simply spirit. And yet, there is still stupidity around. I mean look at this…" He handed us a newspaper clipping from the wall. "Read that."

MAGIC AND FOOD, CAN WE SAFELY COMBINE?

Jeffery Sanderson, the health minister of Western Happendance has reopened the debate on using magic in food production. For millennia it's been taboo within the Wizarding society, but Sanderson reckons a safe way can be found to aid the slow production. The debate rises after last year was the worst crop yield in a century leading some to question the rising price of food. "If we can experiment and find a way of safely integrating the production of our food with magic that would surely be good for everyone. Cheaper food means more people can afford to eat and eat well. A Wizard cannot last on the measly diet that the minimum gold allowance permits. It's not possible, something must be done."

"The Twitch costs our Healing rooms nearly eight million gold peices a year," says Susan Kennedy of the Council of Healers. "But the homeless and hungry need to eat. It's a tricky dilemma."

"This debate should be off the table," says Golandrian celebrity Jack Hummingbird. "We all know the effects of this awful combination. We need to look at new ways of producing enough food, not ridiculous ways like this. We might as well cast illusions of full banquet tables for all the hungry and be done with it. A tax on the very rich would be a start, they don't need all that gold do they? Surely they can spare a little more? And then we can close this ridiculous debate down once and for all."

"*Ergh*, they spelt peices wrong." I said, before the ghost snatched the clipping back off me.

"There's no cure for the Twitch," he said before whizzing off, as he did so I noticed that a very feint blue chain, thin and delicate looking trailed from his ankle. In fact, now I looked closely, all the ghosts had those thin blue chains — some of them were tangled with other ghosts chains… what on earth was it?

In the first week of December my misery slowly reached fever pitch. The routine became too much, the getting up at five every day to go and do the cooking, followed by backbreaking building. Then the lessons — not being able to concentrate through lack of sleep, lack of food and most of all, lack of friends. I hardly saw Robin, or Tina, or Ernie — sometimes he waved to me from his form table in the Chamber, before resuming with his work. Ernie was widely recognised as the most talented pupil in the school and was looked up to by all. I wondered what would have happened if everyone knew it was me that defeated Malakai? I wonder. I felt an all-encompassing despair wash over me, maybe they would have treated me differently — treated me like a saviour, not the outcast belonging to an evil family. It's a weird feeling to have but I wanted Mother. Not my Mother, *a* mother. I wanted a nice Mother who could hold me and tell me everything was going to be ok. But, I didn't have one like that. My mother was evil. I don't think she had ever hugged me in my entire life.

My misery compounded totally after a particularly hard lesson with Magisteer Commonside, in which he tested our knowledge of the numerological table over and over, until I fell asleep. Robin wasn't in the lesson, he was sick — reckons he ate a dodgy pie and spent most of the night in the Healers room. Poor guy. Commonside was enraged at the apparent apathy in his lessons and barked at us: "It's as if you don't think Numerology worthy of your time! Let me tell you this, if you are ever to pass your P.W.W's, then you must know the difference between a number under the Law of Richardson and a Solvent number!" It was the most animated I'd ever seen him. "You don't bother with homework, or learning the chart—" he blew, red-faced.

"Sir please," said Florence. "All our free time is spent rebuilding the Riptide Stadium."

"Yeah," said Grettle. "We don' have the time to do 'homework and such."

Commonside sighed and told us to leave early. When we left, relived, I saw Tina waiting outside for me. She looked happy and was smiling, she was so beautiful — her wavy brown hair was up in a bun and her eyes dark, twinkling and wonderful.

"Hey," she said smiling that wondrous white smile. But before I'd said anything, a voice behind me said: "Hello gorgeous," — Jasper Gandy pushed past me and took Tina's outstretched hand. She grinned up at him, before turning away and walking off down the stone stairs as I stood dumb in the corridor, quite alone.

"Don' they make a lovely couple..." said a passing Swillow.

Utter rage pierced my heart. Pain like I've never felt before boiled inside my stomach — I bent forwards feeling sick. She didn't even see me? I was standing right next to her and she looked straight through me. Nothing felt worse than that. Jasper Gandy? Really? She was going out with him? Ok, he was tall and good looking, with his nice skin and hair but just... *WHY?!* What had I done to deserve this? I thought she liked *me?* She cried at the end of last year when I left to go home—I assumed that things would carry on as they were from the end of last year. But if that disgusting vile witch Simone hadn't have put me in detention, then this would never have happened! All of a sudden blue light popped up in front of me.

"NO!" I cried, but I was too late. The apparitions evil face blasted me with freezing cold ice water. "*AHHHHH!*" I screamed.

"NOW get to your DETENTION!" it called before shooting away.

I was drenched and shivering. Nothing could get worse than this. I fell to my knees, hot tears warming my freezing face. I stood and started in the direction of the kitchens — the rage inside me irrepressible.

"AHH!" I screamed swinging my hand at a suit of armour. It exploded in a flash of bright orange. The air fizzed and crackled as the rage inside me threatened to explode like a bomb. The suit of armour lay scattered in pieces, but it did nothing to replace the torrent waves of emotion that now swept through me like an avalanche.

WOOOO—WOOOO! Came a shrill noise behind me. A big white Occulus jumped past me and whizzed down the corridor, making a loud siren noise. Now I was in for it. But I didn't care.

I couldn't sleep that night. The image of Jasper and Tina hand in hand swirled through my mind. I tossed and turned in bed, the writhing sick feeling in the pit of my stomach just would not budge. Robin was in the Healer's room so I couldn't tell him. I just always thought me and Tina would... I don't know. Go out? But then who was I kidding? I was small, scrawny and had a sloping, un-symmetrical face, as Mother always reminded me. I couldn't compete with someone like Jasper. She looked at him earlier, like she looked at me last year.

Hatred for Jasper streamed through my veins — I hated him more than anyone, even my family, and that was saying something.

Expecting more punishment for smashing the suit of armour, I was surprised when nothing materialised — no one came to tell me that I would now be in the kitchen for the rest of the year. In fact, there was some good news. Hunter and I were told we had finished our detentions.

"Thought I was gonna go mad if I had to another day in there!" said Hunter, heading straight towards the Chamber rubbing his stomach.

***

After a few days off, Robin was better again and came back to our dorm. I was using the time I had back from not having detention, to sleep. It felt wonderful, except for the fact that even in my dreams Jasper's laughing face cackled next to Tina — her face dreamy and docile, spellbound by love spells.

"What's up with you mate?" said Robin coming back from the showers drying his hair. All the other boys were outside, relaxing in the glorious sun that was beating down very hot for December. I rolled over on my bed and said it was nothing.

"That's a lie," said Robin. "I know I've been sick but I'm not blind. Is it the building work?"

"No," I said a little impatiently, rolling over again.

"What then? You should be happy, no more detentions, the stadiums nearly built, we'll be back to normal soon."

I shrugged. "Normal. What's that?"

"Goodness me, you are depressed. I'll have to take you to the Healer's room if you start sounding any more down."

"Don't be stupid," I said pulling my blanket a little closer. This time last year I was living in the clock tower high up in the school. A big part of me felt like running back up there.

After dressing Robin sighed happily, saying he felt much better now. "Done any homework?" he said.

"Sod homework."

Robin put his towel in the wash basket. "Come on, let's go for a walk round the grounds. It is Sunday, might as well go enjoy your new found freedom."

Robin could be persuasive and I felt myself wander after him around the sunny grounds. I scowled, the sun giving me a headache, I wasn't used to it. Nearly everyone was out here which annoyed me even more. I just wanted to be alone. Not even the wandering trees who bowed to people as they passed cheered me up. Or the statues that were serenading a bunch of fifth years with a small water show.

"You are really grumpy," Robin laughed.

"I saw something when I fell from the stadium," I said bluntly. "I think it was responsible for the swinging rafter."

"We were all talking about that, no one understands who it could be. I thought maybe it was David Starlight. Sorry I'm rambling, what did you see?"

"It was… a hunched figure, cloaked, I couldn't see what, but it was small."

"Well, that narrows it down. So you think someone tried to… *kill you?*"

I sighed. "I don't know… maybe, as revenge for Malakai or something. Your guess is as good as mine."

"Is that why your depressed?" said Robin.

"What? No!" I sighed and kicked at the gravel. "It's… Tina."

"Tina? You two had an argument?" he said puzzled.

"No, she's going out with Jasper bloody Gandy!" I said unable to control the emotion in my voice. Robin's face lit up with surprise. "I saw them the other day, she looked straight through me like I was invisible. They held hands."

"They're actually official then?"

"What?" I said sharply.

Robin stopped. "Don't tell me you couldn't see it happening? It was obvious!"

CHAPTER SIX
The Jasper Gandy Show

If anything, I felt worse after telling Robin. It was now common knowledge about Tina and Jasper. I had no one to talk to, or moan to rather. Jake gave me a sympathetic look as I sat glum by the fireside in the dorm, but then he told me to pull myself together, in typical Golandrian style (lot's of swearing).

Christmas was fast approaching, the weather the biggest giveaway. Frost clawed at the window every morning, our breath reaching out in front of us as we woke, before someone aimed their arm at the fire and pumped some much-needed heat into the room. It didn't do anything to thaw the icy shard that had pierced my heart though, at least that's what it felt like. A sick, crippling feeling that rendered me useless, nothing interested me. Lessons? Pah. Food, no chance. Homework? Definitely not. Robin tried his best, offering me countless walks around the grounds. "I said no!" I cried, causing Graham to drop his ink pot all over the floor before glowering at me.

"Do you know how much these cost?" he barked. "I am not rich like some people who come from castles."

I ignored him and rolled over in bed. Idiots.

Everyone was talking about their Christmas plans, which annoyed me. I didn't like Christmas, what was there to like about it? If you'd have grown up with an evil family you'd know what I mean.

Yearlove prowled around the outside of the circle of chairs. "So, Freddie if you wanted to stop an attacker in their tracks, what two spells would you fuse together?"

Freddie, a tall boy with bad skin from the Swillows form pitched his face in concentration, as Robin twitched next to me, desperate to answer. "Erm… is it… Dancidious and…" he swallowed, then shook his head. "Don't know."

"Dancidious is correct, that's the first… Jasper, what's the second?"

"*Prohebe* Sir?" said Jasper smiling sickeningly.

"Correct," said Yearlove surprised. "That's the first person to have got that right in this stage of lessons for a number of years. Well done." A shiny gold star popped into the air and flew over to Jaspers robe, pinning itself proudly on his robes. Tina looked up at him adoringly and mouthed *well done.* It was enough to induce a vomiting attack. I felt my eyes roll, I couldn't stand him. The way he spoke, his smile, his horrible voice, the way he and Tina held each others hands under the chair — just all grated on me. I sat seething silently, sinking down as far as I could into the high-backed chair, hardly hearing a word Yearlove was saying.

Robin sighed. "I knew that!" he whispered. I smiled, as Robin now glowered over at Jasper who received adorning glances for the first gold star handed out by Yearlove. "That should have been mine."

"Now then… for another gold star, who can tell me what this spell is called?" said Yearlove, an illusion of a cartoon man stood in the middle of the room. Then suddenly he collapsed like a puppet into the ground. Yearlove looked around as Robin nearly jumped out of his seat, raising his hand high into air. "Yes, Robin?"

"It's—"

But before he could say anything, Jasper butted in. "— *Tabeo-Ossa* Sir? It liquidates the bones…"

"Correct!" cried Yearlove, flashing his hand as another golden star flashed towards Jaspers chest.

"*Whhaaaat?*" was all Robin could manage.

"You flipping git!" I called at Jasper angrily, unable to help it. "That was Robin's turn to answer you stupid glory seeker!"

"Avis?" said Tina. "Calm down."

"Chill out my friend," said Jasper snarling as the gold star fizzed on his chest. The rest of the class were all looking at me with curious looks. I swallowed and sat back in the chair.

Robin whispered under his breath. "You didn't have to do that mate."

"Like I said at the start of the year," said Yearlove. "There are no rules in this class."

"Yeah well maybe there should be." I couldn't help it as a few people clenched their jaws awkwardly. Yearlove chewed his lip looking peeved, before choosing to ignore me and move on. I didn't care. Why should Jasper get away with such rudeness? It just increased my dislike of him a hundredfold.

At the end of the lesson Yearlove asked me to wait behind. I stayed in my chair as Robin indicated that he would meet me in the Chamber for lunch afterwards. I nodded, moodily awaiting my fate. More detentions? Talking broke out amongst everyone as they packed up. Tina and Jasper packing their bags together as Freddie turned to them both.

"Tina, did you know your boyfriend is the best Riptide player in our form?"

"Really?" Tina crooned, grinning a bright white smile up at Jasper who grinned. "I learn of his many talents each and every day."

A couple of other boys from Tina's form chimed in. "He's actually probably the best we've played against at lunch time," said Henry, a blonde, rather unkempt boy.

"Unplayable!" said Jeffrey Parsons, from Tina's form. He had longer hair than most girls. The kid looked like an Orc.

"Oh please you lot," said Jasper. "You'll make me blush." Again, the sickening tone he used went right through me like fingernails on a chalkboard.

Tina grinned. "There's defiantly something attractive about a great Riptide player…"

After a short talk from Yearlove, I saw Ernie coming the other way down The Big Walk away from the Hall. He was carrying a huge mound of books that teetered, he said something and they hovered into the air behind him. "Homework!" he cried.

"Seriously?"

"No, not seriously. They're books for Dad, I mean, Magisteer Partington. I'm trying to get on his good side, because he keeps nagging me about getting a hair cut," he laughed.

"It's not that long."

"If you know my Dad, you know the only way to stop him nagging is get on his good side. What's up with you?" he said frowning at my dark expression.

"Nothing, just…"

"You know you can tell me anything right, after what happened last year I owe you big time."

I sighed, while that was true, I had told Ernie a lot of secrets when he was a ghost and could probably trust him with anything, the fact is, the reason I was so miserable was to do with his sister. And that was the one thing I couldn't talk to him about. "No, it's nothing. It's er… actually you can help me. Did you play Riptide when you were——"

"Alive? Of course. Just go down the West Wing, near the Lily's office where all the trophies are," he said winking.

"Oh really?" I said as some giggling girls from the forth year passed by pointing at Ernie. "So… what would I need to do to be really good? Are there any… *secrets* that could help?"

A thick grin crept across Ernie's mouth. "It can be… *easier*, when you know what to look for," he teased.

"Like what?"

"Ornaments. They are placed in the Habitat by a spell formula. If you can work out the formula, like I did, then you can work out where they will most likely be," his words sunk into my brain like a revelation.

"What formula?"

Ernie laughed and looked around. "You'll have to find that our for yourself, like I did." He flicked his finger at the books and marched off. "Check the Library," he called.

"What did Yearlove say?" said Robin scoffing a large slab of jam tart and custard.

"Asked me what was wrong. I said nothing. That was about it."

Robin wiped his chin. "I like Yearlove, he's nice. Anyone else would have given you detention for a year," he said indicating Simone at the Magisteer's table.

"I was only standing up for you, that was out of bloody order what Jasper did!"

"Language!" said Dawn. "I don't want to hear words like that at the dinner table."

"Well, spell your ears shut then!" I cried. Everyone on the table gasped. I felt my face grow a little red as I shrunk back in the chair scowling, feeling all their shocked eyes rest on me.

Ellen put her sandwich down. "Avis, you can't speak to Dawn like that, nor anyone."

"Say sorry," said Jake.

"*Whaaat?*" I said, balking at Jake's serious stare. I looked around at their expectant faces. "Fine! Sorry Dawn." Dawn sniffed.

Robin leaned closer and whispered "You need to get your temper under control," he said, looking down his nose at me with a serious expression.

"Whatever. Listen, you know our Riptide matches will be just after the Christmas break right?" Robin nodded. "If it's going be anything like last year then it will be another utter humiliation…"

"Yeah so? What's your plan?" said Robin impatiently.

"I spoke to Ernie a little while ago, he reckons that there is a *formula* to finding the Ornaments. And that there are books in the Library about how to win. Imagine it, actually winning at Riptide?" Robin's eyes lit up, imagining the success and fame that being a great Riptide player brings — one look over at the Centaurs table told you how highly Wizards prize Riptide players — it was packed with adoring fans.

"But… won't it be like… cheating?"

I couldn't think of anything to say and paused a second too long. "No… it's just… giving ourselves an advantage." Robin was almost sold. "Imagine, everyone in the crowd cheering your name as we win with a Libero-Manus! All the girls coming to watch…" something changed in his face. He was sold.

I'll be honest, it was a crafty move. I had an inkling that he liked a girl from the year above us, which was hilarious enough — but I had no idea who, he wouldn't tell me, denying all knowledge whenever I mentioned it. Robin always kept things close to his chest. But this, I knew, would seal his inclusion in my dastardly plan.

***

"You are second years now, of course you are allowed in the Library," said Partington.

Robin scoffed, as if it was a joke, then seeing Partington's puzzled face said. "When did this happen?"

"All second years are allowed in the Library, just ask the librarian what you are after. She's very nice and will show you around."

I sighed, all this year we could have walked straight in? "Why aren't first years allowed in Sir?"

"Don't want them seeing things they're not ready for," said Partington, his owl-like face fixed on fiddling with something on his desk. "Blowing their spark and such, very messy for all involved. No, it's much safer to just wait until the second year when you've build up a resistance to it, and your subconscious has let all the information sink in."

Graham, who was rocking back on his chair then chimed in. "Sir, when are we going to practice Riptide?"

Partington chewed his cheek. "Obviously the stadium falling down put a dent in that. But, as soon as its back up, we will be able to put our name down on the practice sheet and be allocated some time slots."

"But Sir," said Gret. "Da' season starts almost as soon as we get back from Christmas?"

"Well, we shall have to fit it in wherever we can."

A part of me sensed that Partington had all but given up any hopes of us doing well in Riptide.

"I can't believe no one told us that we could go straight to the Library," I fumed.

"I know!" Robin steamed sharing my frustration, he liked books almost as much as me. "Not one Magisteer mentioned it! Think of the homework I could have improved!" he whimpered.

"Why do you want to go to the Library?" said Hunter disdainfully behind us, clearly he didn't think they were much fun.

"Because," I said. "They have books. Books have information. Information is powerful."

"Pfft, I'd rather go do fun things with my free time, what there is of it," he said following Graham, Simon, Jake and Gret outside with two flounders under their arms, (flounders are Riptide balls, one red and one blue).

Robin and I pushed the huge golden trimmed double doors of the Library open and walked inside. Noise hit us like a steam train, it was absolutely crammed full. Every available space was taken up with someone — people climbing huge ladders to the top of teetering bookshelves that reached as high as the cathedral high ceiling. Tables were crammed full of sixth and seventh years hunched over books and piles of paper. Haughty, flitting blue ghosts zapped from one place to another tidying books away, and snapping at anyone who made a noise.

"Ouch!" said a third year boy who was shaking the ladder of his friend and giggling, until a fat ghost clapped him round the head.

"Ok," I whispered across to Robin. "We just need to find some books on Riptide…"

But something very frustrating happened. Apart from all the people getting in the way and constant buzz of low-level noise, there was the incredibly annoying factor of ghosts popping up in front of us at almost every book shelf.

"You can't go down here!" it whispered loudly, for the fifth time.

"Then where are we allowed?" I said, before receiving a very hard, cold slap.

"Keep your voice down! Second years are allowed over there, those three bookshelves."

"*Three?*" I said before it disappeared. Turned out, we may as well not be allowed in the Library, for the three bookshelves we were allowed to read from where useless. Introductions to things we already knew, or some other pointless, useless drivel — entry-level books.

"It wasn't like this when we broke in last year," said Robin. "There were no restrictions then, look over there where those fifth years are, that's where I read that book about *Dancidious*, the spell blocker."

"That settle's it," I said. "We break in. Tonight."

We tugged the loose grate away from the bathroom wall, revealing the small, dark hole. I slid through first into the impenetrable darkness. Only a thin ray of light from the dim bathroom crept through the hole, showing a black, jagged wall. Robin slipped down ungainly behind me and pulled the grate back into place.

I flashed my hand at the river. "Severton," I said, the blue flash temporarily illuminating the dank passageway. There was a sealing, crunching sound as the spell froze the river solid. The black rock roof was low, causing Robin to duck as we slipped all the way along the frozen river. The river passage opened out directly into the centre of the Library. Small boats were frozen stiff against the side of the wall. We clambered up the stone steps and gazed around at the majesty of the empty Library. It was bigger when no one was in here. Robin and I shared an untold passion for books, and this Library held a special place in my heart, it had to be said, for in here there were more books than I'd ever seen.

But then there was a peculiar scratching noise that made us both stop dead. I couldn't work out where from. I tilted my head slowly round at the door which was locked shut, and then through the dimly lit bookshelves. The only light came from the crescent moon shining in through the tall windows. Robin was terrified, he slowly lifted a finger, pointing at the frozen lake. The scratching noise was coming from the tunnel. I don't know what I was expecting to see, but certainly not... an enlarged white eyeball, scratching across the ice on three tiny legs towards us.

I glanced once at Robin, but what could we do? Slowly I started to back away towards the nearby bookshelf, we could hide behind it. Robin cottoned on and followed, tip-toeing backwards. We lost sight of the Occulus as it dipped below the rim of the river. We darted behind the bookshelf as quietly as we could. I cupped a hand to my mouth and ducked backwards into the shadow of the wall. We waited, trying not to breathe. After a minute I glanced at Robin, I couldn't hear anything, maybe it had gone back? We stepped forwards, out of the shadow and peered round the corner. All of a sudden the moonlight reflected across Robin's glasses — the light flashing across the books in front of us. We both stopped. Dead still.

"Come on," I mouthed. "Let's get out of here."

Suddenly, Robin gasped. A chill shot down my spine. Directly ahead of us, staring silently, was the Occulus. For a second it just stood, its dark pupils contracting. Tiny three-toed-feet tapped the carpet nervously. Then, all at once, a prod shot out of the top of its head and a fleshy mouth suddenly began wail!

WOOOOOOO — WOOOOOOOOH!

"Get it!" I cried. The Occulus darted away with the agility of a cat. As it turned to speed down to the lake again, I raised a hand at it.

"Avis *NO!*"

"Pasanthedine!" I called, a shot of wind blasted from my hand and missed the Occulus by an inch. The spell hit a boat, which made an awful crunching sound before shooting into the air. I ran to the river railings and aimed my hand again. But the Occulus had vanished down the dark passageway, the siren call echoing deafeningly under the passageway.

"You can't do spells in the Library after dark remember!" cried Robin.

"Come on!" I climbed down into the icy river, but it felt different, less stable. Lights blazed on from all round, as running feet echoed in the corridors outside. We scrambled and slipped along the ice towards the passageway. Noise and light now clouded my senses as I made a desperate scramble for safety.

"...*AVIS! AVIS!*" Robin called.

"What?!" I turned. Robin was stood in the middle of the river, not moving. The door to the Library was being unlocked. But Robin was pointing to a very large crack that had just appeared in the ice between his legs. The boat that I accidentally spelled into the air had left a big watery gap, which sent cracks shooting through the ice. The Library doors burst open.

CRACK! The last thing I saw was the Lily, Harold, Partington and Straker, before falling into the icy depths below.

Needless to say, no one believed us that we were 'sleepwalking'. I think it made them even more mad. They raised us both out of the water, put some sort of heat spell round us and turned off all the sirens, noises and lights. They still echoed horribly in my ears as black spots were dancing in front of my eyes.

After a few rounds of questions, we told the Lily most of the truth. That we wanted to look at books that we couldn't during the day. Robin whimpering slightly next to me. Surprisingly, the Lily didn't exspell us, or suspend us, or even make us do a years detention. On the contrary, he was understanding. Each Magisteer behind him had a different expression. Partington looked relieved but sheepish, Straker looked surprised and stormy, and Harold looked a strange mixture between angry and proud. It was hard to tell with him.

We were sent on our way, shivering all the way back to our dorm. All the boys were awake, sitting up in bed with half a light on.

"Knew it!" said Dennis as we both trudged in. "We knew you two were up to something, when the sirens went off and we saw you were missing… what were you doing?"

"Yeah come on, what happened?" said Graham, sitting up in bed a little more. Even Hunter had his eyes open.

So we explained as we got changed out of sopping wet clothes, dried, put on fresh pyjamas and got into bed — that we wanted to go the Library and find good books about the secrets of Riptide, so we wouldn't be humiliated again.

"You mean cheat?" said Jake, tutting.

"It's not cheating, it's just…" I struggled for the words.

"Informing ourselves of all the rules," Robin offered.

"I'm up for that," said Hunter. "Anyway, all us Outsiders don't have a chance, we need to know this stuff. You Wizard lot know it all, you've grown up with the sport…" Jake sniffed and muttered something that sounded like: *"would be useful I suppose."*

***

On the way to Wasp's lesson the next day, all we could hear was people talking about the siren's going off — the boys in our form turned with grinning faces to me and Robin.

— "I heard it was Henry Zanders who set the sirens off on purpose," said a girl from the forth year. "He's such a joker."

— "Well, I heard it was a dare by the sixth year Werewolf form, you know James Lock and Shabnam and Abdul Choudhry?"

Another passing fourth year group said—"I think having Occulus spying on us is wrong anyway."

— "We're used to it, us Outsiders."

Wasp's lesson was okay. The enthusiasm he brought to the class made it interesting, his rather squeaky voice rising in pitches as he became even more excited about a certain AstroMagical sign. Often we would ask him questions midway through the class, something about himself, as we knew he would go off topic and tell us these great long stories about how he used a particular spell under a certain sign of the AstroMagical chart to defeat a foe. And he would thrash about in mid air, arms waving along as he recreated the battles. Spinning popping lights flashing around him with the excitement. Then, at the end of the story he would forget what the lesson was all about.

Next lesson was Yearlove's, which I should have loved if were not for the fact that I had to sit and endure two hours of Jasper and Tina. I couldn't help the envious sourness creep into my mind as I sat back in the comfy chair. Yearlove was sat in his own chair, a rather battered brown thing that he said was '*his favourite*'.

"We were so lucky last night. Why do you think he let us off?" I whispered as we got our stuff out of our bags.

Robin nodded. "I thought we were going to be expelled. If that was Simone, can you imagine?"

The midday sun crept through the clouds and pierced the stained glass window. A shot of red, green and gold lit the floor in front of us.

"Wow," said Yearlove. "That is beautiful." There was mutters of agreement as we stared at the spinning colours.

Then I sincerely heard Jaspers awful voice whisper: "*Not as beautiful as you T.*" Others must have heard it? Or had they pretended not to out of embarrassment? But she actually smiled at him, her eyes melting. I felt like being sick all over the floor just to prove a point. Hunter was staring across at them with half a curious, half disgusted face before Yearlove jumped up and began the lesson.

"Riptide is a great example of *bridge spells*. Can anyone tell me what the first part of a bridge spell is?"

"*Returious*," Jasper called out.

"Yes! Well done Jasper," called Yearlove. I rolled my eyes, unable to help it anymore. I knew that it was Returious, everyone knew. It was basic. "Can you tell me then Jasper, an example of the second part of a Returious spell?" Yearlove raised his eyebrows and stroked his beard.

"Well Sir, depending on the situation, your allowed seven spells for Riptide, which is more like twenty-three with counters. But I suppose the most recognisable one's which are not used in Riptide much are: *Catarsis*, *Pasarè* and *Nitäl*. These are used for creating an emotion ball, so that others can better understand your feelings, alerting someone how far you are away from them, and lastly the translation spell for speaking when abroad."

"A very concise and clear answer, and absolutely spot on," said Yearlove taken aback. "That's another three stars for the Swillow form."

Jasper's form burst with applause, and his tall friend Freddie next to him said: "How many's that now? *Nine*?!"

"None," whispered Robin preempting my next question about how many the Condors had.

I sat back in the chair and tutted, simultaneously jotting down the three spells Jasper the git had mentioned. For the rest of the class I sat glumly while Jasper answered all the questions correctly, it was like the *Jasper Gandy Show*. What annoyed me more was the fact that Hunter, Joanna and Gret were starting as adoringly at Jasper as Tina and the rest of the Swillow form were. Did he have them all under some kind of spell or something? Because they looked utterly spellbound.

"And what — and this is a tough one," said Yearlove. "Is the name and process of a Solvent spell that could break the bonds of the infamous red-chain spell?"

"Obviously that's a trick question Sir, as the spell to remove a *Sanguis-Catena* spell is not a Solvent spell at all... You would need a Chaos magic spell for that, something like *Recludo-depellerant?*"

Yearlove stared for a moment. "How do you know all this?" he said dreamily.

"You're amazing Jasper," crooned his friend Henry in a dopy voice.

Something snapped inside me, I couldn't take it anymore — suddenly a voice burst out of me: *"This is the only spell known Sir, well Sir, two bags full Sir..."* I cried, mimicking his perfect voice, as the ball of rage squirmed. *"Oh no Sir, please, let me answer all the questions because I am so brilliant and worthy and geeky..."*

Robin and Ellen sniggered next to me as did a few boys from Hubris form who looked equally bored. But I regretted my outburst.

Yearlove stood, brow furrowed. "I've spoken to you before about this Avis, starting to live up to your family name I see? By disrupting my lesson? Go and wait outside."

"Oh for god sake!" I cried dropping my paper all over the floor. "All we've done this lesson is sit here and listen to him waffle on about how great he is, well I'm sick of it!" I cried, a burning cauldron of fury erupting, as Robin and the others gasped.

Freddie stood up sharply. "Whatever you got to say to Jasper, you say it to me first."

"Oh, do yourself a favour and sit down. You too," I called as dopy Henry stood. "Why don't we just rename this class, the *Jasper Gandy appreciation society*?" A few more people laughed now, complete with a few claps of appreciation from some. Jasper looked affronted, and Tina downright stormy, glaring across the room at me with a thunderous expression. I didn't care anymore. I couldn't sit here a moment longer listening to how great *he* was.

"Maybe," said Yearlove. "But if you would knuckle down and answer some questions then maybe we'd all start to appreciate how brilliant you are."

"Yeah maybe, but maybe no one else can get a word in edgeways! And maybe, I have got better things to do with my time, than sit here listening to that pretentious gnome-faced, Orc eared, goody two shoes waffle on anymore!" I grabbed my bag and turned away.

"Please don't come back to this lesson for a few weeks, until you've calmed down," called Yearlove.

"Whatever," I turned out of the room slamming the door.

I marched off quickly to the bathrooms, my heart beating a million miles an hour, hot blood beating around my body after that awful confrontation. Dumping my bag down I began splashing cold water over my face. That was better. It felt hot after that fiery encounter. I sighed and looked around, it was bigger in here than the bathroom on my floor—more people used it probably—a huge chandelier hung from the centre of the bathroom with burning candles and dripping wax. It was quiet too and every footstep echoed as I wandered aimlessly around the bathroom kicking out at the toilet doors as the last conversations reverberated around inside me. It made me so mad. I had such high expectations for that class. But everyone seemed utterly spellbound by Jasper? Why?

BANG! I kicked another door open. I mean yes he was good looking...

BANG! And clever...

BANG! And apparently brilliant at Riptide...

BANG! But so what? I wandered back to the sink, and stared into the mirror. My face looked sour, red and blotchy. It did that sometimes when I was annoyed or stressed. I leaned against the sink and stared at the ground. I sighed, a great wave of tingling negativity swept over me. I was the one who was supposed to be with Tina, not Jasper. Tina and I, had something special. I saved her life, and her brothers life — except no one knew apart from Robin and the Partington's. I felt betrayed. Why had she ignored me so much? It was rude, after everything I did for her! The way she looked at him haunted me. That loving glint in her eye, in fact, not just in hers, but quite a few people's when they looked at Jasper. Then something slid into my brain... what

120

if he really did have them all under a spell? What if he really was a dark Wizard? Out to avenge Malakai? That would totally explain it—he knows everything about magic, he could know powerful love charms, that's why Tina was ignoring me. That's why everyone loves him. He was out to do Tina harm, to get back at me for defeating Malakai. Or, he could be Malakai? Perhaps the only thing he could do after I defeated him was go into another body, I've heard of that... *possessing*. He was possessing Jasper. Yeah, that would be it, he was out to get me, make me look like an idiot, steal Tina away from me and then get his revenge.

Something made me look up. In the corner of my eye I was sure I saw a shadow move... must have been a sprat. There was a sudden hissing noise coming from behind me, echoing across the large empty bathroom.

Sssssssssssssss...

And then more hisses, rising louder and louder. It was coming from the taps. I stepped back curiously. What on earth were they doing? And then, without warning, they burst. The metal tops blasting into the air, one by one, causing an explosion of water to come raining down around me.

Pop! *Bang*! I spun around, who was doing this? The water was soaking me to the skin, but there was no one here! Then, a flash of white light lit the air. Scorching through the fountain of water and hitting the chandelier above. With a sickening, snapping sound, it fell. I launched myself backwards, skidding through the water. Crashing back into the wet floor. The chandelier crashed hard, sending a tidal wave of water shooting over my head, missing my legs by inches. The echo rang true around the bathroom. I stood up fast and looked around, the person who had done that was in here.

"I know you're in here!" I called above the noise. "Jasper? Is it you?" the flash had come from the toilet cubicles at the end of the bathroom. Laying in the water I scanned underneath the toilet cubicles for the culprit. In the fifth cubicle along I saw it. But, this wasn't Jasper, indeed it didn't look much like a person's feet. Dark, thick torn black rags hung down beneath bare dirty feet. What on earth? And then it moved. Under the cubicles it zapped like a shadow. Passing through the walls of the toilet cubicles as if they were not there.

"I can see you!" I called, my heart beating fast, I raised my hand towards it. "*Severton!*" A flash of icy blue light flew out of my hand toward the mass of small black rags. It hit the toilet door and froze it solid. "Dam!" I called. There was a flash of black behind me, I spun round. The creature in black rags darted out of the bathroom. "Stop!" I called racing out of the bathroom, charging after the flashes of dark rag that whipped around corners. Until... I lost it. Standing and panting hard, my chest set to explode, I gave up. Whatever it was, was gone.

I trudged back towards the bathroom. No amount of explaining would get me out of this one. But this was the strange thing — there were no Occulus's down here. Not one. So, even if I was to tell the truth about what just happened, there would be no way to prove it. Trying not to panic, I waved my arms around myself reciting the heat spell that Partington had put on us when we fell into the Library river. It worked. I felt the fiery rays breeze through my robes. Steam erupted into the air as the water evaporated.

Now to sort the bathroom out... but how? The only person I knew who could help me sort this out was in a lesson. Robin would be out in five minutes, I'd have to wait for him.

I waited near enough to Yearlove's classroom, hidden down a dark corridor nearby, behind a large statue of some animal. I didn't want anyone else from the class to see me. The bathroom was a little way away down the long passage,

I just had to pray no one alerted anybody of the carnage before I, or Robin could fix it. My hands were shaking as I waited. Must have been the shock, something had just tried to kill me. The same thing that had tried to get me when building the stadium. What on earth was it?

Soon enough, I heard a door open, then chattering. "See you all in two days!" cried Yearlove cheerfully. I peeked through the statue and saw them all filling out. There was Robin at the back, talking to Joanna. *Hurry up*, I thought ducking back into shadow as Jessie, Tow and Karma from Hubris passed. This was absurd, hiding like this. I turned back to look — Tina was hugging Jasper, did they ever give it a rest? And now Robin was speaking to Yearlove about something! Tina turned off the other way as Jasper slowly made his way along the corridor, smiling to himself. I snuck back into the shadow as he passed.

"Think I can't see you?" he said slowly, without looking. "*Tut, tut, tut*, you were a naughty boy," he stopped, turning his head slightly to look at me. I nearly choked with fright, how on earth did he spot me? Jasper shot forwards, grabbing me by the collar and shoving me backwards into the dark corridor.

"Get off me you git!" I cried. "ROB—" I tried to call, before he slammed a hand round my mouth.

"How *dare* you call me Orc eared!" He spat, his handsome face enraged. "Your jealousy of my superiority is plain for all to see, you ridiculous relic of a failed family name." I pushed him back with all my strength as he relinquished his hold.

"Jealous? Of you? Pah! You have a high opinion of yourself!" I called, heart beating fast. "And you—"

"SHUT IT!" He punched the wall next to my head, which cracked, plaster and brick falling over my shoulder. "I've had enough of you Avis. What even is your problem? Is it Tina?" he smiled menacingly, nothing like the pretty, handsome charming boy he was in class. "*My* Tina. And yes, she's told me *everything*. I can be very persuasive…"

"I doubt that," I said smiling to myself, if she did tell him *everything*, then the pact we'd made last year would have done something horrible — like tattoo her face with swear words.

"I SAID SHUT IT!" he cried again. I wished Robin would turn around that corner right now and help me. "That she would choose to associate with a Blackthorn is a clear mark of her lack of maturity last year. She has since matured and realised what you are," he leaned in close, until I could smell his rose scented breath. "I can make sure she never, ever speaks or looks at you again. Is that what you want?"

I didn't say anything, I couldn't. My hand was still shaking. He saw it and began cackling. "*Pahaha!*" he riled into the ceiling. "You are pathetic! This is what I suggest… you stop coming to Yearlove's class, or if you do, please just sit there and *listen*, you might actually learn something," he grinned. "Now please excuse me, I have to go help those less fortunate than me, learn something about their signs…"

Jasper smiled again and wandered off whistling, pleased with himself. I stood against the wall for a good minute. I had frozen — he'd scared me. I was already in a state of shock from what happened in the bathroom. It pained me to stand there, weak and feeble, his spitting remarks burning my ears like acid. Slowly I moved away, then began jogging, before sprinting back to my dorm.

I slammed the door shut to the empty room. I breathed hard and got my Seven League Shoes out from under the bed and hurriedly put them on. They had saved me before when Ross had tried to attack me, maybe they would again if that *thing*, or Jasper went for me. Just in case.

***

124

"Apparently it was some wayward ghosts," said Graham.

"No," spluttered Simon. "It was more than likely the dodgy spell-work on the taps. They could have been lethal! Thank god no one was in there…" — They were talking about the destroyed bathroom, everyone was. It was an apparent mystery, since no Occulus' were around to record the incident.

I still hadn't told Robin about what had happened, I just hadn't got round to it. I was walking along with the rest of the boys from my form, preferring to take safety in numbers. Besides, I wasn't going to go to another bathroom alone. It was ten o'clock and I felt exhausted by the day's activities. Besides getting caught in the Library last night, trashing the bathroom and getting sent out of lessons, I then had to make my way outside into the freezing December cold to lift extremely heavy rafters, drapes and metal poles. My hands were really sore too, the rope had slid out of my hands earlier, causing a huge friction burn, followed by a sharp electric shock from caretaker Ingralo.

"You're quiet?" said Hunter, behind me.

"Long day," I offered.

"Yeah and getting sent out of lessons, naughty boy!" Hunter laughed. "Mind you I did agree with what you said, that Jasper kid is a cringe."

"Why are you wearing shoes?" Simon sneered, peering down at them as if this was the most unfashionable thing in the world — they were all wearing slippers.

I sighed, too tired to think of an explanation. "Because I couldn't be bothered taking them off," I said wearily.

"Will you stop 'dat!" said Jake turning to glower at Hunter as we turned the third corner, mid way to the bathrooms. "He keeps trying to trip me up, thinks it's funny…" he said as Hunter giggled.

I sighed. "As long as you don't do it to *meeeeeeeee!*" I said, just as Hunter clipped my heels. And now, golden light suddenly flashed from the shoes. In barely the blink of an eye I was off! Shooting at break neck speed down corridors. The feeling of wading through treacle returned, as I sped round the school corridors in golden loops, arriving at the entrance to the bathroom, dazed and wobbly. I looked down at the shoes as the golden light evaporated. They had worked again? But I wasn't in danger? And they had taken me exactly to where I wanted to be. My brain was frazzled, I couldn't think what this meant. Soon enough the other boys turned the corner with quizzical looks on their faces.

"Why did you just run off like 'dat?" said Jake. "We got scared, thought there was something afv'ter us!"

I wobbled on the spot. "Did you not see the golden light? Or see me whizz off?"

Robin, who looked as tired as me with his glasses dropping down his face, frowned. "What golden light? We just saw you leg-it down the corridor."

"Have you been practicing sprints?" said Hunter. "You're really quick."

Simon sneered again. "So just to get this straight, you didn't see anything odd? No ghosts?" he smiled.

"Hey," said Jake. "Save your energy for Riptide. We could do with speed like 'dat."

Jake had said something that remained with me. Referring to Riptide, he said that we *could do with speed like that*. None of them had seen the golden light, nor the fact I basically flew at break neck speed around the corridors. They hadn't noticed at all, they thought I was just quick? I didn't get long to think about it that night as I slept almost as soon as my head hit the pillow. It was uncomfortable sleeping in the shoes, but needs must.

Snow fell thick and fast during the night. Upon waking and drawing back the curtains, a good three feet covered everything in sight. Caretaker Ingralo was madly zapping around the Riptide Stadium with a heat-spell gun, melting all the snow so that we could go out there and carry on working. That is until the Lily told him to stop. We cheered from our bedroom and danced around as if we'd just won the cup, chanting: "*The Lily! The Lily! We love you!*" A day off from building at last! And to make matters even better, at breakfast it was announced that all lessons were cancelled for the day. A massive eruption of cheers broke out reverberating the Chamber until it shook.

"What lessons we missing?" said Hunter after he calmed down.

"Well," said Dawn sharply. "It's a Friday isn't it? So if you check your timetable, you'll see we are missing Numerology and AstroMagic."

Hunter stood and punched the air. "Thank you god for making it snow."

We carried on eating in very good mood, taking our time over breakfast, still all in our pyjama's and dressing gowns. Jake and Gret read the Herrald sport pages together. Graham and Simon started a game of magic cards, which caused Graham to be told off by Magisteer Dodaline who heard him swear loudly as he was bitten by the lizard queen card. Hunter joined his friends Jamie Brown and Kenny McCarthy on their table and was laughing away in his deep booming laugh. I just sat, feeling quite good about having a free day, but with the previous day's events like the splinters in my hands — unable to get them out. Jasper wasn't in the Chamber, neither was Tina. Good.

I could feel someone watching me, the hair on my arms stood up. I glanced around, in my peripheral I saw Harold, my brother, turn his attention away. He was up at the Magisteer's round table in the corner, now inspecting his porridge sourly. Then, a full head of white hair popped up in front of him. It was Zara from his form. She was gazing at him with the same adorning glaze to her eyes that Tina had for Jasper. She asked him something and he nodded slowly, before she left again with her friends beaming wide.

"What you looking at?" said Robin looking up from his homework.

"Nothing," I said shifting in my chair and looking the other way. "Why you doing homework?"

He looked down his nose at me with a big frown on. "It's got to be done hasn't it? I mean, it's not going to do itself. Might as well use this day to catch up."

"Spose'… hey, I need to tell you about what happened yesterday."

Robin looked up sharply from his homework and fixing me with a deep stare. "Why, what happened?"

All of a sudden some people came storming into the Chamber crying: "SNOW FIGHT!" there was a mass shuffling of chairs as people raced outside to the snow. Robin and I looked at each other, before jumping up and running after them.

"I'll tell you later!"

***

"So, what was it you wanted to tell me?" said Robin taking off his soaking wet clothes and standing by the roaring fire in just his pants. It was not a pleasant sight. I was already nice and dry, having said the heat spell a couple of times on the way back up.

We'd had so much fun in the snowball fight I'd almost forgotten about everything else. I hadn't had that much fun since the end of last year. David Starlight thought he was brilliant at snowball fights and was running around totting up how many people he'd hit, I could hear him counting as he ran, but not before Robin, Jake and I smashed a big snowball right in his face, causing him to lie on the ground for a good minute, before being helped up by his friends. The Lily was watching from his office high up, I could see him out of one of the long windows surveying the action below. I bet he wanted to join in, I would if I was old.

Magic snow balling is different from ordinary snow balling when your little and magic-less, or an Outsider. It was a little unfair at times, the sixth and seventh years were absolute magic masters and knew how to make their snowball fire like a homing missile! So I, and many other lower years, received so many clouts to the face, that it went completely numb.

"So?" said Robin satisfied that he was dry enough as he dressed into his robes.

"Well, there's a couple of things. Firstly, you know the bathrooms near Yearlove's?"

"That was you wasn't it?" he said wide-eyed.

"No, well, not exactly. Just listen... I went there after I walked out——"

"Sent out."

"Whatever, listen... something attacked me. I saw it and chased it. It made all the taps explode, then the chandelier fell on me. Got out of the way though, then I saw it in a cubicle. It wasn't a person, it was small and dirty and dressed in black rags."

Robin slipped his jumper on. "How didn't they know it was you in the bathrooms?"

"That's the other wired thing, there are no Occulus' up there." Robin looked up at the ceiling as if he could see straight through the floors above. "After that lesson I waited for you, but you took ages! Then Jasper saw me and pushed me down an empty corridor. He told me not to say anything else in Yearlove's lessons, and that he can be *persuasive*, and that he can make Tina never talk to me ever again. And other nasty stuff. I was... a bit scared."

Robin shook his head. "Who does he think he is? How dare he use that as a threat, Tina can talk to whoever she wants!"

"And then..." I said flicking my shoes up to my gaze. "My shoes, they——"

"Your shoes?" said Robin turning to look at them. "What do you mean your shoes?"

"At the end of last year, the Lily gave me these in the black leather box. You got the same box. Well, me and Tina found them originally in the passageway near where Malakai used to go."

"And?"

"They're Seven League Shoes."

Robin took off his glasses and stared open-mouthed at them. "Of course."

"They work, except I don't know how, they've saved me like three times now from danger. And last night when I ran off to the bathroom. That was the shoes! There's a golden light around them, and then I feel like I'm running through treacle, but I'm going so fast... And it got me thinking... what if, like Jake said, I used them in *Riptide?*"

Robin shook his head slowly. "They would know. Underwood does a check before every match."

"Well, that's what we need to find out," I said clicking my fingers. "We need to get to the Library again."

"What?! You must be kidding, after the last time? No way! We'll be exspelled instantly!"

I got off the bed. "Listen mate, if we want to find out how to make the shoes work and become brilliant at Riptide, then we need to get into the Library at night? We can't go during the day because we can't look at any books! All we need to do is work out how to take out the Occulus," I said, but Robin was shaking his head.

"No way, we were lucky not to be exspelled last time."

"Fine. I'll go alone," I said sitting back on the end of my bed listening to the shouts of joy from outside as the snow fight continued. "Just didn't want to be the complete losers of the school again, like we were last year. Ernie told me there are books up there that he used to be great at Riptide."

"Is that why he's on like twelve Riptide trophies?" said Robin. I nodded slyly. He rubbed his forehead and sighed. "I'll see what I can do…"

***

Snow continued to fall for the next week, newer flakes falling on top of hardened icy ground. Snowballing wasn't fun anymore, it hurt. Lessons resumed as usual, but obviously I wasn't allowed in Yearlove's lessons. Didn't want to go anyway, didn't want to be anywhere near that git Jasper. I had to find out who he really was. There was no way he was the same age as us, he knew too much — his eyes, when he was staring at me in the gloom of the corridor were… evil. I was sure of it. He was either Malakai, or a Malakai supporter, out for revenge. And he was using Tina to get at me.

"Only a week until Christmas!" Dennis cried at the dinner table, wrapping the wood with his knuckles excitedly. "Oh I can't wait. Going to have a lovely big Dandy bird, and lots of presents!"

"What the hec's a dandy bird?" said Graham looking perplexed.

Dennis scoffed. "You don't know? It's the most delicious bird ever, all Wizard's eat dandy's on Christmas day."

"Except vegetarians," said Joanna sharply, who was an ardent vegetarian.

Hunter was nodding at Graham and Dennis with a bit of bacon hanging out of his mouth. "We have—" GULP. "We have turkey don't we Graham. Outsiders always have Turkey."

"What on earth is a turkey?" Simon sneered. "Some sort of potato thing? Outsiders eat lots of potatoes. Their diet is almost exclusively potato."

Hunter scoffed. "No, it's not a potato thing. A turkey is a bird."

"And is it as delicious as a Dandy?" said Simon.

"Doubt it," Graham muttered. "Who's coming to the Hubris girls party tonight?" the majority of the table nodded, except me.

"What party?" I said.

Jake looked at me quizzically. "I thought out of everyone you would know. Tina Partington's party?"

"Oh yeah that, *pfft*, forgot didn't I?" I said clapping a hand to my head. Jake passed me a small purple leaflet to '*jog my memory*,' I looked at it hard without seeing it for a minute, as I let my red face pass.

You are invited to a small gathering in room 32z, floor four on the 18 th of December to have fun and party and celebrate my 13 th. Just turn up at 8ish. Not robes allowed. Tina Partington.

Why hadn't she told me about this? Or how had I not known about this? Robin was inspecting his toast very closely. "Did you know about this?" I said flashing the leaflet at him. He looked up from the toast, pretending to draw a blank, shaking his head dreamily.

"Noooo— not sure… maybe…"

"You did didn't you?"

"Yes," he nodded sullenly.

"Why didn't she tell me?"

Robin shrugged. "I honestly have no idea."

"Must have forgotten," I said, hopefully.

***

I was a bit nervous because I knew Jasper would be there. I put on my tartan shirt and nice jeans, keeping my Seven League Shoes on for good measure. Robin had put on his best denim jacket. The other guys were walking just ahead of us nervously, Hunter in a big shirt and drape that was actually the curtain from our room, he said he wanted

132

to go as *a prince*. We tried to remind him that it wasn't fancy dress, but he wouldn't listen.

Music drummed outside room 32z as Jake wrapped on the door. A second later Jessie opened it, squealing with excitement as if she didn't think anyone would turn up. We piled into the big room, it was the size of our bedroom, without any beds but the entire place was filled with decorations and banners. The fireplace was lit, but the fire was crackling multicolour fire, spinning dancing rainbow lights around the room. I could hear him before I saw him, Tina under his arm by the fireplace. Jasper was explaining to some third years how he had created the fire and the decorations.

"Easy really, when you know how," he yawned. "A simple bridge spell."

"Wow, you're so clever," said the third year. "I don't even know any of this stuff yet."

The party was actually quite good. One boy, Hayden Carmichael was in the corner of the room, doing the music behind a couple of large speakers: *The Orc Triad*, *Yearning for Slackerdown* and *Gnippoh Culture* were followed by the Happendance folk band *Leprechaun Landing*.

Food popped onto the tables around the sides of the room where me and Robin lingered, hot nibbles on silver platters and sweet smelling pastries drew me in. Hunter smiled happily as if this was heaven and dived in. Then, the girls from our form made their way in slowly. Jess and Florence looked amazing as usual attracting a lot of attention from the boys. Dawn hung at the back in a big flowery dress, with Ellen and Joanna, none of whom looked remotely comfortable.

There were a lot of people in here now, of all different years. Then as yet more people arrived, it became quite cramped. "Hold on," cried Jasper jumping forwards. "Let me enlarge the room." Then, with a big puff of his cheeks, the room extended — the walls made a crunching sound as they slid further away, the corners of the room moving outwards a couple of feet.

"Woah!" went a chorus of people, before a huge round of applause. I didn't clap. Show off.

Another knock at the door, and Ernie entered. Girls all around us crooned silently. He was very dashing, dressed in a long silver robe, with his long curly hair combed back.

"Ernie!" cried Tina, relinquishing her hold of Jasper and hugging Ernie tightly. Just behind him were the Snare form, who came in tentatively waving at Tina who beamed wide and hugged them all. Zara, the white haired girl made my heart start to flutter uncontrollably. She wore a causal black dress with lace arms. It contrasted well with the long white hair. While Robin had his eyes glued to a patch of third year girls.

Ernie grinned at me conspiratorially. "So Avis, Robin, have you… you know, found out anything *new* about Riptide?" We looked at each other, before quietly telling him about getting caught in the Library. "Yeah, that takes me back. The amount of times I was caught," he chuckled shaking his head.

"I want to go back at night, but Robin isn't convinced are you?"

Robin looked sheepish, rolling his head from side to side. Ernie's blue eyes gazed up at the ceiling as he seemed to search for the right words. "You have to take risks if you want to be great. That's all I'll say," he nodded. Robin's eyes blinked rapidly behind his spectacles. Thank you Ernie.

After a long chat with Ernie who told us about settling back into school life, he suddenly looked around. "32z? This rooms bigger than it should be?"

"Yeah Jasper enlarged it," Robin said pointing at him in the middle of the room.

"Did he? I thought he was a second year?" said Ernie.
"He is."

Ernie raised his eyebrows in surprise and turned to look at Jasper. "That's impressive."

"I can't stand him," I said, unable to help myself. I wanted Ernie to hate him too, but he just looked at me sympathetically.

The night sky darkened to a puce purple, the full moon beaming luminescent over the walking trees below. They were huddling together now as they went to sleep — they didn't have leaves anymore, so they must be cold.

"Come on!" said Florence dragging Robin and I forcefully onto the dance floor, where I nodded along self-consciously to The Mad Hatters song *Spelling Alive*. After a while however I got quite into it, the mango perry helping a touch. Then, I saw Jasper staring at me through the crowd of people, looking livid. I turned away ignoring him and saw Zara dancing with her form. A mad torrent of weird feelings tore around inside me. She was so beautiful, but then I looked at Tina and the same thing happened but mixed with horrible gurgling regret and jealousy.

"Her name is Zara Faraday," said Robin loudly in my ear. "Want me to go and—*hiccup*—say hello to her for you?"

"What? No!" I cried over the music. "Please don't."

"You *like* her…" he sang pointing at me madly, as he flailed around attempting to dance. I smiled, before Robin saw the third year girl making her way over to the food stand and followed her. I stood alone on the dance floor mimicking Simon's awful dance moves without him realising.

Then I felt something wet go right down my front. "*Whoops…*" said a voice. Jasper! I looked down. He'd poured an entire glass of blood orange juice down my front. "That's what happens to those who aren't invited," he spat. I quickly looked around, no one saw, everyone was dancing. "Nice shirt," he smiled.

"How dare you do that to me!" I cried, fury boiling over. Without thinking, I pushed him as hard as I could. He sprawled across the floor falling backwards into some fourth years who dropped their drinks everywhere.

"*WOAH!*" they cried as Jasper jumped up and lunged at me, pushing me to the floor.

I clenched my fist and quickly said: "*Pasanthedine!*" Jasper shot into the air away from me, as I jumped up quickly. Then he smiled, raising his hands, a black shot of smoke punched me hard in the gut.

"Ahh!" I toppled forwards into dancing feet, hugging my stomach. Anger and frustration boiled up inside me. I stood quickly, raising my right hand at his throat and yelled: "*Aperchino!*" red wind burst out of my arm like fire. A satisfied glow lit up inside me, as my skin tingled. I felt myself fall back into the ground with the force as the red wind zapped towards his face. A silvery shield spell erupted in front of him. The red wind bounced off. There was a sudden and colossal *BANG*! As it hit the huge mirror above the fireplace, shattering it into a million pieces. A chorus of screams echoed deafeningly. A white layer of mist shot across the heads of all — Ernie's hands outstretched, as the shards of sharp mirror bobbed up and down above the white mist, just over the top of everyone's heads. Hayden stopped the music. Silence fell as eyes moved around to Jasper and I, standing with our arms out at each other.

"WHAT ON EARTH DO YOU THINK YOU ARE DOING?" Jasper called. "I know you don't like me, but there's no reason to do that!"

"*Whaat?*" I said as people started to look round at me with horror struck faces. "You started it!"

Tina stormed forwards through the crowd, then grimaced, pained as she saw me lying soaking wet on the ground. "What do you think you're doing?"

"He poured drink all over me, then—" I said, but she just closed her eyes, too angry to even look at me.

"You tried to ruin *my* party, and I NEVER EVEN INVITED YOU!" there was a horrible silence.

I swallowed. "But... why not?" I managed in a small voice.

"Because I knew what would happen. Because of how nasty you've been to Jasper lately. Because you are jealous of him!"

Ernie stepped forwards. "Tina," he said soothingly. "Come on it's fine." I could sense apprehension in his voice. He was trying to say more than he let on, communicating the fact that we had all taken a pact after I saved both of their lives last year.

"No Erns, I don't want him here..." she said flatly. Her words cut through my heart like a knife. She looked down at me with utter disdain. Whatever love she had for me last year was gone, dead.

Jasper marched forwards, picked me up by the scruff of the collar and pushed me out of the room. "Don't mess with people who are too clever for you," he spat in my ear. "I always win!"

"I'm gonna get you back for this!"

"What you gonna do? Set your brother on me?" he cackled before slamming the door in my face.

Blood curdled hot inside my veins I thought I might melt. But I wasn't just furious, I was sad, and frustrated. I had been made to look like a complete idiot. And Zara had seen it too. Everyone had seen it. I sighed, my nice shirt was sticky and stank of orange and my hands were trembling. I had been on the end of Tina's anger before, but not like this. She had looked at me like I was some disappointment, something nasty to be avoided. She had nothing left for me. I trudged off, back towards the bathroom to get washed. Then the music restarted, echoing along the corridor, as if nothing had happened.

Click. The door opened again. "Wait for me!" it was Robin, he lummoxed towards me like something on stilts. "I just told them how out of order they were. Don't think they were listening. I didn't see what happened exactly, but I believe you."

I told Robin what Jasper had done, he sighed shaking his head. "How did it go with that girl," I said.

"Pah, I er… I never actually spoke to her. Too nervous," he said.

"Oh for goodness sake," I laughed and we trudged along back to the dorm. "You didn't need to leave with me you know."

"I know, but I wanted to. Anyway, I needed to talk to you when we both wouldn't be overheard. I did look into how we could get past the Occulus and I think I might have found a way…"

***

"Let's go now," I said pumped.

"Now?" said Robin, sitting on the end of his bed frowning. "But it's… we need time to—"

"Think about it," I said. "Everyone is either at Tina's party, or asleep? If anyone asks what we are doing out, we say we are on the way back from the party? It's the perfect time."

So, with Robin reluctantly agreeing, we set off. We walked slowly and casually in the direction of the Library. As we got closer, Robin decided that the Occulus' were getting suspicious the further away from the party we went.

"Do it now then, see if it works," I said.

Robin pulled out a small brown box, inside was a pair of old spectacles with a wire frame. He slipped them on, putting his normal ones in the box. He blinked a couple of times against the apparent light that he was seeing. The spectacles he was wearing were special, they allowed you to see magic, past and present. Magic that had been done, even years in the past, showing up as colours. Tina and I had found them in the locked passageway last year and gave them to Robin as a present for saving our lives.

"There's three of them up there," said Robin peering round the corner. "Only looks like one without these on." He was right, it did only look like there was one Occulus, glaring in our general direction.

"So the spell?" I said.

Robin took a deep breath and aimed his hand round the corner at the cluster of Occulus'. "Ok, here goes. *Returious-Tace-Usqe-Glacientor...*" For a moment I didn't think it had worked, for nothing had happened. No whizzing lights, no sound, nothing. But Robin was smiling. "It worked."

"Are you sure?" I said, following him around the corner.

"See for yourself." He handed me the specs, I put them on and saw the blinding swirls of coloured light from all around. The brightest was a light blue trail of pulsing light from exactly the place that Robin's hand had been. The blue line continued all the way to the Occulus', which now stock still. "They won't notice a thing, hopefully. Even if they do, they won't be able to do anything... I reckon we have a good few hours before it wears off."

"Nice one!"

Robin beamed. "I couldn't use a spell that made any noise or sound, they would notice it and set off a siren." I followed Robin to the Library doors. "*Partimo-Sesamea,*" said Robin in a funny voice, his hand pressed against the door handle. With a long, slow *clunk*, it unlocked.

I grinned at Robin. "You're a genius."

We began our search, thankfully unhindered. The music from downstairs making the floors thud. I purposefully took off my channeller and put it on the nearest table, if we did any magic, however small, we'd be in for it. I kept glancing at the river, worried that an Occulus might come sailing down it and catch us again. I really hated those things.

Robin and I searched far and wide for anything that could be of use, we needed a book that had the secrets of

Riptide. Or something that told me how to use my shoes at will. Either would work.

I was searching a very tall bookcase at the far end of the Library, where all the big, dark books were kept. One caught my eye, for I recognised the title — it was the book I read last year, about ghosts. I pulled it down and struggled back down the ladder. Not using magic really was a chore. Putting it on the pile of big books on the table, I began leafing through them. Robin joined me a few minutes later, with an armful of books of varying sizes, placing them gently on the table he sighed happily before commencing. After a while I found the same chapter I'd read a year before, this time a new passage jumped out to me:

Ghosts, very often and over many years forget why they are ghosts. Indeed, the chain's which bind them to this mortal coil get so tangled in amongst themselves and other ghosts that it can be impossible to lead a ghost back to the source that led it to become one. Very often these chains will take you to gravesides, tombstones and old houses, indeed anything that caused the deceased to have 'unfinished business', a term we use called an 'anchor', for, like a ship which anchors at port, a ghost is anchored to a place which it witnessed trauma—very often ghosts will have faded memories of their past life, wandering for so long across the lands that they can forget even, who they are.

It is however big business for Wizards, and, speaking as a Wizard, in our interest that they don't remember. Otherwise we will not have our breakfast served, our clothes laundered, our morning alarm call...

Reading this left me feeling a little cold and I didn't know what to think. My mind went back to the ghost girl in the kitchen who was about my age. I remember the chains, all tangled and in a mess. I sat back and wondered what would have happened if I'd have stayed a ghost.

"I don't believe it," said Robin after a while leaning over a big book. "Listen to this... *Ornaments give off a magical effervescent ray, much like an old spell. Some have the talent of being able to see effervescent rays, while there are some rare instruments that allow one to see these rays, dubbed 'effy-rays' for short…"* Robin looked up as if he'd been struck dumb and pointed to his glasses. "That's what these are! I'll actually be able to see where the Ornaments are on the Habitat!" we laughed softly and high-fived.

An hour later I let out another soft *"Harrah!"*

"What is it?" said Robin dropping his book. "Found something?"

"Oh, of course!" I said, slapping the side of my head. The book I was reading was called *Magical Myths, Hidden and Real in Fairytales: #3 — Magical Artefacts.* "This is so weird. I opened this book and it just fell open at this page…" I turned the big, crusty book towards him pointing at the title. "Listen to this… *Alice Norton, the inventor of the only original pair of Seven League Boots, sold her blueprint to the mad inventor Septimus Libramus, a fair man who presided justice over Southern Farkingham in the mid-1830s. Seeing the potential in boots that could help you travel many miles in merely a few steps, Septimus set about making them for the mass market, his dream being that all should be able to travel wherever they must at will.*

But, after producing and selling just seven pairs, a Wizard who had taken offence at one of Septimus' justice rulings, burnt his house down, with him in it. Alice Norton's original blueprint was destroyed. Before anyone could track down Alice Norton, who had taken a spell of anonymity, she died (at the age of 92), taking her magic boot blueprint with her to the grave.

Thus comes the fairytale 'Septimus's Special Shoes':

Septimus walked on creaking bones barely far enough that day,
'If only I could have a pair of shoes that could walk for me', he'd say
So, off he set, on a journey to find that magic,
Over many miles he trod, with each step his dream enlarged,
Neglecting his duties as justice-giver,
And promoting his apprentice who was barely able.

But one day he found what he'd always hoped,
In a little village with cottages and such,
He stayed at the inn, where he ate and drank,
Listening to the conversation of the village folk,
Who laughed about the mad old woman who ran everywhere,
'How can she run so fast at such age?' they'd say.
Septimus listened intently this way —
Gathering an idea of the old woman from number 13.
Of the magic he was convinced, she was no fraud.
She let him try out the boots himself, of which he was amazed,
He offered her all the gold he had for the plans she had made,
She accepted barely one coin, and gave him the plans.
And a borrow of the boots, saying
he should bring them back when he had studied enough,
She pointed to the heels and said: "Tap-tap to go. Tap-tap to stop,
Wear them now, and be home in a pop..."

I stopped reading. I'd never heard this fairytale, but it sure added up in my brain as memories were zipping around, piecing together like a puzzle.

"So?" said Robin shrugging. "It's just a story?"

"Didn't you spot it? At the end?" I said incredulously. "Listen, the last time I zoomed off, was when Hunter clipped my heels. The time before that I tripped up. Like it says here, *Tap-tap to go. Tap-tap to stop.*"

"*Ahhh*, I get it. The famous *double tap*," said Robin leaning back wistfully. "Of course!"

We returned to the dorm late. Very late. The others still were not back! Even though I was tired, I couldn't sleep. Robin looked up from his pillow and spoke dreamily. "What do you think they'll do if they catch us wearing effy-ray spectacles, and Seven League Shoes?"

I sighed softly. "They won't. That magical artefact book said they are basically undetectable. Underwood will be searching for charms, hexes, hidden spells that might give us an advantage. She isn't going to notice a change of glasses, or shoes," I said, hopefully.

"Yeah, that's true. These artefacts we have, they don't *contain* spells do they?"

"Don't think so," I said lying, I didn't actually have a clue. All I knew was, we needed as bigger an advantage as we could in the fight to not be the *loser form*. And beat Jasper.

The other's returned half an hour after we got back, in very high spirits. "*What a party!*"—"*Did you see Herbert dancing? He was atrocious*," They stopped talking when they saw me propped in bed reading over my notes. I think it rather perturbed them that I was smiling — they were expecting me to be near to tears after the run in with Jasper. None of them mentioned it, although Simon did have an evil glint in his eye.

As soon as I was sure they were all asleep, slow, soft snores rising and falling in tiny cacophonies, I slipped out of the covers and laced up the shoes. I was too excited not to try what I had found out. Anyway, I wouldn't be able to do it during the day with everyone around would I? Even though my eyes felt sore, I put on my dressing gown and crept into the dark hallway outside. This was it, time to try them out. I looked ahead at the long stretch of black darkness.

I took a deep breath and raised my right leg, ready to tap it against the left. *Tap-tap*. Nothing happened. I looked down, they didn't do anything. I sighed, typical wasn't it? I actually thought for a moment that I had cracked it, but no —*fizz, crackle*—what was that? Golden light suddenly burst into the hallway with the force of a thousand spells! I left my stomach behind as the shoes shot forwards at break neck speed. My legs moved in a walking motion, but I was now zapping around the corridors faster than a thunder bolt. One corridor, two, three, four… it took barely a second to zap from the start to the end of them. And I needn't even move or turn when I came to the end, they just did it for me. It was incredible. My dressing gown flashed behind me as I whizzed along, torches on the walls lit up as I passed in a flash, Occulus' peering round, but barely catching sight of me. I even passed Hayden Carmichael coming out of the toilets, he jumped against the wall double-taking as I zoomed past, probably just a flash of light to him.

I wanted to stop, but how? Of course, the double tap again. *Tap-tap.* I stopped so quickly, that I went skidding headlong into a large tapestry on the fifth floor. As soon as I took stock, shaking the dizziness and the tapestry off, I heard a horrible sound.

WOOOOOO-WOOOOOOH! Came the Occulus's siren call, loud and clear across the silent night. It was directly above me, peering down large and frightening. *Whoops.* Then, more sirens began shooting around the corridors from all over the school. This meant trouble, I had to get back to my dorm, now! I fixed my mind on my bed, and double tapped the shoes. After a second they lit up again and I flashed down the corridors, until I stopped directly outside my dorm. The shoes golden light diminished as I wobbled slightly on the spot. I crept inside, slipped off the shoes, sliding them under my bed, took off the dressing gown and got into bed. My heart was beating like a clapper, but I kept my eyes closed as the door opened. The room filled with blue light and Partington's soft voice.

"See Jenks, my lot are all accounted for..."

CHAPTER SEVEN
The Happendance Carnival

Fortunately nothing came of the early morning sprint around school. Hayden Carmichael hadn't mentioned it, nor had he even looked at me differently. Some of the Magisteer's were becoming increasingly frustrated with the all night siren calls from the Occulus — they seemed to be getting paranoid, going off whenever someone went to the toilet. A few days later, on the 21 st of December, it was time for all those who wanted to go home for Christmas, to leave. Most did, including Tina who I heard was going to Jasper's for Christmas. I stood in the hallway waving off Hunter, Dawn, Dennis, Jess, Florence and indeed everyone from our form except Jake and Gret, who said it cost too much to get back to Golandria this time of year. The Hall was packed full of people waving goodbye to their friends, exchanging small wrapped gifts before running outside to catch their carriage. I looked around for Robin but he was no where to be seen. I presumed he would be going home, back to Yorkshire.

"I'm off," he said behind me, causing me to jump — then he leaned in closer. "You gonna be alright on your own?"

"Think I can handle myself," I said pointing subtly down at the shoes. "Take care, have a good Christmas in Yorkshire."

"Cheers," he said laughing.

"What's funny, did I say it wrong?"

"No, it just sounds weird you saying *Yorkshire*," with that he waved and marched out with his bag floating behind his head, getting in a carriage with Graham — apparently they lived close to each other. I was alone again. Jake, Gret and I stepped outside with the few other people staying at school for Christmas, slipping along the ice to watch the carriages launching into the air and shooting away. Ingralo was dragging a large Christmas tree through the snow, before propping it up in the Hall. Some, for want of anything better to do, helped decorate it. I sat on the steps and watched glumly. What could I do for Christmas? My mind skipped back to me and Tina spending Christmas Day together last year, that was fun. Who did I have here now? Jake and Grettle? I don't think they even believed in Christmas. I suppose I had homework to do anyway.

Christmas consisted of mainly being bored. I was free to explore and explore I did, but I didn't have Tina. I had gone and lost her completely — and I had no idea how. Soon enough I had completed all the homework set, sitting by the fire I'd ploughed through it with an intense fury. The Library was locked and I couldn't remember the spell Robin had done to unlock the door or tame the Occulus'. I thought about using some of the gold I still had leftover from *Granddad* to purchase some books from the catalogue at the back of the Herrald, but all the good books had age restrictions.

I read the Herrald each day at breakfast in the sparse Chamber with Jake and Gret, who spoke to each other in Golandrian. *Rude.*

Walking around the school and the grounds alleviated some of the boredom. I'd walk along the long corridors and hallways aimlessly, looking at the paintings, noticing the coloured carpets that corresponded to a certain years dorm and passing other bored looking people. I passed the trophy cabinet near the Lily's office. It was full to the brim of all sorts of different things. And there I saw, *Ernest Partington* emblazoned across several of the trophies: winners of the

Riptide Cup, the League, and top scorer for three seasons running.

Once or twice on these walks, I'd bump into a Magisteer who was staying behind at the school. Magisteer Mallard nearly took me out as he came out of the drama hall, with a mask on.

"Sorry dear boy, sorry!" he called as I marched away a little frightened. Yearlove was in his room too, I could hear him talking to someone. Maybe I would go back to his lessons after Christmas, it depended on if he was actually going to teach all of us, or make us listen to Jasper.

You had to wrap up warm if you wanted to go outside, it was freezing. Every day I'd go for a solitary stroll in the grounds, round through the forest, past the lake where me and Tina had spent that glorious day last summer. On Christmas Eve I went for a stroll, wrapped up to the hilt in borrowed gloves and a scarf, this time I went around the forest and back past the trees who bowed as I passed, along to the edge of the canyon. Over a long drawbridge was the floating island — it was wonderful, suspended in mid-air and covered in benches, rabbits and an angel statue. A great waterfall also fell in long gushing waves down its edge. There was no way I was crossing that drawbridge, I hated heights. My breath came out in long misty streaks ahead of me and I supposed I should go back soon and get some lunch. But then I spotted someone on the island. All I could see, sitting on her own on a bench, was a big flock of bouncy white hair. Zara Faraday was sitting alone on one of the benches, a rabbit on her knee. My heart fluttered and my throat went dry. This was the perfect opportunity to go and talk to her, except, I liked Tina. Or did I? I didn't know anymore. Anyway, I would probably only mess it up.

***

"Merry Christmas everyone!" called the Lily, looking ridiculous in a pink paper hat.

"Slancher!" cried Jake and Gret. I didn't know what that meant. A great big roasted Dandy bird with all the trimmings burst onto the tables. Partington and Ernie sat together at the Magisteer's table, along with the Lily, Dodaline, Mallard and Yearlove who were pulling crackers and laughing. Christmas music played while we ate.

I sat back in my chair feeling full, Zara and three of her form were having a great time together, playing some game that one of the Outsider's had brought in with little houses and paper money. I was staring at her watching them play, when all of a sudden she looked up and saw me staring. I blinked and looked away, my heart suddenly jumping to life as I tried to look interestedly at the ceiling. How embarrassing. I quickly glanced up at the Magisteers table. The Lily was licking his fingers after a sumptuous Christmas cake. And then something just behind him caught my eye. The door behind the stage was slightly ajar. Peering through the darkness were glowing eyes, black rags and dirty feet. It was the *thing* that had attacked me. And it was looking directly at the Lily.

"*MEEERRRRRY CHHHRRRRIIISTMAAASSSS!*" Shouted a sixth year at the top of his voice, standing on top of the table and scaring everyone half to death. Everyone laughed, except me. I looked back at the door, but the thing, was gone.

In what seemed like weeks and weeks, yet was actually just a few days, everyone returned to school and the life and buzz returned. Hunter came back wearing a golden earring, which Dodaline told him to remove immediately. "Do you know what will happen if someone does a *zxanbatters* spell near that? Half your ear will come off!"

Robin looked fuller and more rosy-cheeked, as indeed did most, returning looking a little more rounded and happier. There was however a slight spanner about to be thrown into the works. The first day back to lessons, Partington greeted us in form and told us that the second years had an assembly.

"Don't tell me," said Jake. "The Stadium has fallen over again so we have to restart 'de whole process!?'"

"Not quite," said Partington with an air of nervousness.

"Two things," said the Lily prowling around the Magisteer's table. "As you are all aware the second years are taken on a school trip in mid-January to the Eastern Happendance Carnival..." the Lily stopped as excited chattering and loud exclamations filled the air. The Happendance Carnival? I'd only ever heard about it before, but never actually been there. Robin and Hunter, indeed most of the Outsiders looked around blankly, wondering what the excitement was about.

"You will be accompanied by your form tutor, and will stay for two nights. This is a learning trip, not an entertainment one. *However...*" he said, drawing out the last word making everyone look up anxiously. There was a snag, why was there always a snag? The Lily nodded slowly. "There is one condition. Magisteer Simone has said that due to slow progress on the rebuild of the Riptide Stadium, that if it is not rebuilt by next Friday, which is the last day before the trip — then everyone stays behind to finish it and misses out on the school trip..."

There was a huge exhale of air, as everyone sunk deflated like a hundred blow up snowmen. There was no way that the stadium was going to be finished by then. Muttering comments about Magisteer Simone filled the air, along with stamps of disapproval — the stupid witch!

"Unfortunately, I have to agree with Magisteer Simone, the first Riptide game is scheduled for the start of February and we have many checks to do before then." After letting the Chamber calm down, the Lily waiting patiently with his hands pressed tightly together, then he resumed. "Lastly, there have been a lot of complaints about the Occulus'," several Magisteer's pursed their lips. "But, again, I am afraid to say, they are here to stay. I have personally conversed with them about being a little more... lenient, but as they were sent by the school councillors, my hands are tied."

***

For the next week we worked harder than at any time I can ever remember. Simone and Ingralo stood watching, perturbed by our frantic, yet organised teamwork. The goal of getting to go to Happendance Carnival all in the forefront of our minds. We had to make it. And so on we pushed, skipping lessons, breaks and lunch, working through to the small hours of the morning. We continued pulling rudders into place, push wooden rafters into their slots and hammer in hundreds to thousands of long magic nails. Through wind and rain, cold, biting January frost and a harsh, face numbing sleet we persevered.

After the fourth day there was a moment, as the last nail was hammered in. The girl who was hammering stepped back, we all did, and looked up at the colossal building around us. We had done it, all of it. It was so nearly there. The supports, stairs and surround were completed, now we had two days to fit all the drapes around the outside and all the seats.

Simone took her time summoning them, but finally they popped up in a giant box ten times as big as her. On the last night we were *exhausted*. We were running from job to job, lifting each massive drape and fixing it to the outside of the stadium, hanging it from giant metal hooks. Each drape a new illustration of each form—Manticore, Centaur, Hubris, Eagles, Condors, Hesserbout, Jaloofia's, Phoenix, Snares and Swillow's, amongst many others. Then we jumped up the massive wide staircase we'd constructed and into the seating area where we began laying seat after seat. They had to be fixed to specific markers, and had to be absolutely spot on before the bolt would grasp the magical nut and fasten into place. It was tiring waiting for the nut to grasp. The feint moon shined through silent drifting clouds above casting it's white light across the proceedings. We had less than an hour until time was up. But then… Kenny McCarthy ceremonially raised the last seat into the air, and placed it into the nut, as the entirety of the second year stood and watched.

"*HOORAY!*" we all called jumping for joy, we'd done it!

We traipsed down to where Simone stood at the foot of the stone stairs. "Quite an achievement," she said with an evil glare in her eyes. I had a feeling that she was about to say that we'd forgotten something, like laying the pitch, or something stupid. But she didn't, she turned and beckoned us forwards and muttered that we must sleep now for we had a busy day tomorrow.

***

The mega-carriage landed with a bump in the middle of a large field littered with carriages — the Happendance Carnival carriage parking lot. Some of the carriages were emblazoned with strange words and colours. My muscles ached like never before as we got out. David Starlight tried to trip me up. I turned and glared at his smug little-pinched face. That was close, he'd nearly tripped my shoes into blasting me off. Robin pushed past David and came to my side.

Sound rippled across the fields. Far below us, in the valley, was the biggest, loudest, most colourful sight ever — the Magical Eastern Happendance Carnival — it looked to be in full swing too. My eyes drifted to the lines and lines of colourful magical stalls and markets, a bubble of excitement shooting through my insides. I'd never really been anywhere like this before, my parents didn't believe in fun.

"Now," said Partington getting out of the carriage, and picking up his triangular hat which fell off as it hit the top of the carriage. "There are some rules to this carnival which we'd like you to abide. Stick in twos, no wandering off on your own and if there is any trouble, send a *red miseria* flash into the air, me or Magisteer Straker will come and find you." Straker raised his eyebrow. "You are free to do as you please, but first let us show you the tents you will be staying in, you can put your stuff down there first."

Partington led the way down the hillside towards the carnival. Other second years appeared from all around, walking with us until we merged into a large burgundy mass.

"Here we are!" said Partington in front of a white tent near the back end of the carnival in a muddy bog. "Inside, come on, quickly... Well, you won't be in here for long, you'll be out all day exploring won't you," said Partington in response to Simon and Graham's moans about the state of the inside of the tent.

Small, very old, camp beds lay haphazardly upon the grass. Small, wet carpets lay strewn across the grass in no particular order. "As I said," said Partington. "We won't be spending long in here, just to sleep. *Thankfully*," he muttered. We all glanced around at each other. Hunter jumped on a near by bed and cried as he fell through it. "Be careful with the camp beds, they are very old..."

After Jake and Dennis helped Hunter out and we all set off together for an explore of the famous Happendance Carnival.

Our tent was right at the back near all the carriages, and storage units. Charming. Graham didn't look pleased, rolling his eyes at the puddle of mud that surrounded our tent. "I don't suppose the school could've paid for us to stay somewhere a bit nicer... like that?" He said, pointing over the carriages where a huge red and gold tent sprouted up around the edge of the forest, far eclipsing any other tent near it, for size and looks. A flag hung above it reading "*Farkingham Mystery School.*"

I didn't know there were *other* magic schools. I just assumed Hailing Hall was the only one. "Don't be stupid," said Simon when I said this out loud. "Of course we're not the only one. Farkingham's is much better."

We wandered over towards their tent, the inside was absolutely colossal. Bunk beds ten high reached the ceiling with magical ladders. A huge walking bookshelf, tons of comfy armchairs, a kitchen piled high with food and a room just off the main, was filled with games.

"They don't even need to leave their tent!" said Hunter dreamily. Some of the Farkingham's emerged slowly, dressed head to toe in black. A tight black cape huge from under their chin, falling down to their shoes. The faces that greeted us were dark and glaring—I could feel their thoughts echoing towards us: *why are you standing near our tent. Why are you watching?*

"Think we should leave," said Robin starting to move away.

The sun beat down hot golden rays, tingling my skin. Robin, Hunter and I wandered aimlessly in no particular direction. Robin said it reminded him of a *car boot sale* to which Hunter disagreed and said it was far better, for this was magical. Long extendable tables were crowded with things—all magical. Each table and stall were different, some had a billowing drape roof, others selling things out of the back of a wooden cart. One witch was selling things inside her carriage, I pulled Hunter back as she beckoned us forwards, shaking my head at him slowly. God knows what was inside. The stuff available was too numerous to mention in its entirety, but each stall had a theme. One sold charmed cauldron's that stirred your potions, another sold hexed gifts for enemies (I considered purchasing two), there was an animal foot talisman stall, a witch selling charmed chains that captured a ghost (making it your slave), a breast pocket bookcase stall, a caravan of magical creature's available for purchase, a magical clothing stall where the clothes shrunk or grew to match your size and a charmed mug stall that always kept your drink topped up. And that was just a snapshot. Hundred's of bric a brac stalls of varying, dizzying array with opportunistic looking owners littered the walk. Some looked perfectly pleasant, while others looked downright dodgy.

My heart nearly melted when I saw the magical creatures. I had a soft spot for animals, and the ones in these cages looked sad. There were three small monkeys, sitting quietly, picking each others fur. There was a dog looking glum under a table. Four cats, meowing at us, as if screaming for us to please release them from their cages. Some sprats in a cage, ten krede hoppers in a water tank, some talking turtles which sat in silence, two chameleons whom were bight orange, contrasting with their grey, sludge filled tank.

"Think they're trying to make themselves *seen*," Robin whispered. "So that we take them home?"

"What dya' want? Wan' me to cage a couple up for ya?" said a fat, grubby man.

I shook my head and shuffled backwards. "No, no, just looking, thank you."

"All right," he said affronted. "But this ain't no zoo—it's a shop."

Robin and I left feeling terrible, those poor animals looked so unhappy and I couldn't do a thing about it. Neither Robin nor I had anywhere near enough gold to buy them all.

The tents grew in size. Large colourful, billowing tents spread out in no particular order with large signs outside reading: *'Rupert Greers Hypno-Magical presentation, starts at*

5.43pm. Be prepared to be hypno-ed!' Some of the tents had presentations and shows, some had talks with famous Wizards, Witches and Warlocks (some had books to plug), all talking about a different subject to do with magic. Surrounding these large tents were smaller one's selling sweet smelling food that drew Hunter towards them like a magnet.

We sat on the hillside over looking the carnival. Hunter was moaning and rubbing his feet, while stuffing his face with a pie, then a chocolate eclair, then a Dandy Sandwich. As night drew in, the carnival buzzed with a close, electric vibe. Robin, Hunter and I joined Graham, Simon and Dawn outside a tent and went on to watch several shows. Some were great, others were awful — Jake bought a bottle of mango perry and shared it round, easing our aching muscles nicely. The first show we watched was presented by a tall woman going by the name of Eliza Buckleworth who raised a demon inside a glass cage, it was truly terrifying, Hunter covered his face. Then, Eliza vanquished the demon, and it shrunk back into the ground — followed by a round of applause. As we left I saw Straker in conversation with my brother Harold at the back of the tent, I knew they would be pals.

The sleep in the tent that night was the most uncomfortable I've ever had. The camp beds, were more than old. It almost disintegrated as I got in. Loud squeals echoed whenever anyone moved, and my feet were wet as the carpet next to the beds was soaking. Loud music thumped rhythmically, causing the tent to shake. I was so tired. When did the festival finish? When did everyone go to bed? Graham had shoved two socks in his ears, a practice which most of us followed. I wish we had a good tent, one that blocked out noise. The lights from the carnival were frighteningly bright, the tent material might as well of been see through. I pulled the covers over my head and tried to block it out.

— *"That Hummingbird man was awesome."*

— *"Yeah, he was really something…"* said two voices coming into the tent.

"*Shhhhh!*" Hunter cried. "People are trying to sleep!" he lay back down gruffly, the camp bed gave a squeak before he fell through it again.

***

That morning I woke to pure, blissful silence. The only sound that filled the air was the snores that reverberated softly around the tent. Cold air swept through my clothes as I slipped out of bed and put my shoes on. The tent was stuffy, I needed to get out. The sun shone brightly over the hills. I breathed in the clear, fresh air. A wonderful smell of bacon leapt under my nose — breakfast. I began to walk through the muddy bog towards the smell.

"Can I have one of those please," I said to the woman, she was short and fat with greasy blonde-ish hair.

She sniffed sleepily and rubbed her eyes. "Of course me dear," I licked my lips as she stacked a roll with crispy bacon. *Hmm*, yummy. The small white food cart stood near the large presentation tents, just past all the stalls which were just setting up. I stood and watched them putting up their tables, some with magic, some not. Then most proceeded to lay out their produce, before taking a seat and snoozing.

"Here you go ma' dear…" I thanked the ugly woman, paid her a quarter gold coin and bit into what was, the best bacon roll I've ever had. Slowly I mooched between the stalls, I was the only one around. The air was fresh, the grass crisp and bouncy and they sky clear. Large black and white creatures I'd never seen before were munching grass on the hillside. As I walked slowly, finishing my roll, I had time to think about Jasper and Tina, I mean I tried not to but it was like they were set to default in my mind. I just couldn't get my head around it. Something about Jasper irked me. There was a connection, I was sure, between the beloved-by-all Jasper and the short ragged thing that was after me. I just couldn't piece it together.

"Come and get ya' trinkets and antiques!" bellowed a loud course voice, barely an inch from my ear. I jumped back and glared up at the man who didn't seem to have realised someone was walking past him. Idiot.

I nosed around the bric a brac stalls. I had enough gold left for something amusing, but that was about it. One stall was set out just away from the rest, on a large ornate oak table, next to a purple carriage. Over the table bloomed thick velvet purple drapes with golden tassels. It was intriguing. A middle-aged woman, who looked like she was once beautiful, stepped out of the carriage carefully, for her purple dress was long. She noticed me and smiled sweetly as she set about arranging her things. The things looked no different to the hundreds of other pre-loved trinkets. But she treated them all with upmost care, placing each item softly in its place on the velvet cover. She didn't say anything as I stood. The table wasn't crammed like the others, everything had a place. A row of golden rings to the left of the table, stood next to a circle of black and silver pendants.

"So what are all these things?" I said softly.

The woman placed an ornate silver tea pot down. "These are all rare items that my father collected over many years," said the woman in a soft, sickly sweet voice. "Each item has a unique quality. And yet..." she stood up straight and smiled. "I have no idea what. He died before he could test them all and I am not proficient in his magic to be able to fulfil his work. So, I must sell them as seen. Could be cursed for all I know," she shrugged, a strain of sadness behind her eyes.

"I see. Like a lucky dip then," I said, but she didn't smile. "I was joking."

"Oh I get it, yes, like a lucky dip…" she laughed, but it sounded forced.

And then I saw something that looked… familiar. Behind the woman in a box of things she was unwrapping was some sort of ornament. Except, it had a mark on it that looked exactly the same as the one on my channeller. I pulled my pendant out and glanced at it quickly — it was definitely the same mark. How strange. Now, I know nothing about runes or ancient markings, but I do know about following hunches. And there was something about that ornament that made me want it.

"What is that?" I said pointing at it.

She reached round and picked it up, pulling the rest of the paper off and handing it to me. "Just an incense holder. Nothing special, I don't think." This incense holder was a cold golden metal. It was shaped oddly—like a tall, cylindrical lamp, with a small hole in the top. It was black with dirt, but on the side was that mark, the black indented squiggle.

I swallowed. "How much?"

"Oh, I can't sell to children dearest, I'll get in trouble," she said looking pained. I sighed and went to put it back, but saw her eyes flash with regret. I glanced upwards at her unkempt hair, her hand washed dress and shaggy carriage. On a hunch, I reached into my pocket and pulled out my last three gold coins.

"Will this do?" I held my hand with the gold coins towards her. Her arm jerked towards the gold coins, but then stopped. She looked around quickly, eyes darting.

"Fine," she said, snatching the gold. "Here, let me wrap that thing up at least." I thanked her, clutched my paper parcel and moved away.

"You know you're not supposed to walk around on your own?" came a sly voice behind me. I jumped back, clutching my chest. Harold, my eldest brother stood with one eyebrow raised, eyeing me inquisitively.

"You scared me!" I said. "I know we're not, but... anyway what do _you_ want?"

"Nothing. I am merely commenting on your attention to the rules of this visit. What do you have in that paper bag?" he said suspiciously.

I rolled my eyes. "Nothing to do with you. Anyway, why are you teaching at the school? Mother and father want you to keep tabs on me? Make sure I don't _embarrass the family_?"

"Not quite. I am afraid that not everything in this world is about _you_. As much as you'd like it to."

I swallowed at his cutting remark. "What are you are doing, working at the school then?"

Harold smiled. "I thought I was the one questioning you?" he smiled his perfect white grin. "All this sneaking around, getting caught in the Library, attempting to murder a form mate. You reminded me of myself when I was your age."

"I am nothing like you—"

But he wasn't listening, he had shot away with a flash of his black coat. "We _might_ make a Blackthorn of you yet," his voice said, magically carrying on from where he had stood.

I rejoined everyone in the tent as they were all getting up, hiding my ornament in my bag and moving along with them for a day of fun activities.

***

We sat eating a late lunch on the hillside with the cracking view across the entire carnival. The girls were lying in the thick grass, eyes closed, soaking up the illustrious Happendance sun.

"We didn't come all 'de way to 'dis amazing carnival to do sunbathing," said Jake.

Florence smiled. "Oh it's not for long grumpy pants. We're just enjoying being free of some responsibilities at last!"

Dawn was stroking one of the large black and white things, called *cows* apparently, and Joanna was platting Ellen's hair while she read a new book that she'd bought. She was a more voracious reader than me and Robin put together.

"No way!" said Simon pointing across the fields.

We all looked round. "What?" said Gret craning her neck to see.

Simon pointed frantically. "It's the Lily. Over there! I didn't think he was coming?"

"That's not the Lily," said Robin peering. "He's just dressed like the Lily? Why is he dressed like the Lily?"

"Perhaps he's impersonating him," said Hunter.

Graham rubbed his cheek, "That's illegal isn't it?"

"No…" said Grettle as if she couldn't believe how stupid we were. "Are you guys total morons?" she spluttered as Ellen laughed too. "That is just *another Lily?*"

Ellen put her book down and turned to us. "Someone is called a Lily if they reach the last five levels of magic. It is said that on those last five levels you become *pure of heart*. It becomes a ceremony, and you are *en-gowned* with the white robes and your title."

Dawn didn't seem convinced. "What, so there is more than one Lily?"

"Well yeah!" said Gret.

"I never knew 'dis," said Jake looking curiously at his sister.

As the sun began to set that night, our form went different ways, all wanting to watch different things. Robin, Dennis, Joanna and I went into a tent where a man was demonstrating raising a discarnate spirit from a cursed slipper. It was all rather exciting, as he recited the incantation and the slipper began darting around the room. Until, we were escorted out of the tent by a guard who pointed to a sign which read: *"P.W.W's only."* — Professional Working Wizard's that meant.

"What can we go and watch now? All the shows have started?" I moaned.

"I know," said Robin. "What about that over there? *A talk with Hummingbird?"*

"Hummingbird? That rings a bell, think some of the others went to see him yesterday. Come on."

As we entered the small tent the first thing that hit us was the smell. A choking, burning smell went right up my nostrils and down the back of my throat, causing me to choke.

"Its good to CHOKE!" called a loud voice through the thick smoky haze. I could just about see an outline of a figure sitting cross-legged in the middle of the floor. "Come in boys, come in. Take a seat." There was a smattering of people already in here, sitting cross-legged on thick carpets around the man. "You must surrender to the incense, it's clearing your mind." The smoke was so thick the only thing I could think about was not choking to death. Through the haze the man slowly came into focus. Thick long hair hung past his shoulders across a bright purple and turquoise jacket, which, if it were not so dimly lit in here, would have been blinding me with colour. He grinned a wide toothy grin which shined white through the haze. He was unutterably in control, power and confidence seemed to exude from his every pore. His face was round and body wide, but sat with the flexibility of a cat — legs crossed impossibly tight, he seemed to hang just above the carpet on a thin layer of air exuding personality and charisma.

"You are not late. I was waiting for you," he nodded slowly. "My name is Hummingbird, I am a Golandrian. Many of you may have already read about me — I ask you to forget that fiction and concentrate with all your might on the here and now. Make yourself fully present." He closed his eyes for a second. But then, another face of his appeared translucent next to him, the eyes opening. A full second body slowly materialised downwards from the neck until the exact same man sat cross-legged, eyes open, next to himself.

"To clear your mind we must close our eyes," I followed along, closing them. "You can see darkness, but still life persists in visions flashing upon that dark screen at the back of your eye lids. Like an annoying screen you cannot switch off. I need not tell you how important in magic it is to *clear your mind*. Now, when a thought enters, recognise it, but then watch it shrivel and fall away like a browning leaf."

I watched the lights dance in front of my eyes, thought after thought burst across my vision as I followed Hummingbirds soft voice. The vision of the mark on my pendant drifted through to me, and the mark on the ornament I'd bought earlier. They hung there persistently, my brain itched — then Hummingbird spoke again. "*Everything*, must be forgotten."

When I awoke, I felt completely at ease. I wasn't sure how long I'd been asleep for. Usually I would be panicking, worried if I had been snoring, but I felt good. "Are we all awake?" he said. "Illusions are powerful magic. Only the best are conjured with a clear mind. Practicing visualisation daily will help. I want you to picture something in your mind and we will make it appear in front of us."

Hummingbird closed his eyes. A second later we were sitting in the middle of a desert. Hot sun blazed overhead, I blinked and shielded my eyes. Soft sand lay underneath, as tall dunes stretched off far into the horizon. Tall palm trees the only visible life. But it was hot, so very hot… moans from everyone in the circle echoed as we tried to shield ourselves from the scorching sun. A second later and we were back in the cool tent. "A good illusion can trick the mind into anything it wants…"

After a lengthy explanation of how to make the vision in our mind come out, we set about one by one making them appear in the middle of the circle. "So remember, visualise, feel, see, project. You first." The first person in the circle who I couldn't see through the smoke shuffled for a second. Then, in the middle of the circle a tiny vision of a green front door appeared. It was translucent and it kept flickering — "That's it, keep it fresh in your mind. Wonderful stuff."

The next person made a fist, which knocked on the door. Then both vanished. Hummingbird then pointed to Robin who made a funny nervous sound before closing his eyes. "Visualise, feel, see, project..." came Hummingbird's soft voice.

A soft, hazy vision of green hills started to take shape in the air above us. Then slowly it grew in detail. Grass began to swoosh, stone walls began to build and yellow buttercups sprung up through the grass. Robin opened his eyes and smiled. "Yorkshire Dales..."

"Very good," said Hummingbird impressed. "You next..." he pointed across the circle at someone, peering through the haze I suddenly realised who it was. Jasper! He was sitting cross-legged next to Tina. He closed his eyes, grinning. A bubble of fury popped in my stomach. Trust us to come in here when they were. Tina will think I am following her now! A hundred perfect red hearts floated up from the ground, before spinning round into a long, perfectly detailed rose.

"Well I say," said Hummingbird, his face lit up red from the light of the rose. "That's quite something."

Jasper turned to Tina. "For you."

"You next," said Hummingbird smiling at me.

I closed my eyes and concentrated as much as possible, trying to clear my mind. But the rose still hung in the air, Jasper thought he was so clever. I visualised as hard a possible. I envisioned fire — opening my eyes, I watched the flames erupt into being, burning the rose to ash.

"That's certainly one way of doing it," said Hummingbird as Jasper glared at me through the haze.

CHAPTER EIGHT
A Magical Multicolour Jumper

'Is Malakai Back?' — read the Headline in the Herrald. I had come to the Chamber for breakfast a little late and saw every table anxiously reading the paper.

— *"Thought he was gone!"*

— *"I thought Ernie Partington claimed to have done him in?"*

— *"Not according to this, look!"*

Robin at our form table, peered over the top of the paper at me and frowned. "This doesn't look too good, what do you make of it?" I took the paper and read:

Today, we bring you the startling revelation that the mass murderer and high Sorcerer known as Malakai, is back! — Hundreds of witnesses last night claimed that they saw the mysterious man, in various towns across the Seven Magical Kingdoms. This follows a spate of murders in the same areas. It seems his rise back to power has been rapid. No one knows where he was hiding all this time or what he was doing, but we are sure Ernie Partington, the teenager who claimed to have defeated Malakai will be answering a lot more questions very soon. Last April it was reported that Malakai was defeated—some commentators said even then, that you cannot suppress a force such as his. "It will take a lot more than whatever Ernie Partington, a teenager, did, to keep Malakai from returning..." said Grenville Summerville, WMP for Defence for the Magical Council. "Defeating someone is not the same as ending someone." Witnesses have released the photo's that they bravely took of the returned Malakai.

I glanced at the pictures. Yes, it certainly did look like Malakai. But something about it wasn't right. I mean, that could have been anyone in a long black cape and horns. Partington was sitting at the Magisteer's table, a spoon of porridge half raised to his mouth and a glazed, gormless expression on his face. I put the paper down and shrugged, Robin watching me closely.

"I bet it's nothing," I said. "I mean, if we could dress up and look like him. I am sure someone else can." Robin nodded sagely and seemed buoyed as a large pit of fear swelled in my stomach.

At dinner that night, in a packed Chamber, I had the worst thing ever happen to me, and completely out of the blue…

Our table was talking about Riptide, we knew the first match was coming up very soon.

Graham spoke forcibly. "I am just saying, if we speak to Partington about tactics, because if us quick runners take the wings we will be harder to defend."

"Well that depends on the Habitat," said Jake pointing his fork.

Simon swallowed before butting in. "Well, I think we should copy the Centaurs tactics… we need three attackers and the rest defend. So me, Jake and Graham in attack—"

"*NOO!*" came a chorus from around the table.

"Goodness no!" said Joanna. "It doesn't matter now, we just need to find a system that plays to *our* strengths."

From the corner of my eye I saw a girl enter the Chamber with her friends who were supporting her. She was sobbing uncontrollably, head in her hands.

"Partington doesn't have a clue about tactics, so it would be useless asking him," said Florence nodding at the still glazed expression of Partington. Dodaline was prodding him in the arm with a chopstick, and he didn't notice until she wrapped him across the knuckles with it.

And then the loudest screaming wail echoed across the Chamber. Everyone stopped dead still and silent. "MY PARENTS, MY HOME, EVERYTHING… *GONE!*" Screamed the girl. And then, she looked up and saw *me*. Her brow furrowed. "*AHHH!*" she charged! In a flash of blue light I was lifted off my chair and slammed into the floor. "Your family! Your sick, twisted family! Have KILLED MINE!" she sobbed uncontrollably as I stood sharply, shocked by this sudden attack.

"I'm really sorry I don't know what you're talking about," I said softly.

"BLACKTHORNS! ROT IN HELL!" she screamed. "Your family burned my parents house down, WITH THEM IN IT!" A large sigh of disapproval rippled through the Chamber. What on earth was happening? I glanced up at the Magisteer's, some of whom were making their way over. But then in flash she was on top of me. Twice as big and maddened, she punched me hard in the face! Some people nearby leapt across and dragged her away, as I scrambled back across the floor.

"You murdered my parents!" she cried. "MURDERERS!" she charged with murderous menace. Her hand stretched out and... clawed at my face.

"*AHH*!" I cried, as her nails pierced my skin. I jumped backwards as Yearlove spelled the girl away from me. The Chamber gasped. I felt my face drip hot blood.

"What do you think you're playing at!" Robin cried at her, jumping to my side. Dodaline, Mallard and the girls friends took hold of her as she sobbed hard, escorting her out of the Chamber.

"Let's get you to the Healers room straight away," said Yearlove. I nodded as red blood dripped across my vision. The Chamber was stunned, no one knew what to do or think as muttering broke out.

— "She's usually really quiet that girl, never thought she had it in her."

— "*He* does have previous, remember last year?"

The scratches felt long — pain went from my forehead, down my nose and stopping before my lip. The Healers room was big with lots of beds, tall windows but most glamours of all, a big floating green sun called Jade, whose green light healed everything it came into contact with. As soon as I entered the Healer's room, green rays of light began coursing towards my face.

After one night in the room I was free to go. I glanced at my face in the mirror before I left, the Healer smiling behind me, there was barely any sign of the scratch marks at all, thank god. I was still a little shocked after the incident, I mean, why should I take the flack for my parent's wrongdoings? I didn't kill her parents. My mind was also still on the news of Malakai's apparent return, so as soon I left the Healer, I went looking for Ernie.

I found his room on the seventh floor and knocked. It was a Sunday, so he should be indoors — hardly anyone would be outside as it was raining. "Come in," he called. "Avis, hello how are you?" said Ernie, standing and removing his glasses. Around him on a magically increased desk was more paper and books than I had ever seen in my life. The whole room had near enough been taken up. "When the other's leave I make it bigger," he offered, watching me look around the room. "I heard about what happened, you ok?"

"Fine," I said closing the door and sitting on a nearby bed. "I was just wondering about what was... in the Herrald."

"About Malakai?" he said. "Whether it's true what they are reporting, it's correct that he will return at some point."

I swallowed. "What, so even though we defeated him, he can still come back?"

"Someone as powerful as him will always find a way," Ernie put his glasses back on and peered around his desk. "Sorry Avis, I am quite busy. You know, what with my P.W.W's coming up."

"Oh right, of course." I said, standing and leaving, feeling rather deflated.

That night I struggled for sleep, we had lessons tomorrow and I was trying to decide if I should go back to Yearlove's lessons. He was nice to me yesterday, I supposed. I was running everything through my mind: why that fourth year girl (Kelly Canon, I was later told), had decided to attack me. What were my parents up to? Kelly had been escorted to the Lily's office and he must have sorted something out because she wasn't in school anymore. I didn't realise how much that incident had effected me. My chest felt tight ever since the incident, and I felt jumpy — even the crackling fire had me on edge.

A tear welled up in my eye and I didn't know why. I supposed I didn't want people looking at me like I was scum, or horrible or evil. I didn't burn her house down did I? On the way back from the forest after playing Riptide with my form earlier, a gang of fourth years sat watching me — faces stormy. Then some fifth years stood in the doorway and wouldn't move out of the way as I tried to enter.

I rolled over. So, apparently Malakai had returned. Was it true? If it was, then I knew full well who he would come for first. It was only a matter of time.

As the clock finished chiming for two o'clock, there was the strangest noise. As I lay there, wide awake listening to the delicate snores, pattering rain and crackling fire, I suddenly heard this feint ticking sound. *Tick, tick, tick, tick, tick, tick, tick…* before stopping. I stood up and looked at the clock above the fireplace. It had come from somewhere far away… or did it? *Tick, tick, tick, tick, tick, tick, tick…* it went again. It was coming from somewhere close by. I leaned forwards and peered under my bed slowly. A feint gold light flickered, from the inside of my bag. The noise was coming from the incense holder I'd bought from the Carnival! It was moving ever so slightly on every tick, as if someone was tapping it softly. I reached under the bed and pulled it out.

Tick, tick, tick, tick, tick, tick, tick. It rocked gently on the covers. I placed it back in the bag underneath my bed. It was too late to start working out what it was doing — I just hoped it wasn't cursed!

***

"How's the face?" said a snooty voice. I turned to see Jasper standing smugly against the wall. "Didn't think you'd be back to Yearlove's lessons *so soon*," he smiled as some fourth years passed by glaring at me.

"Well, I couldn't miss out on your fountain of endless knowledge could I?" I said as sarcastically as I could.

Robin cleared his throat. "Just ignore the git," he whispered. "Your back in lessons, that's all that matters."

Yearlove started the lesson by asking us what we learnt at the Happendance Carnival. "We accidentally watched a whole show about spirits, which was just for Professional Working Wizards only!" said Henry.

Yearlove prowled around the outside of the circle. "So, what did you learn from it?"

"Well," Henry said, looking into the ceiling and grinning, before turning to Jasper for help.

"…That you can spot a spirit inside an artefact with a couple of things…" Jasper started. "If it has strange markings on it and odd things happening around it."

"Very good," said Yearlove. "But you forgot about the other thing — does anyone else know?" Jasper looked affronted as Yearlove glanced around the room.

"If it makes a noise?" I said, inwardly smiling to myself.

Yearlove snapped his fingers. "Correct!" he called. "Welcome back Avis. Were you in that tent too?" I shook my head. "An even bigger well done then," he smiled and I felt warm and fuzzy at his praise. "Yes, the three things you use to distinguish a normal magical artefact with that of an artefact with a *spirit* inside are…" Yearlove counted on his fingers as he walked slowly. "Markings on the object, often imbued upon it when the spirit becomes fused with the object. Next would be odd things happening around the object, the spirits magic is restricted, but clever spirits will find a way of causing disturbances. And finally, noises — one of the things a spirit will do is to make a noise. The last two, it does to alert those around it of its existence…"

"But why would it do that Sir?" said Tina.

Yearlove tipped his head. "Well, for one very good reason. To increase its chances of being freed, usually on the precursor that the one who frees them gets a wish…"

"A wish?" said Hunter, his eyes lighting up. "What, so it's literally like the myth of the genie and the lamp?"

"Yes," Yearlove smiled devilishly. "In exchange for its freedom."

Muttering broke out around the room about this exciting news — but inside me was a tumultuous rip-roaring kaleidoscope of happy emotions… butterflies whizzed around my stomach at the speed of light because… I was in possession of one of those items! I was sure of it.

"What can you wish for?" said Hunter. I sat back trying to hide the elation that was flooding into me.

"I don't know," said Yearlove. "But please, even though they are extremely rare and it's unlikely you will ever come across one in your lifetime, do NOT go searching for them. The spirits inside are immensely dangerous, and if they can cause you damage for any reason, they will. Often the wish you request will come back to bite you. Now… what else did we learn?"

I didn't really listen to much else, my mind was whizzing ahead. I had a spirit and a wish. What could I wish for?

I saw Tina, her hand resting softly on top of Jasper's who sat glumly — annoyed that I got that answer right earlier most probably. I could wish for him to vanish, or to get expelled?

No, I knew what I would wish for. Visions of people staring at me like I was a criminal, even though I'd done nothing wrong just because I was a Blackthorn influencing my decision. But I couldn't actually do it, could I? Not after what Yearlove just said — it was dangerous.

***

"No way!" said Robin. "You can't, I mean… are you sure?"

I nodded. "Look…" I handed him the incense holder which immediately began to make the knocking noise. Robin held it at arms length away from him with wide, terrified eyes.

"Avis, you're not seriously considering raising the spirit are you?"

I went over and poked the fire. The rest of our form had gone to dinner, I wasn't hungry. "Pass me a log," I said.

"Avis, seriously? You want to get into all that trouble for what? A wish?" he said dropping it on my bed.

I made my mind up earlier and had to tell Robin out of pure excitement. "I am going to do it yes, once I find out how."

"You're mad," Robin sat on his bed and rubbed his eyes. "I don't want anything to do with it," he said standing and leaving me in the room with a hard silence.

I was still going to do it, this was a perfect opportunity, it's not often something like this falls in your lap. I needed to make that wish, and I knew the perfect place to do it.

After dinner I lay in bed and waited as patiently as I could. Excitement poured through me. I had a plan, an excellent plan to make everything better again. When everyone was in bed and quietly snoring away, I pulled out my Seven League Shoes and put them on, lacing them tightly. Stepping out as quietly as I could into the dark

172

corridor, I tapped them twice. At breakneck speed I whizzed along in a haze of golden light, fixing the Library in my mind.

I slipped inside the Library doors alcove away from the Occulus' stares as quickly as I could. I put my hand gently on the door handle and whispered: *"Partimo-Sesamea…"*

The door clicked open — I had been very, might I say, clever. At dinner, just as pudding was being served, I wandered over towards the Swillow's form table. They all glared at me as I passed. But then, I turned to Jasper. "Oh, I almost forgot to mention, Yearlove told me to tell everyone that he wants us to do homework, five paragraphs on spells and charms that unlock things. Don't look so worried, I am sure I can spare some time to help you out."

"Don't need any help from you," he spluttered, buying my lie, hook line and sinker.

"Oh yeah," I smiled sweetly. "Name one of the door unlocking spells then?"

He snorted as if it was obvious. "What, you mean *the* door unlocking spell, *Partimo-Sesamea?*" he said fluttering his hand as he said it. "There's only *one?*"

"Yes, I know…" I said noting down mentally what he'd just said. "Anyway, good luck," I smiled before sauntering away out of the Chamber and writing it down as soon as possible on a napkin. I had to do that because Robin refused point blank to tell me.

And it had worked! The doors gave a tiny click, before unbolting. I slid inside the doors as quietly as I could and began to search.

***

The Lily's bald head shined like a flounder under the fire bracket. "Riptide match schedules have now gone on the great wall for you to all peruse and note down. Lessons will be accommodated throughout the matches as best we can," announced the Lily standing tall at the front of a packed Chamber. "We have a great tradition in this school of nurturing the finest Riptide talent, many of whom go on to become professionals. This is not to say you should abandon your studies. Everyone, even I, must have a *plan b*. This year we will give you all personalised Riptide schedules which will appear on your tables right about... now." *Pop*! Went the papers onto our tables, making me jump. "There has been some confusion in the past with the schedules only being on the great wall, and people writing in their diary the wrong days," the Lily's eyes rested on several people in the room who he perhaps thought were serial offenders. "I need not remind you all of the rules, but if you need another quick brush up, then Magisteer Underwood will only be too happy." Magisteer Underwood raised her eyebrows. "We will be using the old format of Riptide to make the league fairer and the cup competition more exciting. You will see this on your schedule. And we will have no more than two matches a day. The marathons of last year were not fair on anyone." I was wondering when he would mention the bit about the entire Stadium being rebuilt by us? And perhaps some thanks?

"Oh look," said Graham. "We start our first match against the Happerbats in our year, then the fourth year Jaloofia's in the cup a week later!"

"I see," said Jake inspecting the paper closely. "The leagues are now split up into year groups, so we will play our year only. But the cup..."

"We play all years!" said Gret excitedly.

I was not really concentrating. I was thinking more about the book in my bag I had stolen from the Library which had step by step instructions for raising a spirit from an artefact. Robin wasn't talking to me properly, he'd made himself perfectly clear — he wanted nothing to do with it.

As the crowd dispersed from assembly, I used the cover to sneak away. Up the stairs and into the Big Walk. I jogged ahead, along the free corridor, down a route I knew well. Along to the winding staircase and up. Up, up and up.

I pushed open the hatch to the clock tower and sneezed immediately as the dust plumed around my face. It smelt exactly the same — dusty, old and cold. I put my bag down and sat cross-legged with a view out of the clock face. I pulled out the incense holder and the book. Then, I pulled out a large drape and covered them both before repeating the Riptide chameleon spell *Goaternut* over them until the drape turned the same colour and shade as the wooden floor. My incense holder and book were now invisible, just in case anyone did come up here they were properly hidden. I desperately wanted to raise it now, but I had lessons and it would raise eyebrows if I skipped them. But the incense holder and book were safer up here than they were with me. No one ever came up here. Ever.

"We didn't have any homework on unlocking spells you liar!" called Jasper, standing stony-faced with Henry the other side of the corridor, as I tried to sneak out of the spiral staircase.

"Oh really?" I said innocently.

"Yeah!" said Henry. "We just went there to hand it in. He said he had no idea what we were on about!"

I grimaced as they got closer. "Oh, must have been my imagination, what am I like?"

"What were you doing up there?" said Henry pointing up at the winding staircase.

"Nothing to do with you," I said as they exchanged a suspicious look. "Handing in some work to Partington. Thought I'd go the back way, that okay with you?"

Jasper leaned in closer. "I know you're up to something Blackthorn, whatever it is, I will find out."

I grinned. "And I know you're up to something. Or you already *have been* up to something…" I said as menacingly as I could as he towered over me.

"Whats *that* supposed to mean?"

I didn't reply, I left them both with a curious raise of my eyebrows, before slipping away round the corner. As soon as I was out of their vision I tapped the shoes and sped off back to my dorm — that was close.

***

In the middle of the night I was zooming through the school in a blaze of gold light. Shooting up the spiral staircase I landed in a dusty, dirty mess on the clock tower floor. I sealed the hatch shut. There was no moon tonight, only twinkling stars behind sparse clouds, watching me curiously behind the long iron hands of the clock face.

Excitement about what I was going to do dribbled through me, tinged with the anxiousness of unpredictability. I had no idea what to expect. Sitting cross-legged on the floor I undid the *Goaternut* spell so I could see the vanished things. I drew the big book towards me and flicked to the right page. I cracked my knuckles and took a deep breath. Was I really about to do this? Raise a spirit? My mind was filled, like an obsession, I had to get *my* wish. I would do anything for my wish.

Place the ornament so it faces north, sit south of it. It took some working where north was before I did as it asked. *Put the protective charm around you...* I read aloud the incantation: "*Omu-nama, duoma-camer, humda-narda...*" for five minutes I repeated the incantation without a pause. The incense holder began to knock again, this time less frequent, a calmer knocking in time with my incantations. Perhaps it knew what I was doing. "*Loomer-yelder, jarder-zernarder...*" then I stopped as a feint white light pulsed out of me, expanding like a big balloon until I was encompassed by a thin reflective bubble. *Place your hand upon the ornament* — I did. *And say... exsolvo-dissolvo-catena-vanesco...*

My heart was hammering a hundred miles an hour, I took a deep breath — "*Exsolvo-dissolvo-catena-vanesco…*"

A choking smell lit the room as pink smoke puffed out of the top of the incense holder. The thick sandalwood scent burned my nostrils, creating a thick haze. I leaned back as smoke billowed outwards like a steam train.

"YOU FREE ME?" — a deep rumbling voice echoed terrifyingly close.

I looked through the smoke. "*Y-y*-yes," my heart beat fast, stuck somewhere in my throat.

"THANK YOU," it chuckled. Then, I saw it. Part smoke, part translucent light, like a ghost. It sat cross-legged in mid-air facing me. A long blue chain around its ankle connecting it to the incense holder. The spirit was big. And it was a he. He was black with long dreadlocks with metal fastenings and feathers. His deep, dark stare froze me to the spot. "*CHILD?*" he said in a deep accent. He licked his lips and stretched out his long powerful arms. I was scared of him, very, very scared and I didn't know what to do.

"To finalise my freedom, this Djinn may grant you a return favour of any proportion. I must reciprocate your kindness as set out in the rules of magical spirit…" he said, voice deep. "Forgive me, it took me a while to get used to speaking again," he chuckled. "Now please, what is your name?"

"Avis… Blackthorn," I managed.

"You know the rules of raising spirits, or you do so by accident?"

"I knew."

The Djinn nodded once. "Then you know about the reciprocation? Did you have something in mind? For instance a large pile of gold, secret knowledge or…" he looked at me up and down. "Love, even?"

"Love?" I said.

"I can grant you *anything,*" he said tantalisingly.

"I just want to be…" images of the forth year attacking me, the glares and the accusations, just because I was a Blackthorn. "All my problems would go away if I wasn't a Blackthorn."

The spirit shook his big head. "Can't change *you*, that's a rule. Cannot change who you are."

"Ok… well, I suppose what I want really, is to be *liked*. By everyone. You know, so people have no prior judgements, to see all my best sides, not the bad…" I trailed off feeling embarrassed.

"You want to be liked, popular, that's a reasonable request. You want to finalise? Once you've chosen, it cannot be undone," he said ominously through the pink haze.

"Yes finalise it," I sat straight, shoulders raised in anticipation to what he was going to do.

"I cannot spell you directly… but I can do this…" with a click of his fingers balls of all different colour wool burst into his lap. In flashes of rainbow colour he began knitting! A full-length multicolour jumper began to take shape in front of my eyes. There were small flashes and pops of light as he knitted spells into the jumper. Every so often he would hold it up to me to see if the fit was right. Then, finally, he stopped. He held it at arms length, it was the most colourful jumper I had ever seen — every conceivable colour was in it.

"Use it wisely," he said before placing it over my head.

"Thanks."

"No, the thanks are mine to give. You've done me a great duty." The blue pulsing chain that connected him to the incense holder snapped, then vanished with a pop. "Now I am… FREE," he said wistfully. "At last."

The trail of light that connected him to the incense holder morphed into legs. Now, he stood, tall and translucent. He smiled and then jumped backwards out of the clock face window. There was no shattering, he just jumped clean through it as if it wasn't there.

The bubble around me popped and I blinked, standing up feeling giddy. The jumper felt wonderful and warm, but I wondered what would happen now? I picked the book and incense holder up and put them back in my bag. I'd better get out of here.

CHAPTER NINE
The Riptide Advantage

No one suspected a thing. I daren't take off the jumper that night, sleeping with it on. When the clock chimed at seven o'clock I sat up in bed immediately, feeling spectacular.

"Good morning!" I stretched.

Robin sat up in bed, reaching for his glasses and peering around. "You're in a good mood. *Woah…*" he said, catching a glimpse of me. "Nice jumper. I've never seen it before?"

"Yeah, had it ages, it's old, I just never wore it…" I lied.

"Very nice," he said longingly. "We have Numerology this morning,"

Hunter let out a long moan from under his covers. "What is the point of that lesson?"

Robin frowned towards him. "Then AstroMagic…" Hunter made a loud snoring sound, before Robin turned to look towards me, his eyes swimming with colours as he gazed at the jumper. "Listen, I am really sorry about what I said before about not wanting to help you. I was out of order I shouldn't have stormed out like that, it was out of character and I apologise profusely!"

"Calm down Robin. Wait, you're joking aren't you?"

"Joking?" he said as if it hadn't been invented yet. "No, not joking. Do you accept my apology?" he looked close to tears, weird.

"Yeah, course I do mate."

"*Phew*," he puffed, looking genuinely better.

After being complimented several times about my jumper by Graham and Jake who were next up, I went down to breakfast with Robin. I still had the jumper on and bubbles of excitement rippled through me now as I entered the Chamber. What would happen? I wondered, sitting down to butter some toast.

"What do *you* think Avis?" said Dawn staring intently at me.

"About what?" I said, *everyone* around the table looked at me quizzically, eyes fixed greedily on me.

"About the homework? I know you're really good at homework and we were all wondering what *you* would write about?"

I swallowed, a little taken a back. "Well, I wrote about the correlation between Mars and the star sign Ziffers, which has some interesting effects upon the behaviour of hubris."

"Wow yeah!" said Graham in awe. "I never thought of that!"

Jess smiled. "What a great idea, you're so clever."

"He's amazing," said Dawn dreamily. "I never saw it before."

"—Thank you." I smiled, as they all gazed at me wondrously. Some part of me felt like this was all a big practical joke and that they would all start laughing any second. But they didn't. Every conversation we had, people talked to me, included me, asked for my opinion. It was great, but weird.

***

For the first couple of days everything was great. But then, slowly but surely, things began ramping up. First of all was a lesson with Magisteer Wasp. It started off normal enough, but then as we were all talking about *star signs of the fifth quarter*, I noticed Hunter staring dreamily at me.

"You have a lovely voice…" he said.

"*Ok*… thanks." I said perturbed.

Magisteer Wasp came over to our corner of the steps. "You my dear, have a wonderful aura today," he said excitedly. "This must mean that Venus and Saturn are in conjunction with your birth house, very interesting and rare!" he said to himself before turning back.

"But my Birthday is in March Sir?" I said.

"Then it's even more rare! Congratulation my boy, the stars love you!" He twirled on the spot, causing the class to laugh.

On the way out of the lesson, David Starlight of all people was waiting for me and insisted on talking privately. Robin wasn't very happy and stood as close as he could, snarling like a Wolfraptor. Some of the others like Hunter and Jake stood waiting too, their beady eyes watching a nervous David.

"I'll er, catch you guys up," I said before turning to David who looked to be struggling internally with something. "You didn't come all the way up here to see *me* did you?"

"Erm, yeah…" said David, panting and looking sheepish. "Well, the thing is I've been doing some thinking and well… I was really mean to you last year and I… I just want you to know there's no hard feelings. I didn't mean those things and I hope we can be friends?" he looked at me pleadingly. This was incredible strange — this jumper was even more powerful than I had ever thought — but the thought of being friends with David Starlight turned my stomach.

"You want to be my *friend?*"

David twisted his tie round his fingers. "Yeah…"

"But, I thought you hated me?"

David shook his head violently. "No way! I mean, I even suspect that you saved my life. You told Ernie that Malakai was after me and well, he ended him right? Well, that means I owe you. I was too proud to say anything before."

"Right, okay. Thanks." I managed.

"So... we can be friends?" his eyes were lit up like a toddler.

"Maybe, let's just see how it goes yeah?" I started walking down the stairs as he followed.

"It's just... everyone really likes you, and I do too, don't get me wrong..."

I managed to finally get rid of David by pretending to have to go to the toilet and insisting that he couldn't follow me. As I stepped out of the toilets, faces leered out of the shadows.

"Riptide tonight?" said Hunter, causing me to jump. "In the grounds again?"

"Yeah you up for it?" said Joanna.

"It will be fun!" said Ellen. "We don't want to unless you come."

I put my hands up to calm them. "All right, all right, if you'll let me speak... yes I will come and play Riptide. How did you know I was here?" I said, indicating the empty corridor.

"Cool, is he coming?" called Gret walking out of an alcove. "We are meeting at five by the lake."

Robin poked his head out from behind a statue. "I followed you," he said. "To make sure David didn't try anything."

"Cheers... I think," I said as we entered the Chamber for lunch.

"Hey Avis," said Ernie, who was just leaving the Chamber with a pile of books floating behind him. "Did I hear you mention Riptide? Some of the lads and I are going to go and play down by the river later, do you want to come?"

"*Ahh*, I would, it's just that... I've said I'd play with my form today."

"Ok..." he smiled, before walking off looking put out.

"I really am... sorry..." I called. I kicked myself, I should have said yes. The seventh years offered me a chance to go and play Riptide with them? This was madness.

That night, I took the jumper off and placed it carefully at the top of my wardrobe. People liked me now, it was nice. The girl who had scratched my face had come back to school, when she saw me she came straight over. What followed was lot's of crying and a begging of forgiveness before she leapt on me again, hugging tightly. The Magisteers stood close by, just in case she tried to murder me again. "…And it's all turned out ok, I get to live with my Grandparents who are lovely so it's all ok now…" she said in between sobs. When she finally relinquished her hold, the entire Chamber applauded.

No longer did I receive those horrible glowering glances from the forth years, nor anyone. In fact, quite the opposite — girls would giggle tweely as I passed and once or twice I heard: "*Go talk to him…*"—"*No! You go!*"

But the best thing of all was… I had Tina's attention. In a lesson with Yearlove, as we took our seats and pulled our notes out, I saw Jasper and Tina sitting next to each other still, but with a gap between their chairs. And they weren't holding hands.

"Today, we are going to be talking about *unlocking* charms," said Yearlove with a flurry. "Someone gave me the idea of this when they brought me some homework I hadn't asked for." Jasper sat forwards smiling, ready to take the praise. "So well done Avis…" said Yearlove. I nodded my thanks as the class burst into a smatter of applause.

"*What?*" said Jasper affronted. "It was me who gave that —"

"It was Avis's ingenuity, his foresight, his entrepreneurial spirit that made him decide that *he* would set the agenda. We need more people like you Avis. People to cut a new path, not people who can tread the same old paths over and over. Now can someone name two door-unlocking spells?"

"Yes Sir…" said Jasper as if he couldn't believe his luck, leaning forward with his finger out.

"I think you're trying to trick us Sir," I butted in. "There is only *one* spell that unlocks a door, *Partimo-Sesamea*… however, there are countless *charms*."

"Wow, excellent knowledge my boy!" Yearlove cried as another round of applause came my way, followed by a gold star which suddenly blazed on my chest. Tina's gaze was fixed upon me. At last. Jasper slumped back in his chair, arms folded looking cross. The rest of the lesson was magnificent, I managed to persuade Yearlove to tell us *all* of the unlocking charms — which I wrote down as quick as I could in my workbook.

Jasper was suspicious, for some reason the jumper didn't seem to work on him. He left the lesson watching me curiously as Tina waved goodbye grinning before following her friends — going the opposite way as Jasper. It was working, it was really working.

***

In my dorm room that night, Robin and I were just finishing our homework. It had been a long, exhausting day. Simone had set us *ten paragraphs* on our experiences of rebuilding the Riptide stadium (the jumper didn't seem to work on her either). I was into paragraph five, tutting as Robin told me three lines probably didn't constitute as a paragraph.

"I might go down and get a snack," I said.

"Me too," Robin said putting his pen down and watching me fixedly, as if I might disappear at any moment. "Don't go without me."

"I won't." This was becoming a slight problem, Robin would not leave my side.

"I have an idea," I said, something bubbling into my mind. "Put your special glasses on, I want to try something."

"Okay," he said instantly, before rummaging around for them in his bag, and putting them on. Something seemed to happen almost instantly. He shook his head as if waking up from a dream.

"Bloody hell Avis!" he said. "That jumper's full of magic!" he stood.

"What can you see?" I said.

He blinked, shielding his eyes before glaring at me over the top of them. "Light, spinning round really fast. Where did you get it?" I didn't say anything. "No way! You went and wished for it!"

"Keep your voice down, the other's will be back any minute!"

"I don't care, do you realise how stupid you've been!?" he cried.

"Wait a minute. You're not being nice to me…"

He blinked confused. "What? Of course I'm not, you've been a *class A* idiot!"

I stood feeling affronted, but something more important had occurred to me. "Robin, those glasses make you immune to this jumper."

"Do they?"

"Yeah," I said. I didn't know how to feel about that. "I might go and get a snack from downstairs…"

Robin looked at me and shrugged. "Well, don't expect me to come with you, gotta finish this homework."

"Okay," I said smiling to myself for I had the normal Robin back. "Oh and Robin, keep the specs on."

Robin complained as we went down to the Chamber that his spectacles were hurting his eyes — apparently there was "too much bloomin' light and magic about…"

When we got to a sparse Chamber, small platters of supper laid out across a few tables. I felt several gazes look up and watch me. The first was David Starlight and his friends, who approached submissively. David tapped me on the shoulder as I was putting some bread and butter on a plate.

"Hi David—" I said.

"Avis hi! I was just wondering if you'd thought anymore about being my friend. I mean I know we haven't seen eye to eye—"

Robin stood tall and pushed him in the chest. "What's your game exactly?" he said, equal mixture of suspicion and confusion.

"Game?" said David snorting a little with his three friends. "What game? We just want to put the past behind us and be friends with Avis."

Robin swallowed. "You can't, he doesn't like you."

David's bottom lip trembled. "Fine. Avis, we'll come back when the dragon bodyguard isn't around!"

"Good luck with that," said Robin watching them all the way out of the Chamber before turning to me. "You going tell me what that was about? You're not friends with him now are you?"

"Course not!" I said placing some cookies and milk on my plate. Now a girl from the third year approached. I felt Robin recoil next to me. When I looked up I saw why, it was Felicity Merrilyn, the girl in the third year that Robin had a crush on. He'd tried to talk to her before at Tina's party, but never managed to introduce himself.

"Hi!" she said staring at me with wide eyes, like she was meeting a celebrity or something.

I looked away. "Hello," I put some more cookies on the plate and hoped she would start talking to Robin. But she ignored him, preferring to stare at me. She was quite plain looking, with small glasses on a merry face — in fact, she looked a bit like Ellen.

"Erm… can I help with anything?" I said as Robin shifted on the spot, bright red in the face.

"Yes, well, I just wanted to say that my friend wanted me to come over, well she didn't *want* me too I don't think, but she likes you and… we were wondering if you would go and talk to her at some point?" I felt Robin let out a huge silent sigh of relief.

"Erm, sure? Maybe another time, bit… busy right now."

"Of course, I understand you're busy," she said sweetly.

"But…" I said. "Can I introduce you to my *best friend*, Robin Wilson." I stepped out of the way as Robin went scarlet.

"*H-h*-hello," said Robin stammering and holding his hand out.

"Hi, so you're the best friend of Avis?" she said, shaking his trembling hand.

"Yep. Best friend," said Robin.

"Really? Awww," she cooed. Robin was taller than Felicity even though she was in the year above and they carried on talking as I quietly slipped out of the Chamber and back to the dorm.

Ten minutes later Robin came back. "She wants to meet me one lunch time!" he said, tongue poking out as he nodded at me with a big wide grin on.

"Nice one mate! You finally did it!"

"Yeah… And I know what that jumper is. I've worked it out…" I turned, he stood tall, his shadow cast long by the moonlight outside, a fierce glaze on his face. "You *wished* for it," he said, slowly stepping towards me as the fire crackled. "You released a Djinn!"

I told Robin everything I'd done as we sat by the fireplace into the small hours of Saturday morning. "In the Chamber, I could see, that *something* was making people *like* you."

I nodded. "Yeah, the jumper." I smiled, but Robin didn't share my smile.

He shifted in his seat uncomfortably. "Don't you see though Avis, you can't manufacture popularity, you have to earn it."

"Robin, I am a Blackthorn. I am starting a hundred points behind you!"

"Well, that's even more reason to win people over using your personality, not a jumper! You were doing so well, I mean I know it's hard what with your family, but you could have shown that you are different from them. But also... you shouldn't care so much about what others think."

I knew he was right, but I had come too far already. "I'm tired, it's late..." I said before getting into bed. "Where is everyone else?"

"Midnight Riptide apparently," Robin sighed, giving up trying to argue with me. "You do realise I am going to have to keep these spectacles on, so I can't be pulled in by the jumper's magic?"

"Yeah. Sorry," I said quietly before falling asleep.

***

All of a sudden the first match of the Riptide season was upon us. Partington was a little late to form, but finally arrived bouncing into the room wearing a lurid blue and green scarf. "Before you ask, Magisteer Yelworca made me. So, who is excited about the first game of the season!?" he cried, certainly he was. We had twenty minutes or so until we had to go down to the match, so Partington queried us on our lessons. "How are you finding it all, anything you're unsure of?"

"Yearlove is amazing!" cried Florence.

"Yes," nodded Partington sitting across a desk nodding sagely. "Everyone loves Yearlove."

"And AstroMagic is okay," said Robin. "Magisteer Wasp is very…" he searched for the right word.

"Enthusiastic?" Partington offered. "It's nice to have someone teaching you that is so interested in things, don't you think?"

Graham lent forwards with a sly look on his face. "And we were also wondering Sir, I mean, you know we rebuilt the Riptide Stadium, well… why has no one mentioned it?"

"Yeah," said Simon. "No thanks, no nothing!" murmurs of agreement crept round the room.

Partington grimaced. "Well, to be honest with you, I don't know. It's all up to Magisteer Simone."

Joanna and Gret slammed the table. "But she's a tyrant!"

"Ah, but a very effective Physical and Mental Training Magisteer," said Partington with a wry smile, before standing and changing the subject quickly. "Are you all excited about your first game of the season? Who are you playing again?"

"Happerbats!" said Dennis.

Florence gazed towards me. "We should be ok Sir, we have Avis…"

"That's very true you do," Partington's eyes rested on me and he blinked a couple of times. "My, what a wonderful jumper that is!" Robin sighed quietly next to me.

***

"PLEASE WELCOME OUT" cried Underwoods voice. "THE LORKERDOS!" The Lorkerdos were a fourth year team and wore blue and green, that must have been Magisteer Yelworca's form. I'd never seen Magisteer Yelworca, but heard she was regarded in the same vein as Magisteer Simone — a taskmaster.

"Avis?" said Graham. "Wanna put a bet on with me? I'll give you good odds?"

"I would, but I don't have any gold left, sorry."

"No worries," said Graham before turning to Simon. "Oi, git face, a bet?"

Just behind us we heard some giggling and muttering. I glanced around and saw three, mischievous looking first years boys. They stopped laughing almost as soon as they saw me.

"Oh, it's you Avis? Avis Blackthorn..." one of them said as the others stood staring, open mouthed.

Robin turned and glowered at them. "What are you doing?"

"Apologies," said the first in a small voice.

"We were going to play a prank on you, but we didn't know it was you Avis. So sorry!"

"That's quite ok," I said grinning sideways at Robin, who grimaced and turned back. The first years scuttled off again, shoving whatever toy prank they had back into their robes.

"AND NOW... WILL YOU PLEASE WELCOME OUT... THE SNARES!" My ears pricked up instantly. I didn't know they were playing? That meant... The white hair bobbed up and down, held back by a white bandana. The Snares wore all white and marched onto the field with a steely gaze. Harold, my brother was standing at the front of the Magisteer's plinth arms folded, surveying the pitch beneath him. A huge roar of applause rippled around the stadium as the Habitat changed in a flash of white light. "THE FIRST HABITAT IS A FARKINGHAM BOG..."

It was an exhilarating match. Zara Faraday was better at Riptide than all her form mates, and consistently outlasted them. The first match was won by the Lorkerdos 5-3, they were a tough team — slow, but powerful and their spells accurate. Whereas the Snares were quick and flighty, but haphazard. A big fat lad from Lockerdo found an ornament in the mud which made his spells ten times more powerful and he finished the Snare's off in thirty seconds flat.

Brian Gullet and Sarah-Jane Thompson from the Snares took the headlines in the second and third matches — Brian is a notoriously clever magical geek, and did spells I've never seen before. Robin said he was using the bridge spell *Returious* to create an enclosed bridge for Sarah-Jane to run across. The Lockerdos sent spell after spell at the bridge, which crumbled, but not before Sarah-Jane had run the length of the pitch and slammed the ball into the Lockerdos bolt-hole.

In the third match, the bigger Lockerdo boys went straight for Brian Gullet, knocking him out of the game. Then for Zara and then Sarah-Jane, before winning the match with a "*Libero-Manus!*"

The Lockerdos had some interesting tactics that Jake and Gret were analysing. Apparently they were very clever, adapting themselves to different circumstances. For instance one of their team, the large fat one, was a *Searcher*, it was his job to only search for Ornaments. He had someone who guarded him while he searched. Then there were three Lockerdo's who went straight for the best players spelling them out of the game. The rest were the flounder players, it was their job to get the flounders and keep them, they did this by staying in shapes and finding space. Passing around to each other in circles. It was very effective. The Lockerdos, of the fourth year, beat the Snares of the second year by four games to one. Zara, Sarah-Jane and Brain Gullet left the field looking bedraggled and very worn out.

***

"So, what I am saying is this…" said Jake who was all charged up after watching the first competitive game of the season. "We need someone who can be our Searcher—so we have a chance at finding an Ornament. Finding an Ornament can turn a game around."

"He's right," said Joanna. "What's the point in having twelve of us charging towards their bolt-hole if they will just take us all out… the upper years know better magic than us. We need to work in a tactically sufficient way that suits us."

"We should play offensively against teams in the league," said Gret stamping her fist into her hand. "And operate a swift tactical defensive unit in the cup games. We need clear tactics so everyone knows what they are doing."

We were standing in the clearing where we played Riptide debating tactics for what seemed a millennia. Everyone was up for it after watching a master show from the Lockerdos.

"Robin will be the Searcher," I said. "He has a great eye for things like that," I winked at him.

Robin rolled his eyes. "No, no, I don't think the responsibility—"

"Great idea Avis!" said Hunter enthusiastically. "Robin, you up for it?" Our whole form looked longingly at him.

"I mean," Robin glared at me, before sighing. "Sure, why not."

***

"We're still gonna get beaten," said Hunter as we finalised our tactics for the last time with the girls in our dorm room. The fire crackled as Dawn put another log on it.

"What?" said Jake. "Look, we've practiced, we have planned tactics. What else can we do?" It was the night before our first Riptide match and the nerves were getting to everyone.

"Why did you put that log on?" said Simon. "It's too big, this is the boy's fire, only boys are allowed to operate it!"

"Sorry!" said Dawn flouncing back to the armchair. "Can't do right for wrong with these boys," she whispered loudly to Ellen.

My mind was on other things. Earlier, at dinner I was leaving the Chamber and Tina approached me smiling. "Hey you," she cooed.

"Oh hi," I said rather awkwardly.

"Long time no speak," she said seductively twirling her hair. "Good luck with the game tomorrow. I hope you win," she fluttered her long eyelashes at me and pecked me on the cheek.

"Thanks," I said before Jasper's sour face frowned at me from the top of the stairs. I shook my head and pulled myself back into the dorm room.

"I am just saying we need to 'ave a positive attitude about 'dis," said Jake.

We'd been talking Riptide tactics for days and days. We kept agreeing on a final plan, but then someone would come up with a new idea and we would debate it for hours. "Jake's right," I said. "We do need to maintain a positive attitude. What happened last year won't happen again. We had no idea what we were doing last year, it was a nightmare… but that won't happen again. Let's just keep our tactics as they are, nice and simple so we don't get confused and just see how tomorrow goes."

Everyone nodded. I didn't mention the training we had with Partington the day before, because well… it was a disaster. Everything that could've gone wrong did. Hunter face planted the bolt-hole and had to go to the Healer's room. While the *pasanthedine* spell worked (*raising someone into the air spell*), it seems we had forgotten completely how to do *kadriepop* (*to get ourselves down again!*) I hung, limp in mid-air waving my arms round like a lunatic, along with most of the others until Partington let us down, and then left early, claiming he had some very important meeting to attend.

***

The crowds chants rang deafeningly above us as we waited in the tunnel. The Happerbats were already on the pitch and had received a very well rounded applause. What would we get? Laughter probably — *Theres the team that doesn't know how to play Riptide from last year, hahahaha!*

I had the jumper on, underneath my Riptide shirt, along with my Seven League Shoes. I persuaded Robin to keep his spectacles on too. So now, this gave us a couple of advantages (*illegal advantages*). My heart began beating at the speed of knots as Magisteer Underwood came into the tunnel holding the long probe.

"Feet up and arms out," she said. Joanna at the front was searched thoroughly by Underwood before being given a nod. "Anything illegal, please say now, or face the wrath of permanent exclusion."

I froze solid, my heart beating in my chest. Would she recognise the jumper, the shoes, or Robin's spectacles as illegal? I could say I didn't know, that I had no idea that they were magical—surely she would buy that?

She checked Hunter, then Simon, then Graham. Robin glanced behind at me with a panicked expression before lifting his arms. Underwood scanned him, then nodded. All clear.

But, maybe it was just glasses she couldn't see, maybe they weren't magical enough? My Seven League Shoes would surely be found out! *Oh, why oh why did I have to risk using the jumper and shoes, just to give us an advantage at stupid Riptide?!*

This was unbearable. I held my arms out as she approached. I felt her eyes scanning me for what seemed like an eternity. "Ok the Condors, you're all clear. Make your way out now," she said.

My heart jumped for joy, before retuning to absolute fear as we slowly marched out onto the wide grass pitch.

"PLEASE WELCOME OUT... THE CONDORS!" A mix of gentle applause, not as loud as the Happerbats rippled around the stadium.

We marched out, jelly-legged and came face to face with the Happerbats who stood confident, in purple and green stripes. They were a lot bigger than us in size and weight. My stomach turned inside out—this could be another car crash like last year, in front of the whole school. But, then I remembered, we had three distinct advantages.

"Take your positions!" cried Underwood marching into the middle of the pitch. I walked solemnly over to furthest right side of the pitch. Jess and Florence stood just behind me, it was their job to follow me only.

Robin, who was rearranging his spectacles stood in the very middle, guarded by Dawn and Graham.

Jake, Gret and Joanna were standing dead centre in a small huddle — causing the spaced out Happerbats to look quizzically at each other, for this was not usual.

Hunter stood guard by the bolt-hole with a fixed mark of concentration on his face.

I stood anxiously looking around, for in a minute or so that blue or red flounder would be sailing straight for me. We seemed to have to wait an age for Underwood to initiate the Habitat change. All around the stadium was excited faces chattering away. The Magisteer's plinth had Partington standing arms folded, with Straker just behind muttering something that Partington was trying his best to ignore. The Lily sat next to Simone, both staring off into the distance looking bored. Hardly any yellow and black scarves waved in the crowd — it was all purple and green. I saw Tina and Jasper standing together with their forms, all wearing purple and green. And yet, there were some wearing Condor scarves. I looked closer... it was Zara and her Snare friends — my stomach fluttered again.

In a white flash the Habitat changed. Now we were standing in a long swaying grass field. Several sparse trees stood unmoving.

"AN AFRICAN PLAIN!" cried Underwood as the crowd crooned.

A whistle rang true across the stadium and a great roar erupted from the crowd. The blue and red flounders shot up out of the opposing bolt-holes. Flashes of *pasanthedine* spells zoomed towards us as the Happerbats charged as one with an almighty roar. I jumped into the grass, out of the way of three spells. Jess and Florence fired spells back at the runners who were charging full pelt towards us. Joanna, Jake and Gret, with their arms outstretched had grown the grass ahead of the charging Happerbats. In one go their feet became tangled. In panic they stopped, backing away and firing a tirade of spells at the grass — which promptly caught fire. Robin was frantically searching the pitch for an Ornament, squinting hard with Dawn and Graham following. It couldn't have been easy, there was so much magic going on that he must have been half-blinded.

A blue light lit up above me. The flounder was soaring through the air. Hunter had thrown it, but it was going to land way too far ahead of me! With a double tap of the shoes, I erupted up the right flank. It was magical. I saw the Happerbats charging towards me and I darted straight past them. In slow motion, I turned, aimed two hands at the three chargers and cried "*Pasanthedine!*" One blast of white light engulfed them immediately. I looked up at the descending flounder. "*Zxanbatters!*" I called as the magnetic spell drew the ball to my hand with a snap. Up ahead, a big Happerbat guarded the bolt-hole. The speed I was running at was impossible, my legs felt like they were being pushed beyond anything they had ever done. And I was fast running out of space before I smashed headlong into the end of the stadium.

The guard at the bolt-hole had spotted me and was aiming everything she had. In one fluid motion, I kicked off a tree, launching myself up into the air, ten feet above the ground. I double tapped the shoes, and then miraculously, began to slow, descending straight at the bolt-hole. Jess and Florence charged forwards through the fiery grass, hands outstretching as I curled my feet back and pulled the flounder behind my head. Blue and white light burst from Jess and Florence, knocking the guard high up in the air in a screaming fit of anger. I sailed downwards slamming the flounder into the deep, dark bolt-hole goal. A blue column of light shot into the sky. I landed on the raised grassy hill and slid down, feeling a little dizzy as a gigantic roar lit up the stadium.

But I couldn't stop now, the red flounder was in mid-air. Simon and Dennis were standing beneath it, awaiting the fall. The Happerbats were so caught up in the fight with Jake and Gret, that they had forgotten about the flounder. When the ball dropped to Simon, he simply ran through the open space, the Happerbats realising too late as a column of red light shot skywards like a laser.

After the restart the Happerbats had regrouped, and managed to spell Dawn, Ellen and even Joanna off the pitch. They remained resolute for the remaining seven minutes (perhaps the dressing down they received from Yelworca helped), they defended well, not letting us near the flounders. But they didn't get close to scoring either. We were on for a 2-0 win for the first game.

That is, until Robin shouted "*AHA!*" A loud eruption rumbled through the ground. Giant human hands made of grass and mud burst up out of the pitch underneath each Happerbat and took them out of the game.

"LIBERO-MANUS!" called Underwood as a tidal wave of applause threatened to deafen us. Followed by a standing ovation from the Lily. Partington looked overwhelmed and stood clapping mightily. Robin grinned at me, pointing at the spectacles — a broken Ornament in his hands. I grinned back. We were winning and doing well. Confidence coursed through us. We were organised and determined. Jake and Joanna gathered us into a tight circle as we prepared for the Habitat to change for the second match.

It was in the fifth and last match that I heard something glorious ring true around the entire stadium: "*AVIS, AVIS, AVIS!*" — It was undeniable, they were chanting *my* name.

A minute before one tall Happerbat holding the red flounder hadn't noticed me hiding behind a tall brick wall. I tapped the shoes, stepped out and dodged the spell he threw at me, before snatching the ball and spelling him into the air. Now I charged forwards.

Five Happerbats were now soaring through the air towards me, completely blocking my path to the bolt-hole. But, Jake was making a lone run the other side of the pitch.

"*Nouchous!*" I called, causing a blaze of fire to erupt between me and the oncoming Happerbats. A perfect distraction. I pulled my arm back and launched the flounder into the air to Jake as I fell into the fiery grip of five Happerbats, I watched happily as Jake slammed the flounder past the guard. In a flash I zapped back the bench and out of the game. But it didn't matter, we had just won 3-2. That last act of unselfishness hadn't gone unnoticed. Jake grinned across the pitch at me, raising his hands in a high salute as Underwood called time on the match. The crowd suddenly roared. "AVIS! AVIS! AVIS! WE LOVE YOU AVIS!" It was the most wonderful feeling in the world — I was good at something. People loved me.

"AND THE WINNERS OF TODAYS RIPTIDE MATCH BY FOUR GAMES... ARE THE CONDORS!" Underwoods voice called true across the stadium to a colossal roar of applause. The purple and green scarves were now non-existent, replaced by a sea of yellow and black. I smiled at Robin, who had his eye on an adoring group of girls screaming his name, one of them including Felicity Merrilyn. Tina and Zara were now both applauding loudly while Jasper sank back into the crowd until he was almost invisible. We left the pitch, bowing proudly to a standing ovation, followed by "AVIS, AVIS, AVIS, *AVIS*!"

It was the best feeling I've ever had. Ok, it wouldn't have been possible without the shoes, Robin's specs and maybe the jumper played a *small* part. But was it worth it? You bet.

CHAPTER TEN
'Accidents'

The Condor changing room was charged with an electric atmosphere. We jumped around dancing and chanting as if we had just won the *Riptide World Championships*!

"Avis, I can't believe it, you were incredible out there!" said Jake, beaming wide.

"Cheers!" I called. Robin caught my eye and winked across the changing room. It was a humungous room with a high pitched roof and massive animal statues that hung perilously above, strutting out from the walls. A tiger, a hubris, a flutteryout and a dragon — everything else about the room was the same as other bathrooms: cubicles, showers, baths and lines of sinks. Except these Riptide changing rooms had two doors at the end leading to the girls changing area and the boys. Graham had proceeded to push on all the taps and began spraying everyone with freezing cold water, as if he were shaking a bottle of champagne.

"Well, well, well!" said Partington, appearing in the doorway and beaming wide. "I don't think I've ever had a team play *that* well before," he said arms folded, talking as if half in dream. "You gave me quite the surprise."

"Thanks Sir," said Simon as everyone stopped shouting and whooping for a minute.

"Congratulations to all of you, I am so proud of you," with that, he turned and left. After a detailed breakdown of the match and lots of celebrating — which mostly involved Hunter dancing round the room with his trousers on his head — we calmed down a little.

"I might have a bath…" I said looking down at my muddy wet clothes.

"I think I will too," said Robin.

"And me!" said Graham.

We didn't much mind having baths together as the shower curtains around the baths were magical. Once you pulled them around, no one could pull them away except from you — so no one could see you in the nude, which was good, because I don't think I'd have showered or bathed all year if I had to get naked in front of other people. Especially girls.

I turned on the bath before scouring the shelves for bubble bath. "Avis?" I turned to Jess and Florence, both looking a little bedraggled, with so much mud on them they looked like a swamp creature. "We just wanted to ask you if you thought we did a good job today?"

"What?" I said confused. "Well, yeah of course you did. A *brilliant* job."

"We did it for you," said Florence smiling radiantly.

"That's… *nice*. Thank you." I said as they giggled and ran off, this jumper really was powerful.

Now, all I had to do was work out how to get my clothes off without anyone seeing and getting in the bath — I turned off the hot tap and poured in some Chameleon Curd Bubble Bath, I tried not to notice the girls watching me as I dithered about with the water, trying to find the right moment to hide behind the curtains and change into a towel.

"Well, I reckon we 'ave to change up our tactic's slightly for 'da next matches," said Gret.

"I don't!" said Hunter. "This worked so we should stick to it."

Joanna sighed. "Well, you both have a point. But everyone in that stadium will have seen how we played, so Gret's right we might have to mix it up a little bit."

"Guys, guys…" said Dawn. "Let's not worry about this now, let's just enjoy our win!"

I wasn't looking but I heard them all murmur in agreement. "She's right," said Robin. "Let's just enjoy the fact that we smashed the Happerbats and… AVIS WATCH OUT!" he suddenly screamed.

With half my head out of the wet yellow shirt I suddenly heard a cracking noise. Then a rumble. Without thinking, I jumped backwards into the sinks. An almighty, colossal, monumental *BAAAANNNGGG* rang around the bathroom. The giant horned hubris statue had cracked and fallen, smashing into three of the baths sending porcelain, water and stone flying off in all directions.

"*AVIS!?*" called Robin, through the choking dust. "AVIS! WHERE ARE YOU?"

"I'm here!" I called from under the sinks as thick stone dust clogged my throat. I moved towards Robin's voice and out of the dust cloud that now engulfed the corner of the bathrooms — crawling through the debris to where everyone was cowering against the wall.

"You ok Avis?" they chorused — some of them, like Hunter and Jess began fussing over me, brushing the dust off.

"Really, I'm fine. Thanks Robin, you saved my life…" I was about to say *again*, but in present company decided not to.

Robin was frowning hard. "It just, I mean, it just cracked and fell?"

Hunter stepped forwards. "Right, perhaps we better get washed in another bathroom, one which doesn't have falling statues. Everyone out!"

"I will be telling Partington and the Lily about this!" said Simon. "That could have killed me."

***

A week later and we were in Yearlove's lesson. He was teaching us how to charm plants. For they were the easiest things to charm — they can't put up much resistance. We paired off around the massive room with our potted wildflower. Mine and Robin's was a tall, stalky flower with a yellow bud.

"To charm the flower, place it on the table in front of you," said Yearlove as a table appeared in front of us out of thin air, a book a top the table which turned to the correct page. "Then, read aloud the charm, changing the specifics to match your particular plant."

The air filled with charms being read aloud. "We have to face the plant from the North mate," said Robin moving around the table. "Otherwise it won't work."

Soon enough the air was filled with laughing. "Look, it's dancing! Dancing!" cried Damien Duffield. It was too, his potted Dahlia was doing a very merry little jig to itself.

"I can't believe Damien has managed to do it and we haven't!" I whispered as Robin scanned the words in the book for the twentieth time.

He huffed. "It makes no sense…" said Robin. "We've read it aloud and look, nothing. It must be dead."

"Who's ready to show their plant charming skills to the rest of the class?" said Yearlove, it wasn't a question. If it was, we would have chosen not to, on the account that we couldn't do this most simple of tasks. Jasper and Tina had, not only got their pink Rose to dance, but they had also taught it the moves to the *Cauldron Double Clap-Clap* (a very popular Wizard dance).

But now here we were reading aloud a useless charm to a (probably dead) yellow Chrysanthemum that did not want to dance. Robin was so embarrassed, he made me read out the entire charm. When I'd finished however, the plant did do something. It began to wiggle, and move. Robin and I exchanged a glance — had we done it? The rest of the class watched on as the plant stood, and began to dance. Wiggling it's leaves to an imaginary beat.

"High five!" Robin called laughing and looking extremely relived.

"Brilliant work boys!" said Yearlove, and I was pleased to see Jasper looking genuinely annoyed. "Whose next? Jake and Hunter please…"

As we were watching Jake and Hunter nervously read aloud their charm, our flower which was dancing just within my vision began to do something *strange*. It started to grow. It was as if something else had taken over it. In one flash it had reached the ceiling.

"Sir! SIR!" we cried as the shadow loomed large overhead.

Yearlove turned frowning, before jumping backwards. "Goodness gracious me! What on earth could have done tha—" Yearlove stopped. We all stopped, open mouthed as the flower changed dramatically. The light inside the room vanished. The flower widened, stalk thickening. The pot burst as long snaking roots dived into the cracks of the floor. Then all at once, it dived.

"AHH!" Screamed the class falling back, apart from me… snaking up my body were long, green tentacled vines. Thick and waxy, encircling me from feet to chest, winding up towards my head. I didn't even have time to think, it was all happening so quickly.

Yearlove backed the class away and was gazing up at me, suspended in mid-air. I was *so* high, my stomach twisted as I spun like a fly in a spiders web. I tried to double tap my feet, but they were bound so tightly I was all but paralysed, the breath slowly being squeezed out of me.

Raising both arms, Yearlove shouted: "*Relovotessellaregrassus!*" all in one go. There was a flash of brightest orange, as flames suddenly speared the thick snaking body of the flower. Leaves burned, as it let out a screeching cry, before releasing me and wilting away.

Burning to ash as it fell to the floor in a clump of smouldering green debris. I hit the pile of green ash and lay panting, trying to catch my breath.

"Thank you," I croaked at Yearlove.

"That's quite ok my boy!" he said lifting me up to my feet. The colour returning in part to his pale face. He stood looking quizzically, stoking his black beard, glancing from me to the table, the book and the broken flower pot. "I don't know how this could have happened."

***

I couldn't eat. My mind was whirring. Fear had gripped me. like a vice. Wind had filled my stomach uncomfortably, like it always did when I was worried. I needed to let some out, but I couldn't in a Chamber full of people. Or could I? The growth of the flower earlier had scared me. The statue falling in the changing rooms *could* have been an accident. We heard caretaker Ingralo, who in charge of fixing it, talking to Simone about it on the way to a Physical Training Lesson. "Some people 'fink it fell on purpose!" he cackled. "Don' they know how old these 'fings are?"

"Quite," said Simone.

Disappointingly, Partington thought the same when we told him our concerns the next day in form. "Remember, those statues are very old… I don't think it's a *conspiracy*… the Lily has ruled out foul play and that's good enough for me. But what I will be addressing with him is the safety aspect. Some safety spells need to be updated. You were very close to being squished… I mean, I can't have one of our newest high scorers for the Riptide team suddenly dying on us!" he snorted.

I pushed away the pie that Hunter slid towards me. "Gotta' eat!" he said, shaking his head at me before diving in himself. Robin was half-reading and half had his eye on a table ahead, with Felicity on it. She had been most interested in Robin ever since his Riptide heroics.

"Hey, you have to eat that jam tart, it was the last piece," said Dawn tutting at me. I sighed absently and pushed the bowl towards her. "Oh look, you haven't even touched it. Such a waste!" she said, picking up another spoon and diving in.

But not a second later, did something terrible happen. As soon as the tart entered her mouth she promptly began choking. Softly at first, but after spitting out the tart, she continued to choke. Firstly, our table looked up, Ellen clapping her on the back. But then, she continued choking, eyes bulging, face growing redder and redder. Then purple. More and more tables began looking round now. Dawn was standing waving her arms wildly, unable to catch her breath. Joanna and Ellen stood sharply signalling to the Magisteers table. Straker and Mallard appeared next to Dawn in a flash. Laying her on the floor and waving hands over her mouth they became confused, then a little panicked. But then, Straker raised his hand over Dawn's mouth and drew something else out of it. A handful of what looked like moving black fluff jumped out of Dawn's mouth and into his hands. Straker cupped them tightly together. He nodded once to the Lily and mouthed: "*It's a curse*." Before running out of the Chamber with his hands cupped and outstretched.

The Lily appeared next to Dawn in a blaze of white light. He looked down at her, before she coughed and spluttered back to life. Everyone gave a huge sigh of relief.

"You gave us quite a scare," said the Lily. "Do you think you're up to showing me the last thing you ate or drank?" Dawn sat back up at the table, cheeks pale, her eyes wide and watery with shock and embarrassment.

"Of course Sir, it was this…" she pointed to the bowl of jam tart. "It *was* Avis's…" faces turned towards me. The

Lily raised a hand at the pudding and without a word, it burned in a blaze of white light.

***

I couldn't sleep. Snores rang around the room, a backdrop for the wailing winds and rain outside that were battering the window with almighty intent. As I lay, my thoughts slid to Tina — I missed her very much. A tight knot of regret tightened in my stomach. I turned over in bed, clearing my mind. The clock above the fireplace said it was almost three o'clock! I'd been lying here, trying for sleep for nearly five hours. I sighed and watched the fire embers burning, listening to the hammering rain against the glass.

I don't know what I was dreaming about, but at some point a white hot burning sensation began rising up my legs. Then a loud roaring sound, shouting and choking smoke.

"AVIS! *AVIS!*" — I woke and saw immediately why everyone was shouting at me.

My bed was on fire!

"AVIS, GET OUT OF BED!" they cried at me. For a moment I thought I was still dreaming. Orange flames plumed from every angle of my bed covers as smoke billowed into the air. Suddenly I felt the pain on my legs. Extreme heat burning them to cinders! Screaming with pain I jumped from the covers — or, I tried to — my legs were caught on something. I clawed at the carpet trying to pull myself free. But, what felt like… cold hands had hold of my ankles!

"AVIS! WHAT ARE YOU WAITING FOR!" Robin cried, jumping down from his bed and coming as close as he could.

"I CAN'T GET FREE!" I yelled waving my arms out at him. "PULL ME! SOMETHINGS GOT MY LEGS!" I couldn't get free of the impenetrable hold around my ankles. I kicked and writhed, but the hold was impossibly tight. Jake and Graham jumped up and began chanting something. Suddenly, freezing cold water came pouring all over me.

"*AHHHH*!" I cried. Followed by everyone else in the room. The fire was doused. Steam rose up from my bed as the sounds of the fire died. My legs now free, I pulled them out of the covers and stood soaking wet, with a bed that resembling a lump of charcoal. I stood shaking.

"You all right mate?" said Robin, passing me a towel. I didn't say anything, I couldn't.

"I'm soaking wet!" Simon complained, standing up out of his bed now too.

Jake turned on him. "Oh poor you! Sorry we panicked and got everyone in the room wet, but we '*ad to save his life*!"

"Something is wrong," said Hunter who stood shaking by the door. "Too many accidents... I think.... I think someone is trying to *kill you* Avis."

They all looked round at me as if I were a condemned man. "Its kind of undeniable now," said Dennis softly.

Footsteps appeared outside the door before Magisteers Partington and Yearlove appeared. "Impkus the ghost told us there was a situation in your room? Goodness me whatever has happened?" said Partington staring at my bed and coming further into the room. "Ga— I mean, Magisteer Yearlove I think you should come in."

Yearlove did, holding a gas light aloft looking tired. "What happened here?" he said frowning around at the destruction.

"Avis's bed caught fire Sir," said Jake. "We did a water spell to put it out."

"Good boys, well done," said Partington who turned to look at the bed running his finger across the black charred sheets and sniffing. After a muted conversation with Yearlove, Partington turned back to us. "Well, you can't sleep in here tonight, better get you all off to the Healer's room. Looks like Avis could do with some ointment for his legs anyhow…" he said with a worried look at my red legs. They hurt.

Yearlove was staring at the fire with a fixed expression. "Must have been a stray ember," he mused. "I will deal with the mess in here. By tomorrow, it should be back to normal."

No one slept in the Healer's room. Ghost guards were placed at the entrance, their blue light shone under the doors just visible through the dull green light of the sun Jade. "So that's three *accidents* in a week!" cried Hunter. "This is getting out of control!"

"I know," cried Graham. "I didn't think so before, but it's like Jake said, it's *undeniable!*"

"But why would anyone want to hurt Avis?" said Dennis, who was being completely serious.

Robin, in the bed next to me sniggered quietly to himself, then said: "Yeah Avis, I can't think of any reason whatsoever that someone would want to try and kill *you*," then under his breath so only I could hear he added. "*Except the most evil Sorcerer of all time.*"

"Whoever it is," said Jake. "When we find out, we will go after them and give 'em a taste of their own medicine!"

"Yeah!" they all chorused.

It was starting to worry me, something was definitely after me. They could have all been accidents — the falling hubris, the killer flower, the cursed pudding and the fire but that was too much of a coincidence. But who, or what was after me?

I sat up as the wonderful, graceful Healer approached with a bowl of flowery smelling burn cream. "Quiet down all of you," she said sweetly as she swept through the room. Green rays had already attached to me and my burnt legs which began to pulse harder as the cream was applied.

Hunter and the other boys were grinning broadly as the Healer began applying the cream up and down my legs. I ignored them.

"I think my legs are burnt too," said Hunter.

"And mine!" Graham said with a fake pained expression.

The Healer smiled and finished applying the cream. "What you all need is sleep. I want you to all lay back in your beds…" every single one of us did what she said. She spoke in such a soft peaceful voice, it made my brain tickle. "Now let Jade's green rays fall over you as you descend into a long, blissful sleep…"

Zzzzz…

Yearlove cleaned our dorm room completely. No sign of any accident was visible. It was dry, smelt lovely and even had a fire guard in front of the fireplace — which Robin poked, amused. "That's not gonna stop a *curse* is it?" he muttered. Two ghosts were allocated outside our room — Partington was worried, and walked around with a pained expression as if he couldn't tell why on earth someone would try and hurt his form. He kept popping into our room unannounced every couple of hours.

"Hello boys, just checking your all ok," he'd say before disappearing again. His gaze lingering a little longer in my direction. Perhaps he felt like he owed me after I saved his only remaining family last year?

"There's quite a few options…" said Robin to himself staring at the unlit fire with a blanket around him. No one had dared light it again, even though Simon complained of the cold. Jake slapped him when he tried to throw a log on and light it.

They had all gone down to dinner now (it was warm down there), I stayed sitting on the sofa opposite Robin. The rain continued to batter the windows and the wind wailed, causing the chimney to whistle. I was too tired to go down to dinner anyway. "I mean, it could be any number of people…" Robin muttered again.

"What are you talking about?" I said, rubbing my eyes and trying not to pay attention to the massive pile of homework laid out on the table in front of me.

"The person who tried to kill you Avis? You should pay more attention, whoever it is, they're still out there…" he pointed out the window.

"I know," I said, slightly annoyed that he thought I didn't care. "I am thinking about it, how can I not? I nearly lost both my legs last night."

"It has to be him doesn't it? *Malakai?*" Robin whispered.

"Not necessarily, I mean think about it. I did him some damage…"

"But he's had time to recover, it said so in the Herrald, that he was back!"

I scoffed. "I wouldn't believe everything you read in the paper mate!" I said. "I mean think of all the protection that's come to the school specifically to watch out for Malakai coming back, with his reduced powers too."

Robin shrugged. "Who else hates you enough to try and kill you?"

I had a few ideas already. I was running them through my mind and becoming more and more paranoid as the days went by.

The Happerbats? No, why would they try and kill me just because we beat them at Riptide? They didn't seem to hate us, some of them had even shook my hand in the corridors after the game to congratulate me. It must be someone who was immune to my magical jumper.

Jasper? He hated me. But why try and kill me? It made no sense. But what about…

"What?" said Robin looking tepidly at my open-mouthed face.

"It could be Harold?" I said. "My brother. I mean… he starts at the school right after everything that happened at home and... well, he's a master of disguise and cunning. What if my parents want me dead? What if they know it was me that defeated their beloved Malakai?" I stood up, it all made sense in my brain. "Yeah that would make sense, and that stuff in the paper about him returning... *pah*! Load of rubbish. That was my parents! I just know it was. They dressed up as him and attacked places all at once so it looked like he was really back."

"Avis," said Robin sounding apologetic. "I know your parents might not like you, but I don't think they would try and *kill you*. Anyway, if your parents really wanted to kill you, I think they would have done already, don't you?"

His words pierced through my thoughts, popping them like a balloon. I sat back down. "Who then?"

***

It didn't take long until there was progress. On a Wednesday afternoon during free period, our form was sitting in the Chamber. The rain was still lashing down outside, it hadn't stopped for weeks.

Jake and Gret were playing chess, while Ellen and Joanna had their noses in a book. Jess and Florence were comparing the new make-up they'd got from the catalogue section in the back of the Herrald. Dawn, who's appetite had not been interrupted by the *choking incident* was eating three different kinds of cake whilst writing her AstroMagic essay on: *the holes in the electromagnetic Earth beams* (and getting crumbs all over it). I was staring absentmindedly at the essay for Yearlove on charming flowers while Robin was scratching away next to me like a charged entity. The Chamber was packed, because it was raining outside the atmosphere lent itself to bored, cooped up individuals with tendencies towards shouting or running around to burn off the excess energy — until they were told off by one of the equally grumpy Magisteers.

"Hi Avis," said a quiet voice behind me. David Starlight stood awkwardly on his own. "Just wondering if I could talk to you quickly?"

Robin peeled himself away from his homework, when he saw David he growled like a dog. "What's he doing here?" he muttered.

David pulled up a chair and bent over his hands as if he was about to tell me awful news. "Me and some of the Eagles were in detention earlier, cleaning outside the staff room. I overheard them talking about you."

"Me?" I said. "What did they say?" Robin stopped scribbling and turned in his seat to face David, a sceptical look on his face.

"They were talking about the accidents, except some of the Magisteers seem to think that they are not accidents at all. I think…" David leaned in a lot closer. "They think someone is trying to kill you," he said gravely, a look of absolute terror emblazoned across his face.

"Is that it?" said Robin, rolling his eyes. "That's what you came to tell us?"

"I just thought…" David looked deeply hurt as tears formed in his eyes. "If I told you, then maybe you would like me." With his lip wobbling, David stood and marched quickly out of the Chamber.

Robin raised his eyebrows at me. "That jumpers gonna get you in trouble."

"You didn't have to be quite so harsh," I said.

"What? He didn't tell us anything we didn't already know." It was at that moment that Hunter entered the Chamber with a towel round his head, sitting between me and Robin, before grabbing a slice of carrot cake and munching.

"Guess where I've been?" he said.

"Detention?" said Robin without looking up.

Hunter gulped. "Yup."

"There's a surprise," I said chuckling.

Hunter smiled and put his cake down. "I think I know who it was. Who set the '*accidents*' on you..." he said in a hushed tone. "I worked it out earlier."

Robin slammed his pen down and looked up. "Go on..."

"We were cleaning the annex near the staff room, they didn't hear us and in the little bit I was cleaning I could see right through into the staff room. Well, after they were talking about them not being accidents, they started speaking about how much they hate the Occulus's!"

"Right..." said Robin putting his pen down. "But how does this mean you know who it was?"

"Because, I saw Magisteer Simone... *smiling* when they were talking about it — she was sitting there and smiling when they said you were nearly crushed by a hubris statue and she nearly laughed when they mentioned the flower."

"Oh rubbish Hunter!" said Ellen, who, next to Robin was secretly listening. "Magisteer Simone is a teacher at this school, her job is to look after the pupils, not kill them!" But her argument had fallen on deaf ears. I for one could see where Hunter was coming from. My mind whizzed back to the very first *accident*, when we were building the Riptide stadium, a huge rafter came swinging towards me with magic — and I got the blame for it!

"It's worth looking into," said Robin to Ellen's absolute annoyance. She huffed and dived back into the pages of her book.

Hunter smiled. "And I've got a plan..." he whispered.

***

"It feels strange, us sneaking around together. Remember the last time? I almost died," Hunter said stumbling along.

"Yes, don't remind us," I said peering through the darkness at the corridors ahead. "Right, stop here." I held my hands over both of their heads and whispered.

215

"*Avertere,*" they both shivered as the gloopy cold spell dribbled down their spine. I repeated the same on myself, now at least we would only be partially visible.

"There's one up there," said Robin pointing at a far off Occulus. "I'll take it out." He stepped forwards keeping his back to the wall and aimed his hand very carefully at the Occulus.

"Wow," said Hunter greedily. "How did you do that? That would be so useful for me."

"Come on, her late night class is down here…" said Robin. Sure enough, in her classroom at the very end of the corridor we could hear thuds and shouts.

"A class, at this time of night?" I said.

Robin grimaced. "It's the seventh years, they have late night classes."

As we got closer, the barks of command and thuds got louder and louder. Quite obviously the attendance of this class were being worked extortionately hard. We waited in the shadows, before the door opened and lots of sweaty, panting seventh years came puffing their way out and away up the opposite corridor.

"Quickly," said Hunter spotting Magisteer Simone marching off down the adjacent corridor. "After her!"

"No, hang back…" said Robin. "We need to follow from a distance."

We did. Tip toeing slowly, we pushed past the exhausted seventh years and followed Simone. All the Magisteers in the school had their own living quarters somewhere, but they were usually kept secret, so unruly students couldn't find and trash them. Probably. We did our best to keep well back so she didn't notice us following and finally, we saw her walk directly through a tall, green drape.

"What now?" I said, moving into the shadow of an alcove, this corridor was big and lined with tall dusty statues. Tall windows on the right let in the dull light from a rainy night sky.

Robin checked his watch. "Come back tomorrow when she's not in?"

"Pfft! No way!" said Hunter. "Let's search her place now. We need to find a clue that she is the one causing these accidents!"

"Are you mad?" I said. "She's in there right now!"

"No she isn't look…"

I turned slowly, half expecting her to be bearing over us, but from behind a statue I peeked over and saw her walking down the opposite corridor with a towel and wash bag. "She's actually gone for a wash, her first this year!" said Hunter laughing. "Come on!" he marched forward.

"Hunter no!" I said.

"It's all right, he won't get through the drape anyway," said Robin. "Oh…" the smile wiped from his face as Hunter walked clean through the drape and into Magisteer Simone's living quarters.

I glanced at Robin, we both knew that if we were caught now, the least of our problems would be an expulsion but we couldn't just leave Hunter. We tiptoed forwards and through the drape together. Now we stood in a small passageway, the end opened out into a comfy living area and Hunter was already poking around. Light from the fire and a few brackets around the high stone walls illuminated the tidy, ordered room. A leather chair and foot stall faced a television in the middle of the room. Hanging drapes, with feats of accomplishment hung all around the room.

Women's Riptide League Champion — three medals.

Women's Riptide Cup Champion — one medal.

Women's Olympic Witch Heptathlon Event Runner-up — three silver medals.

All sorts of medals and awards, trinkets and honours hung from the wall and on shelves. Framed photo's of her standing smiling (which was odd) next to important looking people. "That's the Magical Council Leader, Bernard Brimming!" said Robin.

"How do you know that?" I said, never having much knowledge of magical politics myself.

"I read," he said, as if suggesting I should too.

"What are we looking for exactly?" I said.

"Clues," said Hunter, before stopping dead. "I can hear something. She's coming!" he mouthed. "Get in the wardrobe!"

Standing in the corner of the room was a large wardrobe. We opened it and piled inside as quietly as we could as fear swelled inside me. Just as the door clicked shut, Magisteer Simone entered the room. My heart was beating a million miles an hour. I could see her through the crack in the wardrobe door. She would kill us if she found us in here. Or eat us. I glared at Hunter through the darkness. This was his rotten fault! We waited. And waited. My legs began hurting. But we couldn't make a noise. She sat down in front of the television with a big box of cakes by her side and began watching. Putting her enormous feet up on the foot stall. I turned to the others through the darkness, Robin had gone so pale with fright I thought he might glow in the dark.

We were trapped. It was like something out of a nightmare. A terrifying monster was eating its way through twelve massive cakes, and we would be next.

I don't know how I fell asleep... but I did — and not just me, the others too. I woke up to Hunter dribbling all over my shoulder. Now outside the room, was quiet and darkness. I peered through the crack and saw no Magisteer Simone. The television and lights were off.

"Wake up, wake up..." I whispered as quietly as possible.

"Please mum, just another five minutes..." Hunter moaned. I punched him on the arm.

"*Shhh*! I'm not your mum. And be quiet."

"Oh god, we're still here?" Robin stirred quickly as I opened the wardrobe door softly and stepped out. Robin rubbed his eyes.

"Time for a quick search?" said Hunter who peered up at the stuff on the walls.

"No, we need to get out of here!" said Robin — this was a stupid plan anyway, I mean what were we expecting to find? A piece of paper that said: '*Kill Avis Blackthorn.*' — I'd only just realised how pig-headed and ill thought out this had been.

"We're doing this for *you*," said Hunter.

"I know, but what are you expecting to find?" I said.

Robin put his hands on his hips. "She's clean," he said as if he was a detective.

"No, she isn't. I just know she isn't..." said Hunter spotting a framed photo and approached it slowly. "It's her and two..." but as Hunter touched the framed photo something terrible happened.

A deep rumbling sound echoed around the room, shaking the floor. Then, I thought my eyes were deceiving me. A giant spiked boulder, as tall as the room, rolled out of the fireplace.

"*AHHHHHHHH!*" we cried. Sprinting for the exit, we burst through the tapestry and back into the long corridor. But, as we turned the boulder blasted its way after us, scattering stone and statue all around... we were about to be crushed and spiked to death!

"SOMEONE DO SOMETHING!" Hunter screamed lagging behind us. I was so startled by the appearance of a giant spiked boulder, that my thoughts were frozen. It was gaining on us, closer and closer. We were running out of corridor! — We were inches away from a very spiky, painful death.

"The shoes!" Robin screamed at me. Of course! I reached behind and grabbed Hunter by the scruff of the neck as Robin snatched my sleeve. I jumped and clicked the heels together twice as the shadow of the boulder engulfed us.

Time slowed. In that second, as golden light filled the air, one of the spikes pierced my shoulder. "*AHH!*" I screamed with pain. Gold light whisked us away, blasting forwards through the corridor. Wind and air beat our faces as we zoomed through corridors at the blink of an eye.

"*WOAH!*" Hunter cried as we zoomed, far ahead and away from the killer boulder and landing in a heap outside our dorm room. Where we lay, panting.

"That was way, way, way… *way* too close!" said Hunter into the carpet. I rubbed my shoulder where small beads of blood had leaked onto my jumper. The spike had made a hole in it! Small threads of wool were dangling, shredded by the razor sharp boulder spike.

"I don't understand why she would have such a thing!" said Hunter. "It could be tearing the school to shreds right now, let alone people… We need to alert everyone! Before they get spiked!"

Robin sat up and rubbed his eyes. "No we don't…" I sat up and looked at Robin. "If we admit to being up there, we will be exspelled, mark my words."

"But mate, people could be dying right now!" I said.

Robin smiled and shook his head, as he tapped the glasses. "No one's going to die. That boulder was an illusion…"

CHAPTER ELEVEN
Distorted Magic

I didn't know what time it was that we got back into our beds. But I sure felt tired when the alarm went off, and we had a full day of lessons!

The hole in my jumper was really annoying, the loose strands hung just in my eye line—I wondered if I could get it fixed? Would I have to get the Djinn to fix it? Hunter was dead sure that because Magisteer Simone had set a booby trapped spiked boulder after us, that it meant she was already guilty of setting the accidents on me. Robin however, was unsure and concluded that perhaps Hunter wanted it to be Simone, because she kept giving him detentions.

Some strange thoughts in my head suggested that perhaps she was in love with Malakai? And found out that I was the one who defeated him and now she set out for revenge. I laughed, what a crazy idea.

The next night I saw someone *staring* at me. It was so weird. I didn't know who the person was, but from their orange robes assumed it was a third year. I was just leaving the bathrooms after dinner, thought I'd get washed early and go to sleep because I was knackered. This person stood staring straight at me along the corridor — like he was in a trance.

"You ok?" I called, as there was no one else around. But he didn't say anything, he just stood staring at me, his eyes following me as I walked away, rather quickly, back to my dorm.

But that was just the start of the strange and weird things that were to follow…

***

I sat up at the call of the alarm, noticing Graham and Simon both sitting up watching me. "*Woah…*" I croaked sleepily. "You both all right?"

"Yes, are you?" they said together, then exchanged annoyed looks with each other.

"I was speaking!" said Graham.

"No, I was!" Simon replied.

"Can I get you breakfast Avis?" said Jake, as soon as he opened his eyes.

"No thanks…" I frowned confused, adjusting the arms of the jumper, it had gone all writhed up where I'd slept in it. I shouldn't have slept in it really, but I was so tired that I couldn't be bothered to take it off.

Jake seemed upset by my rebuttal and left instantly. Simon and Graham then argued with each other about who would be the best person to bring me breakfast, before they both left. Robin looked over his sheets at me with a '*what on earth is going on?*' look.

Throughout the day I noticed strange *looks* in people's eyes. Their gaze lingering on me for a fraction too long. It felt as if they were leering, ready to pounce. If I wasn't already anxious enough, it just made my nerves ten times worse. I stuck as close to Robin as I could. Sitting down to lunch, my table started asking constant questions whether the food was all right.

It was all becoming too much — something had gone wrong, or this was some awful practical joke…

In classes, Magisteer Wasp insisted on only asking me the answers to the questions, even when I know I got them wrong he said I was right. Everyone in the class applauded violently. Except Robin.

In Numerology, Magisteer Commonside insisted that all my numbers were in alignment. "The magical double's are exuding from every pore of your body! Elevens, Twenty-twos! Thirty-three's!" I didn't know what he was on about, but he seemed charged with more emotion than I had ever seen in him.

Robin was becoming increasingly frustrated, especially when Yearlove ignored his homework that he'd spent so long on, preferring to announce that my homework was the best he'd ever seen, without looking at it.

At dinner, I was exhausted. This popularity thing has got out of hand. People were being too nice, it verged on madness. For instance, all my dorm had shifted so close around the table to me, that I had no room to eat. And then, there was an argument as Ramid Khan and Jack Zapper from another form came over and asked to sit with us—or more specifically, with me. Gret, Joanna and Dennis stood, ready for a fight.

"He's *our* form mate!" said Gret.

"Yeah, go get your own, this is our table, it's already too cramped!" said Dennis.

Jake stood and squared up to Dennis. "What is this supposed to mean?"

"You can't hoard him," said Ramid. "It's his decision, isn't it Avis?" I could feel a fight ready to break out.

"Look," I said as all eyes rested on me. "This is very flattering, but really, this is too much—"

"See!" Gret cried. "You've upset 'im now!"

"It wasn't us who upset him!" cried Jack Zapper.

Now Hunter stood pointing frantically at them. "It was too! He was fine until you came over."

I left as quickly as I could, pulling Robin along after me. I was so glad that he was immune to the jumper—for something had gone wrong. Terribly, terribly wrong.

***

"That's the last piece of wood," said Robin, spelling it to the door.

"Do you think it will hold?" I said, biting my nails.

BANG! BANG! BANG! Came the crowd outside our dorm room. They were trying to get in. As we got back to the dorm, person after person knocked to ask if they could come in. But they didn't go away when we asked them too, they just stayed. Then fighting broke out, and now they were all trying to get in.

"Something's gone wrong hasn't it?" I said.

Robin shot me a fierce glance. "Of course it has! It's that bloody jumper!"

"Do you think Magisteer Simone found out and put a curse on me?"

"No!" said Robin exasperated with me. "It's from a *Djinn*! Do you know how dangerous it is to take a prize from a Djinn?! Did you listen to nothing that Yearlove said?"

"Yeah but…"

"Come on mate, admit that it's your fault."

"Fine, it's my fault!" I cried, anger rising at Robin. "It's the spiked boulder that did it. The cut in my jumper, it made all the magic go wrong. Stupid Hunter convincing me to go, and stupid Simone for having a spiked boulder!"

"Don't blame her, *we* trespassed…"

"It was your idea! And I saved your life!"

"It was Hunter's idea actually. And thanks," he said, not very convincingly. BANG! BANG! BANG! Came the crowd outside. Some of the wood on the door splintered with an ominous growl. I was starting to sweat now. What would they do if they did get in? Robin began looking outside the window to see if there was an escape we could make, before he turned back glowering at the jumper. "Listen, you need to take the jumper off…" he said. I hesitated. "You have to take it off Avis!" BANG! BANG! "Do you not understand?

224

It's gone wrong! Listen to them out there, the jumper has sent them *crazy*! Don't tell me you actually enjoy it?"

"Of course not, it's just…"

"It's just what?!"

"It's just nice to be liked, to be popular for once."

Robin stared at me, deep brows furrowed and I noticed large black bags under his eyes. "So… that's what you wished for… I'm your friend. I have stuck by you through everything…" he turned to the window again and looked out, arms folded as another loud BANG echoed across the room. He couldn't even look at me. "You value our friendship that much, that you aspired to be so popular that you wouldn't need me anymore. I am the default friend, the one that will always be here. Reliable Robin waits around for his friend that everyone loves, is that it?" he said in a slow, soft voice.

"No! It's not like that. I just wanted to… I don't know, it was stupid now I think about it. But I never took our friendship for granted. You're my best mate."

He didn't turn around, but stayed stubbornly still with his arms crossed. "Look, I was excited about the prospect of having a wish. When I found that incense holder at the carnival, I bought it because it had the same mark on it as my pendant. I didn't know it had a Djinn inside. Only after our lesson with Yearlove did I realise that. And then, I admit the idea of having that wish consumed me. You only want what you don't have, right? I just wanted people to like me without any predisposition about what my name is. You saw that girl that attacked me in the Chamber, just because I'm a Blackthorn? I raised the Djinn and asked if I could be popular, some part of me thought Tina would… *like* me again. Everything was working fine, until I snagged it on that spike." I sighed as Robin still scowled out of the window. "…I'll take the jumper off…" Now he turned slowly and waited, arms crossed.

Goodbye jumper, I said solemnly in my head. This was the right thing to do, it had gone bad. I sighed and pulled it upwards.

But… it wouldn't budge. I frowned and tried to slip my arms out of the sleeves, but they wouldn't go. The jumpers wool arms contracted, holding onto my arms tight. "I can't get it off!" I said, panicked.

"Oh, you really will do anything to try and keep it won't you!" Robin cried.

"No seriously Robin, help me!" Robin came over and took hold of the bottom of the jumper and yanked, but it just contracted and stuck to me like a coiling snake.

"Oh…" he said confused.

BANG! BANG! EEEEK! — the door cracked in its frame. Bits of wood we spelled to the door were splitting. "We need to get out of here!" I said.

Robin span around. "How? Where?"

"The clock tower."

Robin shook his head. "Yeah but how do we get out of this room first?"

"Isn't there a spell that can help us?" I said hopefully.

"Oh yeah, there's the transportation spell we learn in about six years, or the flying spell we'll never learn if we get killed by the mob out there!" he gesticulated frantically.

"Can't we fire spell our way out? Use it as a distraction?"

Robin just looked more maddened by the second. "Yes, let's do that, lets set everyone on fire!"

"As a distraction?" I offered hopefully as three more loud BANGS split a piece of wood in two.

Then Robin looked at me with an open mouth. "Fire?" he said. "The fireplace!"

"We can't get up there can we? Anyway I don't like small spaces," I said as Robin jumped forwards and peered up it. Then, in a flash he was inside. A second later he had disappeared. As the door smashed once again, the hinges

226

squealing I realised it wouldn't hold any longer. Without a second glance, I jumped into the fireplace after Robin.

It was just big enough. It was a good job we were both thin, Hunter certainly would not have managed it. All I could see looking upwards was Robin shuffling upwards kicking soot and dust in my face. It was black and the smell was awful, like a hundred crap barbecues. I had my feet perpendicular to the wall and slid myself up, getting the jumper all dirty. Then, below us I heard a big CRASH! They had smashed the door open. Now, shouts and cries filled the air, followed by disappointed wails and moans. I had to find a way of getting the jumper off.

Robin pulled me out through the fireplace of an old classroom above. I stumbled through the ash and soot and came to a stand. Patting ourselves down we sent plumes of soot into the air causing much coughing. We were a floor up, above the madness downstairs. It looked like this classroom hadn't been used in a hundred years — old leather bound books lay strewn around on oak desks and the window was boarded up.

"We need to get to the clock tower without being seen..." I said. After performing a couple of spells over ourselves, we set off. Robin unlocked the door of the classroom, I grabbed him, set the destination in my head and double tapped the shoes.

We pushed open the roof hatch and clambered inside. The wooden rafters reached up ever so high into a tall pitch. The room had two very large glass clock faces at opposite sides to each other, telling the time backwards. To the left was a huge bell and a load of cogs and nubbins that made the clocks work. Robin looked better already for being up here in the quiet, calming seclusion of the clock tower. The views up here were outstanding, I had spent many an hour watching the sunset and sunrise over the hills of Happendance.

Robin sat cross-legged and very still, he was more terrified than me, and I was the one everyone was after, the one with the jumper that wouldn't come off.

"This is bad, a Djinn…" Robin kept repeating over and over. "We need to tell the Lily as soon as we can. He will be able to sort this out."

I sighed. "I can't tell the Lily."

"Why on earth not?!" said Robin sharply.

"Because he will exclude me from school!" I said. "Think about it, if I tell him the truth, that I raised a Djinn, he will exclude me immediately."

"Just say… it was an accident, that you didn't mean to."

"He will know it wasn't."

***

At ten to midnight, Robin stood and announced that he was going to get some food. His stomach had been rumbling for the last three hours and now he couldn't wait any longer. "I'll go," I said as Robin laughed maniacally. "What? I can use the shoes, be there and back in a second. Look I can't hide up here forever!"

"You're not going anywhere, just stay here until I can think of a plan!" He marched out of the clock tower slamming the roof hatch.

I sat, on the hard floor feeling useless. Robin was at his wits end with me. I felt like I was treading on eggshells around him, if I said the wrong thing he would just snap at me. After half an hour, Robin hadn't returned. I started to worry—what if they had cornered him demanding to know where I was? What if they had attacked him to get information out of him? But then, my worry subsided as the roof hatch squeaked.

"Your back at last! You took ages," I said. But when I turned I nearly screamed with fright. It wasn't Robin at all. Through the darkness loomed Tina.

"So this is where you're hiding," she said, opening the hatch fully and coming inside. "I should have known."

Tina smiled, but it wasn't the beautiful white smile I knew. It was… *different*. With a knowing knot in my stomach at her presence I noticed that she had the same glint in her eye that the others downstairs had. She came and sat in front of me, cross-legged.

"Jasper wouldn't want me to come here, but I did anyway."

"Oh," was all I could manage. She was wearing her polka-dot pyjama's and a long red dressing gown.

"Avis, I am so, *so* sorry that I haven't been able to talk to you!" she cried, exploding with words. "Just so, so sorry! It was Jasper, he told me that I had to choose and that it would just make it all awkward if I continued to talk to you as well. I am just so sorry. So sorry that I never realised how… *dishy* you were." Her tone changed in an instant — now slow and seductive — dark eyes blinking softly, face leaning in close to mine, her lips pursed. But for one awful heart bursting moment, I remembered why she was doing this. It wasn't me, it was the jumper. I lent back, avoiding her kiss. She looked annoyed.

"But Avis, I know everything is messed up and horrible, but you do still like me don't you? I *know* you do." She lent forwards again.

I scrambled backwards, along the floor. She followed. I backed away, wishing Robin could come back soon. "I just can't help myself… it's not *my* fault we were warned away from talking to you."

I stopped. "What do you mean warned away from talking to me?" I said.

"Me and Erns and Dad, we were warned not to talk to you anymore, otherwise *bad things* would happen. But, never mind that we're talking now aren't we?" she smiled seductively again as I backed straight into the bell. There was no room left to back into. She approached slowly.

I swallowed. "Who was it who warned you away?"

"I don't know, does it matter?" she was closing in, the evil glint in her eye gaining on me. Her lips moved in again.

"I *see…*" came a long slow, poisonous-sounding voice from the other side of the room. "You lure her here to steal her away from me?" It was Jasper. Standing with a face like thunder. I had never seen him so angry. My heart jumped into my throat.

"It's not like that…" I said scrambling away. "Seriously, look can both of you go away."

"You don't mean that!" Tina cried lunging at me.

Jasper jumped forwards and grabbed Tina, holding her tight and inspecting her. "What magic have you put on her? What have you done to make her like this?"

"I haven't done any magic!" I said, strictly this was true.

"Rubbish! This is *dark magic,*" he called inspecting Tina's glazed, maddened expression.

"No," I said, but in a flash, Jasper raised his hands behind his head and threw them at me. Red and blue fire spiralled in the air and catching me square in the jaw. I felt myself sailing backwards as bursts of hot and cold lit my skin on fire. "*AHH!*" I cried as vicious pain cycled through my body. Green wind shot towards me faster than lightning. "*Dancidious,*" I said limply through crippling waves of pain — the black paw swiped Jasper's spell out the air, which spun into the bell — CLANG!

Jasper marched fast towards me. "TELL ME WHAT YOU HAVE DONE!" Hands raised high behind him, streams of red sparks began shooting at every available space of my body.

I jumped to my feet waving my arms in a circle. "Dancidious!" I screamed again, repelling most of the fiery balls. Before screeching with pain as one of them burned my ear with a fizzing sound. "*Pasanthedine!*" the wind shot from my hand, but Jasper cast it aside. "*Sevhurton!*" I called as ice flashed underneath Jasper who slipped, but in a second he reduced the ice to water and steadied himself. I couldn't think of what to do next, but I had to end this.

"STOP THIS! STOP IT!" Tina screamed jumping between us — with a flick of his hand Jasper made Tina slide back along the floor.

"Stay back from him!" He cried, raising his hands back at me, high into the air, a manic expression on his face. I jumped into the air and double tapped the shoes, gold light lit the room and with ten tons of force, charged at him. Hitting him hard in the chest, I knocked him to the floor, pinning his arms back using all of the force I could muster. He kicked hard, pummelling from all sides. But I stood firm. As Jasper struggled, I felt my grip loosen. In a flash he flipped me over.

"Tell me what you did to her!" he spat viscously, his face red and livid. "How did you charge me so fast? What dark magic are you using? Did your parents teach you it?"

"Get off me!" I called — as Jasper leaned over me, his pendant came loose. I stopped struggling for a second — for it was exactly the same as mine.

WHOOSH! — A sudden flash of blue and orange smoke made Jasper fly backwards into the air, hitting the bell which bonged loudly. I stood quickly. Robin was back, hands outstretched towards Jasper.

"What are you both doing here?" Robin called, observing Tina who was standing rather dazed in the corner.

Jasper peeled himself from the bell. "I came for Tina, she's been... spellbound by him!" he shouted.

"We're trying to fix it," said Robin.

I stood panting and brushed the dirt off the jumper, the hole had got bigger after the tussle which would only make things worse. "Aha!" said Jasper slowly coming towards me finger outstretched at the jumper. "Now I get it. This all started when you got that jumper? You did something to get it, but what?" he said, more to himself. "You found something that had a spirit inside didn't you? And you released it. Yes, that's it, it must have given you a wish and you wished for Tina!"

"Not quite," I muttered.

Jasper huffed. "Not quite? So you did wish for Tina!"

"No, he didn't!" Robin cried. "How did you know he'd received a wish?"

Jasper grimaced. "Process of elimination, and certain things I'd spotted this year. The fact that you were sneaking around the school all year. The fact that you could hardly hide your excitement when Magisteer Yearlove told us about Djinn and incarcerated spirits. So you wished for Tina, to try and prize her away from me! You were jealous!"

"For the last time, I did not wish for Tina… anyway you can't wish for *love*." I lied. "I wished for… popularity."

"Oh-*ho-ho*," Jasper cried as if he couldn't believe what he was hearing. "That is a good one." Then he turned back to face me. "You expect me to believe that? Blackthorns don't care about *popularity*, they care about power, greed and possession!" he gesticulated towards Tina. "Everyday I have to live with the fact that my father… my *father*…" tears split Jasper's eyes but he didn't rub them, keeping his fists tensed. "He was a great man. And they… he… Malakai and his band of followers, including your parents… killed him!"

Robin sighed. "Look, Avis is a lot of things but I know full well, that he is nothing like his parents, or family. He is a victim of them as much you are."

Jasper wiped his eye and nodded, smiling viciously. "I am going to tell the Lily everything. Raising a spirit in the school… You will get exspelled for that," he said eyes lighting up.

"Please don't…" I said, but it was no good — there was nothing I could do or say to stop him. He took the dazed Tina by the arm and left, smiling as he slammed the roof hatch.

CHAPTER TWELVE
To Vanquish a Djinn

I was in trouble. Jasper was about to tell the Lily everything. I wrenched at the jumper attempting in vein to remove it, but the harder I pulled, the tightly it clinged to me — until, after a few large yanks I was suddenly gasping for air, the wool strands contracting. Robin stood, looking melancholy at the now dirty pile of sandwiches that were laying strewn across the floor.

"I need to burn it!" I said.

"You can't burn it off, you'll set yourself on fire!"

I stopped and glowered at him. "No! I need to get it off and then burn it. If the Lily finds out the truth I'm done for!"

I pulled and pulled and pulled, but to no avail. I had to find out a way to get it off.

Yearlove's voice began to echo round my head as we shot to the Library in a blaze of golden light: *"The spirits inside are immensely dangerous, and if they can cause you damage for any reason they will. Often the wish you request will come back to bite you."*

Why didn't I listen?

The book about Djinn that I'd stolen from the Library was still in my bag. I reached inside quickly and pulled it out. It was a black leather bound book with red scratchy writing on the side. '*The History and Process of Incarnate & Discarnate Beings and their Uses: A Practical Guide*' read the spine.

Robin didn't know what to say, he had run out of expletives. But I was panicking — I had to do something to save my place at Hailing Hall.

I flicked through the index and ran my finger down the subjects desperately hoping that *how to undo a Djinn's magic* or something would be in there. Robin was sitting quietly, wrapped in a blanket, staring at the moon. The page before the evocation instructions had the chapter headline: *BEWARE*. I read on:

Before you think about raising a Djinn, you must think how much you value your life. As we've discussed in this book so far, the Djinn are an incredibly cunning, clever, and malevolent race. They will do anything to ensure their freedom. Many times, the lure of a wish is too much and one jumps in to get it. However, the Djinn are clever, they give you <u>exactly</u> what you wish for. But this can leave a lot of room for interpretation. Wishes always have a bite in the tail.

I sat back feeling glum. Why hadn't I read this sooner? "Hate to say I told you so..." said Robin still looking out of the window. I felt stupid. Very, very stupid.

All of a sudden, blue light lit up the clock tower, as a glowing ghostly face rose up through the floor. "The Lily would like to see you, in his office. Immediately." Then, the ghost vanished with a pop. Robin turned and looked at me gravely. I felt a stone drop in the pit of my stomach.

Slowly as I could, I made my way down to the Lily's office. Robin walked silently by my side, he knew I was about to be exspelled. I walked as slow as I could, taking it all in for what could be the last time. This school, my home — I had blown it.

The corridors were completely empty, thank goodness. My heart was beating at a frantic rate, my skin felt clammy and mouth dry as chalk. I didn't want to go home! He couldn't make me could he? The long corridor lay out in front of me, the Lily's office with its huge white double doors stretched up as high as the ceiling.

"This is it then," said Robin robotically. "Good luck." I nodded once, unable to speak. For my fate was waiting inside that room. But as I began to walk, I felt something tingling in my arms. Then my chest. Then... my neck. I stopped walking, as I tried to work out what was happening. It was the jumper, it was tightening! The strands were contracting like a snake, squeezing me tighter and tighter. I bent forwards with the pain, all the air being squashed from my lungs.

Robin stopped dead staring at me. "What's happening?!" he cried. "AVIS!"

All I could manage was gasping breaths as the jumper began strangling me with its thick woollen hands! I grabbed fistfuls of wool and pulled. But it was too strong — grip harder than steel. "HELP! *HEEEELLLPPP!*" Robin cried.

Running footsteps echoed up the corridor, then voices and blurred faces. "Oh no!" cried the voices.

Robin cried. "Please, you've got to help him, I don't know what to do!"

"We must help Avis Blackthorn!" they said.

"I want to save him!" said another arriving on the scene.

"No!" cried the sixth years. "We are saving him, now go away."

I couldn't hear the rest, my consciousness was fading. They were arguing about who would be the one to save me, as I lay struggling for breath. I started to see stars, and hazy colours. The energy was fading out of me as all noise and light began to dissipate.

A flash illuminated the hallway. I felt the strangling hands fall away. I could breathe again — great lungfuls of air swept into my body. I could see again… the tall, white outline of the Lily stared down at me.

I sat on a stool in the Lily's office, dazed and emotionless. Clutching my neck and sides as he walked around me in long smooth circles, waving his arms like a conductor. The hole in the shoulder knitted back together, grey flashes sparkled around it.

"Take it off," said the Lily. I felt weak, but stretched my arms out, pulling it up and off. At last. The Lily stared at it in the middle of the floor. White light burst from the seams. Exploding in a fierce fire, the jumper burned to ash. And, was gone.

The Lily sat back at his desk and turned away from me, staring out of the long, tall window that survey the entirety of the Hailing Hall — the grounds, the floating island, the hills and caverns in the distance. He turned back and indicated for me to stand before his desk. This was it, the part where he told me I was out of here and to get my stuff and leave.

"I am not just angry that you knowingly helped a known Djinn find freedom. I am not just angry that you broke into Magisteer Simone's private living quarters. I am not just angry that you searched the Library at night, after you were caught by myself, to look for restricted material. But I am also disappointed because I thought *you* were different. I am disappointed that you demonstrated selfish, self-indulgent and arrogant behaviours. I thought you were different from your family? You stood in here last year and told me that you were nothing like them, you were proud of that. And yet, I find myself having the exact conversation with you that I did with all of your other siblings…"

I felt awful, tears welled up in my eyes and a lump in my throat. I felt ashamed.

"Not just that, but I personally locked away the Djinn you released. In fact it took a team of us, and many months to track and defeat him. In the hope that he should never get to inflict his persons on anyone else in the magical society ever again. And now that work has been reset. Believe me, I can understand *why* you did it," he said softly, his eyes pouring into me. "Don't we all wish to be liked?" then he shook his head. "But that is not the way to achieve it." He nodded towards the small pile of ash which sparked with multicoloured lights. "I would have thought after last year that you would have learned from your mistakes. And strived to do better, proving that you are… *a good Wizard?*"

He had publicly backed me in front of the entire Chamber last year and said that I was a good Wizard. And now, I felt nothing but shame.

"But what are we to do now?" he said. "That is the question." I looked up at him, waiting for the inevitable. The Lily stared up at the white pitched roof, then smiled. "You are the one who released the Djinn, therefore you shall be the one to vanquish it." I swallowed, hoping he was joking. How on earth could I vanquish a Djinn? "Surely you know that the one who released a Djinn is the only one who can vanquish it?" he said, I shook my head slowly. "Djinn will do anything to maintain their freedom. The only way it can guarantee its freedom is… if you die."

"If I die?" I said, and then something popped into my head. All the accidents—the attempts to kill me. They must have been the Djinn!

"The only way it can guarantee its freedom on this plane, is if the person who released it… dies. It's not a nice fact, but it's the truth. And you deserve the truth." The Lily stood sharply and wrapped his knuckles on the table. "Don't mistake this for being let off the hook. I am angry with you. But you can redeem yourself… by vanquishing the Djinn back to the holder it came in. I know for a fact that the Djinn must still be in the school somewhere — it would be too weak in it's released form to travel more than a few hundred feet. It will have stayed here, hidden somewhere to conserve its energy. If you can't do this, then I will have to seriously consider your place in the school. You have until the end of the year," said the Lily finally.

"But, how? I mean, what do I do?" I said.

"You won't go alone, an experienced Magisteer will go with you," the Lily marched towards the big white doors. "Oh and Avis… don't tell anyone about the Djinn or your mission — we will all be in trouble if certain people find out that a Djinn has been let free in school grounds."

***

I woke late and alone in the dorm room. Sunlight streamed in through tall windows showing up the dust in the room. I sighed. I should have been grateful, I was close to never seeing this place ever again.

Walking down to breakfast, I felt naked without the jumper. My stomach rumbling, I slipped into the Chamber as quietly as I could. Instantly, all eyes turned towards me, and then a low booing sound started to echo from all around. They were booing me! I saw the faces that had come up to me when I had the jumper on before, excitedly asking me to be their friend. Now, those same faces were stormy. They certainly did not want to be my friend now— now that they realised their love for me was... *synthetic*.

Jasper was sat with a pleased expression and David Starlight was glaring at me with little more than murderous contempt. I suppose this is what I deserved.

I scuttled, head down, to my table. Glaring embarrassment choking harder than the jumper had. As I sat down, the people on my table didn't look up. Not even Robin, who was staring into his porridge glumly — I saw why, Felicity, the girl Robin had a crush on, was glaring in his direction. I felt responsible.

Partington wasn't in the Chamber. I had almost forgotten what Tina had told me, up in the clock tower — they had been warned to stay away from me.

"Avis! You don't look as dashing in the cold light of day!" cried a voice — Jasper, he was standing, as if about to make a speech. "Everyone hates you for tricking them into liking you with *black magic*," he announced.

Blood burned my veins with anger as he revelled in the audience of the entire Chamber, while I simultaneously tried to think of which invisibility spells I could get away with and which spells to attack Jasper with. "... And they said you were a *good* Blackthorn? Blood runs deep!" he called.

The Chamber watched Jasper with glee, turning from him to me with wide-eyed expectancy. "And I am sure, they will all want to know what it was you did? Well... I will tell you all what Avis Blackthorn did! For I was the one who beat the truth out of him in a duel high up in the school tower!" The crowd bayed, looking around at each other muttering.

"*Don't...*" Tina pulled his sleeve. But Jasper wasn't listening, he was enjoying himself too much, finally the chance he had been waiting for had arrived, and he wasn't wasting a second.

"Avis did black magic to conjure... a *demon*! He used its power to weave a jumper that made Tina, *my* girlfriend, fall in love with him! Because he was jealous!" the Chamber crooned. "But because it was black magic and he didn't know what he was doing, it went wrong, and you *all* fell in love with him!"

Screams of *no way!* And *that's why!* And *I knew there was something dodgy about him!* Rang about the chamber.

"And this is the worst bit..." Jasper cried, one long finger pointing at me. "He... *he*..." but Jasper stopped, shaking his head, as if struggling to utter the next words. Then he shuddered — he couldn't speak. His mouth was sealing shut!

"Spit it out!" shouted Jack Zapper. But Jasper couldn't. I watched on with the rest of the Chamber, as Jasper's lips shut tighter, fading away until... he had no mouth! He snatched at them, trying to pull it open, but to no avail. It was sickening.

"His mouths gone!" shouted Rahmid Khan excitedly.

"That's a black magic spell!" said a fifth year.

My brother Harold was the only one on the Magisteers table who wasn't looking up and continued to sit there while the other Magisteers rushed over to help Jasper. His dark eyes swam slow as a ship along the horizon to me, then away, back to his porridge. It was him. He did that to Jasper. I knew my brother, and I knew that look in his eye.

CHAPTER THIRTEEN
The Seven Sided Room

I was pacing nervously around the dorm. The Magisteer that was helping me vanquish the Djinn was about to arrive.

I had almost worn out the carpet, much to the annoyance of Graham and Dennis who were trying to do their homework together. Graham had been rather behind everyone else in the class and Dennis had taken it upon himself to help.

A short small knock at the door told me the Magisteer was here. A wave of panic ran through me. Who would it be? Partington perhaps? The Lily even? I opened the door slowly to reveal the long, tall, stick thin figure of Magisteer Straker. A cold stone dropped inside me. Of course, it was Magisteer Straker. He looked down at me with all the warmth of an ice cube. He was a strange looking man — he had a completely straight back, with a long neck, and a tall head. His hair was short and black, speckled with grey. The rest of his clothes were grey too, apart from one white lace handkerchief, folded in his breast pocket.

"Come on then," he turned and walked beckoning me to follow.

I followed Straker for what felt like miles, in absolute silence. We walked and walked and walked. Up one corridors and down the next. I looked up at the tall grey figure, gliding along just in front of me with a bored, annoyed face (or was that his normal expression?) We walked all the way along the Big Walk, past all the people emerging after a lovely big dinner, my stomach rumbled.

Then, all the way along the fourth year dorms, past everyone going to get washed and ready for bed.

My legs started to ache, we were high up in the school where the seventh years slept now. Straker continued to walk slowly, eyes fixed ahead and nothing coming out of his mouth. I mean, I would have perhaps liked an introduction like '*this is how you vanquish a Djinn,*' or '*we will walk this way to see if its down there.*'

Maybe Straker would just deal with it if we found it? Yeah, I mean, they couldn't expect me, a child, to deal with it could they?

We were down low, in the cavernous dungeons. The walls were black, there was no light and my skin bobbled with goosebumps. Straker sighed, he looked tired and bored too.

"Erm… Sir, how long do you think we will be… walking."

"Oh it speaks," he said. "I was perhaps under the suspicion that you were a mute."

"But… I thought you didn't want me to speak?"

"This is *your* mission. I am the *helper*," said Straker, rolling his eyes sounding peeved. "I am following you."

"But I was following you?"

"I know you were," he said. I blinked, feeling too tired for this confusion. "You are in charge. You are the boss," Straker had a way of talking that made you feel unsure the whole time, as if, he didn't really mean what he said. "Perhaps you could start by telling me what happened. The truth."

"What you mean about the Djinn?"

"Yes,"

We continued to walk, and I thought about where to start as I peered through darkness. Straker sniffed. "If you want me to make a light, just ask."

"Yes please," I said. A few seconds later a line of blue fire lit the ceiling of the dungeons and ran all the way along. As I looked around my heart started to race, for bones of animals and… things, lay on the dungeon floor. "And…"

"Find a way out of the dungeon?" he offered.

Every night at 6pm on the dot, Straker would knock upon my door and escort me around the school. He was acting like a petulant elemental at first—he wouldn't do *anything* unless I specifically asked him too. After a short while though it fell into a familiar routine. I would gather some food from the Chamber on the way back from my last lessons, place all the sandwiches and snacks into a hubris hide bag that Jake lent me, slung it over my shoulder and waited for Straker. I mean, he almost got used to me too. Last year he hated me — he was the one who found us after Hunter was attacked by Malakai.

Straker was well known to have a soft spot for some of the Blackthorns. I don't think it meant he was a dark Wizard, but he simply admired all magic. Behind the grey and boring exterior, lay an enthusiastic individual, interested in everything. Straker completely surprised me, he was nothing like I had imagined.

As we scanned the fifth floor classroom areas, Straker had his eyes narrowed and walked like a cat, coiled up as if ready to pounce.

"Is there a something I can do to be able to see better?" I said.

"Yes. But you will be disappointed, there is no magic spell," he turned and looked as if he was sniffing the air. "You narrow your eyes until reality starts to blur and flicker."

I tried it, the corridor ahead did blur and flicker about in a sepia haze. I opened them again, not sure how this would help find a Djinn.

"Djinn work on the periphery of senses. Half in our world, half in another. Only by lessening your senses do you sharpen them. When you lessen your sight, you begin to see in peripheral vision, you see?"

"Kind of," I said carrying on walking, slightly miffed that there wasn't a spell. There probably was but he wasn't allowed to give me it. "What do I do if I find it?"

"Don't you know?" said Straker in an amused tone, staring ahead.

"Well, no, that's why I am asking."

"You must learn it fully and commit it to memory."

I nodded. "Of course."

"Ok," Straker smiled. Waving a hand, a pamphlet dropped out of mid-air and fell gracefully into my hand. It was a dozen pages thick or less. The pages were detailed with pictures and instructions.

"Commit it to memory," Straker repeated. I tucked it away in my back pocket and said I would.

We ate the sandwiches in a disused classroom on the third floor, it was a really old one, for it had statues either side of the blackboard. I think I ate more dust than sandwich.

"Don't like *egg* sandwiches," said Straker like a grumpy toddler before eating it anyway. After a while of sitting in silence, my eyes stinging due to tiredness, for it was very late, Straker looked up at me quizzically. "Why did you do it?"

"Do what?" I said.

Straker picked the corner of his lip with a long grey finger. "Raise the Djinn?"

I looked up at the ceiling, I thought everyone knew? "For the wish," I said.

Straker nodded. "And what did you wish for?"

I paused, feeling embarrassed. "I wished for... popularity... to be liked." Straker looked utterly dumfounded, and disappointed.

"You had a wish from one of the most powerful Djinn ever, and you wished for..." he swallowed, the burst of anger subsiding as he looked out the window. Then he laughed. "Goodness me. You could have wished for *anything.*"

"I know…" I said, and he suddenly looked sympathetic.

"You must have been really sick of being unpopular?" he said as if the concept was foreign to him. "There's so much to do in the world. Good or bad, liked or not liked. We as Wizards have that privilege."

"I just… you know, wanted to be liked by people."

"I was the same when I was young," said Straker. "Never wanted to be a Magisteer… I had a good job before, working for the Magical Council in central Dodecagon. It was an exciting job, every day was different and filled with adventure. Lot's of travelling, meeting important people and keeping the peace between rival Wizarding factions. I was what they call a *Mediator*. I made sure that each rival faction offered a fair deal — it could get quite scary sometimes." Straker's eyes glazed over.

"Why did you leave?"

He blinked. "Too much politics… I got too old… too many bad things… many reasons."

When I got back to the dorm room, Robin was still up, standing still over the fireplace. An orange glow reflecting off the front of his spectacles, and a strange pair of khaki trousers on with lots of pockets which were bulging with objects.

"What are you still doing up at this time? And dressed like that?" I nodded towards the trousers and laced boots.

"Sounds to me like you are not having much luck finding it?" he whispered. "You could probably do with these?" he pointed to his spectacles. "And I've got a pocket full of magic. Shall we go?"

I could hardly refuse. I made a pit stop at the Chamber. Lit by one solitary fire bracket, leaving it horribly dark and empty, and poured myself a big cup of stuff the outsiders drink — *coffee*. Apparently it made you more awake. So, with a hot cup of disgusting brown stuff, we set off.

"I had to help," said Robin. "I don't want to be here without a best friend," he said marching so fast along the Big Walk that I was struggling to keep up with him. "Do you have any idea where about's it could be?"

"Up high I think," I said, panting.

Robin nodded fervently with his tongue out, then looked at me. "Can't you narrow it down a bit?"

"The Lily said that it would be *within a few hundred yards from where it was raised.*"

Robin nodded. "Right, let's start up near the clock tower then. *Occulus!*" said Robin, darting behind a pillar pulling me with him. A small white eyeball tip toed silently along the corridor past us. Robin craned his neck watching it disappear down another hallway. "Coast is clear…"

We climbed the spiral staircase upwards, through the slits in the wall all I could see was black, with the occasional white wisp of cloud. Up here were all the turrets, some had classrooms, others were seventh year dorms, private rooms and places to keep people who had been really bad.

I huffed and puffed as we climbed, already having been up and down these stairs twenty times today already. "We're not going to find anything… if Straker can't see anything then I doubt we will!"

"But you're forgetting I have the spectacles of sight." Robin said proudly, he had taken to calling them the *spectacles of sight*, because he thought it sounded clever. I didn't. "I am getting used to them," he said. "I can spot an Occulus a hundred paces away."

Halfway up the spiral staircase, with my legs burning, we exited through a small doorway. We were somewhere just above the clock tower right in the centre of the school.

"So…" said Robin with his hands on his hips and looking around like a builder. "Within this vicinity, to about a hundred feet, the Djinn should be. Do you know what to do if we actually find it?" he said looking at me, suddenly concerned.

I pulled out the pamphlet and waved it. "Should be fine. I've got this, step-by-step instructions on how to vanquish a Djinn…" I said sarcastically, but he didn't notice it — nodding appeased and walking on.

"These corridors go round in one big square," he said. The corridors up here had long windows from floor to ceiling on our left, continuously the whole way around. Pierced only, by long hanging blood red curtains with gold fasteners, brown doors, lots of green drapes and the occasional statue. I knew another secret entrance to the clock tower was up here somewhere, behind a drape, followed by a climb down a rickety wooden staircase underneath lots of spindly beams.

"What was that?" said Robin, holding a handout. I listened. A door was creaking open behind us. We exchanged looks. Robin turned slowly and peered through the darkness behind us.

"What is it?" I whispered barely audibly.

Robin was staring hard through the glasses. Before he started to back away, pulling me behind a curtain. He didn't take his eyes away from the end of the corridor — I strained my eyes and squinted them, but couldn't see a thing.

"*It's…* completely shrouded in dark magic." He whispered as low as he possibly could. "It's gone… wait here." I could hear Robin's heart beating in its cage next to me. "I don't know what it was… it was small and hunched, and cloaked in black…"

"Where did it go?"

"Down the spiral staircase." Robin moved away from the window, suitably reassured that the mysterious thing was gone. "Do you think that was the Djinn?"

"I've already described what the Djinn looks like."

"Hmm… then what was *that*?" he said. We carried on, hearts beating fast. It was well into the morning hours now, and I had homework due in for tomorrow. Magisteer Wasp was not going to be happy. He was already in a mood with me after finding out about the jumper — along with everyone else.

"I was almost getting somewhere with her you know, Felicity. Until you decided to mess it up for me… I blame Hunter."

"Why Hunter?" I said.

"He was the one who suggested we go and check out Magisteer Simone's. That giant boulder that spiked the jumper, made the jumper all weird, got you caught. Made Felicity hate me…" he muttered.

"She doesn't hate you," I said, he was being melodramatic.

Thankfully, he changed the subject. "You know that giant boulder was an illusion? There was no damage in the school. It was a hex — an illusionary booby-trap."

"If it was an illusion, how did it rip my jumper?" I said, after laughing at Robin saying *booby-trap*.

"Illusions can still rip jumpers," he said matter of factly. "It's about your belief of them. The mind is more important than you think."

"Right…" I said, my eye lids drooping. "Can we go back soon?"

"I've just realised that there are no Occulus's up here. Don't you think that's strange?"

"Not really, I don't think there's any point. No one comes up here." As we rounded the next corner Robin stopped again, and began looking around, squinting at the floor.

"Here…" he passed the spindly wire glass frames to me. "Tell me what you see."

I put them on and looked. Instantly light danced around in front of me. Without them on the corridor looked like all the others, drab and grey. But now, there was light… and it was all concentrated in a small stream towards a place in the wall. The light was multi-coloured and it took my eyes a while to sort through it. Thick pulsing yellows, bright burning reds and fizzing purples clumped together like a massive tangle of technicolour string. There was a lot of magic leading directly into the stone wall.

"It all leads into that wall…" I said.

Robin grinned. "It's not a *wall*…" An ordinary drape lay over the wall.

"There must be a door behind it?" I said. But a trickle of fear slid through me, what if, behind that door was the Djinn? Robin didn't look too concerned and was scanning the outline of the wall with his spectacles as I held the drape up.

"It's not dark magic," he said to me addressing my concerned face. "Honestly, I know the difference now… Aha!"

"What?"

"Found the doorknob, so to speak. It's an energetic doorknob." He pointed to a stone that looked the same as all the others in the wall. "These glasses show a very faint hand print. They must have done magic just before they pressed their hand to the wall," he looked at me. "Press your hand onto that stone,"

I did what he said. The wall in front of us evaporated like it was made of mist. A small enclosed tunnel exactly my height opened. We stepped through slowly. Yellow light zoomed around the cracks between the stones in the tunnel, casting a fizzing sound overhead. After four or five steps, I suddenly found myself in a room.

"*Woah*…" said Robin behind me as he entered. It wasn't big, but it was impressive. There were seven sides to the room and the roof pitched high with old hanging beams. Light came from candles, lots of them scattered around the room, burning soft orange light. A comfy chair sat nearest the window, with a plethora of half read books on a stool next to it. In the middle of the room and taking up most of the space sat the oldest, intricate and decadent round table. On it lay more books, papers and magical devices, some of which I had never seen before. A simple fireplace lay with the faintest of embers.

"Someone's been here recently," I said. I mooched around the room quietly. It looked like someone was using this room to work, the books that lay around were some that I'd never seen nor heard of, some were foreign and some were so old they looked like they would fall apart if touched.

I sat down in the chair, *ahhh*, that felt nice. My legs eased their appreciation, my back smiled, everything in my body thanked me. Robin tutted at me for sitting down as he scanned around the room for signs of Djinn.

As I sat there, I saw the spine of a book at the bottom of a large pile — '*The Seventh Sons*' read the title. Curious, I pulled it out. It was a small, thin and bendy. I opened and had a look inside.

Seventh Son — myth or real?

A seventh son is a term used to describe the seventh male born to two parents — in myth, this is a good omen for the parents, for a seventh son is blessed with immeasurable power. Several stories have led to the idea that seventh sons are so powerful they are dangerous to the magical kind.

From my own findings, seventh sons are more compassionate, open-minded and curious, even when their hereditary nature is not to be so, or their environment disruptive. This is interesting, the fact that because they are a seventh son, this influences their personality — changing their hereditary traits.

When the myth was prevalent in the 1500's, many families tried to have as many sons as they could until they reached the seventh. Alas, it seems many attempts were thwarted by nature. Many parents couldn't cope to feed so many children, or fend off diseases, many died. And many grew frustrated when females were produced. The famous incident of Margret and Humphrey Grubriller, who in 1629, attempted magics to influence the sex of their unborn baby — while it worked, they were sentenced to a lifetime imprisonment for Magical Acts Against Nature.

There are many conditions that have to be met to make a seventh son. Some known, some not known. The magic of a seventh son is still firmly in the hands of nature.

I looked up from the book, wondering if it would fit in my pocket for I was just about to read a chapter about the *'powers of a seventh son'*, before looking up to see what Robin was doing.

"What are you doing?" I said.

"What does it look like?" he strained, winding up what looked like a silver thimble. "Laying some booby-traps. These should tell us if anyone comes in here, and what they are — human or Djinn," he winked. "Got them from the back of the Herrald. Pretty cool huh? If it finds something, like a Djinn… it will alert me."

"How?"

"I don't know, it didn't say… It was only two gold coins." Robin finished winding the little objects up and placed them in cracks around the room. I stood, my body screaming out for my bed. Light was just starting to come in through the window above.

"It must be passed five!" I said. Robin gave me a grimace and we set off extra fast for our beds, the tunnel sealing shut behind us.

I felt buoyed, we had found *something*… whether it belonged to the Djinn or not, it was a start I supposed.

Half way along the corridor, Robin stopped me with a long arm — up ahead was the spiral staircase. And now, I could hear small padded footsteps coming up them. "It's the dark thing again, in fact…" Robin gasped, passing me the spectacles.

Putting them on, I scrambled to look — up ahead I could see through the stone to the thing climbing slowly upwards. Dark light surrounded the body, an aura of black, spitting off dark sparks of energy. The figure was tall, cloaked, horned and masked. My heart started to race, my legs turning to jelly. He was coming up the stairs towards us — Malakai was back!

Robin snatched the glasses back and tried to pull me into a shadowy alcove. All I could do was stand, frozen to the spot. The dark figure emerged from the spiral staircase, but… it wasn't Malakai at all… it was someone else, someone very familiar. It was Jasper.

He looked up, saw us and stared with cold uncaring eyes. It was as if he was sleep walking, barely registering our existence. Blinking rapidly, he began to shake, then came back to himself.

"What are *you* both doing up *here*?" he spat, glancing around at his surroundings.

"Nothing to do with you, why are you here?" I called.

Jasper looked around, settled himself, then said. "I like… early mornings." He was lying, I just knew it. For it all made sense now in my brain — he wasn't Jasper Gandy… he was *Malakai*!

"I knew it!" I said. "I knew there was something odd about you." The black energy that had surrounded him before was gone now I didn't have the spectacles — but I knew what I had seen — a full outline of Malakai surrounded him.

"Excuse me?" said Jasper affronted.

I pointed, my heart racing, in equal measures terrified and angry. "You're him aren't you? Out for revenge, out to get *me*?!"

Robin shuffled next to me. "Avis," he whispered. "I don't think that's—"

"*Shh…*" I said turning back to Jasper. "Now I know and I'm gonna let everyone know what you are!"

Jasper stared at me before spluttering with laughter. "What on earth are you talking about?"

***

Jake excitedly reminded us over breakfast, that we were practicing Riptide that night as a form with Partington. I heaved my consciousness back into this reality, for it was beginning to droop into my porridge — I'd barely had an hours kip and I was exhausted. Robin however, seemed absolutely chipper.

"I can't come…" I said. "Oh, what time are we doing it?"

"After lessons?" said Gret.

"Yeah I can't do it then." I said, closing my eyes for a minute.

I heard some of them round the table winding up for giving me abuse. "And *why* not?!" said Joanna, sounding like my Mother.

Robin piped in for me, saving my bacon. "Detention with Straker," he said. "That's why he's so tired, makes Avis walk about the school at night as punishment."

"What for?" said Hunter aghast. Jake and Graham looked at Hunter as if to say *isn't it obvious?* When he still looked blank, Simon chipped in.

"For that poxy black-magic jumper he wore," he said.

I quietly began to eat some toast hoping the subject would change quickly. I had a plan — go to the first lesson with Wasp, get shouted at for not doing the homework, sneak away just before lunch and sleep for an hour, before an afternoon full of lessons — one with Simone no less.

I was already annoyed because I'd tried to get out of today's lessons by pretending I was ill. I told Partington that morning in form that I wasn't feeling good, he looked at me, said I did look pale and sent me to the Healer with a ghost. I was hoping the lovely Healer would say I looked awful and I must have a lie-down. She did say this in fact, but the poxy ghost that was escorting me, consorted a paper list and decreed that *tiredness* was not a suitable reason for having the day off ill. So, the git escorted me all the way back to form — I even tried to sneak back to my dorm, but it began shouting at me.

Back in the Chamber, Joanna put her toast down and got out a piece of paper. "Look at the glut of games we have coming up!" she said. "We need to be fully prepared in all our tactics to be able to have any chance of winning."

"Yeah especially since we've got a cup game soon," said Graham. "And that's likely to be against an upper year form…"

"We need to train, all together," said Ellen.

"Lunchtimes and evenings!" Hunter said with his finger in the air like he was passing a law.

I was terrified. On one hand, I could join them at practicing Riptide, and make sure we didn't embarrass ourselves again. On the other, I had to explore the school with Straker and look for the Djinn and banish it — otherwise there would be no more Riptide, no more lessons, no more school. I can't survive outside of an institution. I'd have to go home, be treated like a sprat, be bored to my back teeth, or even worse, go to another magical school — I've heard how terrible they are.

Jasper's voice travelled across the Chamber as he boasted about something to his form. I knew what I had seen in the spectacles, he looked like Malakai, and the odd behaviour as he looked at us. My brother Ross used to sleepwalk, and it looked exactly the same as that. But then, Jasper had seemed to wake up and be fully aware. If in fact he was Jasper? A pupil was the perfect disguise for Malakai…

***

After Simone's exhausting lesson in which she had us do at least five hundred sit-ups, I went to the Chamber to get some food. I placed some sandwiches in the hubris hide, along with some biscuits and carrot cake, Straker's favourite. My hands felt clumsy, as the tiredness seemed to exude from my every pore. I was surprised I'd made it this far through the day.

"Hello *friend*," said a cold, slimy voice, dripping down my spine like a slug. I didn't bother turning, I knew who it was.

"What do you want?" I said.

"I want nothing from you," said Jasper, standing close on purpose as I picked at the food. "Do you really think I'll forget about seeing you and your deluded friend poking about the castle in the dead of night?"

"Us poking about? What about you? What were you doing up there?" I said turning to face him, unable to help the angry tone creep in. His eyes were even the same glowing blue colour as Malakai's. His face the same pale white. It made sense, he was Malakai. He'd come back here to get me. "I know what you are!" I said. Jasper smiled amused, which just infuriated me even more.

"Here we go again…" he muttered as people in the Chamber began to look round — I felt my face grow red, my voice rising.

"You're him… And I am going to prove it to everyone… that you are… Malakai!" I announced. There was a short silence before, an explosion of laughter.

— *"He's off his rocker!"*

— *"Pahaha! Paranoid or what?"*

— *"He can't be serious?!"*

The next moment I was being escorted from the Chamber by Magisteer Mallard who told me in no uncertain terms that I could not go around accusing people of that, before slamming the Chamber doors.

CHAPTER FOURTEEN
The Volumino

"AND HERE COME THE CONDORS!" The stadium announcement rang around the stadium to a series of shouts, roars and boo's. We were playing the third year form Mermaid's (not real ones — that would be impossible), in our first ever cup game ever.

Unfortunately, I had been unable to attend any of the extra Riptide practices my form had arranged, all my time had been taken up with searching for the elusive Djinn. The crowd roared hard and I felt the familiar terrified gurgle in my stomach. Joanna was reminding the team of our tactics — she had briefly told me at a hundred miles an hour in the changing rooms, but I'd forgotten already.

Robin was warming up close by a collection of third year girls. One of which was looking purposefully the other way. Felicity sported a purple Mermaid scarf and flag and had a snooty look. Hunter stood near the bolt-hole primed like a cheetah, but looking like a fat human. The noise of the crowd electrified the stadium. My eyes drifted into the crowd — the Lily sat straight backed with a bored expression — he kind of looked like he wasn't really here, mind you, he knew magic some people could only dream about. I bet his body was here at the stadium, but he was actually in his office reading or something. Straker and Partington stood close on the Magisteer's plinth, but were not talking. Mallard and Dodaline were in a deep conversation with Commonside, who was pointing angrily at a sheet of numbers. Wasp, Yelworca, and Yearlove were sitting, Wasp talking softly to Yelworca, probably telling him who was going to win because he had predicted the outcome from the stars.

Then, the Mermaids, who were a tall form, made their way out. It didn't take long before I was standing on the line, waiting for the whistle to go — my shoes ready to tap, my hands ready to spell and the crowd awaiting with bated breath.

***

"WE DID IT!" Gret cried embracing Robin and Simon in a rib-cracking hug. I turned round as Dawn picked me up off the floor.

"You were amazing!" she cried.

Joanna was beaming at me. "You didn't follow any of my tactics, but I am so pleased you didn't!"

"Thanks!" I said as Dennis and Jess began a victory dance. It had been a cracking match. The Mermaids were great — scoring three goals in the first five minutes. We thought we were onto a hiding, but then Underwood sent off their captain for two games for an illegal spell — Ruby Knight, charmed the rook turret on the habitat to come alive and start smashing at us. I don't think she quite realised the extent to what she had done. Anyway, we took advantage and won the match with a "LIBERO-MANUS!"

"And when you jumped off that mound and exchanged the pass with Jake!" Gret cried aloud, causing everyone to clap in agreement. "That was something else!"

In the end we had won the match by four games to one and were into the next round of the cup. I'd scored five goals, and by the end of the match the crowd had come round to applaud me softly — even though some refused. It was the most elated feeling I've ever had. They were applauding me, even though I didn't have the jumper.

On the way back up to the castle some first years waited behind for us, greeting us like we were celebrities and following us all the way back up the hillside to school.

"Think about it for a second!" cried Roger Zapper (Jack Zapper's little brother). "You are second years, and you just beat a third year team!"

***

At first I thought that I and the Magisteer assigned to me would be able to sniff the Djinn out in a couple of hours, then work it back into the incense holder and everything would be fine again. But now I realised how ridiculous this was. Every night Straker and I wandered the school trying to get some sight or sound of it. But we got nothing. Zilch. Nout.

Walking around at night with Straker had it's up sides. I got to see things I wouldn't normally. A few times now, we would be walking along and he'd get an alert from a ghost that someone was out of bed. He would then start to march in the direction of the culprit, me in toe, and I'd get to watch Straker give them an ear-lashing.

Three times now Straker had caught a boy in the sixth year called Aaron Fulford, who had been seeing a girl in the same year called… Frankie or something — they kept sneaking off together in the middle of the night. So Straker split them up.

"It is your own fault for getting caught. You're sixth years, I would have assumed you could have thought up something a little more ingenious to cloak yourselves. This is the third and final time. You can see each other in break, lunch times and after lessons," said Straker sounding thoroughly bored with them. Aaron and Frankie stood like naughty toddlers in the bathroom staring at the floor. "Until then, you can't be trusted…" Straker raised his hands towards them.

"*NO!*" cried Aaron, but he was too late. A red crack split the air between them.

"There. Now you are invisible to each other outside of the times allotted. Come to me at the end of the seventh year and I shall remove it."

Aaron looked around madly, so too Frankie — when neither of them caught sight of the other, both burst into tears. "Bed!" Straker cried. "If I were you, I would concentrate on my studies. It probably won't work out between you both anyway," he said slyly as they made their way out of the bathrooms and back along the corridors to their dorms, completely invisible to each other. I didn't know whether to be fearful, amused or to just not care about what Straker had done.

***

"One more match in the cup and we're in the final!" said Robin. "How *mad* is that?" We were staring up at the Riptide Schedule that had been painted large on the wall in the Hall outside the Chamber.

Condors with a picture of a brown bird and yellow and black frame sat in the list of the last four teams, underneath the words *Semi-Final.* There was an excited buzz in the air, a lot of people had filed into the Hall to check out who would be playing who — at midday, the schedule would be chosen.

In a shock happening, the favourites to win the Riptide cup and league, the Centaurs, had been knocked out by a second year team — the Swillows. Unfortunately, that was Jasper's form. In my mind, that was just another reason why he was Malakai, he could use dark magic to defeat the best Riptide team in school.

In our previous cup match, the *quarter-final* no less, we were drawn a fortunate game against a first year side the

Tiddlegawks. It was the easiest game I've ever played and we felt bad, but managed to get three Libero-Manuses.

The Manticores were watching the draw with bated breath, hanging on to each other. Even some of the Magisteers paid an interest — I could see Straker, standing in the shadows upstairs, casting a cold eye over the proceedings. Jasper and Tina were hanging off each other, with the rest of the Swillows watching on nervously. The draw was between us, the Condors, the Swillows, the Hesserbouts and the Manticores — two second year teams and two sixth year teams. I was excited, everyone was excited to see who we would play in the semi-final. Naturally the two sixth year teams, who saw this as their perfect opportunity to win the cup, now that the Centaurs had been knocked out.

The Hall was packed and as the clock hit twelve there was a whistling noise. The huge painted schedule started to fizz and crackle. Then, the icons moved. Our Condor's brown bird, the Swillows white bird, the Hesserbout's silver sprat and the Manticore's scorpion-tailed-lion, all began to move.

The Hesserbout icon moved first, climbing into the one of the four empty spaces under *Semi-Final*. There was an *ooing* from the crowd as the fizzing white stars made their next move. The Manticores painted icon moved slowly, its form dripping upwards along the line, until it came and sat opposite the Hesserbouts.

That meant, that we were playing the Swillow form! I was playing *Jasper*! The crowd in the Hall broke out with talking, and shouts of excitement as the final move placed the Condors opposite the Swillows.

"We've got to *trash* them!" cried Hunter grasping Robin, Jake and me by the necks with his long arms and pulling us into what he probably thought was an affectionate hug, but felt more like a physical duel. I wrestled myself free, before I was hugged by an excited gaggle of Condor girls.

"The Semi-Final! Can you believe it?" said Ellen, followed by the same remark from all the girls. My heart was racing, the rivalry between me and Jasper felt like it had reached fever-pitch. Some of the crowd were now staring between Jasper and me. Robin gave me a *'you alright about this?'* kind of look — I nodded, my chest felt tighter than when that flower had me in its grips.

***

"I don't want to be exspelled," I said quietly as me and Straker walked slowly and quietly along a discarded corridor.

Straker chuckled. "Of course you don't. Who would?"

"I can't go home…" I muttered.

"It's only fair," said Straker stern voiced. "You can see the Lily's reasoning, anyone else would be exspelled for the same crime — this is your chance to recover yourself. He's given you a chance."

"True," I said.

"It's too dangerous to allow you to stay at the school indefinitely, you'll be putting the other pupils in danger. Don't you see? It's only a matter of time until the Djinn is strong again, and it will be in the school… and who are the majority of people in this school? Children. They will be the victims," he said gravely. "Alas, if the accidents we've already experienced continue we could have a hefty number in the Healers room, or worse. If, however you are exspelled, the Djinn has to follow. It cannot be too far away from you until it gains an independent life force."

"Right, this is probably a stupid question but… why can't the Lily just go after it? He's much more powerful than me." I shivered at the thought of the Djinn following me home — as if home wasn't bad enough.

"You're right… it is a stupid question. There are a number of reasons. Firstly, it will destroy the Lily if he tries

261

to find it. Secondly, only the *raiser* can vanquish it. And lastly, it's your fault, why should the Lily clean up your mess?"

I sighed, he was right, but this was all getting too much. I felt like I would never find the blasted Djinn. I would end up living at home, being haunted by a Djinn — an exspelled, unqualified Wizard, forever.

Needless to say I became exhausted by the whole routine. It became an effort to drag my caucus around to lessons, which were increasing — we now had double the lessons we did at the start of the year. As well as constant Riptide training and daily mile upon mile walks about the school with Straker's miserable face next to me.

It crossed my mind to decide to search up high, near the clock tower and *accidentally* find that hidden room that me and Robin found. The room that, in my mind was Jasper/Malakai's room, the place where he hid all the special books, where he read about seventh sons to try and find out how to end me. Why else would Jasper be up there?

This whole year I had waved the possibility of Malakai returning away… but it was inevitable. If so, I was doomed. Not only did I have a Djinn after me, but also the most powerful Sorcerer alive.

In amongst this mess of routine, for I hardly knew what the day was most of the time — I actually forgot that it was my Birthday. Can you believe that? It took me until midday, after a gruelling lesson with Yearlove, while Robin was reading the Herrald, I was nearly asleep in plate of sandwiches when I looked across and noticed the date.

"Is that today's paper?" I said.

Robin glanced at the front. "Fourteenth of April? Yeah why?"

It was my Birthday and I had forgotten. I was fourteen and no one even realised. I didn't know whether to be sad, or grateful. I bit into a sandwich. "It's my Birthday…"

It was late April. Wind and rain battered the school continually. In class you could hear it hammering the windows and doors, the wind shaking them in their frames. The Magisteers had spent all Sunday reinforcing them with rain repelling spells, but it didn't stop the dungeons flooding, or one of the turret roves to collapse. Thankfully the Riptide Stadium stayed upright.

It was a year ago today that I had saved Ernie and Tina. All day I'd been dreamy, thinking about it. Yearlove asked me questions and I didn't notice, Wasp talked about my stars, I didn't care, and Commonside droned on about the numbers showing up something interesting for me soon, but I wasn't listening. My mind flashing back to that fateful day. The fright I felt descending into that dark basement where Malakai was and confronting him. I remember the dread of seeing his form. My thoughts flashed with the spell that killed me. And then... that wonderful feeling as I stepped onto the golden escalator... I sighed.

I had hardly seen Ernie in months, he kept to himself up in his high tower, alone. I heard that he had moved out of the Phoenix dorm because they were too loud and he wanted to concentrate alone on his work. I missed him. I wish he was a ghost again... no, that was a horrible thing to say. But as least I'd get to see him. In fact I wish I could go back to the first year.

And what about Tina? She was with Jasper now, but it would have been nice for her to acknowledge me — I had saved her and Ernie's life.

***

Straker could see I was flagging, my feet noticeably dragging along the floor as I walked. "Here..." he said as I greeted him with barely more than a grimace outside my dorm. I looked at the concoction of thick looking orange liquid in a test tube.

"What is it?" I said curiously.

"It will enhance our search," said Straker, taking another out of his inside pocket, de-corking it and downing the liquid. I raised the orange stuff to my nose — that was a mistake. *Ergghh*, I wretched. "Just drink it."

"Fine…" I opened my mouth and poured in the thing that tasted like: raw eggs, dirt, soap and toothpaste. With the slightest hint of mango, cucumber and… curry. I clawed at my tongue until the taste eventually passed. Straker stood watching me for a second, until suddenly I felt an enormous swirling inside. I felt energy and optimism start to bubble up, I felt pride and courage, confidence and assuredness. My senses sharpening — I could see far father down the dark corridor, my eyes zooming all the way to the end and reading the number *112* on the door. My hearing was pronounceable better too — I heard the creaking of the wood as someone got into bed. I heard the crackle of an ember, the easing of a stone, the pummelling rain outside, the squelching of someone's wet clothes. Everything was sharp.

"I must remind you, not to tell anyone about this," said Straker taking the empty vile. "Otherwise they'll all want some."

We began to walk the familiar route, but everything about it seemed different. My footsteps echoed with a stoney recourse, my breathing long and slow, my heart pumping rhythmically with a great sloshing sound. After a minute or two Straker stopped, we had just entered a dark corridor. He waited, un-moving — the light bracket behind us went out and we stood in pitch black.

"Stand very still," said Straker moving his hands in awkward movements over my head, then his own. My feet tickled with pins and needles, my skin buzzed and felt for one horrible second like it was contracting. Then, two small pops sounded the end of the spell. Straker beckoned me forwards. The light brackets didn't come on and my footsteps were absolutely silent. With the orange potion coursing through me I could see through the darkness as if the corridor was lit by a million candles.

Straker pulled a tiny silver ball out of his pocket, then threw it into the air. It split into two pieces, the parted silver crescents acting like tiny wings beating ferociously. In the middle of these wings was a pure white eyeball. It seemed to awaken, the retina swinging into motion and darting around as the wings beat hard. From out of the retina a bright blue light, laser focused in a concentrated beam, burst outwards. The blue light began scanning every nook and cranny.

"It's an Occulus' that I *changed*…" said Straker. "It will scan the area up ahead for us with its laser light focus, I reduced the eye in size, changed its sight, upscaled it so that it can spot invisibles, spirits… *Djinn*. It's also indivisible to them, but not to us."

"Woah…" I said amazed that anyone could just create something like this.

"I call it the *Volucer-Illumino* or the Volumino for short."

"It's amazing," I'd never seen anything like it, a flying eyeball that hunted for spirits? It flew far ahead of us down the corridor, its bright blue beam shooting into crevices and crannies, leaving no space unchecked.

"Look it's got something already!" — The Voluminio was flashing it's blue light at us. We ran towards it as fast as we could, Straker had his arms outstretched ready to attack.

"No Volumino, that's the ghost of Magisteer Dodaline's old cat. Yes, I am sure it was always that scruffy grey colour." I laughed as the blue light illuminated a bony cat rubbing up against Straker's leg. The Volumino looked very pleased with itself, it had caught something and now it was teasing the ghost cat by whizzing around its head, the cat watched intently, swiping an old paw at it.

"It might take a bit of adjusting," Straker admitted getting a little notebook out and writing something.

"But why are you doing all this for me?" I said, Straker looked over his notebook. "I mean, the potion, the spells, the Volumino…"

"Who said I was doing it for you?" he smirked.

"Well, I thought you were helping me to… find the… Djinn?" I stuttered.

Straker tucked the notebook into his breast pocket. "We were getting nowhere were we? I had to think of something. There is no sentiment here, whatever you might think — I have a job to do, help you find and vanquish the Djinn. And this…" he pointed to the Volumino. "Is me doing my job. Just don't tell anyone about it."

***

Where on earth had the time gone? Only two months of school remained. They were supposed to be for learning, or maybe extra curriculum activities like playing Riptide. They were not for spending all your waking hours searching for one of the most powerful Djinn, to save yourself from being exspelled. And then, just as I was starting to get hopelessly perturbed and panicked by the lack of progress, something happened…

Two weeks with the Volumino and so far it had found: a rat eating demon in the dungeons, a golem pretending to be a wall, a Florax (a kind of devilish, naughty two foot tall creature that likes to collect teeth, fallen out or *not*) amongst other things.

I grew quite attached to the little thing, it was like having a tiny efficient pet around the place, zooming just ahead of us. But on this particular night, all was quiet. We were searching up high, near the tallest turrets in the school — I was hoping there wouldn't be a window because I think I'd have feinted if I saw the drop. Straker and I stood before, what everyone in the school had dubbed '*the death corridor*' — it was just any other corridor, except for the fact that it was very old, and held up exclusively by magic. When looked at from below, the death corridor looked unsafe, suspended in mid-air between two turrets. It was the only way to get across to the other side of the school — this high up anyway.

Even Straker was having second thoughts as we stared along the old passage, but it was too late to turn back now — it would take hours to walk back the way we had come. The Volumino had already zoomed down it, scanning the crumbling walls and sloping mullioned windows. Straker, sensing my panic of crossing the treacherous corridor, threw his hands wide, all the dusty curtains swung shut. I tip toed alongside Straker who strode forwards.

As we reached the half way mark, the Volumino stopped, *flash, flash* went its signal. No, not now!

My breath withdrew inside me, my heart contracting. The Volumino's blue light shot round and for a second, cast light on a small, hunched, dark cloaked figure with blue glowing eyes.

A tiny clawed hand jerked. The tiny Volumino smashed against the ceiling in a blaze of blue fire. Then fell to the floor with a thud.

"Avis—" but Straker didn't have time to finish what he was saying. With no warning, the hunched figure clapped — the spell rippled through the air.

A cracking, splintering noise echoed ominously. The floor was beginning to give way! I looked back, my worst nightmare confirmed... the spell was collapsing the corridor! It was starting to fall in on itself! Straker grabbed me by the scruff of the neck and pulled hard. But, we started to slide down, legs giving way beneath us. Twenty feet behind us was the exit. I had to act, or we wouldn't make it. I jumped up against the almost vertical floor, grabbing a fist of Straker sleeve. CRACK! Went the floor, it was falling backwards — we had seconds! I double tapped the shoes, gold light erupted in a frenzy. I began to run against the vertical corridor as Straker cried out. The shoes connected with carpet. A burst of speed somehow pushed us forwards, scrambling up the carpet. Using everything to scratch our way up. But, a gap had formed between corridor and safety. The corridor had broken away from the turret! I pulled at Straker's sleeve, holding it tight Before… sprinting and jumping. Wind wailed, gold light lit the dark blue sky temporarily as we soared across it. The dark gap yawned beneath us.

And then… floor. We slid into the safety of the turret as the death corridor broke away completely and fell.

"*NO!*" Straker cried, leaning over the precipice. He aimed his hands at the block of falling stone — its descent slowed, then stopped in mid-air. Straker was breathing heavily, arms and hands trembling. His face drawing pale. Below was the fifth floor, the corridor would fall into the school causing unknown damage… I lay useless, what could I do? Red sparks shot out of Straker's hands, zooming across the dark night and into the Lily's office window.

A second later the Lily appeared, climbing his window and onto a stone plinth that appeared as he walked, he raised his hands instantly. The weight of the corridor being taken caused Straker to collapse. The Lily sailed the collapsed corridor gracefully down towards him, placing it neatly on the lawn below. He fixed us a stare from his plinth, a voice next to us suddenly said: "*Come to my office.*"

I lay back on the stone floor. My hammering heart beating like a drum. Straker sat shaking his head. "How on earth did we get out of that?" he said. There was a funny little buzzing noise above our heads. "You made it!" I cried as the Volumino, flapped towards us. It made a funny whistling noise in greeting, beating furiously to stay in the air, it's wings cracked and juddering. The retina and blue light flashing all over the place. Straker cupped his hands softly around it, closing the silver wings over the eye until it stopped moving.

"The Lily will not be happy about this," said Straker looking out of the gaping hole in the turret where the corridor used to be.

"Whatever that thing was, it was powerful right?" I said, but Straker said nothing.

We walked back in silence. The events had clearly shaken Straker up, me as well, I felt giddy. If it hadn't been for the Seven League Shoes we'd both be splattered all over the school roof by now. It couldn't have been the Djinn for that was tall and transparent. This thing that attacked us, was short and stubby — the same thing I'd spotted in under the stadium, in the toilets and now again, but what was it?

Outside my dorm before leaving to go to see the Lily alone, Straker turned. "Can you please beat the Swillow's on Saturday," he smiled then grimaced as he walked away into the darkness. The ominous feeling of something bad being about to happen was a keen sense that I'd developed from living with an evil family. And I felt it now.

***

Partington was pacing up and down, kicking up dust. The dorm room was stuffy and nervous — one more sleep and we would be playing the Swillows in the semi-final of the Riptide Cup. Everyone was fraught with nerves. Hunter kept trumping which stank the room out and Simon had completely chewed his fingernails until they started bleeding. Partington's owl-like face was scrunched up with what looked like painful contemplation. Joanna was reading out tactics to employ against the Swillows based on their apparent weaknesses.

Graham tutted. "Ah, but you see there Jonna what you say about having two people follow Jasper — shouldn't it be three?"

"But," said Joanna. "If we make it three, we will have to sacrifice the defence for Robin hunting for the Ornaments."

"I see," said Partington rubbing his lined face.

"I can help mark him?" I said gleefully.

"No!" said Jake and Gret. "You are our top goalscorer. We need you to do just that."

"Okay, okay, I was only kidding."

Jake huffed. "This is no time for jokes." I thought about telling Jake that we were not going to war, this was just a game. Believe me, I wanted to get one over on Jasper and the Swillows as much as the rest — the whole reason I had risked going to the Library at night was to find a way of being good at Riptide, so to prove a point to Jasper and Tina. And this grudge match would be the pinnacle of that point. But I didn't want to sit here running over all the different tactics that we'd forget as soon we stepped onto that pitch.

"Jess!" said Gret. "Pay attention!"

Jess sat up, looking sleepy. "Don't tell me what to do, who do you think you are?"

"I am someone who want to 'vin this match!"

"So am I!" screamed Jess.

"Ladies, ladies!" Partington cried. "That's enough. Now Ellen, please tell me about this four point plan to counter the threat of their front three."

The past week had been no better, the closer we got to the game the more fractious the energy. Not just between us and Jasper's form in lessons, but between ourselves. There was a clear divide between the team with Joanna, Jake and Gret clearly thinking that the rest of us were not as passionate about winning the cup as they were. I was in the middle of it — small pointless arguments over dinner, little niggly comments in form, pointing accusations in class — it was all building up to a horrible conclusion.

In form one afternoon Dennis tutted when Joanna started to say something about tactics. "Why did you just tut? Is it not important for you?"

"Here we go again!" said Dennis. "We're sick of hearing about your tactics!"

"Too right!" said Graham, slamming a fist on the table waking up Hunter.

"Oi!" said Jake. "Don't talk to her like that. You could do with a boost of passion that she has if we're ever gonna win this match!"

Florence sighed. "There are more things to life than Riptide!"

"That is not the right attitude!" said Gret loudly. Robin buried his face in his book like a turtle every time they started arguing.

"Look guys… *GUYS!*" I cried, finally snapping. I was fed up with it all. I had enough to think about without them bickering. "What is the point?" I said slowly. "What on earth does this solve? Joanna, Jake, Gret… people show passion in lots of different ways and just because they don't show it in the way you were expecting doesn't mean they aren't… *up for it.* We've got this far by being a *team*. Now, the only way we can win the next match, even to have any chance against them… is by being a united team."

There was a big rivalry brewing between the Manticore's and Hesserbout form. They looked as stressed out as we were, but being older I suppose they were used to the adulation and speculation. "That's Connor McKendry," said Dawn with wide adoring eyes looking towards a good looking blonde haired boy. "He's the Hesserbouts top scorer…"

We were sucked into the speculation and gossip as much as anyone else. I would often hear my name mentioned in the Chamber and glance across and see people exchanging gold. The anticipation in the school was reaching fever pitch. Not helping the fact was the rivalry that already existed between me and Jasper — "*All because of a girl...*" I heard one boy say, as if, were it not for her me and Jasper would have been best mates.

Even lining up outside Yearlove's classroom, we stood in our separate forms not looking at each other, and in absolute silence, until Yearlove called us in. I could feel a tight knot in my chest. I desperately wanted to beat Jasper, I mean so very, very much. Partington also said this was the first time in a century that two second year teams had met in the semi-finals of the cup.

That last week before the match was the most tension I've ever experienced. I kept needing to go to the toilet. Whenever I did Robin would either already be in there, or follow me and go again. I was still receiving small hisses and boos around the Chamber when I entered for lunch, the majority still uncomfortable with being conned into liking me. This led to a kind of majority likability for the Swillows, which Jasper was lapping up every second of. He had taken to announcing to the entire Chamber that he'd just received the support of another seventh year, or another sixth year form.

On the wall in the Hall, someone had graffitied over our Condor icon with: '*black-magic blackthorn*' — in our world to be accused of black-magic is pretty horrible. What's worse is that the idiot cursed it to the wall, so that it couldn't be removed.

Next to it, on the wall was an unofficial support wall where people could place a mark showing their support for that team (so they knew how many scarves and flags to change colour before the match). Large markings in different bright colours littered the wall under Swillow's with messages of support and things like: *beat those black-magic Condor cheats*, and even *we'll pay 10 gold for taking Avis out...* and things along those lines. Under our form there was nothing.

It was like a giant boulder of support had careered into the Swillows and suddenly they had the support of the entire school — it became against the grain to say you were supporting the Condors. In fact, everywhere we now went, white Swillow scarves flashed in our faces. They had all changed their ever-changing scarves early, so they could figuratively and literally rub it in our face. I would be lying if I didn't say these things effected me. They did.

That last night in bed I lay, feeling very small. Jasper had won the popularity contest, now I had to make sure he didn't win the match.

CHAPTER FIFTEEN
Semi-Final Foes

I woke with a start, as if prodded awake. At the end of the bed were the yellow and black shirts — with the small addition of a small golden outline around the Condor icon on the breast (for cup matches). I took a deep breath and steadied my nerves. Today was the semi-final, it was actually here at last.

I lay back in bed, the alarm hadn't even gone off yet. Some part of me wished that we hadn't done so well in Riptide, then we wouldn't have to play these highly pressured matches. Moans and groans echoed around the room as the clock jingled.

"Come on guys, let's go get washed. Today is the day!" Jake called. In all respects, the fact that everyone wanted us to lose seemed to pull us closer together as a team. After washing together, we went back and put on our shirts, looking around at each other. Hunter was the first to put a jumper over the top of his — not because it was cold, but because we didn't want to draw attention to ourselves. We all did the same, before traipsing down to breakfast in silence. I don't know why we went to breakfast, we weren't going to eat anything. We met the girls at the table, who looked equally un-hungry. All wearing jumpers and jackets over their Riptide shirts.

"We had a lovely entrance to the tune of *'You're going to get thrashed this afternoon...'*" said Jess eyeing up the Swillow form who were surrounded by supporters waving scarves. The Swillows were proudly wearing their all white tops, while we Condors hid, alone on our table with no support, and with jumpers over our shirts.

"Can't believe we have to go to lessons first!" said Hunter, pushing his bowl of cereals away. I caught sight of Harold on the Magisteers tables watching the melee below with distaste, he hated sports, but I felt like maybe he would be curious to see what a Blackthorn could do. Bah, who was I kidding.

***

"Come on! One of you can answer surely?" said Yearlove who was parading around the circle. "Ellen, can you tell me what the two spells to quell a Happerbat are?" said Yearlove expecting Ellen to come out with the right answer.

But she didn't, she froze and shook her head. "Sorry."

"What is wrong with you guys today?"

"Sir, it's the match today…" said Jasper, voice dripping with intent. "Swillows vs Condors."

"I am quite aware of the match between the two forms but that's no reason not to know the answer to these questions!" he said. "Okay, an easy one… what is the form of charm that the Happerbat uses to travel and stalk prey?" he looked around expectantly, but no one said anything. I kept my head down, my mind on the match that we would be playing in about an hour. Nerves like never before were coursing through my very being. Robin put his hand up again next to me.

"Sir," he said.

"Robin, yes! At last, someone with the answer!"

"No Sir, sorry, it's just I was wondering if I can go to the toilet?"

"*Again?*" Yearlove said blinking perplexed. "Go on then!" he said as Robin jumped up and left. My insides were doing funny things too. The Riptide shirt underneath my jumper was feeling hot and sticky already.

"Jarrold, can you stop shaking your leg!" said Yearlove. "It's annoying."

"Sorry Sir, it's just I'm nervous about the game——" but then Jarrold stopped talking as Jasper hit him in the side, shooting him a fierce look.

"Why would you be nervous Jarrold? It's clear who the winner is already!" said Jasper sneering along with the rest of the Swillows.

"Yeah, they might as well give up now!" said Jarrold.

"Oh shut your gob!" cried Hunter, throwing his book across the room.

Yearlove spelled it into the air. "Oi! I'll have none of that in this classroom."

"Avis!" called Jasper. "Can you tell that great lump that he better improve the accuracy of his throwing or your all done for!"

"Jasper!" said Tina next to him, giving him a glare of disapproval. I stood up, along with Hunter, Jake and Graham. So too did the Swillow boys.

"You'll get what's coming to you," I said pointing into his shiny blue eyes. "You might have got the whole school on your side with your little *PR campaign…*"

"PR campaign?" he laughed. "You did that all on your own when you used dark magic to——"

"—— Enough!" cried Yearlove, before silence fell again. Tina sat back shaking her head and mouthed: *pathetic.*

***

"You got your specs on?" I whispered to Robin.

"Of course!" he said. "Now leave me to go toilet alone." —— he was on the toilet again.

I ran the tap and splashed my face with water. Far away I could hear the sound of the chanting and the noise. In less than ten minutes we would be on that pitch. Nervous was an understatement, sick would do it a disservice, petrified was about right.

The girls sat alone on the benches, staring down at the floor. I looked into the mirror at my disheveled face, I had to pull myself together. We'd be fine, we had the shoes and Robin's spectacles and all those tactics. The feeling of something bad about to happen was pervading every pore of my being. But what? Being trashed by the Swillows? Being killed in the changing rooms by the short, stubby creature? Being murdered by the Djinn? Malakai coming back for revenge?

"AND NOW," came the magical announcers voice. "PLEASE WELCOME ONTO THE PITCH, THE SWILLOWS!" An almighty roar burst across the stadium, causing the wooden rafters above us to shake. I stared at them half in dream, trying to forget about the immense swelling of wind in my lower abdomen. Robin was bent forwards, doubled up with nerves. I'd never heard such a large roar from a crowd.

"AND NOW FOR THEIR OPPONENTS..." Suddenly the announcer was drowned out by booing. Magisteer Underwood beckoned us forwards, out of the tunnel the boo's rang across the Happendance Kingdom, seemingly to drown out all else. I wish I had thought to put a deafening spell on my ears. But then, we were moving. Joanna at the front moved first followed by Jake, then Gret, then Hunter. I was at the back, I could turn and run away? They wouldn't be too mad would they? My feet started to move following the line out towards the pitch.

All around were faces, an ocean of eyes watching us distastefully. The Swillows stood across from us on the grass. Jasper fronting them, arms folded and a gleeful expression on his face. But, I noticed one person in the crowd who wasn't cheering for any side, one person who didn't have a white scarf, or yellow. Tina sat with her head resting on the side, watching glumly.

Magisteer Underwood strode onto the pitch as the announcer spoke: "THIS IS THE FIRST SEMI-FINAL BETWEEN TWO SECOND YEAR TEAMS IN A CENTURY, BUT WHO WILL BE VICTORIOUS? THE SWILLOWS?" An almighty tidal wave of noise erupted from all around. "OR THE CONDORS?" *BOOOOOOO!* Rang out the jeers.

The Lily watched on rather distastefully at the noise as Partington stood by our team bench nervously chewing through his triangular hat. There were a few yellow specks in the crowd... I strained my eyes. Ernie was sitting near the Magisteers plinth with his yellow scarf round his neck. And one other speck of yellow... Zara, the girl with the bright white hair, had her yellow scarf waving above her head, much to her forms bemusement. My stomach did a flip at the sight of her. I shook myself and concentrated.

We waited, the whistle hovering in mid air above Underwoods face. "LET THE HABITAT CHANGE!" she called. The white light collected on the grass pitch, then shot into the air, flashing a blinding white column of concentrated light into the sky. I slipped and skidded on my feet as the ground turned to ice. A cold biting chill spiralled in from all around as a black cloud hovered above and snow began to fall.

"OH A TRICKY ONE! IT'S AN ARCTIC ADVENTURE!" The crowd *oooed*.

Then Underwood waved her arms aloft. "TAKE YOUR POSITIONS..." I marched ahead, legs like jelly — which I had to shake off quick — and stood on the furthest right facing three Swillows. Florence guarding me someway behind.

Joanna, Jake and Gret stood at the front centre as a three ready to try and take out Jasper. Hunter stood primed by the bolt-hole. Robin stood centre ground, guarded by Jess and Dawn.

Jasper smiled at me — but he knew now it wasn't about popularity, it was just us against them. The silence and apprehension were paramount... the snow fell in a soft, slow rhythmic pattern. Not a sound could be heard. Until...

Hweeeee! Went Underwoods whistle.

A roaring wave lit up the stadium. Red and blue flounders shot out of the bolt holes high above. The three Swillows ahead of me charged, hands aloft.

"Duck!" screamed Florence as an electric fizz crackled past my ear smashing the centre Swillow in the face.

"Avis!" Hunter called, pointing frantically at the red flounder soaring through the air ahead of me. But Jasper, who was being pursued by Jake and Gret was after it too. I kicked off the ground and double tapped the shoes with a flurry.

"Florence, you take the left one!" I screamed. But it was too late, the two Swillows had orchestrated a combined Pasanthedine spell directly at Florence with the force of charging hubris. Florence soared through the air and back to the bench, as they fixed their attention to me.

"*Pasanthedine!*" I called aiming my hand not at them, but at the snowy ground just before them — the wind shot out and kicked up an avalanche of snow over their heads. I turned to see Jasper soaring through the air at the red flounder. In a golden flash I burst forwards, running as hard as I could. Snow and wind hit my face as all sound vanished.

Jake and Gret's spells shot at Jasper with the timing of a machine gun, but kept missing! "*Goaternut,*" I said, feeling the inky chameleon spell wash over me. I aimed both arms as I ran. "*Sevhurton!*" I called as the icy blast soared through the air, hidden by the already icy surroundings. It hit him! Catching Jasper on his outstretched arm as he sailed through the sky, causing him to recoil.

But then, the worst happened! As I ran, I must have not been looking — I ran straight into a stray Pasanthedine — wind suddenly engulfed my vision. The next moment I was launched into the air. I hung useless upside down, as spells suddenly rained upon me.

"*Kadriepop!*" I screamed, falling to the floor, narrowly avoiding a fire spell from Jarrold who glared at me from his bolt-hole. But now, Jasper was half way up the pitch with the red flounder — jumping and slamming the ball past the frozen solid Hunter. Red light shot into the sky. A roar erupted across the kingdom.

NO! I looked around at our sparse team: Simon, Dawn, Graham, Dennis, Ellen and Joanna all gone!

The blue flounder was being worked forwards by a group of Swillow girls and now Jasper spotted it. I slipped across a patch of ice. To my left were two Swillows boys trying to free Freddie from a frozen spell. I double tapped the shoes and shot at them.

"*Pasathedine! Severhurton!*" I cried at the top of my voice. The wind and ice froze them solid and launched them into the air.

Jasper aimed his arms at them and shot a Kadriepop spell.

"*Returious-Severhurton-Flund,*" I cried as a burst of white web engulfed Jasper's white spell in mid-air and catching in the fibrous webs. It tried to wriggle away but, a second later, the three Swillows shot back to their bench in a blaze of light.

Then an almighty *BOOM* cracked the ice floor. Robin stood looking victorious, a burnt out ornament in his hands. Jasper clapped his hands to his head as the ice beneath us split, a huge watery black cavern opened out.

The rumble made me slip. Without warning, I fell with a splash into excruciating pain! From all over, everything was on fire! Robin's ornament had back fired. I clambered out onto the ice shivering uncontrollably — the most painful experience of my life!

I struggled for breath, shivering like a dying fish. Robin scrambled to shore too, as Jasper stood on a shard of free ice and aimed two hands at us, spelling us into the air and out of the game. A second later I met Robin shivering on our team bench. "*S-S*-Sorry," he shivered.

Partington gave us a magical blanket and we shuddered back to normal. I put the blow-dryer spell on myself, then Robin until we felt back to normal.

"We need to get in quick and take them out," said Joanna. "Especially Jasper!" she said as he paraded himself in front of the adoring crowd as they won 4-0.

— "*We love you Jasper!*" came the cry of the crowd.

"Agreed," I said. "I need someone else with me," I said. "Florence can't do it all on her own."

Jake nodded. "Yes, I think Simon should go over to the right, as Avis iz' a target for 'dem." Simon nodded, shivering as white light lit the Habitat from all around. A Happendance folk tent field replaced ice — tall white tee-pees poked up from the long bushy grass, amongst a set of small trees.

Fully dried out, we walked back to the pitch to cries of "*you're gonna get thrashed*" — charming. Jasper looked charged and victorious. I took my place on the right of the pitch again as three different characters now faced me — Jarrold, Kelly and Harry.

I turned to Florence and Simon. "*I've got a plan…*"

Red and blue flounders shot into the air. Instantly, Simon and Florence's spells shot at the tee-pee's — expecting them to blow over and into the oncoming charging Swillows. I waited. But the tee-pees stayed where they were! Bummer!

I jumped out of the way as the Swillows charged into us, knocking Simon down. From the ground I aimed my left hand at Jarrold, my right at Harry. "*Pasanthedine!*" I called. I didn't wait to see what happened as a blast of black smoke shot past my chest and lit the grass on fire.

Graham had our red flounder the other side of the pitch, but faced opposition from a wall of Swillows. Joanna yelled to him to throw it to me. I made my run into the space ahead, but Jasper spotted it.

I put a hand behind my back: "*Dancidious*," I said — I felt three spells rebound away as the red flounder came sailing through the air, twenty feet from the bolt hole.

Their keeper jumped from the wooden plinth and lunged for the flounder. Not before I grabbed it as she clawed the air, missed, and toppled off balance into a tee-pee. I had an open goal. I lifted the flounder up ready to slam it home, a swell of happiness coursing through me — before... a wall of Swillows burst out of nowhere! Five of them suddenly blocking my path, it was too late to stop! I crashed headlong into them, dropping the flounder with a thud.

By the time I looked up, I was upside down and they had scored. I zapped back to the bench before I could blink.

That wasn't fair! Surely, that wasn't allowed! I stood up off the bench waving my hands at her, but Underwood wasn't looking.

Partington was staring disbelieving at what had just happened — you cannot use tele-magical-portation. I was the first one back to the bench, what a kick in the teeth! I waved my arms at Underwood as the crowd jeered and booed me. *Oh shut up!* I thought, sitting down with a glum thud. *Cheats*.

We lost the game. The blue flounder pinged around between both teams, until Jarrold, who must have got out of my spell earlier, exchanged neat passes with Jasper and Kelly before bamboozling Hunter and placing it in the bolt-hole, a blue column of light lit the sky. That was 2-0 to them.

Minutes later the announcer called out: "ONE MORE CONDOR REMAINS…" they were moments away from a Libero-Manus, with Jasper and four Swillow's still on the pitch — but they never found Robin. Because he was invisible and hiding in a tent. Too scared to try and do anything to savour the game. They won 4-0, and we hadn't even scored a point yet.

Depression was starting to settle into our bench, but we had to remain focused. We were two games down. If we lost the next game, we were out. And thrashed as well.

We made our way down to the pitch, the Habitat had changed to a Venetian waterway — tall buildings with alleyways and bridges, gondolas and fruit stalls.

As the whistle sounded, I charged ahead. I was going to get their flounder first. Double tapping the shoes as I kicked off the bridge, I jumped into the air as golden light lit the stone beneath me. Kelly the Swillow was running down the road towards me, not seeing me, I took the opportunity and spelled her into the air. This time repeating the spell until she flashed back to her bench.

Up ahead I saw the blue flounder fly over a building, I climbed a ladder up a tall building — just below I heard voices. Harry and Jarrold were standing in a darkened alleyway, trying to disguise the blue flounder, they didn't think I could see them.

"*Reptlylidiulis*," I whispered, aiming my hand just in front of them. A huge snaking reptile rose out of the river and snapping its jaws. In a flash they jumped for their life, dropping the flounder and legging it. I took my chance. I jumped off the building aiming a hand at the ground. "*Pasanthedine!*" the wind took the shock of the fall.

Then raising both hands at Jarrold and Harry's shocked faces said: "Sevhurton, *Pasanthedine!*" they froze instantly, then shot upside down into the air. Hanging like amusing frozen art sculptures.

I picked up the blue flounder and crept forwards, the bolt-hole was no less than thirty feet away. Ahead of me was a rather fat girl blocking the bolt hole. I tapped the shoes and ran at her. Spotting me, she aimed everything she had, but I was ready this time.

"*Dancidious, dancidious, dancidious, dancidious!*" I repeated over and over as spell after spell rained upon me, before being deflected away. Dennis popped up out of nowhere to my right, over a bridge. I saw him out of the corner of my eye.

"Spell her!" I called blocking another tirade. A gust of wind finally caught her ankle and she shot up. The glorious sight of blue light erupting from their bolt-hole caused the crowd to go silent. But there was no time to celebrate, we had to find the other one.

The game was scrappy.

With two minutes to go and 1-0 up, Robin bumped into me in a dark alleyway. "Ahh!" he called, turning to spell me.

"It's me you prat!" I called holding up my arms.

"Oh thank god!" he called putting his down. "Look, I've found this but I can't work it..." Robin held out an Ornament — it was a delicate, small looking vase with yellow dots.

"You know how to use Ornaments Robin?" I said, and he gave me a small look. He was afraid of using it after what happened last time. He didn't want to risk our winning score.

"You do it," he said. I gave him a look, took it and smashed in on the ground. Robin stared at me wide-eyed expecting the ground to give way again.

We both blinked — I could *see*. I could see through all the buildings like they were ghosts. The Swillows lit up red, our form lit up yellow. Our teammates could *see* too, because they were all suddenly charging towards the same place, where three Swillows had a pulsing red flounder.

"After you…" I said to Robin, who smiled, then charged ahead. We ambushed them completely, they were so surprised to see eight Condors sniff them out that they screamed. The three girls shot back to their benches and we slammed the flounder home winning the match 2-0.

The eye sight wore off, but buoyed by our victory — a new found confidence now coursed through us. Jasper was complaining loudly to Underwood as he left the pitch that we cheated. He had a cheek!

The next match was a must win. The Habitat changed again with a flurry, the crowd around us was singing: *"You're still gonna get thrashed,"* but they didn't sound so sure.

The venetian waterways changed to a dense, dark forest. Thick, old oak trees, dark covered forest floor and sparkling green leaves — sun poked through the black cloud illuminating the pitch. Graham clapped me on the back with an encouraging, "Come on! Let's do this!"

"Come on guys!" cried Jake. "We 'ave practiced on this habitat enough times in the forest!"

I went over to the left side of the pitch, swapping with Robin. This time, curiously, no Swillows followed. I could see them huddled together in the middle, through the thick-set trees. What were they planning? Underwood took the whistle to her lips, and blew. A rush of adrenaline flooded through me.

Robin instantly began scanning around the forest floor like a mole, with Simon and Dawn guarding him. Hunter shouting Jake forwards, he and Gret were already sprinting through the woods towards the Swillows bolt hole. But I couldn't see any sign of the Swillows! The blue ball hung above their bolt-hole as the crowd started to look around for them. It worried me, where had they gone? I looked through the deep, dark forest stepping softly upon snapping twigs.

"Florence, look!" said Jess pointing up at the Swillow's bolt-hole — the blue flounder had gone. But who had taken it? This was impossible, they must be cheating!

Joanna barked at Hunter not to release the red flounder until we had worked out what the Swillows were doing. I broke into a jog, keeping my gaze peering through the darkness. The sounds of the crowd disappearing, degraded to all but a dull whisper in amongst the thick undergrowth.

A fluid black shape darted ahead of me. I stopped still and looked back, there was no sign of my entrance, no light behind me or ahead. My heart beat fast in this impenetrable darkness. Where were the others?

A low chuckling noise rippled out just ahead of me. I stepped back, snapping a twig.

"Who's there?" I called, voice trembling. It chuckled again heartily, then a flash of black shot past my vision. It was like trying to look through black ink... "Show yourself!" I called.

"If you so wish," it said slowly. Then, without any warning, an enormous BANG thudded through my body. I felt my nose crack as my head flew backwards. I hit the floor hard. My vision swam, small stars popping in front of my eyes, as my face burned with pain.

Standing nonchalantly against a tree, was Jasper, chewing on a small green stick. "Charbuckle, it's good for your teeth. You will find it growing abundantly in a forest like this."

I rubbed my throbbing face and stood. Blood was boiling in my veins at the sight of him. Suddenly the crowd roared, Jasper lifted his head slightly. "Sounds like we just scored..." he smiled.

"Are you cheating?" I said. "Using invisibility isn't allowed!"

"It is if you know the right Returious spell!" he scoffed. "Which I do," he added.

Slyly, I turned my palm towards him, and whispered as softly as I could. *"Pasanthedine."*

"Oh pathetic!" he said batting it away lazily, as if it were a fly. His eyes flashed. I felt my feet leave the floor, before flying back through the air. CRUNCH! I hit a tree hard and slid down.

"That's how your so good at Riptide…" he said suddenly, staring at my feet, a dawning realisation on his face. "I knew you were a *cheat*!" he said, but he was smiling. "At least that leaves me safe in the knowledge that you are not a *natural* like some of them said you were. We are not equals, not with shoes like that. It explains so much…"

He moved around me, as the tree roots dug into my back. My head ached and I was sure I had dislodged some bone or muscle. "I can read you like a book. You thought, in that tiny mind of yours that by becoming brilliant at Riptide you could what? Lure Tina back into your life?" he looked down pitifully at me. "You really think you stood a chance with her?" he laughed.

"Get lost!" I spat, salty blood leaking from the corner of my mouth.

"Oh look the red flounder…" said Jasper, as bright red light appeared next to him out of nowhere. "Don't worry Avis, I'll score this and then I think we should… *level the playing field.*" He smiled again malevolently. "Catch you later… loser."

With that he disappeared, footsteps crunching away — I wanted him to come back. I wanted to show him how much I hated him. I heard another almighty roar, before the words: *"Jasper! Jasper! Jasper!"* began to ring around the crowd.

Picking myself up I limped away before a white light lit the floor, almost blinding me with surprise. The trees and the forest vanished. The crowd was now visible. The woodland floor had given way, the trees gone.

Now a huge swath of long thick grass with stone mounds and tufts lay across the uneven habitat.

"OH, AND SOMEONE'S FOUND A HABITAT CHANGER!" cried the announcer. "AND IT'S CHANGING… TO ER… A *MOUNTAINSIDE*!" The crowd made a sarcastic *ooing* noise. Jasper was grinning at me as he dropped a spent Ornament.

"What happened to you?" said Robin. "Looks like you've cracked your head open. Blood," he said looking queasy. I wiped the blood from my mouth and felt my head, a wet, blood red hand met me back. "Tell Underwood and you can go off, you need to go the Healer's room," said Robin.

"Bloody Jasper!" I said. "Do you know a spell will disguise this to her?" I said pointing at Underwood.

Robin didn't bother arguing. "Yes," he said reluctantly. "*Pergoaterferace*," my head tingled and Underwoods face instantly looked the other way.

Dawn ran over. "Guys, come on, the flounders are on the way out. Huddle."

We joined the rest of the team in a huddle as Joanna spoke. "This is our last chance to get back at these guys! They are two-nil up, if they score another, they've won then they'll go for Libero-Manus."

"So what's the plan?" said Hunter.

"Erm… well, I don't know. They seem to have countered every tactic we have!"

"Guys they've cheated I know they have," I said — but then the workings of a glorious idea had just occurred to me. "I have an idea… Robin, how quickly do you think you can replicate your spectacles and make them invisible?" he looked at me as if I'd asked him to marry me.

"I can't, they're not… they're…" he struggled for an answer.

"Desperate times…" I called. "And you're the cleverest guy I know."

He looked down at the floor thinking about it as Underwood gave us the ten second wave. "A few minutes?" he said finally.

"We haven't got minutes!" said Graham.

Ellen smarted. "No, we've got seconds…"

"It can work! I promise." I said. "Jake, Gret and Joanna, you go on the offensive, distract attention. Dawn, Graham and Simon protect Robin as he does his work. I'll deliver them all to you. But in the meantime let's make sure they don't score."

"What do they even do?" said Simon.

"You'll see…"

Underwood told us to take our places. It was the only idea I could think of, was it a stroke of genius or madness? I knew that Robin could make a copy of his spectacles and the powers that go with them, they wouldn't last long — copies of things often fade and vanish after, sometimes minutes, but that's all we needed.

The whistle blew again. The Swillows looked confident and hungry. Five charged upfield with the blue ball, I aimed both hands and shot as many spells as I could to disperse them. Robin, with the others hiding over him, was in the corner, hidden by a shield of chameleon spells.

Jake collected the ball from Hunter, and exchanged neat passes with Gret and Joanna through a tide of Swillows. Until Joanna was spelled into the air. But they continued to chase Jake and Gret into the corner of the pitch.

Jess and Florence were now in a tangle with the three offensive players Jasper, Kelly and Harry who were duelling for possession for the blue flounder. I double tapped my shoes and shot across the pitch towards Robin. Aiming my arms towards Jasper I shot six Pasanthedine's, one hitting Kelly in the face and launching her into the air.

"Robin!" I called as I reached the shield. "How many?"

"Four!" he called, hands working furiously beneath him.

"They're amazing!" said Dawn, already wearing a pair. "I can see what spells they are about to throw at me!"

"That's the idea," I said, scooping up the spectacles.

Robin looked up at me. "Tap them twice and they'll turn invisible.

"Dennis!" I called racing towards him. "Put these on, tap them twice!" Dennis took them and promptly began running around the pitch after Swillows.

"Hunter!" I called throwing him a pair. He dropped them. But, gave me a thumbs up as he put them on. I duly delivered them to all remaining players and called at Robin to rejoin the game now we didn't need any more.

I put my pair on and tapped them twice, colour and light illuminated the pitch. For a moment I could only watch. Green fizzing electrical light was forming in the centre of Jasper's chest, then, it shot out of his outstretched right arm towards Gret, who flew into the air. As Jake fought off three Swillows, I spotted a gap. Double tapping the shoes I shot forwards. The pain in my body was excruciating, but I had to ignore it. The Swillows were duelling with us, all in their own half, leaving a gap through the middle.

"Jake!" I called. He spotted me and threw the red flounder high into the sky, directly into my path. I was one on one with the Swillow keeper. "*Avertere! Goaternut!*" I said hand over my head, as I disappeared from view. The Swillow keeper gorped around, the spell brewing in her suddenly came pouring out like a volcano. Green wind shooting all over the place. She couldn't see me, she was panicking.

"*Dancidous!*" I repeated over and over, as I jumped up the plinth, past her and placed the flounder neatly in the bolt-hole. Blue light exploded into the sky, Swillows looking around shocked as I burst back to the middle of the pitch.

Three minutes remained.

"Robin, you lot… all of us, over there!" I pointed at the red flounder and they took note. Robin, Dennis and Dawn charged across in a blaze of green, red and white flashes.

Suddenly, to my left Henry from the Swillow's appeared out of nowhere and made a dive for me. I double tapped the shoes and span out of the way, holding up my left hand I muttered. "*Pasanthedine…*" Henry was engulfed by wind, launching high into the air.

Up ahead, Dawn, Dennis and Jess wrestled the flounder from Jarrold as Jake made a bee-line for the bolt hole, but he hadn't spotted the keeper who had a nasty red spell brewing in her arm that was about to explode out at him. I aimed my right hand and steadied it, she was in my sights.

"*Sevehurton!*" I cried. A blast of ice flew out of my arm in a spurt of blue. The aim couldn't have been better, it sailed true as an arrow. Her red spell was inches up her arm, ready to burst out at Jake who was in mid-air. And then… sweet glory. The ice spell hit the Swillow keeper right in the chest and she froze into a solid blue block. Jake slammed the ball into the bolt-hole and wheeled away.

"AND ITS TWO-*ALL!*" cried the announcer to muted applause. "NOW ITS ALL TO PLAY FOR!"

"You IDIOT!" Jasper screamed at Jarrold.

The last two flounders would come shooting out of the bolt-hole any second now. It was 2-2 — we had to win this match to stand any chance of staying in the tie, and the next goal would decide the winner of the game.

A wet splodge hit my nose from the black clouds that had formulated above. And then, rain. But not any rain, hard, heavy driving rain. Wind whistled, splashing into our faces until it hurt.

We huddled together. "Any more tricks you want to teach us Avis? Any more masterplans up your sleeve?" cried Graham over the howling wind and rain that was now pummelling every part of us, and the Habitat — the green mountainside reducing to muddy bog.

"None," I said.

"These specs will do!" said Florence. "I can see their spell before they shoot it."

"At least we're at equal numbers," said Hunter, pointing at the Swillows who also had seven players left. Joanna, Gret, Dennis, Simon and Ellen were watching anxiously from the benches. Even the Lily was on the edge of his seat.

Underwood's whistle lit the air as the wet crowd roared back to life.

I charged forwards across the slippy mud ground as the red flounder came soaring towards me. CRUNCH! I clattered head long into something… my vision swimming I saw it was Jasper's elbow! He sniggered loudly as the crowd recoiled. I lay back in the freezing mud, my face pounding with pain again. Deflecting his spells I aimed my hand at his departing legs and cried: "*Returious-funis!*" — a line of cord bound his legs and he sprawled through the mud.

"*Zxanbatters*," I said standing, the flounder he dropped magnetically charged to my outstretched hand. I sat up and threw it to Jake who was unmarked and charging forwards.

Suddenly, Jasper looked like a man possessed — Dawn flew into the air, followed by Robin.

"NO!" I cried — but I was too far away to save him.

Kelly and Henry were charging fast towards me with the blue flounder — they stopped as a wall of fire blocked their path. I spelled them into the air and picked up the blue flounder — next to me was a hole under the rock, I slipped the blue flounder inside, increasing the shadow until it was invisible.

The crowd were on their feet, a roaring wave echoing deafeningly. I turned — Jasper was one-on-one with Hunter! He stood tall surrounding the bolt-hole, but there was no way he could stop Jasper. Out of nowhere Jess and

Florence appeared, before wrenching Jasper back by his collar batting the red flounder away!

Jasper aimed spelling Jess, Florence and Hunter into the air with an almighty gust of green wind. His face shot back round to the whereabouts of the red flounder, and he saw my hands raised at him. And he did something awful... he pulled Jarrold, who had just sprinted to his aid, in front of him. My spell hit Jarrold and pulled him into the air — the crowd was shocked. I dived to the floor as a black bolt of fire zipped past me.

"Jake!" I called sprinting forward — he had the red flounder and I was open on goal if he threw it to me. But he was duelling with three Swillows, he was trying to throw the flounder, but couldn't release it. Jaspers black fire came shooting towards me again as I ducked. I raised both hands towards the Swillows and... *WHIZZZ* — two green shots of wind expelled from my arm pulling the two Swillows into the air.

"*AHH*!" Cried Jake, who was also now hanging in mid-air — he and Kelly spelling each other out of the game. With a flash he shot back to the bench.

There was a moment of silence. I stood, soaking wet as I suddenly realised what had happened. I turned. Through the driving rain and howling wind, my clothes billowing on the hillside Habitat, I saw him marching towards me, the Swillows last player — and I, the last player for the Condors.

Who could have predicted it? Jasper and I coming head-to-head for a final duel. Jasper walked slowly, as the crowd stood, watching on in silence.

His blue eyes twinkled towards me as he brushed his soaking hair out of his face, his pure white kit splattered with mud. Like mine. I thought I might feint at any moment, my heart would surely give out and my lungs were burning as if on fire. Everything hurt — and I was terrified.

And then, all at once, we moved. Jasper dashed towards me with the force of million hubris. I moved swiftly spiralling out of his way.

We both continued running the opposite way from each other — I jumped over the hill, slid along the mud and fell down the ravine, pulling the blue flounder out of the crack. The howling wind and rain blocked the noise from the crowd and impaired my vision. I could see the outline of Jasper, standing straight and tall with a red flounder in his right hand — we stood unmoving again.

And he did something that I never expected — he threw the red flounder. It soared high into the air, over my head towards my bolt-hole.

He sprinted — forcing me into a choice, deal with the flounder or deal with Jasper? But, I was quicker than him. With a jump and a flurry, I flew forwards towards the red flounder, reaching the bolt-hole I stretched my arm and caught it.

Now I had both.

Jasper was surprised and breathing heavily. Somehow, I had to get a flounder in his bolt-hole.

Through the driving rain I could see my team on the bench, they were gesticulating towards me and pointing at something. The score board — it showed less than thirty seconds left of the game — if I didn't score this, then we would be out.

With that, I ran. I had no better plan. I pulled my hand behind my head and launched the blue flounder forwards — I needed a hand free. The crowd roared as my legs burned like fire. I launched myself off the plinth and onto the slippy mud. Making a beeline to the edge of the stadium as far away from Jasper as possible, I kept my palm facing towards him.

"*Dancidious, dancidious…*" I repeated black fire came raining after me, singeing my shorts.

But then, something changed, there was a rumble. What had he done? I slipped on the mud, and sprawled along the ground as the rumble juddered the ground. What on earth was he doing? There was a splintering noise, and a horrible bone shattering, cracking. The crowd was looking around, for the noise seemed to be coming from within the stadium. Jasper stopped running. The blue flounder came to a small thud in the corner of the Habitat. Underwood marched out as the rumble began to get louder and louder.

And then it became horribly clear. The stadium was collapsing! The northern part stadium began to sink — the wooden frame bowing and bending as splintering noises erupted into the air. Screams echoed deafeningly from all around as panic exploded.

The Lily stood. Raising both hands high the entire crowd lifted upwards out and above the stadium. White light fizzed and flashed with the effort of the spell.

Noise, rain, and wind filled my every sense. Underwood screamed at us. "You have to get off the Habitat! You can't be raised into the air because you're on the Habitat! Get off now!"

Jasper was panic stricken. The wooden slats to my left began to crack and fall, buckling beneath itself. We had to do something but there was no time! We couldn't be spelled into the air because we were on the Habitat! It had a charm to protect it against outside crowd interference. My heart was racing — if I didn't act soon then we would both be dead. The splintering, cracking reached a crescendo.

"Get off the pitch!" screamed Tina, hanging in mid-air.

And suddenly, we ran out of time. The entire stadium fell.

But I could do something. As wood and debris began to rain down, I raised my hand at Jasper and said: "*Pasanthedine!*" — the wind took him into the air and to safety.

There was nowhere left to run, even with the Seven League Shoes. From all around wood came crashing down. Huge, heavy rafters knocked the wind out of me. I felt myself being thrown to the ground as I slipped through mud and was drowned by a sea of wood. Screams of horror shot through the air like a far-off dream. My face in mud, with the weight of the stadium on top of me — surely, I was dead?

Through the silent darkness under the colossal weight of wood — I saw two shining blue eyes. Drifting forwards from far away, the short stubby creature came into a small patch of light. It's small white face half obscured by hood. A thick grin crawled across its face.

"...Now...you know...what...it feels like...to be stripped of everything. I won't stop here...I will go...after your most precious...things." I blinked, confused, my body trapped. The next moment it vanished. I couldn't move anything. I was paralysed and couldn't breathe. Consciousness was slipping slowly away. Whatever it was had finally got me. I shut my eyes.

Something grabbed my sides, shielding me from harm. A wonderful last dream.

The shock, the panic, the darkness and dust. The noise and the screaming all seemed so fall away.

"You're safe," said a voice, a far-off, unfamiliar voice. Too dreamlike to recognise it as I slipped in and out of dreams. "Brace yourself."

A blast of energy blew a hole in the debris. Daylight and rain woke me slightly back to my painful body. The person held tight before jumping.

We were on the edge of the hole, the top of the debris of wood. All around through my eyes that would barely open, I could see faces staring through the air, as they were suspended by the Lily. Shock and awe gripped them. Before I felt myself going up, gliding away high into the sky as screams of woe rippled outwards, past waves of roaring wind.

CHAPTER SIXTEEN
Burrows and Chambers

I didn't know what was happening. Even in unconsciousness I could feel the pain. Weird dreams flickered across my vision, dreams of childhood, of being persecuted by my siblings. Dreams of having things taken from me by my parents, because a cuddly animal was "*not what evil Wizards had.*"

Had I flown off because I was dead? Or had someone saved me? Had someone had risked their life for me? And did they fly? But who?

These questions, and more slowly thudded around my sore head as consciousness dripped back into my body. I felt groggy, painful all over. I was lying on a hard surface, above me a high-pitched roof, with lots of wooden rafters. Two men were gliding about the room. The fireplace lit, an orange glow warming through the room as rain and wind battered the window. Everything looked foggy and unclear. My head felt heavy, my chest sore.

Slowly, I realised that the two men in the room with me were strangers. The first man was busying himself around me — he was somewhat familiar. The second man was hunched over the fireplace unmoving. He had long black dreadlocks, and long black coat.

Horror took over me, the realisation setting in over who he was — it was the Djinn!

"Chambers, is he ready?" said the Djinn, in a slow, weak voice — my heart raced — what did they mean, *ready?*

Chambers, the first man, put down his tools, scanned me up and down and nodded. I was too panicked to take in what was happening, and now I looked about, I saw that I was in the secret room that me and Robin had found, high up near the clock tower, where we spotted Jasper.

My heart was beating so fast I thought it might jump out. "Come here then," said Chambers, in a thick Yorkshire accent, just like Robins.

The Djinn slowly made his way over to me, his form translucent. He looked weak, breath rattling. Around me were instruments, long silver instruments laid out precisely on the roundtable.

"Please *relax* Avis Blackthorn," said the translucent Djinn in a heavy Jamaican accent. Relax? Relax! How on earth could I relax? I had a Djinn next to me that I had been hunting for the best part of three months, and his assistant, who was now attaching something to my arm.

Tap, tap, tap, he went on the middle of my arm. He attached a long silver tube from my arm to the Djinn's. He was going to take my blood! I struggled, but I had no strength.

And then pain, Chambers shut his eyes, speaking frantically. My head shot back and hit the table as what little strength I had, sapped out of me. Blood dripped through the snaking silver tube, as Chambers read aloud from an old book by his side.

As my blood entered the Djinn, its form began to change. He became fuller, I could see my red blood start to pulse around him causing a cloud of bold. They were bringing the Djinn back to life! Wind began to rattle inside the room, slow at first, but then terrible, frightening and dizzying. The fire went out. Anything that wasn't fixed down began swirling. Pots, books and silver instruments darted around, hitting walls, clanging with loud noises. But I had no strength to argue or complain, I just lay, useless.

***

"It is done." Was the first thing I heard as I returned back to the room some minutes later. The Djinn stood inspecting himself. A second later Chambers was lifting a glass to my lips, I rejected whatever it was he had to offer.

"You must," he said, lifting it again making sure I took a large gulp. The foul mixture burned like fire as it slipped down my throat. Chambers stepped back and placed the mixture on the side. My senses came back in part, some of my energy returned, I felt nearly like me again. I sat up slowly, feeling the pain in my ribs, chest, legs and neck and clutched them sorely. I slid off the table, crying with pain as my knees cracked. I held my hands up at Chambers.

"Back away!" I called, but Chambers didn't move.

"You're mistaken," said Chambers. "We are not here to hurt you."

"Sit," said the heavy breathing Djinn. He wasn't asking, he was telling. What could I do? The two men didn't seem at all bothered by threats of magic. Chambers pointed me to the nearest seat, which slid out towards me from under the table.

My arm tingled, but there were no signs on my arm of having given blood. "What did you do to me?"

"You gave life," said Chambers placing his hands together as if deep in prayer. He was so unremarkable looking, that he could probably get away with never using an invisibility spell.

"Look around you," said the Djinn, as he became more and more humanlike. "If we wanted to harm you, we could have. I could have left you under the stadium. Is that the sign of someone who wants you dead?" The Djinn marched over to the fire and hunched over it breathing heavily as if taking in sustenance from the heat.

"Not all Djinn are bad," said Chambers.

"A horrible myth!" called the Djinn. "Don't succumb to it."

I sat down cautiously. Outside all I could hear was wind and rain, the match seemed like it happened years ago. "Come away from the fire," said Chambers watching the

Djinn carefully. "You don't want to set yourself on fire as soon as you've got your form back."

The Djinn chuckled and stepped back. "Quite right."

"I've just realised who you are!" I cried, pointing at Chambers — "You were the best man at the wedding!" I cried. "Before all the trouble started, you came after me!"

Chamber smiled and shook his head ever so slightly. "I didn't come after you. I was making sure you got away. Had to fend off those pesky family members."

"But why were you there?" I said confused.

"Well," said Chamber still watching the Djinn. "I'll let him explain everything…"

"Yes… I should," the Djinn came across and sat the other side of the roundtable, clumsily sitting into one of the chairs. "It's been a while since I was used to form so *dense*," he said in explanation to his clumsy way of sitting. "My name is John Burrows and this is my assistant Chambers…"

Burrows? He said his name was *Burrows*. Why was that familiar? Then, it slid into my mind as they waited for me. "The man getting married… to my sister Marianne… was a Burrows…" They both nodded slowly.

John Burrows sighed. "My son…Edward, *cursed* by the blasted Blackthorns!" he slammed a fist into the table. "Sorry Avis…" said Burrows in response to him slandering my family name — I didn't care, I hated them too. "I admit, that it must have been scary for us to take your blood like that. But you see, the only way I could return to my form was if I used the blood of a seventh son."

"But… how did you know that I'm a seventh son?"

Chambers sniggered — obviously it was a stupid question. "Because your the *seventh* male, in your family?" he said slowly, as if I was stupid.

I felt my brow furrowing, as I thought back to where the Burrows, the Djinn had come from. "But, the incense holder… if you needed my blood, then how did you know *I* would find the incense holder?"

Burrows stood slowly and waved a hand, a mirror appeared in midair in front of him and he inspected himself. "Magic of course! Nothing is by accident. Coincidence does not exist in magic… Oh, goodness me — I need to get a haircut, a shave, and some clean clothes." Then, with a flick of his hands, his clothes changed. Where before he had worn the clothes of a beggar; black moccasin, brown frayed trousers and a long black undertakers coat — he now wore a smart suit. Okay, it was a bit old looking, a white neckerchief, gold trim and buttons on his navy jacket, with white knee-high socks—but, the overall look was smart(ish).

Chambers sniggered again, cupping a hand to his mouth. "I am afraid you are about two hundred years out Sir."

"Well, it shall take me some time to adjust," said Burrows looking miffed. Chambers giggled to himself again, putting a hand to his mouth as he struggled to contain the laughter he was suddenly experiencing. "What?" said Burrows, watching his servant curiously.

"I've just thought… *he-he-he*…" he laughed. "You two, are related… Avis is your nephew-in-law." Chambers stopped laughing pretty quickly under the stare from Burrows, who, I don't think needed reminding was related to the Blackthorns. Hec, I was annoyed enough to be related to them.

Burrows cleared his throat and changed the subject. "Avis, do you have the number seven on your backside?"

"Er… yeah, I mean I suppose the birthmark is that shape…" I laughed.

"Don't you have an apology for Avis?" said Chambers. But Burrows just looked confused. "What quite do you mean? About the blood?"

"No, about the *enchanted jumper*?"

"*Ohhhhh* yes," Burrows put an awkward arm on the edge of the table. "So... when you asked me your wish, I did as you asked. But, the magic that I can work with at that level is limited. It was not my intention to have it backfire so drastically. As a Djinn you reside in the lower levels..." he pointed downward conspiratorially. "Therefore the magic is naturally of a lower level... i.e, in the same dimension as *demons*. In a sense, the magic itself has a demonic quality."

"Its fine..." I said trying to hide the bitterness in my voice. I looked around the room, I still didn't know what this room was — the theory I had about it being Malakai/ Jasper's must have been wrong. "What is this room?"

Burrows walked slowly using the furniture as aid. "This room is a secret room, found only and used only by the initiated — of the Heptagon Society..." He said grandly, waving his arms into the air.

"I've never heard of it," I said as noise filtered across my senses, gradually at first but then louder. Chambers and Burrows heard it too, turning their heads towards the oncoming sound... it sounded like an angry mob was coming our way. "How did you get in here?" I said.

"Through the window," said Burrows. I grimaced. If they had seen where we had come, then I was pretty sure that Robin would lead the Lily up here (to save me).

"They know where we are..."

"How do they know?" said Chambers.

And I told them, how Robin and I had used his *effy-ray* spectacles to find the tunnel leading into this room. Chambers smiled. "It seems that you seventh sons have a knack of finding things you're not supposed to..." Then he seemed to look through the floor. "We don't have long."

"Then I must be brief and tell you what you must," said Burrows. "This room is where we used to conduct our meetings. Around this very table," he said wrapping his big knuckles upon it. "I am glad that you followed your instincts

303

and found the captor and released me. I am not evil, no matter what anyone says."

"Who used to conduct meetings here?" I said imagining the Lily and the Magisteers sat round the table with Burrows talking.

"The Heptagon Society — a society exclusively for seventh sons. Didn't I mention? I am a seventh son too... that's why I needed your blood."

Suddenly, some things were starting to make sense — the book that I'd read when I was in here, about seventh sons — "It was you who read my book..." he said cocking his head and glaring at me.

"Er... er, what book?" I mumbled.

"The one about seventh sons — it was open on the wrong page..." then he sniggered. "You need to work on your body language, I can read *you* like a book."

"Don't be mean," said Chambers. "Anyway he's a Wizard. A Wizard is drawn to books on magic like an artist is drawn to the canvas..."

"Oh, *and*!" said Burrows fixing me a dark stare. "You must take good care of the incense holder, promise me that?"

"I will... but why?"

"It's more important then you can know right now. Hide it if you must, conceal it, what ever you can. We are both special, there are not many of us and we have a special mission. Things are harder for us, you probably noticed that already." Burrows grinned a wide toothy smile. "There are seven members of the Society... you are the last one, you are the seventh. Together all seven of us, will be able to do awesome things."

The noise outside was getting louder, they were getting nearer and nearer. "Don't listen to what they say about me, they will need you to think I am bad, or evil, or whatever else. Just, be careful of who you trust, the sides of good and bad are not labelled. It's probably a good idea not to tell *anyone* about what I am telling you." He was standing close to me now, this hand reaching out for my shoulder, his big deep eyes stared into mine. "There will always be help for you, from the Heptagon Society. But there is work to do yet to get it up and running…"

Chambers made a signal to Burrows that they must leave, and they quickly set about packing things.

"But, who set the accidents on me?"

Burrows and Chambers eyes swam across to me. "I would've thought by now that this question did not need to be asked? Chambers, my crystal ball."

Chambers gave him a smarting look, tapping his watch, before reaching into his bag and pulling out a big clear glass ball.

Burrows put a hand to the ball and closed his eyes, muttering things under his breath before beckoning me towards it. The images inside the crystal ball expelled outwards into the room. Noise suddenly filled my senses as we shot back to the start of the year…

Piles of students made their way to the main hall, but up high in the school peering down at the masses was the short, stubby creature. It's glowing eyes and bald head cloaked by thick dirty rags. Suddenly, the vision shot upwards through the sky, through the wall and into the corridor — darting inside the creature — now, I saw what he saw and felt what he felt.

I saw myself through it's eyes as I made my way towards the school next to Robin and Tina. I looked so happy. Carriages flew overhead and the crowd greeted each other after a long summer. Anger coursed through it at the sight of me — it's fists clenched, it was all it could do not to come down and kill me there and then.

And then, the vision changed, zapping forwards in time.

The creature had made itself so invisible, it couldn't even see itself. Concealed by spells, it darted from statute to statue along the Big Walk corridor. I, was making my way along with Robin and the others to a class.

Ideas and plans were hatching about the creatures brain for... revenge.

Zap! The vision changed again.

It was nervous as it made its way out of the school for the first time, hiding behind a large stone as children made their way past. It didn't know how the spells would react out here. Ducking beneath the wooden stadium, it darted from pillar to pillar, searching for the boy. And then it saw me, up high... perfect. With the energy stored the creature lifted a bony hand up in front of itself and performed the spell. The wooden rafter that hung by a thick rope juddered, before suddenly making a beeline for me. Excitement coursed though it — running to the next pillar to get a better view of me falling to my death.

And then, just as I was about to splatter into the ground, I was saved — Simone's hands outstretched.

Anger pierced through the creature, greater than any pain, as it scuttled back into the school to recuperate.

Zap!

It was waiting, watching from high above the class — finally a chance, I left the room, I'd just been sent out by Yearlove — it rushed after me, passing through the wall and into the boys toilets. Hidden in one of the cubicles, it set about working on the spells. I was angry, kicking out at things.

This was the boys ending. Revenge at last, thought the creature raising its bony arms at me— the taps burst sending off water into the air — a great distraction — watching me through the translucent toilet door it aimed again, the chandelier above fell, crashing onto me... Yes!

And then, out of nowhere I stood, unscathed and began shouting and searching, seeing feet beneath the cubicle. The creature reacted, he had to get out, away to safety to plan again! Darting out under the cubicle, I saw my angry, scared face aiming a freezing spell which missed. Stupid boy, it thought.

The creature tried many times, to get me — but every time he was thwarted. But, they took time and a lot of recuperating of energies to perform, energy he could have spent in better ways. I thwarted him in the changing rooms when he so very nearly got squished by the statue.

Thwarted him when he refused to eat the cursed putting. And I managed to get out of the charmed flowers grip.

It sulked, everything it tried, failed. The creatures memories flashed around its brain as it lay in the middle of the cold stone floor… the boy striking lucky and defeating him. Oh, the pain of it, the power lost as the boy said his true name for the final time. The creature said aloud the spell that would get him out of that room, away from the boy who knew his true name, and away to safety. But the damage had been done — in this new room, up high, it looked in the mirror, breathing heavily, for the life had been sucked out of it. Before the mirror, it watched its tall form descend, shrink and shrivel up. The clothes now dragged on the floor. Everything reducing in size, he looked ridiculous. He was no longer Malakai…

But he would get his revenge. He vowed, before falling unconscious high up in one of the old school classrooms amongst the sprats and dirt, dreaming of revenge.

Malakai! This whole time.

His form had been completely reduced, unrecognisably after I had said his true name last year — he had stayed in the school since our battle, in that classroom with the dirt and the mark on the wall, plotting revenge against me.

Chambers and Burrows were watching with expectant faces. Chambers with a couple of bags under his arm, the noise outside the room of the mob, getting louder.

"When you are reduced to a form like that, it opens the door to negativity. I mentioned before, that I was governed by different magic when I was a Djinn…" said Burrows. "He probably thinks, that by killing you with magic it will make you come back as a ghost—and I don't think he wants that."

"But," said Chambers. "If he kills you, by *accident*, then maybe he thinks that you will not be able to come back as a ghost and reveal his true name to all."

"I didn't think it mattered *how* you were killed?" I said. "I thought you have to have an anchor to become a ghost?"

Chambers and Burrows smiled. "You do, but he doesn't know that."

"When you are reduced to that form, you develop a kind of stubborn inward madness," said Chambers, with half an eye on Burrows. "I mean I wouldn't know, I'm not the expert but I am sure John would agree?"

Burrows nodded slightly, with a knowing look at Chambers. "He is a sorry, lost creature. But poses a big danger. Before we go, we will help you get rid of it…"

Suddenly out of nowhere a pulse of bright blue light swept through the room. "*AHH*!" Burrows cried out, staggering backwards into Chambers. The noise outside the room was now at fever pitch, they were up here in this turret, hundreds of them by the sounds of it.

"You need to go!" I cried as Burrows stood again, looking weak.

"A poxy dispelling charm…" said Burrows. "I'm too weak to counter it!" he said, before he turned to Chambers. "But we need to help him get rid of the creature—" Another flash of blue light, like a wave, shot through the room causing Burrows to scream with pain. I felt nothing, nor did Chambers.

"We must go!" Chambers cried, supporting Burrows, who held up a long finger at me.

"We must go and find the remaining Heptagon Society members. It won't be easy, but we shall keep in contact."

Chambers and Burrows smiled. A second later a purple light licked the air like a firework. And they were gone, along with everything in the room. It was empty, completely empty.

A voice quiet and soft entered the room as if from a discarnate being, a pair of lips spoke from the middle of the room in John Burrows voice: "I forgot to say… *follow the runes*," it said, before disappearing in a small purple flash.

I sat down cross-legged and awaited the mobs entry, looking as nonchalant as I could. I could hear short discussions between the Magisteers about how best to enter. Thoughts about what the Djinn had just told me raced through my head — what did I tell them when they came in?

A second later, a loud voice echoed. "Any thing that offers harm, please step away. I am the Lily. I am entering…" The tunnel opened out as the Lily, white and tall came striding through with big bold eyes scanning every corner of the seven sided room. Straker, Partington, Dodaline and Yearlove followed up the rear.

"Where is it?" said the Lily, from his body pulsed another wave of bright blue light that shot through the walls.

"Who?" I said as simply as I could. "I haven't seen anyone, I just woke up here." I avoided eye contact, instead I smiled at Robin who had just sneaked inside with his panic-stricken, but relieved face.

"Well, thank God you are okay!" said Partington darting forwards and summoning a towel around me. Outside the room was quite a crowd — Partington spoke loudly to them: "He's okay!" he called. There was a loud, relieved, cheer.

Straker stepped forward with a deep frown on his face. "We saw something take you, it looked like a Djinn?"

"Of course it was the Djinn!" said the Lily, angered.

I stood slowly. "If it was, it didn't do me any harm." I said as they slowly looked around at each other. "But, I do know what has been setting the apparent *accidents* on me and others this year. The collapse of the stadium just now, the falling statue, the cursed pudding, the charmed flower, the fire…"

Yearlove, who was looking out the window, turned. "Yes, yes, tell us then boy! *Who?*"

"*Malakai,*" I said. Robin gave me a wide-eyed look of horror and scanned the room with his spectacles again. "He

309

is in the school, he never left after... after Ernie defeated him last year. It wasn't the Djinn at all, it was Malakai."

"The Djinn didn't hurt you *at all?*" said Partington.

"Not one bit," I said. "But... it saved me, from the collapsing stadium. I wouldn't have made it out if the Djinn hadn't saved me."

"Preposterous, it's modified his memories!" called the Lily, looking around at the Magisteers, who stared back at me. "Magisteer Dodaline, can you send a *ping* around the school to check for discarnate beings like Djinn, and also for any trace of Malakai."

"Certainly can," said Dodaline, before rubbing her palms together and throwing them into the air. A ball of green smoke collected above her head before exploding outwards.

"We shall find out soon enough," said the Lily. And not a second later did the smoke return to a ball atop Magisteer Dodaline's head.

Dodaline closed her eyes. "Well, that is interesting..." she said. "Seems there certainly *was* a Djinn here, not more than thirty-seconds ago... but as for... Malakai — I'm afraid it's found no trace of him."

Eyes turned towards me, Robin looked worried. "I'm not lying!" I said. Partington began checking my arms for any signs of harm from the Djinn — before flashing a light into my eyes and peering inside. "Ahh, *gerrof!*" I called.

"His eyes are fine, no sign of modifications..." said Partington satisfied.

The Lily sighed and spoke as if he were talking to a toddler. "We are talking about one of the most powerful Djinn to have ever existed. It will not leave a mark of its magic."

Partington shuffled awkwardly on the spot. "No, of course not... just... checking."

"Well," said Straker. "At least it's gone, that's something."

Everyone stood in silence, watching me. It was awkward. I'd have killed for someone to just speak, to say something. But they didn't. I stared at the floor, wondering how to get out of this one.

CHAPTER SEVENTEEN
"Kill Avis Blackthorn"

"I don't think I need to remind you that we are dealing with a *Djinn*," said the Lily slowly. "A centuries old Djinn that will say and do *anything* to regain and retain its freedom. You know more than you are letting on Avis and let me tell you now that it's firmly within your interest to tell me."

I stood in the centre of the Lily's office, knees weak. He stood tall and imposing, grey spotted eyes boring into me. I couldn't bring myself to meet them, for I know I would reveal everything to him and I couldn't do that. Not after what the Djinn told me — he said I was a member of the Heptagon Society and they were going to find the rest. The words... *Just, be careful of who you trust, the sides of good and bad are not labelled. It's probably a good idea not to tell anyone about what I am telling you...* seemed to reverberate around my mind as the Lily waited for an explanation.

"I am sorry Sir. I wish I could, but I can't remember anything." I lied, staring intently at a crack in the white stone floor (one slight imperfection in a room of perfection). The Lily stared at me silently, I felt his gaze turn cold. He sighed softly, before turning and running a long finger along his desk.

"Now, you say it was Malakai that set these *accidents* on you?" He said. "Why you?"

"I'm sorry Sir?"

"Why..." he said slowly, "was he trying to kill *you?*"

I swallowed. "I don't know Sir."

"Look at me," he ordered, slowly I looked up and met his gaze. He was silent for a moment. "I would have thought that if he was after anyone, it would be Ernest Partington? Wouldn't you agree?"

"Yes Sir," the Lily was getting impatient. "You do know that the Djinn is tricking you? It has what it needs from you and now it wants you to believe something so as it can cover its tracks. It does not want the person who set it free filled with vengeance — otherwise it could be vanquished, by the only one who set it free. It has spun you a yarn that will make you reluctant to go after it. You are the only one who can get it back into the captor. You are the one that it needed to convince, no one else…"

The rain was splattering against the window, outside the Stadium lay in a huge pile of debris, again. "I'm sorry Sir…" I said. "I don't remember anything."

The Lily cricked his neck and looked around at the walls, taking a seat at his desk and slumping backwards shaking his head like a spurned teenager. "It's a shame… shame… you have to help me to help you. But you don't want to, that's fine."

He stretched out his hand as a glass appeared, filling with orange liquid, which he sipped. "I've come to a decision on the outcome of the Riptide semi-final…" he announced placing the drink down, and pressing his hands together.

"Oh…" I said, completely forgetting about the Riptide match, even thought I was still in my yellow Condor top.

"*Yeeas*," said the Lily slowly. "I am awarding the place in the final to the Swillows."

I couldn't speak, my mouth drying up — was he serious? He was only doing it to get back at me for not telling him what the Djinn said. "But, but… that's not fair!" I cried, the injustice burning a cauldron of poison in my stomach so hot, I didn't even care who I was talking to. "You can't… I mean… I was ten feet from the bolt-hole before the stadium fell! I was about to score!"

"Ah, but you *didn't*. And on the subject of *fairness*..." he said slowly. "Do you really think it's *sporting* to wear the pair of Seven League Shoes?"

"I... *I*..." was all I could manage. He knew, of course he did, that I used the shoes to get an advantage — he was the one who gave them to me.

"I am afraid that is the least of your problems... I don't think I need to remind you what we spoke about before?" he raised his eyebrows.

"Er... what's that Sir?"

"But I am surprised you've forgotten," he chuckled. "The fact that if you did not vanquish the Djinn then I would be forced to *exspell you* from Hailing Hall."

An ominous feeling slipped into my stomach. "And it has gone Sir..."

"Yes, gone. Not vanquished."

He was still going to exspell me? "No Sir, you can't exspell me... I mean, the Djinn has gone, that's what you were worried about?"

"No! I am worried that there is Djinn out there that has a connection to you as it's life giver, and with you in the school, that could pose a security issue for the pupils that are in my care," he said voice rising.

"But Sir... you can't exspell me because... this is my home... I can't leave. I'll have nowhere. And magic, I'll..." tears began to fall from my eyes, I couldn't help it. I couldn't believe that I was being exspelled! What on earth would I do? Go home? No, that was not an option... I wouldn't be able to learn magic fully and I wouldn't be able to get a job without my P.W.W's!

The Lily watched me coldly. "You know the rules, you agreed to my demands of vanquishing it."

I held my hands to my face as hot tears streamed uncontrollably. "But... I cannot just exspell you instantly — I have to satisfy the School Councillors, by providing them with the evidence, it shouldn't be a problem — releasing a

Djinn is a criminal offence. You have until the end of the year to prove that it was Malakai who set the accidents on you, and not the Djinn. If you can prove it, with *evidence*, then you will be allowed to stay. We're not barbarians — innocent until proven guilty. Currently you are guilty and due to be officially exspelled in just under three weeks."

I swallowed and took a deep breath. "Yes Sir…"

The Lily stood. "I'm off for an emergency assembly. I've just told you the contents of it, so it's not required for you to come… wait for the doors to unlock before going to the Healer's room to get checked over. We don't want you bumping into anyone in the corridors as they make their way to the assembly."

My head was pounding. I stood in the middle of the Lily's office utterly dumfounded. If I didn't find evidence for it being Malakai that set the accidents on me, then I would be exspelled!

I felt weak, my knees shaking together so violently I thought I might collapse. It was like my worst nightmare. I'd have to go home and be treated like a scivvy (a magical-less servant). I stood and listened as crowds of people made their way down to the Chamber.

I stood alone in the Lily's office. It was completely white; the walls, the door, even the window frame and curtains. It was strange to see so much white in one place, it kind of dazzles the eyes — like standing in Slackerdown or the Arctic or something. All the things that usually stood in this room — storage units, tables of magical items, bookcases and such had vanished when the Lily left he room. They sunk downwards into the ground — obviously he didn't trust me to be around them alone. The only thing that remained was the Lily's desk. I suppressed the urge to smash it up, for it was the least he deserved. He was being completely out of order.

Click, went the door, opening wide. I walked slowly, the doors clunking shut behind me as I made my way towards the Healer's room. I hadn't been harmed at all by the Djinn, all I did have was a horrible headache which felt like my brain was caving inwards. Perhaps it was the stress.

As I walked the empty, silent hallway a thought occurred to me. A terrifying thought… what if the Lily was right? What if the Djinn had tricked me? What if it had completely fooled me and implanted memories of it being nice and telling me all about being in the Heptagon Society just to keep me on its side? To make me impotent against vanquishing it — if I even could anyway. My mind was a mess, it hurt to think.

Approaching the large double doors to the Healer's room I heard a familiar voice from inside — one I had learned to hate… Jasper's. I tip-toed closer to the door and pressed my ear to it.

"Ouch, that still stings a bit," he said.

"It will do," said the Healer in her soft, wonderful voice.

Jasper cleared his throat. "It's all that Avis Blackthorn's fault… he saved me, now they all think he's a hero — but don't they see? It's his fault anyway! He's the one who set the Djinn free…"

"Ok dear, calm down and stop talking so much. It will help." I pulled away from the door, the stupid git was talking about me — I'd saved his life and he was still moaning. "There," said the Healer. "Keep that held onto there and that should heal in a few minutes or so."

"Thanks," said Jasper. "Oh, there is one more thing, before you go…" Jasper paused, I could sense he was nervous about something. "It's just, well, I was wondering if you know anything about… *blackouts*?" his voice cracked.

"Blackouts?"

"Yeah, well it's silly, probably nothing. Forget I said it actually."

"If you wish," said the Healer. "Your cut looks healed over now, you are ready to leave."

I jumped out of the way of the door and tip-toed down the corridor, slipping into an alcove. The double doors opened slowly as Jasper gave his thanks — I peeked round the corner. He was still in his white Riptide kit. It was muddy and torn in several places. He marched away up the opposite corridor, muttering to himself. I moved out of the alcove and quietly slipped into the Healer's room.

I didn't go back to my dorm room straight away, making a pit stop for the same place I always go when things get tough — the clock tower. I don't know what it was about it, apart from the fact that I basically lived up there for half a year. Maybe it was the dusty floor, the clanging bell, the bird mess, or the damp smell. Still, I found myself climbing up the thin, spindly ladder and opening the roof hatch.

Pacing the floor, I kicked at the rotting beams — I was just so annoyed and frustrated, tears welled up in my eyes. I prayed for this to just be a horrible dream, and I'll wake up in a few hours with everything back to normal. I sat down and stared out of the clock face across the rain battered grounds of Hailing Hall — I couldn't let this be my last memory of this place. If I left, my life would be over… I'd never see Robin, or Tina, or Hunter, or Partington ever again.

A horrible image flashed before my eyes — me turning up to their seventh year graduation to congratulate them, only… they didn't recognise me. I shuddered — currently, in three weeks I would no longer be a student of Hailing Hall.

I didn't know how long I was up there. It could have been minutes, or hours — I should have been able to tell seeing as I was in the clock tower, but I had a dreamy daze wash over me. Making my way out of the clock tower to the darkening sky outside, I stumbled and tripped back to my dorm. Pushing open the door, all eyes turned to me.

"Where have you been?" Robin cried, charging over to me.

"Yeah," said Jake. "We 'ave been worried sick."

All the boys were sitting on their beds looking worriedly at me. With light blazing in the brackets, all the boys looked freshly washed, I suddenly realised that I was still caked in mud and dressed in my Riptide shirt.

"Just been… thinking," I muttered, stumbling inside and crashing down on my bed.

"We watched the demon kidnap you," said Hunter. "Everyone thought it killed you."

"The girls were terrified for you," said Graham. "Someone should go and tell them your okay."

Dennis jumped up off his bed. "I'll go…"

"Well?" said Robin. "What happened?"

I sat up a little in the bed as flakes of mud fell everywhere. I didn't care. "I have no idea," I said. "I was unconscious. Didn't see the Djinn."

Simon recoiled. "Who said it was a Djinn?" he said suspiciously. Bummer.

I squirmed. "Hunter did, just then…"

"No," Simon pointed. "Hunter said *demon*, not Djinn."

"Same difference," I said waving my hands.

Simon huffed snootily. "They most certainly are not the same!" he called. "You must have had some recollection to know that it was a Djinn and not a demon? Anyway, why would it *save* you?"

"We 'ave all been wondering," said Jake sitting on the end of his bed. "It iz' a little strange 'dat the Lily says the Djinn that you released collapsed the stadium, but why would it collapse the stadium on you — but then save you?"

"Exactly!" clapped Simon.

"We kind of put it together Avis," said Graham. "The jumper that you just got from nowhere… it did weird things to people… that was from the Djinn wasn't it?"

My eyes felt heavy and I was tiring, my headache returning as I strained to think of the right thing to say. "Look, it's been a long day… I just want to get some sleep —"

"Yeah but…" said Simon. "You haven't heard the best bit! We had an assembly earlier, the Lily told the whole school that someone in our form *cheated*."

"He didn't say *cheated*," said Robin. "He said *used an illegal spell*."

"Same thing… anyway, it means that he's awarded the place in the final to the Swillows! Which means it's your fault that we are out!" Simon cried — the other boys scoffed at him.

"How do you come to that conclusion?" said Graham.

"Yeah!" Hunter bellowed. "We wouldn't be anywhere near the final if it wasn't for Avis."

I sighed. "I already knew. The Lily told me earlier, in his office. He's angry with me that I wouldn't tell… I mean, that I couldn't remember anything about the Djinn. So he's told me that I'm going to be exspelled in three weeks…"

"*WHAAAAT?*"

I slept like a log. Can you blame me? It was the most eventful, stressful, adrenaline fuelled day I've ever had at Hailing Hall. I didn't even bother taking off my Riptide shirt, nor did I care about them all watching me as I drifted into sweet unconsciousness.

Strange dreams flew around my head for what felt like years — Caretaker Ingralo burst through the bedroom door. CRASH! "Where is he?" he called.

Everyone jumped. "Who? *Who?*" Hunter cried, pulling his sheets up to his chin.

"Avis *BLACKTOOOOORN!*"

"Over there!" said Simon pointing at me. Ingralo charged forwards and grabbed fistfuls of bed cover and leg.

"What are you doing!" I cried. "Get off me!"

319

"Yeah get off him!" said Robin.

"YOU'RE EXSPELLED! OUT! OUT! OUT!" Ingralo got a purchase on my ankle and dragged me hard. BANG! Went my head as it caught the floor.

"Not yet!" I cried. "NOT *YEEEET!*" I put my hands up at him. "*Pasanthedine! Nouchous!*" A whoosh of wind and fire shot at Ingralo but did nothing!

Then, Ingralo dropped me outside the dorm... looking down at me was the Lily, he began to chuckle softly — the fire in brackets dancing white in their holders and flashing on and off. When the light went black — he turned into Malakai! The Lily — Malakai — the Lily — Malakai... I cried out for Robin, anyone, to help me.

"I'll take it from here," said Jasper rising tall behind the Lily.

Suddenly, we were in the Hall. The Lily and Jasper standing over me — the big double doors swung open, rain and wind filled the Hall as lines of pupils around the Hall chanting: "*OUT! OUT! OUT!*" Robin appeared behind me and pulled me up until I was standing.

"Robin! You gotta help me..." Robin looked down at the floor.

"Probably best if you just go," he said, pointing at the door. The outline of two tall figures stood in the doorway, silhouette casting a long shadow into the Hall. I cowered as my parents moved into the light.

"Come along Avis," said Mother. "We could do with another scivvy!" she cackled.

"Indeed," said Father. "Kilkenny!" Our Irish butler appeared by their side in a flash, mop and bucket in hand.

"I think these are *yours* now..." he exploded with devilish laughter.

"*NOOO!* ... Ahhh!"

I woke with a start, covered in sweat. "Please... *huh?*" I was in bed. The curtains were still drawn, but there was light outside. Sitting up, I saw empty beds. Suddenly I was so immensely grateful that I was here — the dream felt so real. I looked up the clock, but I had to wait a minute for my foggy eye sight to adjust — 11am? I'd slept for almost twelve hours? Jeez.

I opened the curtains with a flick of my hand. As I got out of bed crusty mud fell everywhere, but that wasn't all. A small note fell to the floor. I picked it up: *Avis, you were dreaming pretty hard. We left you to sleep in. (Talk later?) Robin.* I put the note down and grabbed my towel — I needed a shower.

When I returned, I dressed slowly watching the rain out side the window. The Riptide Stadium stuck out like the imperfect crack on the Lily's floor — against the backdrop of the perfect grounds. Then I took a seat on the sofa and lay down — running everything through my head.

"Hey Avis? Avis?" Someone was shaking me slowly.

"Huh? What?" I sat up, shaking the sleep away — I'd fallen asleep again? Robin was standing over me, looking concerned. "What time is it?" I said.

"It's dinner. I told the guys to go on without me. You and me need to talk." It was already dinner time? I was starving. The sun was setting over the horizon.

I sat up, my neck ached. Robin took the sofa opposite me, for a long moment he didn't say anything — he just stared. "Is it true? You're really being *exspelled?*" I nodded slowly. "Oh god!" he said collapsing backwards into the sofa, deflating like a balloon. "What happened?"

I told him everything, right from when the Djinn took me to the Heptagon room, it taking my blood and all that Chambers and the Djinn told me.

"So you have… three weeks?" said Robin incredulous. "To find evidence of it being Malakai? That's impossible! How on earth are you supposed to do that?!" I couldn't think of anything to say, so I just shook my head. "If I didn't know any better I'd say the Lily doesn't really want you here anymore. Mind you, when we saw the Djinn fly away with you up into the sky, I thought... well, we all thought, that you were as good as dead."

"I bet," I sighed. "It's all my fault."

Robin's beady eyes flickered behind their glassy frames. "What is?"

"I should have realised sooner. I mean it's obvious now isn't it? I read something last year about true names — and I'd forgotten it, until now. There was some guy called *Tyreko* and he went bad. This woman, I can't remember her name, used love magic to seduce Tyreko and get his true name. Then she defeated him. He reduced in size to a small... stubby... creature in rags." I said, but Robin was still staring at me expectantly. "I defeated Malakai using his true name. And now he too is a small, stubby, creature in rags. The thing that's been trying to kill me all year was Malakai. It couldn't have been the Djinn, like everyone was saying, because the accidents started way before I even released the Djinn. So that's why it's all my fault..." I cried, I couldn't help it. I felt so useless, so stupid. "This whole year I've been an... idiot. Concentrating more on trying to be popular than realising what was trying to kill me, putting my friends in danger."

"Don't get down about it. It's easy to look back with hindsight. Anyway, I want to know what you mean about the Djinn saying you are the seventh member of the Heptagon Society?"

I nodded. "Yes. But, the Lily reckons the Djinn implanted the memory, or that the Djinn was lying to me."

Robin looked to the ceiling. "Could be, but I don't think the Djinn was lying — not about the Heptagon Society anyway."

"What? You've heard of it?"

Robin tapped his chin. "I've read about it somewhere yeah. And you are a seventh son, so it's plausible right?" Robin clicked his fingers, two cups of steaming tea popped into existence on the arm of the chair. With another click of his fingers, some parchments and a pen fell into his lap.

"What you doing?" I said confused.

Robin began scratching on the paper. "We've got to find a way of finding the evidence to stop you being exspelled…"

Stress continually bubbled away under the surface of my mind. I felt hot under the collar, my tie was too tight. Lessons were uncomfortable — I tried my very best to concentrate, to absorb my last remains of magical teachings. But, I just couldn't, it passed me by in a daze. Someone made a joke in Wasp's lesson and I snapped at them to be quiet — I didn't even mean to, it was like someone else had taken over me — my gaze drifting to the floor as wave after wave of sorrow engulfed me.

All I got was sorry glances from all that had heard the news — my form were quieter than usual and kept glancing up at me with sorry grimaces. Word of mouth slowly spread and I walked the corridors to stares and mutters. They had put it together — the Lily announces in assembly that the person responsible for unleashing the discarnate being will be expelled, I had a magical jumper that was most suspicious, and then the Riptide Stadium collapses and I am carried off by a flying spirit.

— "It must be," said the barely concealed whispers. "It all makes sense doesn't it. He released the…"

— "Genie! And he wished for that jumper… I wonder why?"

— "To get Tina Partington to fall in love with him, that's what I heard."

— "Pffft," scoffed another. "You can't wish for love. Everyone knows that."

— "You can too!"

— "Anyway, it's not called a Genie, it's called a Djinn…"

— "Whatever."

323

I was suddenly the talk of the school — rumours flew around faster than the end of school fireworks that Ingralo was carefully placing around the school, concealing with charms so as no one accidentally let them off early, or blew their hand off or something. I gave him a wide berth, remembering the awful dream.

Robin clapped me on the shoulder. "You've gotta get a grip. It's like you've given up already?" he whispered. "We've got three weeks left, that was enough last year... *remember?*"

He was right, I knew he was. But I felt so damn listless. Last year I had less time to figure out how to defeat the most evil Sorcerer in all of the Seven Magical Kingdoms — now I was sure I could work out how to prove to the Lily that I was right and reclaim my space in Hailing Hall. I just had to get a grip, stop feeling so useless and try.

It was around this time that I noticed the seventh years walking around in tall glassy bubbles. That only meant one thing — their P.W.W exams had started. In the Chamber there were lots of these glass balls surrounding the seventh years. They were a clever enchantment, they blocked out all noise and stopped anyone touching or coming near you so they could study in absolute peace. Actually, I think some of them even played soft, relaxing classical music for better concentration. The Magisteers had their eyes on the seventh years, who all had their faces in book and papers, hands waving around softly as they practiced a certain spell. It had given rise to a kind of unofficial game for some of the younger years to see if they could break the bonds of the enchanted glass balls. One girl — Becky Lewis, I think, from the fourth year Flinkydots form was trying to penetrate her brother's glass ball. He can't have noticed much inside because he wasn't looking at her. But then, Becky lost patience trying to distract her brother and instead began slamming her fists into the ball like a madwoman. Magisteer Yelworca stood abruptly at the head of the Magisteers table. The next second an orange smoke arrow shot across the room.

"*AHHOOOWWW!*" Becky cried as the arrow shot into her bottom. She clutched fruitlessly for it as the Chamber erupted into laughter (the seventh years paying no attention at all.)

"And let that be a lesson to all of you," Yelworca cried, taking her seat as Becky hopped around clutching her buttocks before the orange smoke dissipated and she took her seat, looking rather red and embarrassed and sitting down a little gingerly. I looked around for Ernie but, he was no where to be seen. He was probably up high in the school, somewhere he wouldn't be disturbed.

Over the course of the day Robin kept muttering encouraging things to me — I don't know how or why, but it lifted me out of that depressing haze and now my thoughts returned, in part, back to normal.

A defiant charge was beginning to return. Not completely, but I felt a tiny roar of fire deep down in my belly — I hadn't given up yet. As we sat eating dinner, I wasn't too hungry so was just moving a baked potato around my plate, my thoughts began multiplying — I began thinking what I could do to find evidence of Malakai.

That night in bed I realised I only had seventeen days left to save my place at Hailing Hall. I couldn't sleep — the rain outside still poured hard, I wondered how long it could go on for until everything washed away. Hunter snored loudly, while someone else, Simon I think, was muttering softly in his sleep.

Orange glowing embers crackled in the fireplace. I watched for hours, running everything that had happened through my head. It's strange how time puts a new skew on things. I thought right back to that fateful moment the

Stadium fell — I was so close to scoring and putting the Condors in the final of the Riptide Cup. But no, the Lily now decided (after giving them to me) that my shoes were not *sporting*. He was right, they weren't — how could I have thought any else? It was cheating. I had almost convinced myself that I was good at Riptide, that we, the Condors were good at Riptide. We weren't — we just had magic that no one else did, and lots of it. I thought back to the start of the Riptide season. The only reason I decided to wear the shoes was because we were so paranoid about getting hammered again. I had lost sight of the original idea of wearing them, getting too caught up in the hype.

And then suddenly I realised something. The Seven League Shoes — I only knew part of the magic they did... I'd almost forgotten about the time they had saved me from that Outsider who chased me across his field with a pitchfork — his dogs nearly ripping me to shreds — blasting me back to the Magical Kingdoms, straight into a fairy ring and into Gnippoh's. I was on the cusp of understanding a solution, I just knew it...

Zzzz-ZZZ-ZZZ! Went a gigantic snore from Hunter, causing me to lose my train of thought. Dammit Hunter! I was so close to something.

And then it struck me... the shoes had saved me and Straker that time when the corridor fell... when we *BOTH SAW* the hunched figure of Malakai, of course! He liked me now, I was sure he would be able to tell the Lily that we had both seen it, then I would be able to stay! All I needed to do was find him first thing tomorrow morning before lessons and ask him to tell the Lily.

***

It was early, but I was too excited. I rose out of bed after barely a few hours kip. The others were still asleep — I dressed quickly and made my way down to the Chamber. I liked the school at this time, no one was around, except the ghosts busying themselves with laundry and cooking (I did not miss the kitchen). Pushing the doors to the Chamber open I scanned the Magisteers table; disappointingly, only Partington and Wasp were sat up there, both with their heads in the paper. I went over and got a cup of tea. The Chamber was sparse, barely five people sat around quietly reading or doing homework.

"Avis?" called Partington, noticing me. I waved, just being about to leave and try Straker's classroom. But Partington waved me towards him. I sighed softly and approached his table.

"Hi Sir," I said sipping the tea and recoiling. It was hot.

"I wouldn't go creeping around pushing open doors and such..." he said looking down his glasses at me. *Creeping around pushing doors open and such?* What did he think I was, a Happerbat? (*Note: if you are an Outsider then you probably don't know what a Happerbat's traits are — they used to be used by Wizard thieves to sneak into houses and steal the shiniest, most valuable items. They have a tendency to like shiny things, and a good eye for expensive antiques.) "The seventh years are in their second exam right now, and you don't want to accidentally walk in and disturb them."

"Quite," I said. "I was wondering if you could help me Sir. I was wondering if you know where Magisteer Straker is?" Partington's face fell a little — he and Straker had a mutual hatred of each other, bit like me and Jasper.

"I see," he said sharply. "No, can't say I have. He's usually in the staff room at this time. Perhaps I'd try there first. If you *must*," he added sourly — well excuse me for asking, it's not like Partington was going to do anything to save my place at Hailing Hall was it?

I marched out of the Chamber and towards the staff room, on the other side of the school, near west wing. I passed a couple of people who were slowly rising, walking sleepily to the bathrooms with their towels and wash bits. As I got closer to the staff room, I suddenly realised how nervous I was — I had a lot riding on this. The staff room stood a top a small flight of stairs just up ahead. I could hear them inside — I took a deep breath and slowly climbed the stairs...

"Well I think the Jaloofia's deserve best kept form this year," said a Magisteer, it sounded like Yearlove.

"You're only saying that because it's your form!" said Simone.

"Well exactly!" said Yearlove and they all burst out laughing.

I stopped on the stairs, listening. "What about most improved form?" said Commonside's weary voice.

"Well," said Mallard. "Personally I would have said the Condors after they're staggering performance in this year's Riptide, but, as the Lily has suspended them due to apparent... irregularities, maybe another."

"The Swillow's are the first second year team to make it to the final."

"Not the Swillows!" said Straker. Suddenly a warm glow entered my stomach, not just because he was here but because he hated the Swillows too. "I'd also question whether their were any *irregularities* in their play too."

Dodaline laughed. "Just because they beat your beloved Centaurs." Straker grumbled.

"I think the Lily is right in suggesting the special award for most improved person should go to Jasper Gandy, what do we think?" — No way! My knees nearly gave way — they couldn't! Did Jasper have the Lily enchanted? What was going on?

"I mean," started Yearlove. "He has had a rather exponential rise in ability. His tie has changed colour so many times I've lost track."

"True," said Mallard. "I mean I had him in first year, but he was so unremarkable I barely realised he was the same person."

Dodaline chuckled. "Quite, he was so small and unassuming when he first arrived. Very middle of the ground kind of boy, not particularly good at anything."

"Perhaps his father's death had something to do with it?" said Commonside's dull drone. There was a small intake of breath from the collected Magisteers. "What?" he said. "Its common knowledge is it not?"

So even they thought there was something suspicious about Jasper — a few more people were walking along the corridor now and I looked a bit silly standing against the wall in the shadows of the small staircase. I moved up slowly and peered around the door — I'd never seen the staff room before — it was quite unremarkable. Lot's of leather chesterfields, dirty rugs, tables filled with rolls of parchment, as well as a small summoning kitchen table area where they could bring up food and drink from the kitchens.

"Of course," said Mallard sitting in his pyjamas, not noticing me. "He has had a quite remarkable transformation... *Oh!*" he cried spilling some of his tea down his front as he spotted me. I knocked on the door, a little late, for most of the Magisteers had already looked round after Mallard jumped, and seen me.

"Avis," smiled Dodaline. "What can we do for you?"

Commonside looked up from his marking rather dreamily and looked straight through me. "Hello Avis..." he said, before I could answer Dodaline. "I am just marking your work. What a coincidence... well, not if you believe in the powers of numerology anyway," he said wistfully, turning back to it before tutting. "Oh dear, you've not done very well I'm afraid."

"Right," I said turning back, spotting Straker standing expectantly. "Can I speak to Magisteer Straker please?"

Straker closed the staff room door behind us and turned to me on the stairs. "How can I help?"

"Well Sir, I suppose you know that I have to find evidence for Malakai being in school before the Lily will let me stay?"

Straker chewed his lip. "I knew," he said.

"Well… I realised last night Sir, that we have both seen him."

"We have?" he said looking mightily confused.

"Yes Sir, when the corridor fell… that creature that collapsed it, was Malakai!"

Straker waved his arms a little flustered. "*Shhhh*, will you. Don't go around saying that name too loudly just here. People will start talking…"

"The thing is Sir, I thought that if you go to the Lily and tell him that you and I, both saw Malakai, then he will let me stay."

Straker didn't say anything for a second, but looked apologetic. "I'm sorry Avis, I don't think that will work."

"Why not?"

"A number of reasons — I had no idea that it was Malakai — certainly looks different. I assumed it was that Djinn you set free that collapsed the corridor, they take forms like that when they are released."

"But Sir, it showed…" I stopped, I nearly said that the Djinn showed me in the crystal ball. "I've seen this creature, it's definitely Malakai."

Straker shook his head. "You have to understand, even if I went to the Lily and implored him to believe me, it would not make the slightest bit of difference. I've been here many years. The Lily needs actual evidence, if Malakai really was that creature — I must say, it takes a leap of faith — then you need to find a possession of his, something with his magical signature on. Then, the Lily can check it, date it and tell for certain that Malakai was in the school."

The fire brackets popped on as I walked back along the baron corridors. I couldn't believe it, my heart sank and I returned to misery again. My only option had gone. As I was walking, I saw something in my peripheral vision standing in a dark corridor to my right. This person, was inspecting a book.

"Ernie?" I said.

"Ah!" he said jumping and slamming his book shut, turning to glower at me as I moved closer into the dark. "Oh it's you Avis. You gave me a right fright," he softened, straightening his jacket.

"What are doing here? I thought the seventh years are supposed to be in the exams… and why weren't the fire brackets illuminating you?" I said, Ernie looked around searching for the right answer — looking awkward for a second.

"It's true, I should be in my Infusions P.W.W Exam and in fact, I am."

I frowned confused. "What do you mean you *are?*"

Ernie cleared his throat. "Well, and you better not tell a soul about this!" he said sternly. "The thing is… I am Ernie's doppelgänger."

"What, so you're not Ernie?"

"No, I am Ernie. I am just controlling me and the doppelgänger at the same time. It's hard to explain."

"I see," I looked down at the book in his hands *Advanced Infusions* — read the title. "So, I am guessing this isn't usually allowed?"

Ernie grinned a big wide grin at me. "It's no fun if it is." But then his grin subsided and he looked around worriedly. "You here alone?" I nodded. "Good, well… and you won't tell anyone about this?"

"Course not,"

"Okay, maybe I'll teach it to you one day," he grinned. "And if there's anything I can do, you know, in return then you just let me know old chap," he said playfully.

"Well, seeing as you mention it… there is something you can help me with."

***

I stood looking out at the round glass clock face at the impressive view. Heights were not my thing, but up here, they didn't seem to bother me. Rain battered the grounds with a ferocious energy, the grounds had now descended into a muddy, soaking bog, the trees had took cover in the forest huddling together and the statues were hiding in the hedges.

The roof hatch swung open. In climbed Robin, Ernie close behind.

"Woah," he said gazing around. "Haven't been up here since…"

"Since you tried to kill me when you were a ghost," I smirked.

Ernie chuckled nervously. "I never tried to kill you——"

"——You don't have to explain," I said. "I remember what it was like being a ghost."

Ernie had agreed to help me find evidence of Malakai —— and we met in the clock tower to discuss. "So how do you think we can find evidence of him being in the school again?" I said nervously.

Ernie tapped his chin. "Hmm… there's a few things I'd like to try first. Just routine things."

"So…" said Robin, his beady eyes flicking from me to Ernie before he said in a small voice. "Do you think Malakai is actually in the school then?"

I shot Robin a fierce glance. "You don't believe me either?"

"No it's not that, I mean, it's just that the Lily said you could be tricked by the Djinn…"

Ernie got down on his knees, a small rug appearing beneath him. "If Avis say's Malakai is in the school, then I trust him. I have no reason not to. Anyway, I'm gonna perform some checks to see." Kneeling on the floor Ernie pressed his palms skywards and recited something. Green-blue smoke collected above his head in a ball before exploding off in all directions. Ernie's eyes flickered, hands still spread skywards. Five seconds later the smoke returned back to a ball above his head, electricity sparkling slightly as if it had its own atmosphere. Ernie inspected the smoke as if you might a child for nits, then shook his head. "Nothing..." He set about with some more spells, using several candles, talismans and lucky charms — but, after a good hour of trying looked up and shook his head.

"We're not gonna find out where he is by spell-work," said Ernie. "Anyway, I think we should leave it there for tonight. I've got an exam first thing. I'll have a good think and see if I can find some spells that will give us a better indication."

Over the next week, after dinner, we met in the clock tower to discuss, plan and act. Every new day that we came back with nothing made my heart sink a little more. The voice in my head already condemning me to permanent expulsion.

I was laying in bed, trying for sleep as best I could. I was annoyed. Robin and Ernie were trying, they really were, but even though Ernie had a terrific amount of magical knowledge — everything we tried returned nothing. I just knew Malakai was in the school somewhere, I just knew it. The Djinn had shown me a place that Malakai had returned to just after I defeated him — it looked like a disused classroom, but there were hundreds, if not thousands of them.

In the middle of the night I turned over to watch the orange fire embers, everything turning over and over in my head — Hunter snored violently: *zzz-ZZZ-ZZZ!* He went, reverberating the whole room. Something solid clicked into place... I remembered what I was thinking about before... about my shoes. I was sure the answer to my predicament lay in my shoes. At least something in my gut, somewhere deep down was telling me this, but I just needed to extract it to have any chance of staying.

I was pacing the clock tower — Robin and Ernie were late. I paced the floor, kicking up dust and thought about my shoes — at first I didn't know how to use them, then I realised that they took a double tap and whoosh, off I went, at the speed of light. But, it was only when Hunter had clipped my heels that time that I sped off and stopped stock still outside the bathrooms... our original destination — that's when I realised that you had to have a destination in mind.

Suddenly, the thing I had been trying to dig out of my mind had surfaced. The answer.

The roof hatch rattled. "Sorry we're late, bloody ghost asked us what we doing going behind the drape... Ernie used a cracking excuse..." Robin stopped when he saw my face. "What is it?"

Ernie closed and the hatch as the rain outside stopped abruptly.

"I know how to find where he is." — the shoes, they took you to where you wanted to go, so all I had to do was think about where Malakai was — I had to think about Malakai's room, the one Burrows showed me in his crystal ball. Would it take me to a place I'd never been? Would it be blocked by Malakai's magic? I didn't know. But I had to try.

"And you are sure about this?" said Ernie. "I mean I need some books to plan... spells against him."

I scoffed. "He's not that powerful anymore, he's small and stubby," I said but Ernie didn't seem reasonably convinced. "Ready?" I said.

"Ready as we'll ever be!" said Robin wincing. I grabbed both their hands and took a deep breath — I fixed the image of the room I'd seen in the crystal ball, firmly in my mind. Then, I jumped, double tapping the shoes. Golden light leaked out as I felt the power in them whir. I closed my eyes and fixed my attention on the vision of Malakai's room from the crystal ball.

All at once the shoes moved. We began sprinting — Robin and Ernie picked up by the golden light causing their legs to sprint with the same ferocity as mine. The roof hatch burst open, as we flew down the ladder five steps at a time. Through the drape and into the corridor below... Almost immediately we came to a screeching halt.

I let go of them and bent forwards breathing hard as light brackets above us popped on.

"Well that was... *something*," said Ernie, leaning on the wall. I looked around, we were in a corridor that had a large window from floor to ceiling on our left. Statues stood tall, casting long shadows from the starry night sky. The floor was wet in here, rain seeping in through cracks in the walls — puddles lined the corridor like glassy mirrors.

"I know where we are," said Robin. "This is the high-up corridor we found before — we're the Djinn took you. The one that leads to the Heptagon room."

"Yeah I know," I said softly looking around, I guessed the shoes had taken us as far as they could.

Ernie tip-toed forwards, edging round the puddles. "He probably has some pretty strong magic barring us from entry—"

"Hang on," said Robin stopping before a statue. "There's a door here."

Ernie stared at Robin incredulously. "What do you mean? There's no door there, it's just wall." Robin smiled and reached out a long thin arm. Pressing his hand softly to the wall. Like a mirage, it faded up and with a *pop*, became whole.

Robin dropped his hand and took a deep breath. "Found it."

"How on earth did you——" started Ernie before jumping through the puddles to the door. "I'll go first, just in case." He held his arms out in front of him. *Creeeeek!* Went the door. Tip-toeing, we slowly crossed the threshold.

"*Prafulgeo-Lamas*," Ernie whispered, as a circle of soft blue flame attached to the ceiling illuminating the room. "He's not here…" said Ernie, uncertain.

Robin, behind me whimpered slightly —— I moved tentatively behind Ernie, scanning every corner and crevice of this dirty, disgusting room. The blue light above illuminated a floor thick with black dirt, dead rats, and upturned classroom furniture. "What's he doing in here?" said Robin. "Shedding his poxy skin or something?" Robin picked up a pile of crusty black dirt.

I searched the room —— this was perfect, all I had to do was show the Lily this room and it would be proof that Malakai was in the school. I was saved! There was a small scuttling noise, it made my heart leap into my throat. I turned quickly, arms out.

"It's just a sprat," said Ernie without turning. "So we're in an old disused classroom," he said peering up at a huge blackboard that had a large selection of runes in chalk on it. "Runes? Hold on, they're not runes! Avis, your gonna want to look at this…"

I turned and looked —— plastered across the blackboard in every available space was: *Kill Avis Blackthorn! Kill Avis Blackthorn! Kill Avis Blackthorn!* I stepped back, feeling a little giddy.

"Jeez," said Robin. "He *really* wants you dead." I turned away and looked for more evidence, swallowing the fear that was plastered to my insides. Then Ernie scoffed, looking up at something. "He's quite the artist, looks like he's graffiti'ed the wall for some reason."

"How do you know it was him that did it?" said Robin rather impatiently, edging towards the door. "This looks like a rune classroom, or *was*, it could have been anyone in here."

"Because it's recent," said Ernie. "You can tell by the soft glow of the magic used to create it."

I dropped a flaky old book and turned to see what they were jabbering about — and I almost suffered a heart attack. "*Ah,*" was all I could manage. On the wall, painted in thick black paint — was the exact same rune that was on my pendant.

"What is it?" said Robin, his beady eyes flickering around the room.

I pointed up at it. "It's the same rune that's on my pendant. Exactly the same one."

"I'm sure it's nothing," said Ernie. "It doesn't look like any rune I've ever seen. Anyway look we need to get out of here and let the Lily know…"

I gazed it a second longer, then nodded. "Yeah fine."

We exited the dirty, damp room and clinked the door shut. "Hold my hands," I said. "We're going to the Lily's office."

"I'll just go get my dad," said Ernie as we touched down in the corridor outside the Lily's. "He will want to know." Ernie scampered off, running up towards the staff room. "We'll both meet you inside, you two go ahead."

I took a deep breath and looked at Robin, who smiled. "I think you've done it mate."

A grin crept across my mouth and I raised a hand, knocking on the pure white doors. "Come…" said the Lily. Pushing open the doors, Robin and I stepped inside.

"Ahh, Misters Blackthorn and Wilson," said the Lily raising his arms to us. The room was a buzz with goings on — Magisteers Dodaline, Simone, Mallard, Partington and Straker were sat around the Lily's desk, piles of paper, drinks and snacks piled around them. They looked exhausted. The bookcase to the right was spitting out it's books and replacing them in some apparent new order — the papers, which sat in a huge pile in the middle of the floor were sorting themselves into even more piles, every so often one would jump into the fire.

"Sir, it's just…" I stuttered as the Magisteers watched me. "I've found evidence for Malakai being in the school." The Lily's face didn't change.

"Oh?" he said slowly.

"It's true Sir," said Robin nervously. "High up, in one of the disused classrooms."

The Lily turned slowly to the Magisteers, Partington peered down his spectacles at us, before standing. "I must come too," he said.

"Ernie is already looking for you," I said. "He helped us find it." I added as his eyebrow raised.

"I'll come too," said Straker putting his papers down.

"Well," said Dodaline. "If you lot are going, I don't want to miss out."

"Think I'll stay," Magisteer Simone looked miffed somehow and slammed her drink on the desk as Mallard sank into his chair and muttered that he ought to keep Magisteer Simone company.

"There you are!" said Ernie who stopped running when he saw us opening the doors. "Dad, you weren't in the staff room, has Avis told you?"

"He has, we are all coming to inspect it," Partington smiled.

And so off we marched. Robin and I walking ahead nervously, leading the Lily, Dodaline, Partington and Straker to the room, which would guarantee that I get my place back at Hailing Hall.

"How far at the top of the school is this room?" said Dodaline, panting. "And we can we not just get a magical lift?"

I caught the Lily smirking. "Because that would make the pupils lazy Magisteer Dodaline," he said chuckling softly as Dodaline huffed and puffed.

"Here," said Robin leading everyone out through the small exit out of the staircase and into the corridor.

"This place again?" said the Lily curious.

"Yeah," I said, and started speaking a little too fast, like I did when I was nervous. "It's just up here, not much further. Robin saw the door, it was hidden in the wall, concealed, not sure what charm it was or anything, but he unlocked it didn't you? You are clever—"

"It's ok Avis, calm yourself," said Straker putting a cold hand on my shoulder.

"It's over here," I said slower. I walked to the place in the wall where the door was.

"Just here?" said the Lily walking closer and pressing his hand to the wall and muttering under his breath. The door popped into the wall. There was a collective sigh of relief. I glanced at Robin smiling, but he wasn't smiling, in fact he looked concerned. The Lily put a hand to the door and walked inside. He lit the room with light, which blazed bright white.

When I entered, I knew instantly that something was wrong. This was not the same room — this room was tidy, and orderly — not filled with filth and muck like the room before.

"I am afraid I don't see any evidence?" said the Lily, his grey eyes scanning around the dusty, but tidy room.

"This... doesn't make any sense..." I muttered. "This is definitely the right room, but it's not the same." It had to be here somewhere, a room cannot just disappear can it? "We were here no less than ten minutes ago!"

"It's true Sir," said Robin. "Right here, was a mess of a room..."

"But," said Dodaline. "How do you know it was Malakai's?"

Robin pointed at the blackboard. "It was plastered with *Kill Avis Blackthorn!*"

"But, why would Malakai want to kill young Avis?" said Dodaline as if was the most horrible idea in the world. Robin stopped talking — we were in serious danger of breaking the pact.

"The fact of the matter is, this is just another disused classroom," said the Lily. "I don't doubt for a second what you found before, but… it's not here now. I am sorry."

"But, but…" I didn't know what to say, I was flabbergasted. The place where Malakai was… gone. It took me weeks to find it and now… it was gone.

Partington blinked back a tear before yanking the Lily's sleeve. "Isn't there any magic to see if there was a room here before."

"I just have," said the Lily. "Nothing."

"I'm buggered," I said. "Just buggered."

The Lily, Magisteers and Ernie, escorted Robin and I back towards his office. "I really am very sorry Avis," said Straker on the long walk back.

"You should feel sorry for us, we have a full night of marking to do!" Partington blustered, before receiving glances of disapproval from Straker and Ernie. "I meant… that… oh goodness me," he said getting a hanky out and blowing his nose.

The Lily opened the door to his office and let in the Magisteers in. "Straight to bed you two, it's already past bedtime."

"Sir," we mumbled, turning and walking towards our dorm. I felt numb. Completely and utterly numb.

Robin was shaking his head. "I don't know what to say, I really don't understand what just happened."

"Its fine," I said. "You don't have to say anything." I felt hot injustice burning my insides — my stomach was twisted in such a tight knot of pain and fury that I had to clutch it for fear of falling over. When we turned the corner to our dorm, I heard a voice ring through the darkness.

"Why the long face Blackthorn?" A light bracket popped on above his head — Jasper. He was stood nonchalantly leaning against a wall, eating an apple. "You look like you've just had *bad news?*"

"What are you doing here?" Robin hissed, his fists clenched. "Why don't you just disappear!"

"Ok," said Jasper simply, before disappearing in a flash.

I've never felt so angry in all my life. I shook with rage — my vision blurring. In that moment, all sound vanished. All light went dark. I saw nothing, heard nothing, felt nothing as I descended into darkness…

"Follow the runes…" said Burrows. "Follow the runes… follow the runes… follow the runes," Burrows Jamaican voice said over and over again.

Pictures and shapes flashed before my eyes — my Granddad giving me the pendant, with the rune on it — the incense holder from Happendance Carnival danced next to it, with the same rune stamped on the side — then the fight with Jasper, he was on top of me pushing me to the ground and I saw his pendant channeller, exactly the same as mine, with exactly the same mark.

Then, the disappearing room belonging to Malakai, the same rune plastered to the wall — Then Jasper's laughing face echoing around the floating images.

"Follow the runes… follow the runes… follow the runes."

Jasper's pendant came loose and he began waving it round at me. "Follow the runes… follow the runes… follow the runes." Then — Jasper's face transformed — ghostly horns protruded from his head, face turning pale, eyes glowing blue and the aura around him turning blacker than his hooded robe… "Hahaha!" he cackled. "Hahaha-hahaha!"

Then he stopped and bit into an apple… as Tina popped into the air next to him, strings rising in the air from her limbs — Jasper strummed them gently as Tina began to dance. Her face expressionless…

My eyes flew open and I blinked, rubbing my eyes. "Avis? *Avis?* Oh thank goodness your awake!" said Robin. I was lying on the floor outside our dorm room.

"What happened?" I said.

"You feinted," said Robin putting a hand behind my back. "Here, sit up slowly."

"Its fine," I said brushing his hand away. "*He* did this... I just know it..."

Robin stood back up looking perplexed. "Who?"

"Jasper!" — it had to be. He was the one who looked like Malakai, he was the one who had the same pendant as me and the marking on the wall in Malakai's room. And he was the only other person I'd seen up there in that deserted corridor near the Heptagon Room. It had to be Jasper.

"Come on, let's get inside and to bed!" Robin looked knackered, deep black bags scaled his eyes like a panda.

"But Robin," I stopped, a tear falling down my face. "I don't... I don't want to be exspelled... I don't want to go h-h-home..." and I cried. I didn't know what to think or feel anymore. I stopped crying quickly, a thick numbness replacing the pain as I wiped my face.

Robin pushed open the door and we went inside the dark room. Small blue flashes kept going off. Hunter was standing near Robin's bed fiddling with something.

"What you doing?" said Robin marching over to him. "Give that to me!"

"Calm down!" said Hunter. "I was trying to turn it off, can't sleep with that flipping flashing all night!"

Jake sat up. "*Shhh*, keep your voice down."

"What is it?" I said, sidling over to Robin as Hunter got back into bed.

Robin tried to hide it. "Oh nothing, just a... thing..." — he was a rubbish liar, in fact this just made me more curious. As I got closer I saw that he was fiddling around with a little silver thimble-looking instrument.

"What is it?" I said, but then it dawned on me, all at once. It was one of the little devices that Robin had placed around the Heptagon room to tell if someone had gone in.

Robin stopped trying to hide it, turned the top and the flashing stopped. "It did this when you were taken, by the Djinn into that room... where are you going?" said Robin — I knew who was up there, I could have bet my life on it (and I was about to).

"I'm gonna find him!" I said charging away — Jasper was Malakai, I mean it just all made sense. Burrows said *follow the runes* — Jasper had one of those runes — I had to follow Burrows advice, I had to follow the runes... and that meant following Jasper.

"Avis! You can't... the Lily said... AVIS!" Robin cried, but it was too late — I double tapped the shoes, the golden light licking the air before I shot towards the Heptagon room and towards Jasper.

It felt good flying back along the school — up the corridors and winding up the spiral staircase at the speed of light. Why was Robin trying to stop me? I had six days left at Hailing Hall until I was exspelled, I had to take any opportunity that came my way.

I wish the Djinn, Burrows could have stayed, and helped me get rid of Malakai and win my place back at the school. But, the Lily spelled that powerful pulsing blue light causing him and Chambers to flee.

The shoes drove me to a skidding halt out in the corridor where I had been no less than twenty minutes before. I had a trickle of nerves run down into my stomach. Was I doing the right thing? It was deadly silent up here now. But, something had shown me those visions — something was trying to remind me of the clues that led to Jasper, or should I call him Malakai? The curious rise in grades, (even the Magisteers were surprised), the time I looked through Robin's effy-ray spectacles, when he looked exactly like

Malakai. And, we were back up here… the place where I'd found the room with evidence of Malakai in it, and here Jasper was, in a room not thirty feet away.

The vision of Tina dancing on strings replayed across my memory. Fury bubbled up inside and I marched fast towards the wall and without a second thought, pressed my hand to the stone key.

The wall melted, hazy lines fading into a short tunnel. I saw him eyes closed, sitting on his knees. My heart was pounding. But the sight of him made my blood burn like fire. He opened his eyes and looked up. I nearly gasped with fright ⸺ his eyes were completely black.

"You are him!" I cried. "YOU DID THIS!" I double tapped the shoes and charged. Jasper stood quickly, but not quickly enough. Catching him full on I slammed him into the wall.

"Awoooh!" he groaned. A pulse of blue and purple flashed between us, expelling me away from him. But the golden light of the shoes pushed me forwards again. I raised a fist, but I wasn't going to spell him ⸺ I aimed, the fire white hot inside me, and slammed it into his face. He recoiled backwards in shock as pain rose up through my fist in sharp waves.

Jasper's eyes turned back to normal and for a second he looked scared. "Think about what you are doing," he felt his face. "You really want to fight *me*?"

"I don't want to fight you… I want to kill you!"

The room was empty and it was a good job too, for the next second I slammed my hands together. "*Severso-Zxanxirious-Unquart-Vilunos.*" Power and force swelled between the gaps in my hand. Electric fizzes popped in the air between us. Smoke rose from my finger tips. Then, at the full force of the swell, when I couldn't hold it any longer, I clapped.

BOOM! Smoke, fire and wind blasted like a bomb. I flew backwards. Jasper hit the wall with a loud thud, as the floor shook. Then, he was back on his feet.

"You DARE USE THAT SPELL ON ME!" He screamed. I jumped to my feet as he ran at me with wide maddened eyes. He didn't even say anything, before shot after shot of black smoke detonated from his palm like a machine gun.

BANG! BANG! BANG! I tried to vein to jump out the of the way. But one hit me in the shoulder.

"*AHHH!*" I howled as agonising spasms made me convulse. Then another and another — like angry murderous Wolfraptor bites. "*AHH!*" Jasper looked murderous. "*Dancidious!*" I barked — a black paw erupted out of the air in front of me batting away the black fire.

"*Nouchous,*" I said, fire reined down upon him — before a tidal wave of blue water shot up from the floor, over the fire and me. It pushed me backwards and I spluttered as salty water filled every orifice, but Jasper was already acting… he swished his hands around his head and a giant green wind fragmented the air — spinning violently.

"*Dancidious!*" I called, but it didn't work! "*Dancidious! Dancidious! DANCIDIOUS!*" The next second, wind spinning like a tornado filled every sense. It was all I could hear, all I could see, all I could feel. Green spinning wind. I span, round and round, turning upside down. I tried desperately to think how to get down — then Jaspers voice echoed in a high pitched, distorted tone through the wind — "*You really thought you could beat me again? How pathetic you are. All this for her? You think you're saving her from me? When in fact it's more like the other way around… Even your friends are losing patience with you. The Magisteers have certainly. Remember this: I always win. Goodbye Avis…*"

"WHAT DO YOU MEAN *GOODBYE!*" I screamed.

The voice changed into a high-pitched rasp. "*Its time to die… I've killed before. I will do it again. You think people will miss*

345

you? Come looking for you? Not when I plant a memory in Robin's head that says you couldn't face being in the school a second longer and left… not when they find your body on the moorlands — discovering you were set upon by some rogues and vagabonds. Poor old Avis they will think, before forgetting you forever…"

"*NOO!*" — my rage blew up — blazing fury expelling red light from my hands. It felt like someone had lit me like a match — my skin itched and prickled as blinding red lights popped through the air.

The wind stopped. I fell back on my feet. Jasper was cowering against the wall.

"Admit it…" I said.

"Admit what?" he called, eyes wide and bloodshot.

"That you are *him*. That you are Malakai…" the lights fizzed in the dark room — some of the fire brackets put out by the wind.

"That would pretty impossible," said a strange voice — neither me, nor Jasper — it was high, strained. "Because, he is not Malakai… I am."

Between us, in the middle of the room rose a black shape, through the floor. I stepped back in terror. We both did. A small, black ragged creature stood three feet tall in the middle of the room. Eyes glowing blue. The air in the room fell. I couldn't catch my breath. All sound vanished — as if in a vacuum. The room turned, terribly cold.

"You have had… an extraordinary amount of good luck," said Malakai, his voice dripping with murderous contempt. His blue glowing eyes raised from under the hood towards me. "But, now that luck has run out…"

"Ste-e-eeee!" I tried to say Malakai's true name. "Ahh!" My tongue slit again — the name was Jarred — impossible to say.

"Ha-*ha-ha*…" said Malakai, but he wasn't laughing. "Never rely on past glories."

Jasper was raising a hand slowly upwards behind Malakai. "Don't even!" Malakai cried. Something made

Jasper buckle, as if punched in the stomach and he wilted to the floor.

I was so confused — I thought Jasper was Malakai all along, but now here they both were in the same room. "Trying to kill me all year?" I said a little braver than I felt. "And failed? So you've come to try again? Do you know nothing?" I said, buying myself time while I thought of a spell, or something, anything. "If you kill me, I will turn into a ghost — and tell your true name to everyone I can."

Malakai shook his head softly and tutted. "Idiot child. Do you think I wouldn't have plugged that hole?"

I suddenly realised something... last year I had turned into a ghost because I loved Tina — she was my anchor to this world for she was under a curse and I had to go back to save her. But now, my anchor was gone. "The Djinn, it showed me things about you..."

"Like what?" I glanced down at Jasper, who was rising slowly.

"Stuff about me being a seventh son. You can't defeat me."

Malakai spluttered into a squeaky cackle. "Then he's no friend of yours! Think your confused boy! Djinn don't have *your* interests at heart!"

"They do if they are also a seventh son."

Malakai's blue eyes dimmed. "Rubbish! Seventh sons are a myth, that they have any extra power is a —"

Jasper propped against the wall spat out a mouth full of blood — "Then why are trying to kill them all?"

"Just in case!" Malakai barked. "You can be killed as easily as anyone else. It's lovely that you think so highly of yourselves to think you are special! Well, this will be exciting, to kill two Wizards with one spell. Oh, it will be exciting... to watch the aftermath — the rumours about what happened... I could say that you killed each other, over that girl you both love. Or I could kill her too and say one of you killed her, then each other... *yeass* that would work..." he spoke fast, enjoying himself — Jasper caught my eye and mouthed something.

I swallowed the fear. Then all at once stretched out my hands as we both cried: "Returious-*Jacinwa*!" Bubbles of thunder spiralled across the ceiling — Malakai batted it away, blue eyes glaring.

But Jasper didn't stop, he jumped up — a barrage of blue and yellow smoke blasted into Malakai, who squealed as fire licked his cloak, before retaliating. A swarm of maddened Happerbats exploded through the window, biting at every available space on our bodies. I swiped in vain at them, screaming with pain at every bite. Jasper waved his arms and a blue flash froze them in mid-air, before they fell to the floor with a thud.

"You will both *DIE*!" Malakai threw his arms out. What felt like a brick wall smashed into my face, slamming me backwards. I hit the wall hard, hearing something crack and slid down.

Stars and light pulsed before my eyes. Malakai split into two, before pummelling my chest with punches.

"*AHHH*!" tiny fists beat every inch of me and Jasper. I felt weaker than I had ever done as Malakai stepped back breathing heavily. I couldn't hold my body up, I slumped forwards. Across the floor I saw Jasper do the same. His eyes connected with mine — at first I felt ashamed that I had accused him of such a thing, for now we would both die. Green chains spiralled round my legs and began snaking up my body.

A voice inside my head echoed: "*Avis, blink now if you can hear me...*" It was Jasper — I blinked. "*When I count to three you need to grab my hand and say Revelendo-Mallum-Rejicio.*" I blinked again, my heart hammering as the green chain, cold and slimy, climbed past my chest. We didn't have long, before my hands would be taken. "*Wait...*" said Jasper in my head. Malakai grinned down at me, his pale face exorbitantly happy as he raised his hands up behind his head.

Then Jasper called — "*Now!*"

I reached out and grabbed his hand, then as one we cried: "*Revelendo-Mallum-Rejicio!*" — the screeching noise obliterated everything else. Malakai squirmed as a wave of blue light pulsed out of us like a tidal wave.

"*Wahhhh!*" he cried. The join between mine and Jaspers hand pulsed hot blue waves. Another wave echoed through the room as Malakai glared berserk, maddened and shaking before raising his arms again.

"*Again!*" called Jaspers voice.

"*Revelendo-Mallum-Rejicio!*" we called — I shielded my eyes again as the light shone brighter than the surface of the sun. Malakai screeched, echoing long after he'd disappeared. I looked up... Jasper snatched his hand back. The green chain fizzed and fell away.

Malakai was gone. We'd done it!

But there was a problem. The floor was shaking. Rumbling from somewhere deep — stones in the wall juddering.

I glanced at Jasper — "What's going on?" I said.

Jasper sat up quickly then cried: "Get OUT! THE ROOMS FALLING IN!" We scrambled up across the wet floor — darting for the tunnel.

"Get BACK!" I screamed as we reached it. It was falling in! I just had time to lunge backwards as — RUMBLE! CRACK! We did scream, but I didn't hear it. Stone wall collapsed in from all around us and everything went dark.

***

I didn't know how long I was out for but when I woke the first thing I questioned was my mortality? Was I dead? But then, as pain returned I realised I wasn't.

Jasper was sat trying to start a fire. Rubble and stone lay high all around us. We were trapped in a tiny space around the fireplace. I felt groggy, hurting all over. As I sat up groaning I felt a scarf around my mouth. I pulled it off, groaning as my back killed.

"Oh you're awake," said Jasper softly. Then I noticed something sticking out of my arm — it was a long silver tube that ran all the way to Jaspers.

"What's going on?" I said, my voice weak.

Jasper looked bad, his face cut and bruised, left eye half shut. "You needed blood... it was a close call. But I suppose I owed you one after the stadium collapse. So this makes us even now."

"Was I that bad?"

Jasper looked back at the fire and poked it. "Well you stopped breathing so yeah, quite bad. And I put some of my robe around your mouth because of the dust, in case you were wondering."

"Right... thanks," I said.

"I've already looked around, tried some spells to get out of here but... he left us with a parting gift — collapsing this room inwards before he left."

"Can't we just spell a hole through it?" I said.

Jasper shook his head slowly. "No, Malakai cursed it — that makes it next to impossible, unless you're the Lily or something, to find a way out. I've tried to get a message out for help, but the curse just kills it."

"Oh god, so what we gonna do?"

"What can we do?" he sounded mad, speaking in a soft, low voice. "If you hadn't have come up here making accusations... this would never have happened."

I didn't bother to respond — I knew already that this was my fault, all my fault. Jasper had seen Malakai too, perhaps, when we got out, or if we got out, he could tell the Lily what happened. But... the Lily needed evidence and I didn't have any. I felt bad accusing Jasper now — he had just saved my life, if it hadn't been for him Malakai would have killed me.

For what felt like hours we sat together in the small confined space amongst the rubble. Jasper tried and failed to spell a fire — complaining the curse wouldn't let him. The cold crept in and lodged in my bones, a horrible silence fell and didn't shift for a long time. It was impossible to know what the time was — my instinct said it was still the middle of the night, maybe nearly morning. I wondered how we could get a message out to Robin, but even the window was completely blocked. The atmosphere was frosty — he had a right to feel aggrieved, this was all my fault and I owed him one.

"Hold on," I said as I pulled the silver instrument from my arm. "You gave me blood?" Jasper glanced up, his burgundy robes thick with dust and dirt. "But... how?" I said.

His eyes rested on me. "Because I am a seventh son."

Utter shock smacked me in the face — Jasper was a seventh son too!? I couldn't believe it. I felt giddy, as a tingle of jealousy fluttered in my stomach. I thought I was only the only seventh son in the school. Now the silver tube in my arm made sense, he gave me blood because he was a seventh son — Burrows the Djinn needed a seventh son blood to regain life.

"How did you know about this room?"

Jasper dropped his hand away from the fire, giving up. "Someone showed me it. I didn't know about the Heptagon Society until a man in white called Chambers explained it to me. He told me I could use the room — but I found it earlier. There were things in here that proved useful. But after you were taken by that Djinn, it all disappeared," he smarted.

"The Djinn is a seventh son too," I said, but Jasper didn't say anything — he rolled his eyes sat back against the rubble and looked up into the tall rafters.

"Nothing surprises me anymore..." he said, before sighing. "My father, was a good man, he was the cleverest, bravest, most loyal person I've ever known. His life's work was trying to create a peaceful, inclusive society that worked for everyone. Where huge power amongst individuals was reined in, where no one went without food, where everyone was happy... but they killed him. Saw him as a massive threat to their dark plans. Chambers, the man who showed me this room, worked for my Dad — lots of people did, they called themselves the Order of White. Malakai is only powerful with an army behind him... my Dad never wanted violence. He tried to solve everything with non-violence... but for that, they killed him — Malakai and his minions, killed him..." tears fell down Jaspers face making lines in the dirt. "I wanted to kill Malakai so much, I've dreamt about it every night. Even though I know what my Dad would say... *violence is not the answer, peace doesn't arrive by violence, only by peace.* But then, when I saw Malakai earlier — I froze... I couldn't think of anything. I am a failure."

I sighed. "You're not a failure, anyone would have done the same. Anyway, you're the one that saved us. Without you, we wouldn't be alive." Jasper wiped his eyes, and I noticed he was stroking his pendant. "Did he give you that?" I said.

He looked down at it and smiled. "Yeah. He left it to me. It was his," he frowned. "It does stuff. I think it's imbued with magical knowledge, or maybe it remembers the magic my Dad did, because, well I just seem to know so much more magic this year..."

So that explained the curious rise in grades. I wondered about my Granddad giving me the pendant — I didn't feel any cleverer, or have any extra powers.

Jasper sighed and closed his eyes. "You can't blame for me not liking you," he said. "My family were terrorised by the Blackthorns for years. It tore them apart, made my mother a nervous wreck. So you can understand that when you started mouthing off at me, I took that as you being a typical Blackthorn, come to terrorise me like your family before. *They* tried to say that you were not evil. I've had years of knowing the evil families that were trying to do us in, or take us down." A cold breeze drifted through the room. "But I realised, after a while, that you *were* different... after what Tina told me."

My heart jumped in my chest. "What did she say?"

"She said you two had something in first year and you saved her brother —— that you were good. She made me promise not to hurt you."

I swallowed. "What else did she say?"

His blue eyes rested on me. "She said you weren't like your family. I had a hard time believing that one —— especially after you tried everything you could to make me look stupid."

Tina couldn't have told him about Malakai, and nor could I —— because of the pact. "When did you start coming up here?"

"Just before Christmas. I sleep walked up here..."

"You sleepwalked here?" —— the memory of seeing Jasper snap out of something when me and Robin saw him up here before, shot across my memory.

"Yeah well, I've been talking to my Dad in this room," he said wistfully.

"Dad? But... I thought he was dead?"

"Whenever he wanted to talk to me I would find myself sleepwalking up here. That big round table allowed me to speak to him. I would sit in one of the chairs and then... he would appear in the one opposite. Telling me things I needed to know."

"I thought you were Malakai for so long..." I said shaking my head, hoping the pain would fall out if I shook hard enough. "I mean... I even saw you when you came up here and you looked like *him*."

Jasper smiled and shook his head softly. "That was just the same cloaking spell that Malakai uses, with the black aura and horns? My Dad told me to use it when coming up here at night. You won't be stopped or spotted by anything."

"What about your eyes, when I saw you earlier, they were black."

"Like this?" he said, closing his eyes and opening them again to reveal startling, scary black eyes. "It's a bewitchment charm. Rudimentary start to contacting the dead…"

"Who were you… *ohh*… your Dad?"

"Yes. The table was gone so I was trying to do it without. But I couldn't. Slightly annoying, this room used to be filled with books and stuff… but now it's empty."

Silence fell for a few minutes. There was no sound, apart from the wind outside the window — I felt awful. Through the silence something terrifying was sliding into my mind, something I had been wondering for a while. "I'm scared…" I said.

Jasper looked up slowly, the look of deep thought still on his face. "Why? He's gone…"

"Not of him. I'm scared that I am turning into them."

"Who?"

"My family," I said. "I've always been completely opposite from them. They hate me because of it, ever since I was little they knew I was different — not inherent evil like they are. They do things and have done things that I would never dream of. But just this year, I've felt myself turning into them — doing things that they would do… getting revenge, using violence and submitting to the darker side of oneself. I was never like that before. And now I've paid the price, because I'm exspelled…"

"It's your choice who you turn into. No one else's. You can let yourself be moulded by others, or you can take control of your own destiny," said Jasper looking back at the black fireplace. "That's what my Dad used to say."

I was wrong about him, I had judged too early. I realised my mistake now, letting my judgement be clouded by jealousy. This all started because of Tina — I was mad green with envy and could not hide it, taking out my frustrations on him.

Now I rewinded everything through my mind I remembered what Tina said to me in the clock tower when she was maddened by the jumper. Something about being told not to talk to me, being warned away — I assumed at the time that it was Jasper — my hatred of him forming quick judgments, lumping all my accusations at him. When in fact, now that I looked at him, sitting with tear tracks on his bloodied, dirt ridden face, his eyes gazing upwards in mournful recollection — I realised that he wouldn't have done that. It just didn't fit together somehow. Jasper had his face resting on his knees, stroking his pendant.

I cleared my throat. "I don't know if you noticed," I said. "But we have the same pendant."

Jasper frowned and glanced at me — I pulled my identical pendant from beneath my shirt and held it up — the dull golden metal swung softly, revealing the black rune mark cast deep in the metal, reaching the ends of the jagged, uncouth edges. Jasper gazed across at it, a look of utter disappointment on his face. I didn't think it would have that effect, he began shaking his head.

"I thought," he said slowly looking down at his. "I thought this was special." He twirled his own jagged golden pendant with the same black rune mark on it around in his fingers. "Hang on… show me yours again," he said, before sliding across the floor towards me. "Pass it here a second."

"Why?"

"Come on just do it," he said —— I pulled the chain and it clicked off. "Look…" he put our two pendants next to each other. "They fit together perfectly."

He was right. I was flabbergasted —— my pendant's right edge slotted perfectly into Jasper's pendants left side. The two identical runes sitting side by side as one. "What does the rune mean?" I said.

"No idea, it's no rune I've ever seen," Jasper said passing me my pendant back —— I would have expected Jasper to have known, out of anyone. "Don't look so surprised. I am not the fountain of *all* knowledge."

"So what do you reckon they are?"

Jasper shook his head, squinting down at his own with his head cocked because he could only see out of one eye, his left was swollen bigger than puss-filled sprat bite. "Well they look like they were both one, at some point. And were then separated —— I honestly have no idea. The runes look ancient, they are not modern runes —— maybe they are *sigils?*" Jasper shrugged. "Where did you get yours?"

"My Granddad gave it me at the start of the year," Jasper nodded as if all was right. "Except for the fact that he died five years ago."

Jasper stared at me. "He's dead? And he gave you that?"

"Yeah. In the summer holidays, I was running away from my brother and then I found myself in a dark room. He spoke to me about stuff and then gave me the pendant channeller and a bag of gold. I have no idea how that works…"

Jasper grimaced as if it was a particularly tricky puzzle. "Could have been someone pretending to be your Granddad?"

"But who? Who could have got into my castle, who isn't a member of my family, who hate me, to give me something that would potentially help me? Unless it's not to help me?"

"What do you mean?"

"Well, they've always wanted me to be evil. Perhaps this channeller helps make me evil?"

Jasper shook his head. "That's ridiculous. You can't blame what you did this year on that. You have to face up to it — you got jealous." I swallowed — he was right. "My guess is before your Granddad died, and for whatever reason, he put a destiny charm on the pendant — passing it to you. Knowing the others in your family might try and get it. I mean, it can't be a coincidence that we are both seventh sons and both have identical channellers?"

CHAPTER EIGHTEEN
Ghostly Goings On

I forged a deeply uncomfortable patch in which to lie in, sweeping away the rubble and dust revealing a frosty, hard floor, I curled up into my robes. We slept a long, painful, cold sleep — both too proud to get close to each for warmth. That would be weird. Dreams are always strange when you're stressed. Horrible, bizarre visions hurled themselves around my brain. I was sure I heard Jasper crying softly to himself. The urge to lay an empathetic hand across his back and say; *'it's all right...'* never arrived. Instead, I lay shivering hoping that we would be found, wishing to god that this small act I could not bring myself to perform, did not condemn me into being anything like my brothers and sisters.

I don't know when it was — what time, night or day, but I woke to this strange sound. A scratching, scraping then rasping noise was coming from somewhere deep below us. Jasper looked up and put a finger to his lips. I lifted my head, the sound came in rhythmic waves. And then, as it got closer we realised it was coming from the fireplace!

Was it Malakai? Coming back to finish the job? Jasper and I sat up, scrambling backwards against the rubble and lifting our arms upwards at the fireplace. We waited. Breath caught somewhere in our chests. Hearts beating faster than a hummingbirds flap. And then... a head came coughing and spluttering into the fireplace...

"Ahh, *pah! Pah! Pah!*" it went — I grimaced with terror at the horrifying sight. The face of this... *demon?* Was black and grey, its face contorted into a... hold on a minute... this wasn't a demon, it was...

"Robin?" I said. But the face had just got a mouthful of ash and was choking violently.

"Hiya!" he said, before coughing again. "I've found ya', at last!"

"Oh thank god!" Jasper cried with joy.

"I've never been this pleased to see you!" I jumped across to the fireplace as Robin climbed out, and hugged him. Soot and ash went everywhere but it didn't matter.

"How did you find us?" said Jasper.

"I knew Avis came up here after you," said Robin smarting. "But when he wasn't back in the dorm this morning I knew something must have happened. They got ghosts looking for ya' and everything, got everyone up doing a headcount," he said looking about the destroyed room. "What the bloody hec's happened in here?"

"Malakai," I said watching Robin's beady eyes grow with terror.

"What you saw him?" he cried.

"Saw him?" said Jasper. "We fought him, and just about got away with it, until he collapsed this room as a parting gift."

"Goodness me. Right well let's get out of here. I enlarged the fireplaces from below — why didn't you think of doing that yourselves? Then you could have climbed down."

Jasper indicated the boulders and rubble. "Malakai cursed it, we couldn't do any spells from inside the room. Couldn't even light a fire."

"Yeah, well that's probably just as well. I like my face how it is," said Robin — and we laughed, following him into the fireplace and at last — to safety.

Climbing nimbly out of a large open fireplace we stepped into a classroom — this one looked like it was actually being used. I let my arms drop by sides, that climb down was excruciating and now they throbbed. Robin patted himself down, billows of ash flew into the air and formed a thick dirty cloud around him like he carried his very own atmosphere. Jasper finally climbed through the grate and smiled weakly. "Thank god that's over," he said. "Thanks Robin."

Greeting us as we opened the door was a terrifying sight — several Magisteers, fronted by a stony faced Lily. Terror, likened to that of coming face to face with Malakai, filled me. The Lily's grey eyes rested upon us like a Wolfraptor on its prey.

"Thank you Robin," he said — Robin looked down at the ground whimpering.

***

I was getting quite used to being in the Lily's office by now. I had the impression that, had we not just arrived, it would have been a hive of activity. Piles of papers were hovering in mid-air, shaking slightly as they readied to their intended course — having stopped when the Lily walked back in the room — he needed silence to talk to us. Books too, that were on the march in a large circle from one bookshelf to another stopped and fell to the floor with small thuds. An endless assortment of devices littered the room haphazardly, it was not the tidy office it once was.

The Lily walked towards his desk and turned. I knew we were in trouble, even more trouble than I had been before. But how could it get any worse? I was already being exspelled, what worse a thing could they inflict upon me?

"Magisteer Simone, can you close the door please."

The Magisteers followed us into the office and watched mournfully from the either side of me and Jasper, like we were on the march to the noose. The Lily sat down at his desk, sighed and folded his hands, before his eyes came to rest slowly, on me and Jasper — looking like a sorry pair of chimney sweepers. "So, would you like to tell me what happened?"

"Well Sir," said Jasper sounding calmer than he looked. "I was up high in the Heptagon room, out of bed after hours which I am immensely sorry for. Then, Avis charged into the room and attacked me — he kept saying that I was... that I was Malakai Sir."

"Indeed?" said the Lily, his eyes swaying to me. I didn't bother saying anything, what was the point?

"He was mad Sir, berserk even... he tried to kill me, he said as much." — I knew the git would sell me out, as soon as we were out of the room. He carried on. "And then, well he used the *S-Z-U-V* spell on me Sir."

"Not a *Severso-Zxanxirious-Unquart-Vilunos?*" said Mallard who looked shocked and appalled — I was not as shocked as them, in fact I was quite proud that I had managed to do it — for it was a very hard spell to do. I suppose you can only really do it if your pumped full of adrenaline like I was. I found it in on my old list of spells from last year that I had collected from odd, old books and such — not knowing what half of them did.

The Lily sighed. "Violence. Numerous school rules broken. You were already being exspelled. Would you like to add anything else to this growing list Avis?"

I felt a wave of sorrow ripple through me. So many times I had tried to get the evidence I needed to be able to stay at school and every time I was thwarted. "No, Sir."

"You don't care?" he said.

"Care?" I said. "*Care?* Of course I care! This place is my home — more than anywhere else I've felt at home *here*. Now I have to go back to my parents who hate me because I am not *evil*, not properly anyway. I will be their scivvy, their male cinderella, their pathetic magic-less mistake. So yes, I care. I really do. More than anything. I would rather say that I am an orphan than be labelled a Blackthorn."

A silence fell — and I felt a tear roll down my cheek. Jasper seemed to be struggling with some horrible internal problem, he kept clenching his fists next to me, going to say something and then stuttering.

Partington raised a hand. "And if it wasn't for Robin Wilson you'd still both be——" he cried.

"Thank you Magisteer Partington." The Lily waved. "I think we should bring forth your expulsion Avis. I think we need to get you out of this school forthwith. You attacked someone, almost killed them…"

I swallowed. "But Sir——"

The Lily waved a hand for silence. "I will escort you to your dorm where you can say your goodbyes and get your stuff…"

"But Sir——"

"I've heard ENOUGH!" he called. It reverberated hard around the room. I was trying to tell him, in vain, that we had just defeated Malakai. "We will get your things, call your parents and be off back home in time for dinner."

"But…" Tears fell down my face uncontrollably, as reality hit me. I was going home —— I would never see this school, my sanctuary, ever again. I had ruined it —— and it was all my fault, I had lost sight of the bigger picture, of my appreciation of this marvellous place. How it had become my home, away from my parents and most of my family. To a place of safety and warmth and friendship, and learning, and food, and peace, and adventure. And now, it was all gone. Jasper was shaking next to me.

"That isn't all Sir!" Jasper blustered, eventually. "It isn't all, I didn't tell you everything…"

The Lily frowned hard at him. "What do you mean?"

"Well, Sir," said Jasper fumbling around with something in his pockets. "You see, I wasn't entirely truthful. During the time that me and Avis were fighting a voice came out of nowhere. And then… well… *Malakai* appeared —— he's smaller now. He *attacked* us."

The Lily sat back in his high chair and looked up at the ceiling. "So Avis has managed to persuade you to lie for him?"

"It's true Sir! I swear! I wouldn't lie, I don't like... I mean, I didn't like him... but it's the truth and it would be a shame not to——"

The Lily waved a large hand. "Ok..." he said, white face flushing pink. The Magisteers around us did not say a word, but I felt their gaze upon me, bearing into us harder than knives.

"So you have evidence of this attack?"

"But Sir," said Partington. "This is a witness for an attack. Under school rules you only need——"

"Very handy excuse though isn't it? Especially without evidence. Would you have all the pupils running around causing mayhem then saying it was Malakai?"

I couldn't believe it. Jasper had revealed the information that could have got me my place back and the Lily didn't want to hear it. He stood and walked slowly to the door of his room.

"Shall we?" he said looking at me. The Magisteers stood dumfounded at this latest revelation —— Malakai had been in the school. And yet, I was the one being treated like a criminal.

"Wait!" said Jasper who looked frustrated —— he couldn't keep still, his head darting all about the room, hands shaking. "I do have the evidence." The Lily didn't move. "When I spelled Malakai, it must have come off. I found it when Avis was out cold. It's this..."

Jasper pulled a hand out of his pocket revealing a small patch of frayed black material. My heart thundered. The Lily's eyes fixed to it as he slowly made his way towards Jasper —— he didn't say anything, but stared down intently at it, as if it were a fascinating, horrible new breed of magical insect.

"Straker, can you do the honours," he said.

"Of course," Straker took the small patch of black material and placed it on the floor. In a matter of seconds visions and images flooded into the room. A small ghostly outline of Malakai rose up through the floor, and began attacking a translucent Jasper and I. As we watched the events unfold Magisteer Mallard placed a hand to his face, Partington watched through his fingers, Straker's brow furrowed, Yelworca with a pained expression, and Dodaline wiping her eyes with a hanky.

When the vision faded, as rubble and stone fell all around our ghostly doppelgängers, all eyes turned to us. No one said anything for a long time, maybe a minute. The Lily took the piece of material.

"Well," he said. "This is the evidence you needed. This changes things." His expression changed and softened. "I am happy to say that Avis, you can stay."

A flood of emotions entered all at once and I didn't know what to think or feel first. Tears of joy suddenly fell down my face. A small round of applause resounded around the room from the Magisteers. It was over, it was finally over. I was staying!

"What you did was... incredible," said Straker. "You both defeated the most evil sorcerer of all time!" I caught Partington's eye and he winked.

I glanced up at Jasper. "None of this would have been possible, if you were not the bigger man and did the right thing." I said ——— Jasper smiled meekly.

"Right," said the Lily still grave. "And you did *Revelendo-Mallum-Rejicio* together?"

"Yes Sir," said Jasper as the Lily rubbed his chin. "Twice."

The Lily sighed deep in thought. "I think this would have been enough to expel Malakai from the school for good. But, if I know him, he will be back. I will personally do a thorough sweep of the entire school. Magisteer Simone, please call up every single ghost. Magisteers

Straker, Dodaline and Yearlove can you please repeat the *Revelendo-Mallum-Rejicio* spell to make doubly sure that we have expelled him." The Lily looked fiery. "Time to get yourselves cleaned up and off to the Healer's room. Then you're free to enjoy the end of the year, in peace."

***

The news spread like a wild fire in Lunordria (one of the Seven Magical Kingdoms, it's very hot). I don't know how it got out because Jasper and I were in the Healer's room when it happened. Robin came to see us first and we told him what happened.

Green rays from the floating sun in the middle of the Healer's room caressed our wounds and injuries, feint light bobbing up and down. Small cuts healed over and bruises and aches soothed. Robin had wet hair when he came in, having just had a shower and proceeded to sit on one of the nearby beds listening enthralled to the account of us defeating Malakai — shaking his head the whole time as the Healer spread some foul smelling ointment infusion on my neck causing me to gag.

"If it smells bad, it's usually good for you," smarted the Healer before doing the same to Jasper.

"The same can't be applied to food though," said Robin helpfully. She glanced at him, but didn't say anything. The next moment, the double doors opened again.

"Oh my goodness! You're okay!" It was Tina, she marched into the room, flanked by Ernie, and ran straight to Jasper, all but knocking the Healer out of the way before hugging him tightly. "I've just heard, you and Malakai? Is it true?"

Ernie, with a grave expression came to sit next to Robin on the bed. "What happened?" he said, as Tina turned round to listen — I was a little upset that I didn't get a hug. I explained the story as best I could, trying not to gag at the foul fumes from the ointment. I explained truthfully, that I thought Jasper was Malakai, that I went after him for I was desperate and wanted to save my place at this school, the battle with Malakai and the eventual redemption — of which I owed to Jasper, who saved my place at Hailing Hall.

Tina didn't say anything, I don't think she could — caught between anger and appreciation — I had saved Jasper's life at the Riptide Stadium and she knew he was retuning the favour. She couldn't look at me though, that hurt.

Ernie was smiling. "I'm so glad you get to stay here."

"Who told you?" said Jasper. "About Malakai being back?"

"We just heard it from people downstairs in the Chamber," said Ernie. "They were saying *Avis and Jasper had fought Malakai* — I don't know how they found out."

I looked at Jasper who looked puzzled — who could it have been? "This means," said Tina. "That the Lily is going to come under *a lot* of stick."

And she was right.

We received several visits from the Condor boys, then the Condor girls, the Swillows, then lots of people I didn't know. They came in, a few at first, but then more and more and more still… until the Healer's room was practically full to the brim.

— "Why did he go for you two?" said Colin Clapper excitedly.

— "Yeah! What does he look like?" said Herbert Hanningshire.

— "Calm down! Calm down!" called Ernie.

— "How did you defeat him, what spell?" said Hunter.

— "I thought it was Ernie that defeated him?"

— "That's true! So why did he attack you and not Ernie?"

— "How could the Lily let this happen?"

―― "I thought Malakai was gone!"

I couldn't keep up. I lay in the bed feeling dizzy as hundreds of excitable questions rang out at Jasper and me. The Healer became exasperated and shooed them as quickly as she could out of the room.

"This is not a communal space!" she called, ushering Tina, Robin and Ernie out with the crowd leaving Jasper and I to sit awkwardly opposite each other.

When we were finally allowed to leave Robin, Tina and Ernie were waiting outside the Healer's room for us. "Madness!" said Robin. "I wonder who leaked it?"

"It had to have been someone in that room," I said. As we walked the Big Walk corridor, eyes fixed to us as we passed. Conversations were on the apparent return of the most evil sorcerer of all time. And why he attacked *us*. They stopped talking as soon as they saw us ―― eyes turning to watch greedily.

The Chamber was no better, I was starving, having not eaten for a good day. Lessons had been cancelled which did not help with the on flow of people who wanted their own personal interviews. We sat together, Tina next to Jasper, Ernie and Robin next to me.

Noise and commotion from outside suddenly flooded in ―― the Chamber doors bursting open as ten to fifteen reporters from the Herrald swarmed into the room like Wasperats. With tape recorders at the ready, their eyes darted around the room, several going for the Magisteers at the top table.

"*Avertere*," whispered Ernie, holding a hand above my head, before repeating the same over Robin, Tina and Jasper's.

"Look here Nigel!" called Yearlove at the head of the Magisteers table. "I've known you since you came here as a boy ―― you know the rules, no reporters are allowed into Hailing Hall!"

Nigel, the lead reporter held up a large microphone. "Magisteer Yearlove, can you tell us what you know about Malakai returning to the school?"

"No he can't!" cried Dodaline. "Get your men——"

"Magisteer Dodaline! Good to see you again, can you please tell us what you feel this does to the Lily's reputation now that Malakai has been seen coming into the school for two years straight?"

Magisteer Trunwood stood tall over three of the reporters and bellowed. "You heard them, they asked you to LEAVE!" he called. Steel bars jumped into place around the three reporters and trapped them in a small cell. "And tell your cronies to follow suit!" The cell lifted and began floating out of the Chamber.

"Surely," said another reporter coming forward out of the pack. "The welfare of the students cannot be trusted with the Lily? He's already on thin ice is he not, after last year? The Occulus surely a sign that the councillors don't trust him?"

It took for Magisteer Simone to be called until all the reporters finally left, scrambling away under a tirade of bellows and spells from the humungous woman. The Chamber was buzzing. "Let's finish eating then go," said Ernie his eyes trained on the room.

We all took a hideout in Partington's classroom, he saw us on the way up from the Chamber and told us to go there.

It wasn't long however before he came back into the classroom looking puffed out. "The Lily has... called an assembly... everyone must... attend..."

"Another one!" said Tina jumping off the table. "That's how many now?"

As we stood, a ghost drifted up through the floor and said lazily. "The Lily has required all of your attendance in the Chamber for assembly. This is not on your timetables. It starts in ten minutes." It droned, before slipping back down through the floor.

We raced back downstairs and into the Chamber, taking a seat together near the back. Most people were already in here talking amongst themselves.

The Magisteers stood, looking rather ruffled, at the front and to attention. Eyes kept swaying to Ernie, Jasper and I at the back, until Ernie repeated a few spells and they stopped. When the Chamber was full, the doors sealed shut with a *clink* noise. In a blaze of luminous white light sparking like electricity, the Lily appeared at the foot of the Chamber — and began prowling around with a thick worried expression.

"I've called you all here today to set the record straight," he called. "I am not happy with some things — I am aware that group mentality can lead to strange behaviour, but I thought better of you, especially you upper years. Rumours and lies can easily cause undue damage. So let me explain…" You could have popped the silence with a pin. "I have to admit that yes, Malakai has been in the school. It was Malakai that collapsed the stadium — it was *not* the Djinn. However both are gone." Whispers broke out, but the Lily held up a hand. "Last night, he attacked two of our pupils — thankfully, they managed to escape with their lives… I hope this clarifies things. I will not be answering questions. The reporters have been *Barred* from the school, yet, if they do manage to find a way in, or ask questions then I implore you not to talk to them. I am fully aware that my reputation will be challenged, and my ability to take care of you questioned. Understand: all I care about is your continued safety and education."

***

Robin convinced me to go for a walk in the grounds, out the way of the questioning crowds and awkward questions.

I agreed and we followed the rather subdued crowd out of the Chamber.

I looked around the grounds, I could finally relax and enjoy the last few days left. "Come on, let's go across to the floating island!" Robin said.

"No flipping way!" I cried.

He watched me sorrily. "Avis, it's magic, it isn't going to fall! It wouldn't be there if it was unsafe!"

"Hmm," I hummed glancing across at the Stadium. "Course it wouldn't."

After a few minutes of pestering, I reluctantly agreed. Approaching the cliff edge I went a bit funny; weak at the knees, dizzy and nauseous. Robin raced ahead along the drawstring bridge. "Come on!" he called as I navigated my foot onto the thin wooden slats, taking each step tentatively, my heart in my mouth — I absolutely hated heights! "Don't look down," he called. I looked, and nearly feinted. It was the biggest drop I had ever seen. Clouds formed around the beaten rock faces, with moss and small, perilous trees which clinging to the sides. A rushing sound echoed as water fell from the island in a long cascading waterfall down into the canyon below, a rainbow split the air across it. I went dizzy.

"Too late!" I shouted, turning back. But as I did, some sixth years had just stepped on and were waiting for me to move forward. I swallowed and not wanting to look like a weakling, began to tip-toe back towards Robin as quick as I could with my eyes half shut, heart hammering hard in my chest.

When I finally reached the floating island, I clutched the grass gratefully praying my thank you's.

"Have you seen the drop?!" I cried.

"Magnificent isn't it!"

"Not the word I had in mind."

We sat on a bench and watched the view, it was spectacular. You could see the entire view of the Hailing Hall grounds from here, people playing and frolicking around chasing the trees and statues who loved to join in with the games.

Small white rabbits fussed around my feet, Robin bent forwards and picked one up. "They're so tame," he whispered stroking it's long ears — it looked a bit like Sedrick, my fluffy teddy rabbit. I hoped he was okay.

"Can I sit here?" said a voice. It was Zara, the white haired girl in my brother Harold's form. I nodded stiffly, my heart lurching into my throat as Robin stood smiling slyly and shuffled off with the rabbit, winking at me as he passed. What was she doing here?

Horrible gas filled my stomach and my mouth went dry. This was the girl I'd been trying to talk to all year, but never finding the courage and now here she was coming to talk to me!

Zara sat down in Robin's old spot. "I just wanted to say I think you're really brave."

"Thanks," I said trying to smile as I gazed at her beautiful white face, her hazel eyes spinning with adoration. "Wait, I mean, what for?"

"Oh come on." she said smiling. "It was you wasn't it? Who defeated Malakai?"

I glanced away. "How did you know?"

She huffed as if this insulted her intelligence. "Come on!" she laughed. "Everyone knows — you and that Jasper fought him didn't you? Anyway, I just came to say that I think you're really brave. Because, you know, what with your families *allegiance* and everything."

"Yeah," I said softly. "That is a problem."

"Thing is though, your brother, my form tutor, doesn't seem evil at all."

I smiled. "He's a good actor."

"Not like you then?" she chuckled.

"Not like me at all."

"You and Jasper friends now then?"

I laughed. "I wouldn't say friends…" I swallowed, feeling immensely nervous, wondering if the effects of the jumper still lingered on me and if that was the reason she was coming to talk to me?

I cleared my throat, she was looking at me, waiting for me to say something. "Anyway…" I finally managed. "Enough about me. I don't know anything about you."

What followed was a wonderful afternoon talking with Zara. After an hour Robin got bored and re-joined us. It felt so normal, so refreshing. Zara's friend Sophie came over too and we sat on the grass playing with rabbits and talking. Zara was wonderful. I couldn't believe my luck — not only did I get to stay in school, but now the girl that I couldn't take my eyes off all year had come to talk to me! She was from Gilliggan in Happendance and was the youngest of two sisters and three boys. Her Dad was a magical carpenter and her Mum an embroiderer.

I was messing about with daisies, picking them and making them into a chain as we sat talking. "Aww," she said, when I linked it together. "You've made me a daisy chain."

I smiled and slipped it onto her wrist. "Something to remember me by."

"Why? You're not leaving the school are you?" she said frowning.

"No. But I don't know what the summer holds. Not with… everything that's happened."

Zara scowled. "I'm sure," then she stopped. "Well… I know a spell that will make this daisy chain permanent." She whispered something and the chain fixed solid. "There," she said. "Now I will remember you, if you die or anything." We laughed. I hadn't had this much fun with someone since me and… Tina.

Robin and Sophie were also getting on very well. She was lovely, with her spiralling locks of red hair and talking Robin through the small pile of books she had with her.

"I've read that one," said Robin inspecting the pile. "But not that one. *Bartram's Runescape?*"

"Its good," she said. "Well, I figured I have a lot of catching up to do, seeing as I am an Outsider."

"Me too!" said Robin.

The conversation drifted on into the late afternoon. I loved the white rabbits, they were so funny and tame and just ran around chasing each other all day. They were crazy. One, a little tired out came and sat in my lap and I stroked its long ears. I'd never touched a rabbit before. It was the cutest thing I've ever seen. I wanted to keep it.

***

"Come on," said Robin shaking me awake as I yawned. "We have our appraisals today."

I frowned. "Our what?"

Robin sighed, slipping a jumper over his head. "Our appraisals? The end of year classes with all the Magisteers. Come on, all the other guys are already at breakfast."

Magisteer Wasp, eyes closed, danced to the music around the centre of the AstroMagical room hardly noticing our entrance. Jake cleared his throat softly, but Wasp still hadn't realised, seeming to be in utter ecstasy at the soft, violin concerto.

"Sir?" called Dawn. "*SIRRR!*" she screamed, causing everyone to jump, not least Wasp who was so surprised he fell off the plinth.

"Thank you," he said brushing himself down and waving a hand at the music, stopping it. "These are your end of year class appraisals where we can assess how each other has done this year. Individual appraisals don't start until the forth year, so these class ones are useful to find out if we've missed anything. Now," he said brushing back his hair. "Learning AstroMagic is about constant daily reminders. Wizards often forget to consult the chart and wonder why their spells are ineffective?" he laughed as if they were so incredibly stupid. "This year I have been impressed with the diligence and willingness of your form," he smiled. "Much more so than other forms who regard this lesson as nap-time… or of not being worthy to them," he said bitterly ——— Robin and I glanced at Hunter who looked sheepish, he was the worst for falling asleep in Wasp's class. "Individually, I have these notes… Avis your knowledge of the sign of Handen and its fall impressed me, but please work on your homework grades. Simon your aptitude has impressed me, keep up the good work. Ellen, your Main Book has been top notch and Hunter… erm… well done, and… please can you try and learn… *any* of the AstroMagic chart over the summer?"

We all sniggered, poor Wasp had tried his hardest to get Hunter to learn AstroMagic, but Hunter seemed repelled to it, like a magnet. "I will have you all again next year, where we are going to push on to learning all aspects of the particular signs and their effects on not just a Wizards spells, but on our entire physiology. And I will expect you to all come back knowing the AstroMagical chart off by heart!"

Yearlove walked slowly around the circle playing with his black beard. Jess, Florence and in fact most of the girls had their eyes trained on him adoringly. Tina sat glumly, Jasper now some way from her, a visible gap between them.

"Quite an eventful year," started Yearlove looking around, eyes dashing between Jasper and I. "I think you will agree that spell-craft is more than just saying funny words ——— to properly command a spell you need guts, spirit, *something* deep inside that commands the spell. We will resume our learning next year when we will dive head first into: Solvent-Spells, the Law of Richardson and the Novo ——— or the forging of spells. We will learn how to make ice and fire combine. Earth and water separate. We will charm the grass to talk, flowers to sing and trees to jump. We will learn about hexes, curses, bindings and talismans. Next year will be very exciting!" I glanced at Robin as everyone looked around and I couldn't help but meet his grin with my own — next year sounded amazing. Yearlove pulled out some papers. "In particular, special mentions in this class are to given out to: Gemma Dean, Freddie Garbutt, Robin Wilson and Jasper Gandy — all of whom have excelled in their studies and showed remarkable knowledge in Spell-craft. Keep up the good work and for the rest of you, next year I will be giving out prizes — not just any prizes either — so, by improving I will reward you fully."

A buzz of excitement rippled around the room at Yearlove's promise of prizes. Not excluding me — I vowed to *really* concentrate next year and get one of those prizes. I didn't know what it was, but I wanted it. "So, what do we think? What did we learn?" he said dark eyes scanning the circle.

"I very much enjoyed charming 'de flowers Sir," said Gret with an evil wink at me, as the class laughed, me included.

Yearlove chuckled. "Yes, that gave us all quite a shock."

My heart did summersaults on the way to the Magisteer Simone's room, because it meant seeing Zara again. Simone was sitting behind her desk reading the Herrald and gruffed as we walked in, her eyes trained closely on Robin, Hunter and I. Joanna, Gret and Ellen lurked at the back of the room in the darkness as the Snare's entered slowly, putting their bags at the side of the room. Zara entered last with Sophie. I felt Robin stand taller at the sight of Sophie.

"So. You all thought that because this was the last lesson of the year you could all turn up five minutes late did you?" said Simone from behind the newspaper. "You thought because it's not a real lesson, that you didn't need to make a concerted effort to be here on time?"

No one said anything — I could feel what was coming '*a million push-ups!*' or something. Magisteer Simone put the newspaper down. She looked even more ugly than usual, her monobrow bristled like an angry hedgehog. Her brow furrowed, her thin green lips pursed, dirty brown teeth snarling like an old bear. Then she stood, brown robes hugging her impossibly tight as she moved with all the grace of a colossal bag of wobbly custard.

"You began the year as weaklings, muscular wimps, amoebas, sad little worms and what are we now?"

"Strong worms Miss?" Hunter called, causing muffled laughter.

"NO!" she cried, spit blasting Hunter's face. "You are still weak, still wimps, still sad little worms. My seventh years can do a thousand press-ups in one go," she said proudly. "Remember what I said? A Wizard has to be tough, strong — a weak Wizard is a poor Wizard. Next year we will be doing weights…" suddenly the room filled with metal dumbbells. A wave of groans echoed. "That's it, moan! Moan at the pain you will feel. I tell you this, the more you moan, the more I will command you to do. And if you don't, it will be detention. Boys…" she looked at me and Hunter. "Tell everyone about your detention."

"I enjoyed it!" said Hunter causing Simone to wince, her hands curling into fists, she hated Hunter. Now she looked at me.

"It was hard?" I offered. "Working in the kitchens, downstairs, with the ghosts every free hour you have."

Simone smiled. "The thing is, you are all a lost cause. You are too molly-coddled. If I had my way, we'd have Physical Training daily, no, twice daily!" I glanced around, I had the impression that we all felt that it was a very good job Magisteer Simone did not get her own way.

We waited outside Magisteer Commonside's room for fifteen minutes before he showed up. "Have you guys been to see Simone yet?" said Graham. Robin, Hunter and I nodded. "Isn't she just the worst?"

"I could swing for her," said Gret raising a fist, nodding at her twin.

"Such a bad attitude problem…" said Dawn causing some of us to snigger Dawn was no Gilliggan lady herself. "What? I'm just saying, she's horrible, but she'll get what's coming to her."

"Why do you say that?" I said. "Do you know something we don't?"

"No," she spluttered. "It's just, you know, what goes around comes around. Karma and all that." Jake and Simon rolled their eyes.

"Oh?" said Commonside poking his head round the door with a mouthful of doughnut. "I thought I heard voices," he said dreamily, swallowing the mouthful. "I had quite forgotten we had this lesson…"

"Appraisal Sir," said Robin.

"Quite right, yes, I meant appraisal. Should have realised, today is a *numerological geminus day*, perfect days for wrapping things up."

After sitting down and listening to twenty minutes of Commonside's explanation of double digits and what you should be doing on a double digit day, Hunter had had enough.

"Sir!" he called. "It's an appraisal, not a lesson!"

"Right, right…" said Commonside, putting on his glasses and going to his desk, shuffling through piles of paper. "Really should number these," he muttered. "Aha, right yes appraisal… you are the Swillows—"

"Condors!" called Ellen, Jess and Florence all at once.

***

"Well that was awkward," said Graham grimacing. "Why did Commonside ask us what we thought of him, if he wasn't expecting us to tell the truth?"

Joanna smarted. "I felt sorry for him, he tries his best."

"Unfortunately his best is useless," Simon laughed — I had to agree, I really didn't see much point in learning Numerology for a start, I'd never heard my parents talking about it.

"At least next year we can use that class for getting some extra kip!" said Hunter, tripping up the first step of the spiral staircase causing the entire Condor form to laugh — we made our way up and into Partington's classroom.

"Well this is very exciting," Partington prowled the front of his classroom, triangle hat perched on top of his head. "I have followed the progress of your studies this year and I am pleased by what I have seen. Next year will be a culture shock, you have double the classes and double the work," he said, one eyebrow raised. "Which I'll come to in a moment. Your Main Book's have overall been excellent, the marking has been a pleasure. But I will stress that neatness is an issue with some of your books…" Partington picked out and held up one book, ink dripped out of the bottom of the pages all over the desk. "I don't even need to look at the name on the front of that book. Hunter?"

"Sorry Sir, it's just I'm still trying to get used to the pen and ink thing."

"Well get used to it a bit quicker, I go to bed soaking some nights after marking your book. Now, I've obviously been talking to your Magisteers over this year and they've filled me in on your progress. I am delighted to say that our form is third, to the Eagles and the Swillows in the *marking tables* — so keep up the good work. Next year, the gold stars awarded in classes will be added up and the form with the most will be getting special prizes at the end of year awards." — more prizes?! "I was hoping to be able to tell you who you will have next year, but, due to the delicate nature of recent events that looks unlikely. They have not been finalised just yet... so you will find out on the day you get back here. Now, have a great summer!"

***

I awoke on the last day of school to sun streaming in through the tall bay windows — the rain had finally stopped?

Gradually all the other boys woke and sat up in bed — Hunter was the last, being shaken awake by Jake — he would sleep all day and night if he had the chance.

"So this is it, last day already..." Simon said gloomily.

"Don't be sad it's over, be 'appy it's 'appened," said Jake, brushing his blonde hair out of his face. "Anyway, we'll be back in seven weeks."

The summer sun was starting to warm through the school. I thought about home, there was no sun there — my parents had it charmed so that the castle was in constant darkness.

We washed and dressed together and went to breakfast, there was a strange palpable emotion in the air that I hadn't spotted at the end of last year. The first years still walked around a little non-plussed in their turquoise robes and ties — a little overawed by everything still. I put a few extra sugars in my tea — today would be a long day, I could feel it in my bones. Hunter ate breakfast with the tenacity of a Lardpard (a ferocious animal from the cat family that looks innocent, but will swallow you whole if you get too close).

"Slow down," said Jess. "You'll give yourself indigestion."

"Won't," said Hunter gobbling up beans and sausages. "I won't get a chance to eat like this over the summer. Might as well make the most of it while I can." — Jess raised her eyebrows in apparent disgust while Gret watched amazed. "Free innit!" he cried looking to the boys for approval.

The newspaper popped onto the tables. I noticed a big picture of the Lily on the front next to the headline: *Hailing Hall — Can We Trust The Lily?*

I didn't bother reading it, I knew what it would say already. I sat back and relaxed. The only thing worrying me now was… going home. I mean, if my parents were as annoyed with me as my brothers had been when I escaped from the wedding at the start of the year (and crashed their carriage in the Outside world), then I would be in serious trouble.

But, I had heard nothing from them at all. If they were that annoyed with me, then why hadn't they come to get me? I glanced across at the Magisteers table where Harold sat. When I found out he was working here, I assumed that he would be carrying out my parent's orders and bring me back home, or punish me, or *something*. But he hadn't, in fact, he'd barely said a word to me.

Now that the feud with Jasper had cooled off, my mind switched to other things. Arguably, more important things… going home, John Burrows the Djinn, being in the Heptagon Society (whatever that was), the rune on my pendant. I wondered what it all meant, but my mind returned nothing. Tina no longer dominated my thoughts like she had done, my jealousy had subsided and collapsed like a glacier. Anyway, they didn't seem to be getting on particularly well.

On the way out of the Chamber Robin and I heard a voice. "Hey you two!" we turned, Zara and Sophie walked out with us.

"Alright?" I said.

"Yeah," said Zara grinning wide and filling my stomach with butterflies. "Fancy going to the flying adventure play area?"

"Sure!" Robin and I cried together.

By the afternoon we were returning to the Chamber, walking in with Zara and Sophie, who smiled their goodbyes and joined their form table.

Robin grinned at me. He had Sophie's phone number, and I had Zara's (not that I knew how to use a phone), they wanted to meet up with us over the summer holidays! I was gobsmacked, honestly. My knees felt weak and I couldn't quite believe that she wanted to see me outside of school. It was like I was someone else, or I was in a dream or something. We took our seats back at the Condor round table as everyone piled in ready for the end of school assembly. Seventh years piled in amongst the others for what would be the last time, with hands over their mouth, hardly believing that their time was over.

I picked up a glass of mango perry, it's frothy bitter-sweetness making my insides go all fuzzy. Harold, Dodaline and Straker took their seats at the Magisteer's table. Then, Ernie came in with an emotional Phoenix form, Magisteer Nottingham bringing up the rear with his hands to his face, small watery eyes blinking rapidly. The girls on our table were already half crying, (except Gret).

"I can't watch others crying," said Florence. "It makes me go."

I tightened my tie and did my top collar button up, everyone looked so smart.

Ernie had some of the Phoenix form in a hug as they sat down. He had spend the best part of seventeen years here. In fact, he had been here longer than most of the Magisteers!

The huge red velvet drapes were pulled across the stage, any second now the third years would perform the end of year play. I was excited, if it was anything like last year then it should be a hec of a laugh! As every seat in the Chamber was filled, the light brackets suddenly went out, as silence fell…

"In respect of the events of last year and in solidarity with our Hailing Hall brothers, we now perform... Ghostly Going's On..." came a shrill voice from behind the curtain, before, it opened.

I blinked unbelieving, for on the stage was a perfect recreation of... the clock tower! Then, a boy dressed all in blue with a rather crude spell that made him kind of transparent floated around the stage.

"Oh! Oh! Why must I be like this? Why? Why?" cried the boy. *"I must reenact my revenge..."* — he was playing Ernie!

I glanced across at Ernie who was watching with a big smile, they must have asked him if they could do this beforehand — Partington didn't look pleased.

"Being a ghost is not all it's cracked up to be," said the boy playing Ernie, he had his likeness and voice down well. *"You never sleep, you're always bored, and you constantly think about that moment you died..."* Suddenly, the clock tower faded away, as the third years at the side of the stage commanded a wind spell, which blustered through the Chamber. Then a huge black shadow cast long across the stage as Malakai — stood over Ernie, who lay on the floor. *"I will never submit to you!"*

"But I will kill you!" cried the deep, rasping voice. *"Now tell me where it is!"*

"I will never tell you! You'll have to kill me!"

"You can make this a lot less painful for yourself."

"I will never tell you."

"TELL MEEEEEEEE!" screamed the voice, scaring me half to death. The goosebumps on my arms and neck standing as the wind swelled round the room. A drum beat ominously as Malakai's arms extended towards Ernie.

FLASH! The brightest spark of purple smoke shot around the Chamber as a scream echoed deafeningly loud. *"NOOOOO!"* through the purple smoke, Ernie slid off the stage as Malakai disappeared. He fell in slowly motion from the ceiling, through flashes of thunder, wind and smoke in complete silence.

BANG! Ernie vanished. Drum's tapped softly as the clock tower returned and Ernie the ghost sat up.

It was the best play I'd ever seen. At the end, the entire Chamber stood and cheered as the boy playing Ernie took his bow next to all the third years and Mallard, who looked extremely relived.

"Who was that third year playing Ernie?" said Robin clapping hard.

"I don't know but he was great!" I cried. Ernie was grinning broadly and cheering as hard as he could. Glancing across at Tina I saw she had a face like thunder.

"And NOW!" the Lily bellowed, taking to the lectern which shot up in front of him as he approached. We all sat. "We crown this year's Riptide *League* Champions. Please put your hands together for…" We all began drumming on the tables. "The CENTAURS!" — A huge eruption of noise filled the Chamber as they jumped up out of their seats. They had won again?!

"Madness!" cried Jake. "They are just *too* good!"

Golden confetti streamed down from the ceiling covering the Centaurs as they made their way over to pick up the trophy.

"That's three years in a row!" called the Lily.

Receiving their medals were Gemma Icke, Marshall Compton-Campbell and Jenson Zhu — the stars of the team. Ingrid Bloater, the captain picked up the big golden trophy and lifted it high into the air.

"We have it on good authority," said the Lily, grasping the three stars of the team. "That our high scoring trio have been scouted for the Merlin Premier League! So *huge* congratulations to Marshall Compton-Campbell, Gemma Icke and Jenson Zhu! Let's hope you will be able to juggle your seventh year studies and practice," said the Lily ushering the Centuar's back to their form table.

"Now on the subject of Riptide, some of you have been anticipating my decision on the Riptide Cup Final and here it is…"

The Hesserbouts had hands over their faces — it had been said that this was their best chance to win the cup, since the Centaurs had been knocked out by the Swillows. I was still a little raw about the Lily's decision, but how could I argue against it? Jake, Gret and Joanna were shaking their heads slowly, they still couldn't believe it.

The Lily sighed. "I've cancelled the final." Silence.

The Hesserbouts stared forwards, unmoving. The Swillows hardly reacted either, Jasper just dropped his head. "Since we found out Malakai had been coming into the school and attacked one of the finalists, we cannot trust our security. Let me reiterate, this is not *my* decision, but the Magical Councils."

The Hesserbouts collapsed into long moans and groans — that was bad luck, that was their best chance of winning the Cup in years.

"Oh well, you still owe me two gold pieces," said Simon nudging Graham in the side.

Graham glanced sideways. "What you on about? Did you not just here him, he said it's cancelled."

"Yeah I know, but you bet me two gold pieces that the Centaurs wouldn't win the league again." — Graham grimaced muttering something about hoping he'd forgotten that before fumbling around in his gold bag.

I made up for the lack of recent meals by stuffing lots of pudding down myself — three helpings of jam tart and custard. I loved the ghosts jam tart. I was cautious to try it at first, as I had once been persuaded to eat some my sisters had made *especially for me*. I was in bed for three weeks afterwards.

The Lily re-took to the lectern. "And NOW…" he waited for silence. "The Hailing Hall School Awards! Given out to those pupils who we, the Magisteers think deserve it.

So without further ado... the winner of the best kept dormitory is... the Phoenix girls!"

A round of applause echoed hard around the fish bowl roof as seven pristine girls went up to collect their hexagonal leather boxed prizes.

"And the winner of the most improved students of the year are... the Flutteryouts!"

"*Wooo!*" They cried jumping up and running to get their prizes — then raising them into the air as if they had just won the Riptide Cup.

"Now for the *special awards!*" bellowed the Lily, a little tingle of excitement rushed through me — I remember winning one last year. "This one award goes to someone who has not just excelled spectacularly in their studies, not just excelled in their Riptide performances, not just charmed all the Magisteers and myself. But also, faced things that no boy should have to face, the loss of a loved one and the wrath of the most powerful Sorcerer of all time. So this very special award goes to... *JASPER GANDY!*"

Small fireworks erupted into the air — a bit over the top if you ask me — but still, I stood with everyone else and clapped hard. He had saved my life and my place at Hailing Hall, I suppose. He stood and walked up slowly, taking a place next to the Lily.

"It takes great guts to think of a plan under pressure, but you did it. Saving many lives in the process and expelling Malakai from the school."

Tina was standing and whistling loudly, clapping, along with everyone else. "Well done Jasper!" the Lily called and Jasper marched back to his seat at the Swillows table, getting mobbed by them.

"I do have to admit one more thing. However, this is not exactly an award, more of an... acknowledgement. But before we do..."

The Lily flashed his hands around at the first year tables. White puffs of smoke shot off in all directions and immediately covered the first years faces. Their heads became engulfed in white smoke balls, until they looked like dandelions. But, they didn't seem to notice, move or care. The Lily seemed happy that their vision and hearing was suitably muted.

"You will see why that is necessary soon," said the Lily to our perplexed expression, except all the years above us and the Magisteers who looked as if this was perfectly normal and part of the process.

"Near the start of the year, the Riptide Stadium fell down…" the second years perked up. "And the second years were charged with the complete rebuilding of it under the supervision of the Mental and Physical Training teacher, Magisteer Simone." She gave a small nod, grinning her horrible brown teeth. "The task was used to build up the teamwork, the mental strength as much as the physical and we regard this experiment as very successful," the Lily grinned. "But we have a small admission to make. The Stadium, at least the first time this year, was collapsed on purpose…"

A small break out of muttering filled the air, mostly from us second years — what was the Lily talking about?

— "They did it to us on purpose, the sly gits!" said Hunter over the noise with a resentful glance at Simone.

— "I can't believe they'd do this to us…" Gret slammed a fist into the table.

"*Shh*! I want to hear what he says!" I called at them as the Lily raised a hand and silence fell again.

"We collapsed the Stadium on purpose, not because it was old, but because we thought some *practical teamwork* and a common goal would pull you together much more than a round of exercises. And I think, it was a success. Would you not agree?"

Small mutters of resentful agreement flittered around us seconds years. Mind you, we all knew there was something fishy going on at the time, why us? Why ask the second years to re-build a Stadium, surely the seventh years or the Magisteers would have been better placed to do so. But it all made sense now.

"I must also remind you that we do this to *every* second year, every year. There is no year above you that has not had to do this. Nor would the upper years be able to tell you, for we *Barred* them from doing so. Not that they would," said the Lily smirking. The upper years were sniggering at the trick — they knew all along for they had gone through the same thing — they were probably laughing at us the whole time while we were doing it.

"A round of applause for the second years!" The Lily put his hands together and began clapping, all the upper years and Magisteers joined in grinning proudly at us — we had passed the test. Hunter stood and took a theatrical bow, to much laughter. Suddenly, a light began to pulse around all of the second year tables — it was coming from our ever-changing ties! The turquoise lit up white hot and began to change.

"We're levelling up!" called Jack Zapper.

The Lily threw his arms wide. "You are indeed! Now that you have realised you re-built the Stadium, the experience has moved you up a level!"

"Woo!" cried the rest of the Chamber (except the first years).

Looking down, the turquoise tie I'd had for almost two years was changing to maroon — not a second later it morphed into white. I looked around and everyone else on our table had the same colour. Only Brian Gullet and Jasper Gandy had different colours.

"You will start rocketing up through the levels now, mark my words!" called the Lily.

Graham was observing his tie like it was a map. "So… turquoise is one, maroon is two, white three and purple four?"

"Well actually, three is ivory and violet is four," said Ellen.

"What's the difference?" said Graham shrugging.

Dennis snorted. "Only about ten shades and fifty levels!" he cried, rolling his eyes.

The Lily waved his arms again at the noise until all attention returned to him. "I almost forgot to mention — after investigating the most recent collapse of the Stadium, we realised it has been cursed. Which means, my usual method of quickly rebuilding it by spell-work cannot be achieved — therefore it's going to take the summer holiday's to get it rebuilt. We're going to be using Golems. So, if some of you do see these on your way back please do not be alarmed." The Lily waved a hand and the grey smoke that covered the first years faces vanished, they looked up as if nothing had happened. "Now let us proceed with our celebrations!"

A great roar erupted as music suddenly blared out of ten gramophones that burst invisibly through the walls playing: *The Hexes 'Black Cat's and Broomsticks'*.

"What the hec's a Golem?" said Robin, over the music.

Dawn gave him a sorry look. "Thought you were clever?" she said causing Robin to scowl. "They are creatures made out of clay by a Wizard and given life for a set amount of time."

"They are perfect builders because they are strong and do whatever you tells 'dem too. Our entire village was made with Golems," said Jake. Robin nodded impressed.

What followed was a glorious afternoon of music, food, drink and dancing. I didn't dance, Zara tried to make me, but I refused. I did not dance.

"Come on moody pants!" she cried jigging around next to Sophie, but I honestly couldn't bring myself to —— that part of my Blackthorn blood just would not allow it.

"That's it!" cried Sophie as Robin jigged around like a puppet, being pulled around by strings. "You're a brilliant dancer!"

"Come on!" said Zara grabbing my hand and pulling me toward her. I saw Tina over Zara's shoulder, watching curiously until she quickly looked away. The next moment trumpets blared out across the Chamber as the bell in the clock tower rang deafeningly above us. The tables and chairs suddenly shot to the sides of the room with a loud scraping noise.

"Seventh years!" the Lily cried. "You've completed your time with us. The Magisteers, your fellow pupils, myself and all who have shared in your time here, will forever remember you."

The seventh years, dressed in their long bottle green robes came forward, sniffing and welling up with tears. The Lily walked solemnly through the middle of the Chamber.

"When things get tough out there, remember you belong to the Hailing Hall family. Now go and be great Wizards!"

The suits of armour pulled their trumpets out and blew as ghosts burst through the walls in one mass of white and blue and began to sing…

Seventh years, you have been here for seven years.
All of your peers give you our cheers and joyful tears,
And say… thank you very much!
Part of the family, of the Hailing Hall gang,
Go out now and make your mark with a bang!
As best you can: stand up for good, and weed out bad.
Use your memories and knowledge as your launch pad!
Your time here is over, but remember all the good,
Use your memories as beacons, and help all that you should.
Go forth into the world as professional Wizards,
Spells to help and heal, even stopping blizzards.

Whatever you can to make the journey of all…
Better, fulfilled and happy, this is your call.
Thank you seventh years for your time here…
Stand back now as your peer's CHEEEEEER!

And we *cheered*! The seventh years hugged each other and us. I didn't know any of them but that didn't matter now. They were leaving, what was their home for the last seven years — I wondered what some of them would be going out to do in the Seven Magical Kingdoms?

"Oh Lauren," Zara cried hugging a girl with bright white hair like hers. "I don't know what to say…"

"Don't say anything," said Lauren — they looked identical, the same brown eyes, lightly freckled face and naturally bright white hair. "I'll see you at home, just a few days and then I'm off with Dan and Helen. We're going to America?" she said, (I'd never heard of it. I think it was a city somewhere on the Outside — I'd heard about on TV before). "Who's your friend?" said Lauren pointing towards me as I lurked awkwardly.

Zara smiled. "This is Avis,"

"Nice to meet you Avis," said Lauren.

I went red. "Nice to meet you too, I wish you all the best on your travels."

Lauren left with a knowing look at Zara, who flushed pink. Robin, Sophie, Zara and I followed the flowing crowd outside. Carriages were lined up ready to take the seventh years onto their next destination. The Magisteers stood as one, creating a bright white light which lit up the sky and burst. A gigantic rainbow arched across the school, spinning multicolour stars down onto our heads.

Ernie remained standing with Partington and Tina on the steps of the school, waving madly to his friends who got into carriages. Lauren Faraday with her two friends tied her scarf to the carriage door before getting in and shooting into the sky. Zara and Sophie were jumping up and down into the air. "*BYEEE!*" they screamed.

Simultaneously, loads of carriages shot upwards, scorching purple contrail lines through the rainbow.

"Our turn to leave," said Sophie. Our luggage was just inside the Hall with all our names on it — I felt sick. I didn't want to go home.

"Robin," I said as we began stepping back towards the Hall.

"Of course you can," he grinned. "You were gonna ask if you could stay at mine this summer right?" I nodded grinning back. "Get ya' bags then and we'll go!"

Just as we stepped inside a large shadow filled my path. "*Ahhh*, Avis there you are." Harold, my brother stood in my way.

"Hello Magisteer Blackthorn," said Zara.

"Miss Faraday, a pleasure to see you one last time," Zara seemed suitably charmed and shot after Sophie and Robin to get her bags.

Harold's dark eyes came to rest on me. "It seems a shame to waste two carriages on the same journey doesn't it?" he said slowly — I looked down at my feet, dam it! He was onto me. I looked around for support or inspiration, but Robin, Zara and Sophie were way inside the Hall looking for their bags amongst the others. If I went home, they would never let me out of their sight, they might not even let me go back to Hailing Hall! Never mind making it out for one day to see Zara.

"I was going to go and stay at my friend Robin's house for the summer. He lives on the Outside."

"What a generous offer," said Harold in a low, cold voice. Stepping closer until his shadow engulfed me. "But I am afraid I must decline it for you. Come to my office and wait for me to pack, we will take a carriage home together." Harold stepped closer. "If you fail to show up, I will come looking for you, wherever that might be." I swallowed. I thought about clicking the shoes together and running off somewhere, anywhere. But Harold wasn't joking around.

He would come looking, he would find me and I didn't want to think about the consequences.

"Fine," I said, deflating. Harold smiled, straightening up and went back inside. Robin walked out with his luggage and frowned.

"I am guessing that means you won't be getting to see Yorkshire this year then?" he scowled.

"Doesn't look like it no…" I kicked at small tufts of grass. Stupid Harold! "I'm sorry mate."

Robin smiled. "Don't be, it's not your fault. We've had a funny old year haven't we?" he said softly as multicolour rainbow stars continued to fall over our heads. "Just make sure you can make it out for that one day with Sophie, Zara and me. And if you need me, this is my address and telephone number. Instructions on how to use them are on the back —— I prepared it already," he said handing me a detailed piece of parchment.

"Thanks," I mumbled as Zara and Sophie made their way out with luggage floating behind their head. Sophie pulled Robin into a big hug.

"Avis," said Zara softly, her brown eyes twinkling. "I wish we could have got to know each other sooner. See you over the summer yeah?" she grinned, before I hugged her tightly. "Our carriage is here, Sophie!" Zara and Sophie climbed into an all-white carriage with white horses before sticking their heads out the window and waving as they took off into the air. Robin and I watched it shoot upwards into the rainbow and away, until it was just a spec.

The rest of the Condors moved out of the Hall and onto the grass. The grounds were filled with hugging, crying and waving people. The Magisteers stood as one on the Hall steps and waved away their pupils.

"Here's me ride!" cried Hunter jumping forwards and clapping me and Robin on the back, before doing the same to the rest of the Condors. "See ya' guys!" he cried before getting into a brown taxi carriage and shooting into the air.

"Ah... here's mine," said Robin surprised, as the small carriage with *The Outside* written on the side. He waved at Partington, Yearlove and others on the steps — Commonside didn't wave, having his head in a book of numbers. The carriage door opened and Robin took one last look back at the Condors, then me.

"Look after yourself mate. You know where I am..." the door clicked shut as the horses charged forwards — my best friend Robin Wilson shot up into the air and was gone.

Not long after that Jess and Florence took a carriage together. Then Jake and Gret took their very gothic, blacked out, lanterns lit and black lace curtained carriage.

They were followed by Graham, then Simon, Dennis then Ellen, Joanna and finally Dawn. I stood for twenty minutes waving them goodbye and watching all the people I knew get into carriages and shoot into the air. Others were passing through the iron gates, walking to the train station.

Straker stood glumly, having just said his goodbyes to the sixth year Centaurs. He glanced at me as I went to go back inside. "Wait," he said turning away from the other Magisteers. "Look..." he held out his cupped hands and opened them revealing something with small metallic wings encircling a large, round eye.

"The *Volumino*!" I cried.

"Shhh!" he said putting a hand to my mouth. "I want you to have it."

I swallowed, taken aback. "But Sir, it's yours, I... *I*..."

"Just take it before I change my mind," he said smiling. "I am pretty sure you have more need of it than I."

"I don't know what to say," I said taking the Volumino, which felt soft and warm in my hand. It was so small. Its eye closed and cupped.

"I fixed it. You know how to work him." Just then, Hayden Carmichael approached and tapped Straker on the shoulder. I turned away smiling from ear to ear. I couldn't believe it, the Volumino was mine!

I placed the sleeping winged eye into my robe pocket, before collecting my bags. "*Nomusco*," I said and the bags shot into the air up behind my head — I moved up in the direction of Harold's classroom. As I reached the top of the stairs I heard a voice call my name. I turned, standing in the doorway behind the Magisteers, was Tina. "Wait for me," she said. A little butterfly jumped in my stomach — but why did she want to talk to me now?

"Arn't you going to Jaspers for summer?" I said as we moved through the desolate hallway.

"No," she said. "He's going to come to mine for a week, *maybe*. Let's go up to my Dad's classroom. I want to tell you some things..."

Partington's classroom looked strange with white sheets covering everything. Tina sat on one of the tables and flicked the hair out of her face. Outside the window, carriages continued to launch into the air, flinging up making a noise like a charging Wolfraptor, with lines of purple smoke contrails streaming through the rainbow sky until it looked like some amazing colourful artwork.

"I can't be long," I said. "I've got to go and find my brother Harold soon, he won't like me being late," my tone was short. I felt annoyed at her, really annoyed of her treatment of me over this last year and I couldn't hide it in my voice.

"That play about Ernie was... something wasn't it?" she said monotone.

"Suppose so."

Tina leaned forwards. "I really am sorry," she said softly, her beautiful face flashing imperceptible white lines in the sun light — the scars from last years Malakai attack. Her eyes swam with tears, but none fell.

I swallowed as a year of hurt bubbled to the surface. "Look, I am not jealous of you and Jasper, not anymore.

I'm not even sure I was in the first place. Think I was just frustrated because I thought we were friends and then we weren't. I didn't get an explanation…" I sighed, leaning back against the table as her glassy eyes watched me. "I know we would never have gone out, just friends I know that. But after everything we went through in first year, after the pact, I thought at least we had an understanding? And I know its my fault I accused Jasper of being Malakai. I really am sorry about that. I let the… frustration cloud my judgement and that was stupid. But I'm not jealous of you two being together, in fact, I think you are a brilliant pairing. He is a better man than I'll ever be." I couldn't help the cold, resentful tone creep in as I spoke.

Tina looked up slowly, lip trembling. "But I do like you, don't you see that? I really, *really* do. I never stopped liking you." A lone tear spilled down her face. "You don't just stop liking someone. And I saw you and her together…"

"Who?"

"Zara Faraday. I got jealous. I can admit it." She wiped her face — I couldn't believe what I was hearing.

"Why haven't you spoken to me all year then?" I said incredulous, all the lost time we could have spent together flashing through my minds eye.

Tina rubbed her eyes. "I really like Jasper too though, that's whats messed up. And I caused all the problems this year. Nearly got you both killed!" she cried. "I was just trying to do what was best…"

"I don't understand," I said utterly confused, my heart beating a million miles an hour.

"I thought the pact would be safer if we stopped talking and going out with Jasper and being friends with you just complicated things. So I had to choose. Also, if I broke the pact Ernie would get into trouble and I didn't want to lose him again, not so soon after… everything. Him taking the credit for defeating Malakai has put him in a really precarious position you know that right? Now, he's got to watch his back constantly, that some Darksider doesn't try and put a knife in it."

"Is that what they're calling people like my family now? Darksiders?"

Tina sniffed. "All those evil families like yours, belong to that side, Malakai's side. And now Ernie's a massive target."

"So, you stopped talking to me to make sure the *pact wouldn't get broken?*" I said unconvinced. "Really? That's why? What about that thing you told me before, in the clock tower about being *warned away from me?*"

She shook her head and slipped off the table. "That jumper sent me *mad* Avis! You can't believe what I was saying then."

Rubbish!" I said slamming a fist into the table, she was lying, I just knew it. Eventually she sighed and held her head for a long moment.

"We *all* were. Dad, Ernie and me. All warned away from you… this *vision…*"

I frowned. "Vision?"

"I don't know who sent it. But it was terrifying okay? It plagued my dreams for weeks — Dad and Ernie had the same thing, appearing in the middle of the night at the foot of their beds. Flashing horrible things through our minds. Then, it told us: '*keep as far away from Avis as possible, or a fate worse than death will greet all of you…*' Dad took it seriously. He was terrified for us — can you understand? He didn't want to lose us both again. Not after last year…"

I swallowed and slumped back against the table as Tina rubbed the tears away. It all made sense — someone had scared them away from me — but who?

Someone suddenly appeared in the doorway carrying large boxes. Ernie peered round them to see where he was going and saw Tina crying "What's going on?" he said, placing the boxes down.

"Why are you *carrying* the boxes?" said Tina curiously rubbing her eyes.

Ernie blinked. "Its good to use your muscles sometimes," he said flexing his arms.

"Tina was just telling me how you were all *warned away from me*," I said.

"*Ahhh*," he said softly looking at his feet, before moving to sit next to Tina. "It was scary stuff."

"So it's true?" I said.

Tina shot me a fierce look. "I wasn't lying!" she cried.

"Alright, alright..." said Ernie soothingly. "Look, something or someone, did not want us Partington's being anywhere near you this year Avis. I've spend the year trying to figure out who, and why, but however or whatever it was... I have absolutely no idea."

I sniffed, a short silence fell and the things Tina had told me flashed around my head like a thunderstorm. But then, the rolling thunder passed and I felt a serene calmness. This was my last chance to say goodbye to them before next year.

"So, what you going to do now?" I said nodding at Ernie's packed bags.

"Firstly, I am going to help father redecorate the house. It's in serious need of paint work. Then, I am going to go travelling. I was planning to meet up with some of the Phoenix form out in Hellernot City in Slackerdown. After that, I thought I might go and visit some of my old friends, you know from before I died — most of them have got kids and stuff now," he chuckled. "So that will be... *fun*." Ernie tucked his long hair behind his ear and crosses his legs, he looked forlorn — worry lines ran down his face, past his electric blue eyes and Partington nose. "Look..." he said. "I am sure Tina feels the same. But I really am very sorry about not... being there this year. We really were scared for our life. I couldn't let anything happen to my little sis, not again," he hugged her.

"I don't blame you, I'd have done the same." I lied, they both smiled.

"I will get to the bottom of it, I promise," said Ernie, leaning forwards and laying a hand on my shoulder. His blue eyes so much older then the eighteen-year-old body they occupied — I would severely miss him when he left.

"*Ahh*," said a long drawn-out voice. "So here you are…" Harold was standing in the doorway smiling. "And consorting with such unsavoury characters too, I thought you'd have known better Avis," said Harold slowly, his words dripping with unsaid meaning and menace upon every word. I didn't say anything for suddenly his presence alerted me to the fact that: Harold was the most advanced Wizard I knew (apart from my parents). If anyone had set that vision on the Partington's then he would be top of my list. "Come Avis."

Harold's classroom was just as I expected — dark and ominous. The window's had been covered by wooden screens. Large tables lay around the room which had a low, black and dank ceiling dripping condensation and whatever else. Cauldron's lay out neatly on tables. A very big fireplace with green fire was sending waves of hot air around the already boiling room. A small stream running green water ran directly through the centre of the room, with small bridges crossing. The walls were littered with shelves of jars, hundreds and hundreds of ready-made infusions as well as powders, stones, minerals and indeed anything you can imagine that might be used for an infusion. It was all here.

Harold took his time, waving a hand his case opened. Clothes folded and placed themselves neatly inside. Flashing his hands, things began flying from all around the room into the suitcase. It was impossible to hold that many things inside the bag, but slowly, the huge pile of things forced their way down, until the lid shut.

I leaned against the fireplace watching the green embers spit at me. Even Harold's fire didn't like me. Above the fireplace was a tiny urn, dark red in colour — something jogged in my memory, I had seen it before I was sure. I leaned in closer over the fireplace and saw that it had the same rune mark as my pendant! The same mark that had popped up on just about everything this year. But what on earth was it?

"What is this?" I enquired as nonchalantly as possible.

Harold glanced slowly. "Granddad's ashes," —— I gulped and stepped back. Granddad's ashes? My dead Granddad who had come back to life at the start of the year giving me a pendant with the same mark on it as his ashes urn? This was getting weirder.

"Why do you have them?" I said.

Harold glared at me as he sorted through his bookshelf. "Why not?" Ten books floated into an expandable box.

Soon enough five bags and lots of boxes floated up behind us as Harold locked the door to the Infusions room. Walking down through the deserted school corridors was weird, it seemed bigger somehow, now it was completely empty. As we reached the grounds outside, I saw the Partington's getting into a carriage together, it looked rather beaten and worn and chugged like a puffed out seagull as it lifted into the air and shot through the darkening sky.

I had a lot to think about this summer, if I had any chance to think about it. Fortunately, there was no wedding (that I knew of) so that was something. Harold clicked his fingers and a large black carriage came shooting forwards from the parking lot. After putting all his bags and boxes inside, there now only remained room for one person —— he did it on purpose.

"Oh dear," said Harold. "Look's like you'll have to go on the roof."

"Pah," I laughed. "Very funny." But Harold just stared, he never made jokes. "I can't get up there, it's dangerous, I might fall off! I hate heights!"

Harold raised his eyebrows. "I know. Up you get."

"It's ok, I'll get the train. Or I'll jog home…"

"I said *up you get*," said Harold menacingly. I looked around at the empty grounds, the waving trees, the bowing hedges, the adoring statues —— there was no one here to help me. "Either that, or stay here and play with the Golems."

I looked across to where Harold was nodding. Next to the Riptide Stadium were the Lily, Simone and Ingralo —— stood together building tall mud mounds, which were rising and forming into strange shapes.

With that, I put a foot on the wheel arch and lifted myself onto the roof, praying for my life. Harold chucked my bags up to me before getting inside. The carriage juddered and began to move. I had to think of something fast! Aiming my hand at the luggage I said, rather reluctantly:

"*Sevhurton,*" my bags froze to the roof in one solid icy mass. But then, it started moving forwards along the carriage runway. I fixed my hands to the metal roof and cried above the wind that now shot through my ears: "*Zxanbatters!*" A magnetic click forced my hands to the roof of the carriage as it suddenly shot into the air. "*AHHHH!*" I screamed through the hurling winds. This was not how I wanted this year to end. Not at all!

To be continued…

DID YOU ENJOY READING?

If you enjoyed it then I would be honoured if you left a review. When you turn to the page after next, Amazon will ask you to rate it…

I would ***really, really, really*** appreciate it if you left a review!

Thank you for supporting my work!

If you would like to contact me about anything, then please email: jack@jacksimmondsbooks.com

YOUR FREE BOOK!

A Prequel to the Wizard Magic School Series

Available on the following devices...

amazon kindle
nook kobo iBooks
 Windows BlackBerry
ANDROID

Just go to: jacksimmondsbooks.com to get your FREE copy of the Prequel to Book 1…

ABOUT THE AUTHOR:

Jack Simmonds was born in London U.K where he still lives, writes and drinks tea. Lots and lots of tea.

I love to hear from my lovely readers! — You can **connect** with me here:

You can follow me on twitter — @thejacksimmmonds

On Facebook you can like the Avis Blackthorn page for updates on future books:
https://www.facebook.com/AvisBlackthorn

Goodreads: https://www.goodreads.com/jacksimmonds

I look forward to hearing from you.

All the best,

Jack Simmonds

CPSIA information can be obtained
at www.ICGtesting.com
Printed in the USA
LVOW11s1540010817
543282LV00005BA/379/P